OBLIVION

Andy Blinston

Book 1 of the Rakkan Conquest series

Falbury

Oblivion

First published in Great Britain in 2018 by Falbury

Copyright © 2018 Andy Blinston

The moral right of the author has been asserted.

All characters and events in this publication are fictitious and any resemblance to real persons, living or dead, is purely coincidental.

Part 1 in the book series Rakkan Conquest

Third Edition, 2020, Andy Blinston

A CIP catalogue record for this book is available from the British Library

ISBN: 978-1-9993139-2-0

Falbury Publishing

To my mother and father,

Carole and Keith

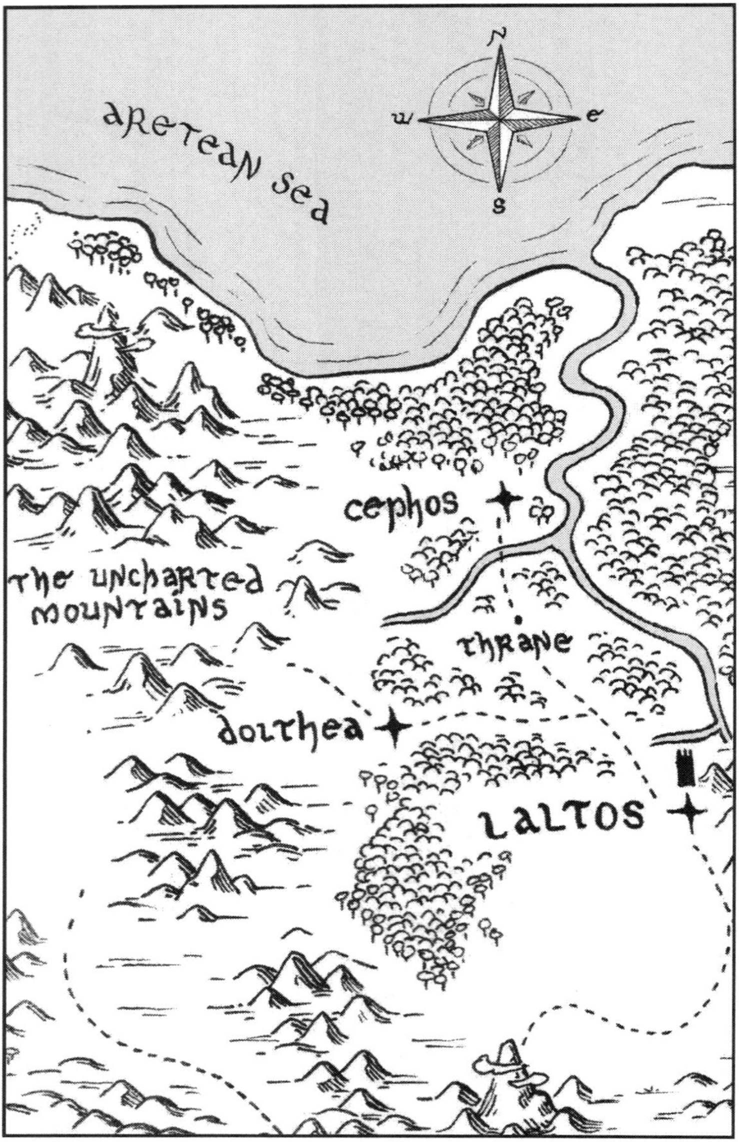

Aretean Sea
N
w
e
s
cephos
The Uncharted Mountains
thrane
dolthea
LALTOS

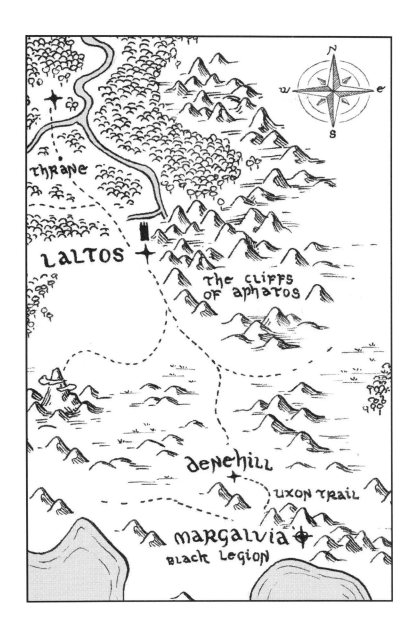

Prologue

A protruding nail stabbed the back of Darius's head as Mum crammed him into the cupboard. She pushed his baby brother into his arms.

"Don't make a sound," she hissed as she pressed the doors shut, squashing him in the dark space almost too small for a six-year-old.

Someone hammered at the front door again, rattling its hinges. Baby Amid whimpered in Darius's arms. *Shush. Don't wake.* He kissed his brother's head through the wisps of chestnut hair and held him tight. Mum told them to be quiet. If Amid cried, things would turn bad.

The nauseating smell of the old olives under his backside grew stronger with every panicked breath. Darius peered through the crack between the cupboard doors into the candlelit cabin, his hunched neck already beginning to ache. Despite the low vantage point, he could see most of the single room they lived in, from the straw bed in the corner to the shuddering front door. Even by slave standards their home was small, but the seclusion it offered was worth any discomfort.

Mum opened the door a hand's breadth and muttered to someone Darius couldn't see. From the back, her curly brown hair shook as she spoke, becoming ever more dishevelled across her grey shawl. A man barked orders as he pushed the door open and stomped inside. His heavy boots thumped against the floor and his skirt of leather strips swayed with each step. The iron helmet on his head covered his whole face except his angry eyes, mouth and chin. The bad people were here, clad in scale armour that was worn and battered from many fights. They'd found him again.

Where was Dad? He'd been gone for hours, leaving just Mum and them in their tiny home. Dad was strong; they needed him.

The man shoved Mum and she cried out as her elbows hit the wooden floor. Darius's rapid breathing threatened to give him away but wouldn't cease, no matter how hard he tried to calm himself. They were hurting her again. Mum sobbed while he watched, helpless, through the crack in the doors.

An older officer limped through the doorway, hunched over a walking stick. The two men's outfits were the same except the new arrival wore a blue officer's cape but no helmet. He shouted in a gruff voice, "Where are your children?" He hobbled past his soldier and jabbed Mum's side with his cane.

"Their father took them," Mum cried out. A lie, but lying to the bad people was fine. They came with swords, shields, spears, fists—always looking for them. Darius was special. They came searching for *him*.

Baby Amid snivelled. Darius put a hand over his brother's mouth. Warm breath brushed his palm. *Be brave, Amid. Dad said be brave like a warrior.* His brother squirmed, letting out a cry.

"What was that?" the soldier asked, looking around the room.

Mum yelled and grabbed his ankle. The soldier tried to wrestle his leg free but couldn't. With a sharp movement, he slapped her face.

A whimper escaped Darius's lips. *Be brave, like a warrior.* Dad wasn't coming soon enough. No one would save them. Darius had to fight and protect Mum and Amid, just like Dad.

He slowly eased Amid past his legs and onto the floor of the cupboard, freeing his arms to fight. The two men were tall. Against a normal six-year-old, their size, armour and weapons would give them the advantage, but Darius had one thing they didn't. He was different. Despite his age, he moved with a speed others couldn't reach. Only other special people could match him.

The officer hobbled around the room, scouring every corner. Soon he'd open the cupboard—there were few places to hide—and then Amid might get hurt too. Mum's sobs filled Darius's ears as the soldier towered over her, sword drawn and ready to make her talk. Darius had to act.

He burst out of the cupboard towards the soldier.

"Darius, no!" Mum screamed.

The man barely had time to turn before Darius's flying kick smashed into his groin. As the man folded over and groaned, Darius whipped a knife from the soldier's belt. Dad had taught him how to use a weapon. Now he'd make Dad proud.

He leapt onto the soldier's back. One hand grabbed the cold metal helmet for support. The other hoisted the dagger, ready to stab the shoulder of the man's sword-wielding arm.

"Stop!" the officer shouted from across the room, near the now-open cupboard. Amid dangled in his grasp, a sword pricking the baby's gut. The walking stick lay discarded on the floor. "Easy, little one. We don't want to hurt you or your family."

That's what they all said. Dad said to never trust them. Mum lay on the floor in tears and now they wanted to hurt Amid too. Darius tensed, the blade trembling in his hand.

"We only want to talk," the officer continued, "then we'll leave your mother and brother alone." His wrinkled smile was wide but fake, like the smile of a street seller.

A faint blue light glinted in the officer's eyes.

Darius's heart pounded. A blue glow meant the officer was special too. What should he do? *Where's Dad?*

"I'm an algus," the officer said. "You see that, don't you?" The scruffy grey hair on his head made him look like a beggar but the eagle crest on his belt buckle confirmed the truth. *Algus.* Darius should have seen it before.

He nodded slowly, as if a sudden movement might risk the officer sinking his sword into Amid's belly. Algus were rare, the ruling class of the Torian Empire. They looked normal, but they fought like gods.

If only Darius had known the man was an algus... Where was the usual algus armour, the chain vest under a black leather tunic and the gleaming blade? He should have stayed in the cupboard.

"I'm like you." The officer's voice turned coaxing. "You can trust me. Now come down from my friend so we can talk."

What else could he do? Darius slipped off the soldier's back, keeping the knife high and ready to strike at the first hint of trouble.

"Good." The algus smiled widely again. "Now put the dagger down and come over to me."

"Don't, Darius," Mum cried out. "Save your brother."

The algus scowled at her, eyes flaring more brilliant blue. "Take her outside."

The soldier dragged her to her feet as she screamed and struggled. Darius's blade came within an inch of the man's leg, but his arm shook, refusing to close the distance. If he saved Mum, Amid would die. His brave little brother hadn't even let out a cry.

"He's lying, Darius," Mum yelled as the soldier hauled her across the room. The man's free hand sought to stifle her words, but she twisted her head away. "Don't trust—"

They tussled through the doorway and into the field outside. When her cries had faded into the distance, the algus's eyes slipped back to Darius. There was no one around to hear her but them, no one to offer aid.

"Don't worry," the algus said. "She'll be fine. Now, as I was saying, you can trust me. I was like you once, but now I'm doing my part in the war. We need everyone we can get. So why don't you put down that knife and we can talk?"

No, liar. Darius's fingers tightened around the hilt. A warrior's weapon was his life—Dad's first lesson. If Darius gave up his blade, the algus could do anything: kidnap him, kill Amid, kill Mum.

Darius shook his head, not breaking his stare even to blink. *Don't trust.* Mum had told him to save Amid so that's what he had to do.

The algus's left hand had held the cane, which meant the left leg was weak. Take out the right, and they could escape.

The algus frowned. "You're a stubborn one, I'll give you that. There's…"

Darius let the man's words fade into the background. He focused on the blade in the algus's right hand. The polished steel moved as the man talked but always remained too close to his brother's flesh. The sword had to be farther away if he was to save Amid.

"Hey!" The algus raised his voice in a sharp bark. "You listening? I told you—" As he spoke, the man turned the blade and pointed it at Darius's head.

Darius lunged forward, raised his dagger ready to slash the algus's right hand. The officer pulled back before Darius swung, positioning Amid between them like a human shield. Despite his infirmities, the algus was swift.

Ducking, Darius used his small size to pass under the officer's arm. His free hand swept the flowing blue cloak aside while he slashed with the dagger. The blade sliced into the back of the algus's good thigh, cutting through the rough muscles.

The officer yelled in pain. Screams erupted from Amid. Blood showered the floorboards and the algus collapsed to one knee. With a final swift movement, Darius withdrew his knife and stabbed the man's neck, cutting off his cry. Spluttering, the algus slumped to the floor with Amid still tight in his arms. Gore pooled around his body. His gurgling breaths faded, buried beneath Amid's shrieks.

Darius had done enough. He'd been brave. Dad would be proud.

Screams rang in Darius's ears as he ripped Amid from under the algus's body and brought the soaked boy to his chest. Blood flowed from a deep wound in his brother's belly. Darius sucked in a breath. A sword plunging into his own stomach could not have hurt more. He had to get away from there.

As Amid's cries grew more deafening, Darius bolted through the doorway and into the field, heart pounding in his throat as the grass whipped his ankles. Amid was slippery to hold, but he'd never let go.

The baby's screams made him wince. They'd never been so shrill, so laced with pain. *Be brave, Amid.* So much blood. Tears welled in Darius's eyes, making it hard to see, but Mum and the soldier were up ahead. She was still standing, still alive.

When the soldier turned towards the sound of the cries, Mum took her chance to twist from his grip and dash away. Ignoring her, the man raised his sword as Darius hurtled towards him.

Darius had to hold himself together a little longer, to see off this last foe. He slowed enough to drop Amid in a patch of thick grass before readying the knife he still clutched tight. *A warrior's weapon is his life.*

The soldier swung wildly as Darius approached, back-stepping with fearful groans accompanying each stroke. Fleeing was the usual reaction to one with Darius's natural speed. He dodged through the slow swings with ease and slashed the man at the knee. With a whimper, the soldier turned and fled, hobbling away as quickly as his injury allowed.

Darius paused, his blood-smeared chest rising and falling rapidly. A common soldier was no match for him. The man wouldn't be back.

Silence filled Darius's ears, with only his own panting breaking it. He looked back at Amid. Why had he stopped crying?

Blood had stained the grass red around the baby. Amid's belly was sopping wet. A coppery smell hit Darius's nose and made his stomach churn as he knelt by his brother.

He gathered the baby into his arms. "Amid?"

Tears trickled down his cheeks. He shook the baby, wishing for those deafening cries to return, those big eyes to open, that tiny nose to scrunch up. Anything.

Blood soaked through his clothes as he hugged his brother tight. "Amid!"

Footsteps approached and he jerked around.

Mum's shocked eyes met his for an instant before she screamed and ripped Amid from his arms. "No, no, no," she wailed, over and over.

Darius collapsed onto his backside. So much blood. He'd never seen so much blood. The red mess overwhelmed him and he bent to vomit into the grass.

When the retching ran dry, he shuffled towards Mum, arms outstretched, yearning for her to take away the pain, to make everything better.

She screamed and slapped him, knocking him back into the dirt. "You got your brother killed! You're no warrior!"

The sting lingered in his cheek while tears flowed from his eyes. *She's right. I'm no warrior.* He stayed collapsed on the ground, not daring to move an inch.

"Get up!" Mum grabbed him by the arm and hauled him to his feet. "We have to go. More will come." Each word sounded like a sob.

"Dad," Darius whined. All he wanted was Dad. Dad would make everything better. Darius could almost feel his warm embrace, hear his soothing voice. *It's going to be all right, Darius.*

"We don't have time to wait for Dad." She paused, trying to compose herself. "We're going to Margalvia. We'll be safe there."

Cradling Amid's limp body, she took off running and Darius followed. Each stain left in their wake was another reminder of his failure.

"Margalvia?" Darius whispered. The fortified city in the south?

It didn't matter where they went. He'd failed. He hadn't been brave enough, or strong enough, or clever enough. His baby brother was dead. Because of him. If only he was a real warrior.

1

The wet soil soaked Darius's backside as he sat. Heavy rain pelted his head through the branches of towering pines. Where was he? He scratched his chin, shocked by the thick, black beard that met his fingertips. How old was he? The last thing he recalled was a fuzzy memory of fleeing with his mother, but that felt many years ago, with nothing between then and now as if he'd been lost in a deep slumber.

He turned to see a soldier's eviscerated corpse lying next to him, spilling gore which Darius now sat in. With a shudder, he lurched to escape the repulsive pool, scrambling to his feet. The chainmail under his trim, black leather tunic scratched as he moved. Stiff bracers bearing fresh scars of battle clutched his forearms. His belt buckle bore an eagle emblem. Why was he dressed as an algus?

The corpse's pale face stared upwards, jaw clenched. A single slash had lacerated the man's scale armour, deep enough to disembowel and all but sever the spine. But it hadn't killed quickly enough, apparently. Judging by the heavy bloodstains on the man's chest, death had come from the stab wound to the heart. *How merciful.*

The evening light waned and dark clouds cast shadows, making it hard for Darius to see past the pines. Their branches swayed and their needles hissed as the wind and rain tossed them. Other bodies lay scattered around, one without a hand and leg, another with a skull caved in, dripping onto the stained soil. The gory sight brought bile to the back of his throat. It reminded him of Amid. *So much blood.*

Footsteps splattered in mud to his right—three pairs. Darius stooped and snatched a sword from the dead soldier's grip, thankful the rain had washed it clean but ready to dirty it again.

The blade was well balanced though a little short for his liking. He ran the edge briefly across his bracer cutting a shallow scratch. *Damn.* Half as sharp as it needed to be to hack flesh effectively.

How did he know this?

Three soldiers emerged from the trees, hoplites wearing dirty scale armour identical to that of the strewn corpses. Iron helmets offered them some protection from the rain. *Not algus.* They paused at the sight of him and raised their circular shields.

Darius didn't move. His hand clenched his new sword tightly.

While he watched, they looked at one another. The dim light cloaked their eyes, making it impossible to judge their demeanour.

"It's him?" one whispered.

"Turn and be gone," Darius said, forcing his voice low and steady. With any luck they'd credit him with the many bodies at his feet and leave. Who knew, maybe it was credit due?

The centremost man ignored the warning and rushed forward with shield raised and sword tucked beside, ready to stab. Darius dodged to the side, startling himself by the speed at which he moved. Instinct smashed his sword across the man's helmet. The blade couldn't cut the metal, but the man fell to the mud in a daze as Darius turned towards the other two. He was even faster than he'd been as a child.

The two soldiers swung with wild arcs that were easy to dodge between. He grabbed the shield of one, ripped it from the soldier's arm and smashed it across the face of the other in the space of a heartbeat.

The evening's fading light now allowed him a glimpse of the fear in the remaining soldier's eyes. The man stood shieldless and defenceless against Darius's speed. He punched the man across the jaw with the hilt of his sword as easy as hitting a target dummy and watched the final soldier crumple to the dirt.

Why did these men fight him?

A crash of metal broke through the patter of rain and drew Darius's gaze to the side. Within the trees stood a tall, dark figure, wearing a cuirass of black metal across his chest, as thick as the plates covering his forearms and shins. His exposed biceps and thighs were thickset, like a centurion from a nightmare. Darius stared. The figure's helmet covered his whole head and face. It swung in his direction, gaze surely fixed on him. Swords gripped in each hand swayed slightly as the giant man breathed.

Armour creaking, the figure strode towards him. *Oh, hell.* Darius brought the shield tight to his chest as the soldiers weakly scrambled on the ground beside him. They could wait. He wouldn't take his eyes from this newcomer. This one wouldn't be as easily subdued as the others. Even the air seemed to flee before the looming figure, howling as it rushed through the trees.

A few feet away, the man raised his right sword.

Darius braced.

The man's first swing came down, but instead of striking for Darius, it severed one of the soldiers' heads.

What the...?

Another two slashes caught the necks of the other soldiers leaving only Darius and the man breathing.

Darius held the shield out enough to block the sight of the gore. His eyes tried to read the giant's helmet. Dark metal grating masked every inch of the face as if whatever lurked beneath was too ghastly for the world to see.

"What is this?" the man growled, his hidden gaze pressing down on Darius. "Why do you just stand there?"

Unsure how to respond, Darius didn't move or speak.

"Darius, what's wrong?" The man stepped towards him.

Darius backed away, raising the shield's cold metal plating to his eye line. The man knew his name. His mind was blank, no memories of friends or foes. Yet he could name a thousand ways to kill a man in a single blow.

"Who are you?" Darius asked.

The man paused, his silence underscored by the still howling wind. When he spoke at last, his voice held a note of trepidation. "What? It's me, Felix."

The name stirred no thoughts or feelings, and his mere presence made Darius nervous. "Do I know you?"

Felix dipped his head and growled, the hilts of his swords creaking as his hands squeezed them. "No. This cannot be."

Felix's blackened iron cuirass was nothing like Darius's own armour, which felt more oiled and fitted for posturing than battle. Didn't that make Felix less likely to be an ally?

"Why did you kill these men?" Darius asked. "And what do you want of me?"

"*I'm* not killing everyone," Felix shot back, "I'm cleaning up *your* mess."

Darius scanned the corpses, the blood that repulsed him. "Would I make such a mess?" A fighter with his speed wouldn't need to hack so clumsily...unless he didn't care. No matter how much he wished it, still no memory of how he came to be here would surface.

"You mean your revulsion at blood? Trust me, you grew accustomed to holding back the chunder, though you hurl your guts out after a fight."

Felix was either perceptive or did indeed know something about him. Darius let his grip on the shield relax a little. His next question began to form on his lips, only to be interrupted by a shadow approaching between the trees. Tensing again, Darius took a step back and kept both the old threat and the new in sight.

Another man walked towards them, thick metal greaves thudding with each step. He was armoured like Felix, with a similar dark helmet covering his head, but he was shorter than the other warrior. A bloodstained hammer was slung over one shoulder. Darius felt the blood drain from his face. Another man that looked fearsome enough to scare away death itself.

"Darius, finally. We need to fall back," the new arrival said. "There's more on the way, and the goman isn't far. This ambush has been folly."

"Brutus, we have a problem." Felix pointed to Darius. "The goman's taken his memory."

Brutus's helmet dipped. "No. That's not possible."

"He doesn't know who we are."

Brutus stepped closer to Darius. The smell of ash on the warrior's breath was thick. "What do you recall?"

What the hell was a 'goman?' If this was a ruse it was elaborate, and they'd wasted ample opportunity to kill him. Their thick greaves and encasing helmets told him they were clad for the front line of battle, and long-since healed scars on their arms and above the knees showed they were no stranger to it. Brutus looked strong enough to wrestle an ox into submission. To take them down, Darius would have to aim for their bare thighs or stab through the armpit into the heart when Brutus lofted his meaty hammer. Again, his thoughts turned only to slaying.

"I remember nothing about myself." His one memory was best left untold.

Brutus cursed and slammed his hammer into a nearby tree. The trunk shook under the blow and the hammer's spiked head sank into its bark. Darius flinched as he imagined his own head on the receiving end.

The warrior's shout hung in the trees for a moment before dissipating in the rain's hiss, not quickly enough to go unheard by anyone nearby. Outbursts like that would only cause Darius more trouble if danger still lurked nearby. *Great. I'm stuck with a hothead.*

Still, their knowledge of his name and his personality kept him rooted for now. He had so many questions they might be capable of answering—provided they spoke the truth.

"Why should I trust you?" Darius asked.

Brutus scoffed and turned to Felix. "You'd think I didn't raise the lad."

"Raise me? You mean you're my father?" A surge of anger made Darius clench his sword as he recalled the yearning for Dad to rescue them all those years ago. Before he could accuse the man of causing Amid's death, Brutus spoke.

"No, your father passed. I took you in. You want proof? Here." Brutus brandished his bulging arm, and Darius could just make out an "M" tattoo in the dim light.

"Is that supposed to mean something to me?"

"Margalvia."

Darius's heart skipped a beat. "What?"

Brutus leaned in closer. "Margalvia. Your home."

That name... His mother murmured the same name in his only memory. It enticed him.

"You have the same tattoo," Brutus said. "Check below your belt."

Dropping the shield, Darius pulled aside his tunic and stretched out the waist of his trousers. Sure enough, a smaller but identical "M" was tattooed below his navel.

"You had to have it in a more discreet place given you're posing as an algus," Felix said.

Darius couldn't find a hole in their story. Margalvia, the tattoo, knowing he hated blood. They likely did know him.

He relaxed a little and picked up his shield. "Fine. I'll go with you." Margalvia sounded like a good place to start looking for answers.

Brutus tore his hammer from the tree. "We'll make for the bridge. With this rain, the river will be fit to burst. We'll wreck the crossing behind us so they can't follow. If they heard us—"

"You," Darius interjected.

"*Us*," continued Brutus, "then they'll be on us soon. Let's get moving." He paced away with broad and heavy footsteps splattering in the mud.

"Is Hothead there always so stealthy?" Darius asked Felix.

The warrior let out a chuckle then set off after Brutus.

They walked silently for a while until Felix shook his head and sighed. "Archimedes will know everything."

The name sent chills through Darius's veins deeper than the icy rain had reached. "Who's that?"

"The goman. Archimedes has many powers, among them control of your mind. He can pluck out memories for himself and even poison you to believe untruths."

Darius didn't care to meet anyone that struck fear into these two brutes. Whatever Archimedes had wanted, he'd taken it and left a blank slate behind. But left Darius breathing…

"Why did he leave me alive?" Darius asked.

"I don't know. You were hiding amongst them, gathering secrets for us and killing people of importance."

"I was uncovered?"

"Hardly. You tried to kill Archimedes—well, we did, to prove your loyalty."

"Who to?"

Felix groaned. "We don't have time for this. The plan was folly."

"Stop grumbling, you two," Brutus said, having stopped to wait for them. "The plan could have worked but he knew we were coming. I think someone betrayed us."

Great. Even they don't know who to trust. Despite the cold wind and rain, sweat covered Darius's back and chest, and his skin chafed against his layered linen undershirt as he walked.

As they trekked through the forest Darius caught the sound of grass rustling behind him in a manner unbefitting the wind. He looked back and saw movement. Then, a panther emerged from a patch of tall grass and bounded towards him.

His stomach sank. He turned to face it, shield and sword raised ready to swipe at the beast's head before it had a chance to sink its fangs into his flesh. As he made to swing, Brutus grabbed his arm and clamped it in place.

"Damn. He doesn't even recognise his own escort," Brutus said.

The panther slowed and came to a stop just shy of Darius's feet. Its amber eyes gazed up innocently and a sense of relief fluttered inside him, but it was as if the feeling wasn't his own.

"My escort?" Darius said. The cat seemed tame enough now it wasn't charging towards him. A panther may be of use in a fight, especially one with rippling muscles that looked to weigh as much as Brutus. Useful for hunting too should this forest keep him long enough. But how did he control such an animal?

Brutus hadn't relaxed his iron grip. Wincing, Darius twisted the captured limb, trying to break free. The warrior noticed his struggles and released him. If that hand ever took hold of his throat he was dead. *Be sure to stay out of reach of Hothead.*

The panther skipped to the side away from Brutus. *Curious.*

"We haven't the time for this now," Felix said. "Let's—"

A blue light flickered in the shrouded depths of the forest and caused the three of them to pause. After a few heartbeats, it flashed again.

Felix gasped. "It's an algus. Darius, you'll have to fight them."

"No." Brutus shoved Darius to the side. "Run!"

2

The panther loped behind them as they fled, splattering through the mud. Something about the cat's presence gave Darius comfort. His legs moved stiffly as the cold bit them, but he knew he could run twice as fast if necessary. Charging off alone into the darkness seemed foolish, however. He needed answers, and his companions seemed to have them, or at least might lead him somewhere he could learn more.

Ahead, Felix slowed. Another flicker of blue appeared in front of them and the two warriors skidded to a halt, ducking behind a nearby uprooted tree. As Darius ducked next them, a protruding branch scraped his wet hair.

Felix raised a finger to the grating over his mouth and poked his head above the trunk to look out. Darius followed his lead but saw nothing except thick trees fading to blackness.

The warrior scanned for a while then dipped back down. "They haven't spotted us," he whispered, only a fraction louder than the wind.

"We can barely see ten yards," Darius whispered, holding his sword free and ready. Could the man see in the dark now?

"Use Lyra." Felix nodded to the cat crouched beside him. "Her sight and smell go far."

Lyra. She turned to look at him as if aware his thoughts surrounded her. How could he 'use' her?

Brutus crept over, scraping his armguards across the ground. "There's a group up ahead with an algus. Archimedes mightn't be far away. We'll go around. Quietly."

Darius frowned, finding it hard to imagine either man moving stealthily in that armour. The rain was loud, but not loud enough. Perhaps taking another path would be best, away from the algus. Just hearing that word made him twitch, reminding him of his solitary memory. Had Archimedes left him that one memory to taunt him?

"If events turn sour," Brutus turned to Felix, "I'll handle it. Just make sure he gets back to Margalvia." He planted a hand on Darius's shoulder and squeezed. "You don't look half as afraid as you should be."

The words echoed inside the metallic helmet, sending a chill through Darius's body.

"Send Lyra ahead," whispered Felix. "We'll follow her."

Darius looked down at the panther. Those big amber eyes were still staring at him, waiting like she already knew what to do but needed the command from him.

He motioned in front of her. *Cat, I command you to move ahead. Stalk.*

Her gaze remained locked a moment longer, then she turned her head away, nose rising into the air as she ignored the order.

I know you understood that.

Poking her nose a little higher, Lyra turned farther away.

Perhaps a different tact was required. *Lyra.*

She half turned her head towards him with what he swore was a raised eyebrow. A better start.

25

Stalk ahead, pleeease.

Lyra gave him a look and a blink that he swore meant "fine, you sarcastic git" before sinking her body to the ground and prowling forwards. *Interesting girl.* He liked her already.

He scooped a handful of mud and smeared it on his metal-plated shield to make it less of a reflective target for archers. Should he have to duck for cover, it'd help conceal him too. There were masses of trees around, at most twenty feet apart, but some weren't wide enough to fit a shield behind.

Lyra's tail vanished into a shrub ahead.

"Let's go," whispered Brutus.

Darius's heart pounded. "Wait. Something's wrong." Fear. The feeling felt foreign, divorced from his thoughts. It was from Lyra.

Two streaks of blue light darted through the air toward them. Brutus rolled as two blue arrows grazed his shoulder and stabbed the mud where he'd lain.

Darius leapt up, abandoning all suppression of his blistering speed, and darted for the closest tree that would shield him from the arrows' sources. Felix followed his lead while Brutus roared and regained his feet but made no move for cover.

Darius slammed his back against a trunk and ducked, bringing his shield to his breast.

"Get him away," Brutus cried, before charging towards the shooters.

Darius peered around the tree and was almost speared through the eye by a blue-tipped arrow. He knew of many weapons but not these. Whatever glowing substance topped the arrows' heads, it was safest to assume it could pierce armour and shield. Brutus was a fool for charging in but Darius admired the man's bravery.

"Run!" shouted Felix, setting off towards the river.

Darius sprinted after him, the cold rain prickling his exposed arms. The stiffness of his thighs made it feel as if he ran through shallow water, yet the trees tore past.

Lyra burst from some bushes nearby and dashed alongside him, barely keeping up. In the shadows, the odd helmet and shield flickered past. Shouts rang out as his passage was noticed but he paid no heed. The bridge was all that mattered. Brutus had said they'd be safe once across, one step closer to Margalvia.

A glance back showed that Felix had fallen behind, no doubt with hordes of determined men close behind.

The trees thinned ahead, and a low groan of rumbling water grew. Darius soon broke from the cover of the forest and was greeted by the banks of a swollen river. Lyra skidded to the edge and watched its thundering waters toss and spew white froth. The splintered wreckage of a bridge poked from the shore a little farther down. *Damn.*

Felix bounded from the forest with two soldiers right behind. He ground to a halt and spun, taking a giant swipe behind him and catching the necks of his pursuers. Their haemorrhaging bodies slumped as Darius turned his gaze to the river. Its dark, raging surface washed the red from his vision but could do nothing for the fear tightening his chest.

"What now?" he asked.

The towering warrior didn't reply. The waters may as well have been a wall twenty feet high. Nothing could pass through.

The rattle of iron grew closer, rising above the pattering rain. Soldiers running, not yet in view. Too many to count. Hopefully they were as slow as the last lot and would fall to Darius's sword.

He swallowed at the thought of gushing blood. Options were few. If it was either get bloody or die, he'd rive men until the river flowed red.

Shimmers of armour came into view from the shadows, stretching as far as he could see. Helmets bobbed; swords and shields glinted. The odds were not in his favour. Even with his special ability, he had limits.

Felix stood beside him with two swords drawn and an eager stance, prepared for the coming fight. The man's dark armour looked thick enough to withstand plenty of blows. Still, two could not hold against a horde forever. Darius's gaze fell briefly on Lyra, now standing by his side. *Three? Still poor odds.* There was no sign of Brutus.

As two soldiers charged ahead of the rush, Darius surged forward. He side-stepped and sliced across one man's bicep. The soldier yelled and dropped his sword. Batting the man aside with his shield, Darius stabbed the next soldier's throat. His sword's point dug into the spine.

Blood. Sputtering. The algus on the floor of their home. Amid screaming.

Darius shook off the memory as Felix came charging past. His companion hacked his way through the wall of soldiers, aiming at knees and shields and helmets.

A blue arrow streaked from the woods, darting towards Darius's thigh. Instinct taking over once again, he skipped aside and sliced through the shaft.

The army of men pressed against Felix but the warrior held his own. He fought with the strength and heart of at least five men. Lyra had joined him and was busy mauling a soldier's arm.

Darius started towards her, uneasy at the sight of his escort exposed without the time to think why, but he paused at the emergence of a new figure from the shadows. This adversary sported no helmet or shield. She wore oiled leather identical to that which covered his own breast. An eagle crest on her belt matched his, but she was no friend. Her eyes flashed blue, trained on him with nothing but malevolent intent smeared across her face.

She rushed at him with the speed only those with his gift could reach. He readied his shield and blade. Her sword flared cobalt blue as she swung for his knees. Darius dove over the arcing blade and rolled away, unwilling to risk blocking a weapon that looked as if it would cut his shield like parchment.

First the arrow to the thigh, now she tried to knee-cap him—all non-lethal blows. Should the fact they wanted him alive make him less or more afraid?

She whirled and charged, slashing low as he backed up but her blade managed to score both his legs. The pain was superficial. He shook it off and dodged again, searching for an opening. Her tight stance and movements showed she was well trained, but her swings were a tad wild, often leaving her left side exposed—a weakness he'd seize upon.

As she raised her arm to swing again he lunged and jabbed his shield into her wrist. It hindered her just long enough for him to thrust his sword halfway through her armpit. She cried out as he drove the dull blade deeper, scratching across her ribs. His sword was blunt, but it did what was required.

He let her body fall with the bloody sword buried in her and snatched her weapon. Now extinguished of its glow, the blade was simply sharp, clean steel. Bile stung the back of his throat, but he swallowed hard and turned to the ongoing fight.

Before he had a chance to re-join the struggle, a weakness swept across him, as if invisible vines crept up his arms and legs. Strength bled from his muscles. He strained to tighten his grip around the sword but it fell from loose fingers. The shield soon followed. *What's happening?*

He backed towards the riverbank. Lyra darted after him, seemingly unhindered by the strange force that held him captive.

Felix, however, faltered midway through a hefty swing of his sword. The man wavered then collapsed onto all fours. His arms shook with the effort of holding himself up.

Darius's knees strained as if a boulder were slung to his back. Closing his eyes, he focused solely on willing strength into his muscles to keep him upright. He found a smidgen of energy to trudge backwards, small steps, as if an inch farther away made him safer.

When he opened his eyes, the flash of a blue arrow caught his gaze. It darted from the forest and pierced Felix's thigh.

The warrior grunted in pain and his leg slumped to the soil.

A nearby soldier grimaced and stabbed a sword into Felix's neck. Blood gushed but Darius couldn't look away. For a few seconds, his protector held defiant, growling as his arms trembled against the pressing weight of death. When the man collapsed, Darius's odds of escape fell with him.

Brutus was nowhere to be seen. Darius was alone but for Lyra now standing behind him. More soldiers emerged from the trees, among them an algus and a masked man unlike any other.

The masked man was tall and wore similar leather attire to Darius, though it was stained green instead of black, melding him into the undergrowth. Long, dark dreadlocks hung from his head to his midriff and he brandished a charred staff in his hand that looked ready to crumble to ash.

Darius looked around desperately but there was nowhere to run. The river cut off any escape he had. The soldiers fanned out to surround him, and the masked man walked forwards.

Darius recoiled. The man wasn't wearing a mask at all. It was his face. He had no mouth, just smooth bare flesh where his mouth should have been and the gaze from his sunken eyes held a darkness that made one want to cower.

"*Darius, I'm so glad we found you,*" the man whispered in Darius's mind as if stood beside him.

Darius inched backwards until he felt Lyra's tense frame pressed against his legs. *How do we fight him?*

She growled and stayed shielded behind him. Icy spray from the river warned him of its proximity.

"Who are you?" he asked in a barely intelligible groan.

"*We're here to keep you alive.*"

"Archimedes?"

The goman's eyes narrowed, arms almost within reach. The mere sight of that mouthless face twisted Darius's stomach. He had no choice. Summoning all the energy that remained within his faltering body, he leaned backwards and let himself fall to the mercy of the raging waters.

Dragging Lyra from harm with him, Darius felt her surge of fear but the icy water ripped the pair apart the moment they hit. His body stiffened at the sudden freezing rush over his skin. The torrent slammed his body into a rock, a sharp edge grating his elbow as he was dragged onwards. Lyra's panic faded, leaving only his own for company.

Before he could regret her loss, strength poured into his arms and legs as if he'd been cut loose from shackles. Darius thrashed to push his head free from the rapids that tossed him about, but to no avail. Each jagged stone he struck was too slippery to grasp. Pain gripped his chest, his lungs crying out for air. At last, his face twisted free of the water and he caught a breath.

The mail vest and leather dragged him down. It was better to lose them than his life. Darius grappled with his belt buckle and rid himself of them. Even without the extra weight, he still struggled to tread water.

On and on it went, repeated submersions and frantic attempts for air. All sense of time drifted. Every part of his being focused only on the next breath. The waters sapped his energy, yet he found just enough to keep fighting. He knew he couldn't keep it up forever, but still he strained for each gulp of air.

By the time the river carried him to a calmer stretch, his feeble strokes were barely enough to keep him afloat. Nothing but blackness met his watery gaze. The last vestiges of his strength waned. His mind slipped too close to slumber and he sank for a moment before resurfacing with a splutter. *Is this how it ends?*

Darkness pulled at him, beckoning his consciousness away. But as he yielded, something tugged at his collar.

3

Nikolaos searched the furious river in vain as he ran alongside it. *Nothing but froth and gloom.* His flaming torch didn't reach far enough. Darius couldn't be found until morning, if he'd survived, and there went Nikolaos's chance to impress Archimedes.

Despite this failure, Nikolaos couldn't contain the smile on his face. Tonight had gone as he'd planned and Archimedes blamed his uncle, the head of the Laltos Guard. Finally, his uncle would be swept aside to make room for him.

He burst through a cluster of branches and in his haste almost collided with another dark-clothed algus standing by the river.

Lex shoved him as he stumbled past, barely managing to keep his footing. She glared, her torch-lit face fierce.

"Apologies, Lex." Nikolaos winced. He preferred to appear graceful around her, not like a lumbering bear.

A glint of blue light flickered in her steely eyes as she regarded him, her raven hair tied tight behind her head.

"Find anything?" he asked.

She gazed pensively over the dark waters. "Not yet."

The remnants of her bow's laminate finish reflected the torchlight as she shifted it onto her back. Nikolaos recalled the day she'd bought it. Made of the finest wood and bone, it had cost more than his entire armoury at the time. How many rakkans had it now killed? Five hundred? A thousand? Few truly deserved the title of algus—divine defender of humanity—but she was one of them.

The worn bow stood in contrast to her fine algus clothes and the engraved sword at her waist. His eyes followed its thin, dark metal edge—kuraminium, the strongest but heaviest metal known to man. *Being a daughter of the Regent of Laltos has its perks.*

She turned towards him, her eyes glazed over as if other things played on her mind. "I've only just arrived after speaking with Archimedes. He has an important request of me."

"What request?"

Lex frowned and looked to the sky, face paler than usual. "My falcon searches overhead, but it's too dark."

Evasive as usual.

"Something troubling you?" he asked, placing a hand on her shoulder.

"He asks much of me." Lex's nose flared a little, a sign of buried anger he'd recognised since their youth.

"If there's anything I can do…" Provide her with soldiers, weapons, a naked body to grind against… A man could dream. As a handsome man he'd sampled many women, but none so stunning as her.

"It's something I must do alone," she said. "And I don't relish what it entails."

She was too often out alone. If only she weren't so reticent, even with a long-time friend like him. Reading her was like reading a scroll in an ancient language—difficult to interpret and deceptive.

"I've not seen you so troubled for a long time." He gave her shoulder a gentle squeeze. It had been years since the last time, since she'd tried to step off one of Laltos's highest towers.

The only reason she still breathed was Nikolaos's swift grasp.

She shook off his hand. "I know what needs to be done. I just don't like it."

"Enough to even speak of it, apparently. Has it anything to do with Darius? If we capture him, we'll get the lead we need on the rakkans."

"Rakkans? You know what Archimedes is like." She sighed and looked him in the eye at last. "I'll take my leave. I pray I'll see you again."

"Lex—"

Without another word, she turned and strode into the forest. Nikolaos watched her go, frowning. *What did she mean by that?*

4

Darius awoke to the screeches of birds and the accompanying stench of droppings. A cough rattled from his chest. Shivers shook his body, roots and leaves scratching against his skin with each shudder. Cold, hard earth lay beneath him. *So cold.* Only the warm, furry body clutched in his arms had kept him from death's grasp through the night. *Thanks, Whiskers.* Lyra shifted in his embrace and growled—not a fan of nicknames, apparently. Best to lay off them considering her huge claws.

They lay under a thick-leaved bush which housed at least two pairs of birds that refused to cease their incessant squawks. His head pounded. Lyra must have dragged him here and snuggled up to keep him warm. Why would she risk her life to save him? He hadn't commanded it and surely she didn't need him to survive. His thoughts drifted to Felix. What made Darius so important that someone would die attempting to save his life?

He cursed. *Unfathomable.* That was his current situation. What had transpired in all the years since his brother...passed? No answers presented themselves. Felix, Brutus and this goman who hunted him only raised more questions.

After sharing Lyra's warmth a little longer, Darius crawled out, driven by the hunger rumbling in his stomach. The bush's heavy branches snared his hair and clothing as he wrestled free, but he welcomed the distraction and was thankful for the thick cover they'd provided. His struggles scared away the birds, bringing relief to his ears, but sharp pain throbbed in his shoulder as his efforts disturbed an open gash. Must have come from a rock in the river and, with the freezing cold, had gone unnoticed until now. The sight of congealed blood banished any desire for food.

Though shallow, the wound was large. It needed cleaning to stop rot. A yellow-leafed Seplyga would do it. He could picture the plant with ease, though his childhood self wouldn't have recognized it. Yet more knowledge that pointed to him being a seasoned warrior, one that had failed in some ambush according to Brutus. Why, was a mystery. Surely the answers lay in Margalvia, wherever that was. He had an inkling he'd find whatever friends and family he had there.

Lyra.

His panther roused and crawled towards him as Darius looked around for any loose branches that would serve as a weapon. Those soldiers would still be on the hunt for him. Being without a shield and armour was manageable, but not a weapon; even a club would do.

Lyra gazed at him with tired eyes.

Thank you again for rescuing me yesterday. Now what else was she good at? *If you know the way, lead me to Margalvia.*

Lyra raised her head and looked around, ears trained in each direction she surveyed. He prayed she knew. Cuts and scratches adorned her paws and back, not serious but they'd need cleaning as soon as they happened across that plant.

With a flick of her tail, Lyra set off, a strong sense of purpose emanating from her. *Perfect. Old Darius chose a good one in you.*

5

Nikolaos watched his uncle squirm in the noose. Webs of blood vessels stretched across his scarlet face and bloodshot eyeballs which now fixed on Nikolaos.

The branch of the pine tree groaned under the weight of the hanging man but eased as his struggles ebbed second by second. *Weak in both life and death.*

Nikolaos grinned.

Only then did his uncle see, realisation dawning and making his eyes swell with rage all too late.

Yes. It was me.

The groans, splutters, chokes ceased. Red eyes turned away as the corpse swung and twisted from the struggles and the breeze.

The algus and soldiers watching the execution turned to return to duty but Nikolaos lingered. A sleepless night hunting Darius had left his eyes heavy that morning, but he'd savour this picturesque moment.

The tree stood in a small grassy clearing next to a green tent. Inside the cloth structure, Archimedes held discussions. He'd not even ventured out to witness the execution, instead leaving the few people to observe as they awaited a summons.

Finally, years of coaxing have paid off. His uncle had spearheaded a catastrophe. They all thought the events that had led to the attempt on Archimedes's life were a string of chaotic occurrences, but Nikolaos knew better. Behind the chaos spun an intricate web that had culminated in him being closer than ever to heading Laltos's armies. After the fire of failure, opportunity rose from the ashes. He just needed Archimedes to name him the algus to succeed his uncle to Laltos's most respected position below regent.

To stand a chance, he needed to know what Archimedes was planning inside the tent with his Numbered. That's where Nikolaos's escort was most useful. His dormouse crept out of his boot and scurried through the grass towards the tent. Archimedes may have lacked physical speech, but his communications were nonetheless vulnerable to intrusion. A fact Nikolaos was about to exploit.

He discreetly mopped the sweat from his brow and tried to keep his nerves cloaked. Eavesdropping would get him crucified like a slave if discovered, but great rewards required great risks. Besides, escorts were rare among algus and no one knew he had one, let alone that he'd chosen a pathetic dormouse over the usual bellicose creatures. Escorts were only available to a select few willing to submit to the virtues of the new religion, the Diagathic Order. No one knew how they made the link between man and beast except the Chief Priest.

"*...I grow tired of this war.*" Archimedes's voice filled Nikolaos's mind, as sonorous as a voice from the underworld. His mouse's sensitive ears picked up every word now that she was close enough. "*I fear one of these men will be the death of me. I would see the war ended swiftly.*"

"Then let's make haste in finding the location of the mine," a woman's voice replied. "The algus argue our efforts are best spent coercing captives, not seeking one man." Nikolaos couldn't place her voice; the Numbered all sounded alike, monotone.

"And for how many months have we coerced, revealing naught?"

Too true; seizing the mine was vital. Some thought Archimedes's possession of the Staff meant victory over the rakkans was assured, but Nikolaos knew better. Wars were lost through complacency, as many kings had demonstrated throughout the centuries.

"Point conceded," the woman replied. "But—"

"As I say, I grow weary and dream of more tranquil pastures. This war will be won, but it will be by my methods. Unless revoked by the King, my word is law and those that need will be reminded of it."

"Yes, master."

Master. Nikolaos grimaced at the title. Only a Numbered would refer to Archimedes as such. He found it surprising that they debated strategy when alone yet never questioned the goman's commands in company.

"I succeeded in severing most of Darius's memories from his consciousness but couldn't extract all of them in time before he escaped me. Adult minds are so difficult to manipulate."

"Surely another knows the location—"

"A fruitless search given rakkans are immune to my powers. I must find Darius to finish what I started."

"I saw you didn't entirely remove his ability to fight."

"I was greedy and sought to count Darius amongst my Numbered. His mind was more resistant than I'd envisaged. I'll need help if I'm to turn him, perhaps an algus to persuade him the human way."

"What did you do to his strength? He's dangerous, but far less powerful than he was."

"I was greedy, but not foolish. I handicapped his ability, for now; it should be enough."

Silence hung for a moment. *"Send in Nikolaos."*

Curses. No mention of the Laltos Guard or any clue as to how Nikolaos might guide the goman towards the best man for the job—him.

The tent flaps opened and Nikolaos turned with faux surprise.

"Archimedes will see you," Thirty-seven called flatly, long black hair fluttering in the wind.

She was his favourite Numbered—because she bore a striking resemblance to the raven-haired beauty Lex now heading on a mysterious quest.

Nikolaos sauntered up. "A pleasure to see you again." He took Thirty-seven's hand to kiss it but she pulled it away. *Typical.* Those Archimedes sank his claws into were stripped of everything they were, especially compassion and warmth. New thought patterns urged them to ignore such impulses.

"Thirty-seven, please," Nikolaos said. "A little sympathy. My uncle was just executed." He spoke in jest, knowing her inevitable reply already. *Why should I care?*

"Why should I care?" she said.

It was an ingrained response in the Numbered. And none of them could answer that question. What reason had they to care about others?

The algus already ordained were careful around Archimedes to ensure he didn't tamper with *their* minds. They were fortunate he'd agreed not to so much as graze their skin.

They were even more fortunate he was the only goman in the Empire.

Before heading into the tent, Nikolaos straightened his leather tunic and adjusted his belt. Ascendency began with appearance.

Thirty-seven led him in. The tent was lofty and wide but bare except for a wooden table at the centre and a single stool, on which Archimedes's dark figure sat. They hadn't even bothered to cover the soil underfoot. The tent merely blocked the wind from scattering the parchments on the table and cast a deep shadow over them all.

Archimedes was reading a letter intently, small beads of sweat covering his dark brow as they always did. Nikolaos had never discovered why the goman always sweated, even in the chilly hills.

"*I take it Darius still evades you,*" Archimedes's voice boomed. One never grew accustomed to talking with someone with no mouth, whose words simply filled your mind like a headache.

"There's no sight of Darius. The forest is dense and my men too few. The rakkans may have found him and hidden him already." That was as good a hint he could muster off the cuff that he needed more men, the whole Laltos Guard perhaps.

The goman looked up at him, dreadlocks slipping back across his cheeks. "*I'd apologise for your uncle but neither of us care that he's dead.*"

At least Nikolaos needn't worry about outmanoeuvres and political games given gomans couldn't lie or deceive, but the problem was, what the goman lacked in deception he more than compensated for in perception and intellect.

"I mourn the death of any of my family. But one can't overlook taking the Staff of Arria without authorisation." Nikolaos struggled to contain a smirk.

"*Don't think I'm unaware of your conniving.*"

Nikolaos's blood ran cold. If Archimedes knew his orchestration then he'd be crucified, algus or not. "I assure you I had no part—"

"*No, but you threw your uncle to the wolves to save your own hide. Such political deviance may serve you well in Laltos, but in war I need algus with an eye for battle not gaming. I won't name you as your uncle's successor.*"

The damned mouthless swine. Who was he to say Nikolaos hadn't the knowledge of battle? He'd directed his men in plenty.

"A position I wouldn't have accepted had you offered," Nikolaos said, keeping his voice even. "It is for the Regent of

Laltos to determine who leads his city's defences." He'd take his chances buttering up the Regent, even though the man disliked him. Pity Lex was in the wilds on the goman's orders. She could have helped persuade her father.

Archimedes rose from the stool, a towering figure. "*I will command the Guard directly for now. We move for Cephos.*"

"You wish to halt the search for Darius?" Odd for the goman to concede so quickly and move to the nearby forest-town.

"*Yes.*" The goman's dark eyes clouded over. "*I already know that is where Darius will be.*"

"I'll relay your orders to the men," Nikolaos said, his mind already working on a new scheme to take the Laltos Guard for himself.

6

Darius crouched at the riverbank and ripped the thick Seplyga leaves from the ground, praying he hadn't confused it for a poisonous plant. At least bending eased the hunger and thirst pains jabbing his stomach.

Water streamed mere feet away yet his lips stung, cracked and dry. He hadn't noticed the water's peculiar taste when drowning, but had when he'd taken a drink. Contaminated. Lyra wouldn't so much as touch her tongue to it and that was enough to keep him away. The odd puddle would have to do until dire thirst demanded he drink from the water flowing mockingly by.

The corruption had to be man-made, tons of bodily waste being dumped farther upstream, most likely from a large city best avoided.

He broke the Seplyga stems and squeezed the seeping contents onto his shoulder. It stung as if rubbing in salt and he stifled a howl. The sight of the wound brought back more images of Amid's bloody body, that single memory raw in his mind. He'd tried to reason why it haunted him but remained flummoxed.

Why should I care? It was as if a voice whispered the question at the back of Darius's mind whenever he thought of caring.

No answer came.

Thankfully the sap soon hardened and sealed the wound. He rubbed a little on the bruising across his chest and back, gasping at the burn. Lyra padded over through the bushes, her tail lashing at the sound of his choked cries. Similar gashes and cuts spoiled her fur.

"Lyra, come here."

She backed away as he held out the yellow leaves, ears flattening against her head.

You're too sharp for your own good. "Stop."

She halted, amber eyes wide and trained on the plant in his hand.

"This'll help you." Darius knelt beside her and began rubbing the sap into her wounds, half expecting her to bite him for the effort. She squirmed and tried to wriggle away so he wrapped an arm around her and held her still. This cat was worth her weight in gold and her attitude did have its charms. Plus, having her made him feel less…alone.

After he'd treated her wounds she calmed, her warm body vibrating as she purred. He ran his hands through her fur, softer than the finest silk, or so he imagined having no memory of such fabrics. The gentle rise and fall of her chest rocked his heart into a calm rhythm. Peace.

A luxury he couldn't afford to enjoy any longer. His stomach growled, demanding more than the few berries he'd foraged the day before. Lyra had yet to show any signs of hunger, but she was likely as thirsty as he was. In spite of that, she paced by his side as they set off again through the undergrowth bordering the river. Darius carried a long pointed stick, the closest thing to a spear the forest granted him. Travelling without a weapon was worse than without a cloak. He knew how to fight and little else. *I guess you were the brains of our duo, Lyra.*

Questions had circled his mind all day to the brink of insanity. A raid of his pockets yielded no insights, only a few silver coins that, thankfully, he remembered the value of. They'd perhaps buy him a ride somewhere, but not far. Wouldn't an assassin or spy need more money for bribes or a few cups of firewater to loosen a man's tongue? Yet another question for the endless pile.

As evening approached, stealing away the sun's warmth, another night of disturbed sleep crammed in a bush loomed ahead. To survive the night, he'd have to risk drinking from the river. The idea repulsed him. Darius looked down along the riverbank, wishing for a source of clean water, perhaps a stream or brook meeting the river.

Something ahead caught his eye. A large stone wall arched over the water and stretched in each direction into the forest. Peeking over the top of the wall were pointed wooden roofs entangled within more trees—a settlement, finally. Water. Food. Weapons.

He slinked through the brush all the way to the wall. It stood twice his height, with moss and ivy clawing the ragged stones. Trees encroached on the whole construct, resting their branches on the top as if the stonework had been built through them without clearing the forest. *Bewildering.*

Lyra. Get higher and sense what you can of guards atop the wall. Crouching, Darius scratched her behind the ear to pacify the potential rebellious streak he'd learned to expect from her. It worked. The panther began clawing her way up a nearby tree while he wondered how she'd relay whatever she found.

This town would make for an easy siege. There was poor visibility from the wall, and the trees still had their lower branches, offering an easy climb for invaders. Sooner or later, the townsfolk would wake to their throats being cut. Though perfect for a rogue like him, it was not a place to linger for long.

Perched on a high branch, Lyra scanned around but seemed relaxed enough. Worst case scenario, she'd missed one or two waiting guards behind the wall that Darius would have to silence. It would even give him the opportunity to secure a weapon.

He made his way quietly up the tree, his parched tongue almost able to taste the water awaiting him inside the town. The top of the wall came into view. Only one guard visible, far away and facing in the opposite direction. *Kill them and take a sword and armour?* Maybe later. His need for water was most dire.

Darius moved across a branch like a squirrel, his gift granting agility even with muscles threatening to cramp. Soon his feet landed on the solid stone of the wall and he dropped down to a thankfully deserted street below, Lyra following.

The ground was hardened dirt with the odd bit of flagstone to even it out between roots and lumps. Stone buildings stood cobbled together under the shade of great trees; some even leant against them for support. None had windows that would allow him to swipe a bottle or cloak. He slinked to the narrowest street he saw and began to scavenge.

Would Lyra draw attention? Perhaps, but he'd risk staying with her to put her senses to use. And she desperately needed water as well. The makeshift spear was less necessary, so he snapped it in half, tossed one piece aside and leaned on the remaining shaft like a walking stick.

A sweaty, plump woman with a hulking sack over her shoulder was the first to happen across him. Both her hands were visible but she could have a knife concealed under her fleece. The paranoia of his thoughts surprised him, but this warrior's instinct had kept him alive so far.

She caught his eye and bowed to him, as best she could under the weight. *Strange.* Giving her a nervous nod in return, Darius continued walking. He took the next turn he could, only to almost knock heads with a soldier.

He adjusted his grip on his staff as the man shoved him back.

"Watch it!" The hoplite glared, looking him up and down. Lyra growled, drawing the man's gaze, and his expression softened.

Darius paused, waiting for the man to draw his sword before he struck.

"My apologies, algus." The man bowed his head sheepishly, backing away.

This attention and reverence Darius could do without. He waved his free hand in a dismissive gesture.

The soldier turned and scuttled away as Lyra watched with ears stood to attention.

As the sun set, the shadows in the streets he traipsed lengthened. *We should get inside, my whiskered friend.* Darius set off again through the town, passing ragged people as quickly as possible. After a few streets, he came across a building with a battered wooden sign reading "Cephos Inn." The inn leaned from the side of a tree, with a crooked wooden roof that looked as if it would slip off at any moment. *It'll do.*

A peregrine perched on top of the building and Darius swore it was looking at him. Keeping one eye on the bird, he entered a narrow room with scattered wooden tables and chairs. Floorboards creaked and a stale smell of sweat floated in the air. The place was deserted except for a man and boy leaning across a table in quiet conversation. Drinks stood near their elbows.

Their discussion cut off as he came in and they looked at him.

The man stood up, slim except for his large protruding belly. The few hairs that remained on his head were grey and straggly. He looked Darius up and down then glanced at Lyra, a mix of confusion and disbelief on his face. "May I help you, algus?"

Darius rushed over and snatched the man's half-full cup. He downed the bitter ale so quickly some spilled into his beard, but he didn't care. Cold liquid soothed his parched gullet. With a sigh he set the cup on the table. "Apologies, but I'm in dire need of water. My escort, too."

"Get water." The old man nodded to the boy who rushed off into the next room.

"I need a room for the night, also," Darius said. He'd rest, eat his fill and be gone by morning.

"Well," the innkeeper walked from behind the table, "there's a fine guest house on the east side of town, owned by Ismene."

Darius didn't need comfort or more wandering the town. "Do you not have rooms here?"

The man scratched his peeling scalp. "I do. You mean to stay here?"

"Is that a problem?"

"Well, of course not, algus. I just…" The man's eyes relaxed as though a pleasant thought had occurred. "Pardon my asking, but you're dressed as a vagabond, and you finished the last of my ale. Do you mean to pay?"

His question implied Darius's algus status might let him off on an empty purse if he wanted. *Good to know.*

Darius pulled a silver coin from his pocket. "I'll give you a crest at the end of my stay, as long as it goes undisturbed and unnoticed by all." Better to rely on men's greed than their discretion.

The old man's eyes widened and he grinned. "Let me show you to a room and I'll bring your refreshments up."

He grabbed a couple of clay oil lamps and led Darius and Lyra through a corridor and up a staircase so steep it was virtually a ladder. Based on the condition of the place so far, it wouldn't be comfortable, but just a bed would do. Now that Darius had a respite from soldiers, rivers and dangerous forests, the stress had eased from his muscles and left them tired, worn and bruised.

"Here." The innkeeper opened the door to a cramped room, bare but for a single bed and small wooden desk and chair by a thin window. He handed Darius a lamp. "I'll be back with supplies soon."

"Bring me a razor, too." Removing his beard and hair would make him less recognisable.

The man nodded and left.

Darius let Lyra in then closed the door and set the lamp down. He peered out of the window for a while, taking in as much of the town as he could, trying to jog any memories. Only a bloody Amid came to mind, best wrestled back into the shadows of his thoughts. *So much blood.*

Outside, a pair of iron-capped soldiers patrolled the streets, wearing the same attire as the ones he'd fought only days ago. Perhaps they wouldn't recognise him, but it wasn't worth the risk. Darius turned back to the room and eyed Lyra, who had made herself comfortable on the bed and lay dozing.

"Oh no. You're not getting the bed." He walked over and nudged her shoulder.

She flicked a paw at his arm but barely roused.

"Fine." He squeezed himself onto the straw mattress next to her and let out a deep sigh. Not even the hard lumps in the bed digging into his lumbar spoiled this rare moment of peace. He'd drink, eat, sleep then get back on the road to Margalvia. Something there may trigger a memory. Someone could help him. He had a good inkling about it.

Footsteps approached and there was a knock at the door.

"Some bread and water for you, algus," the old man called.

That was more luring than sleep. Darius got up and opened the door. "Thank you." He took a crusty loaf and bottle from the innkeeper, not hesitating to bite off a chunk of bread. A bit stale, but more than satisfying for his gnawing stomach.

"Apologies, but I don't have anything more. No one really dines here."

"Bread's fine for me," Darius mumbled. "But she needs meat." He nodded over to Lyra's slumped body.

"It shouldn't be hard to find some. If you call at the butcher's down the street he will have some chickens."

"Will you get some for me?"

The man shifted uncomfortably. "But…it's getting dark outside."

Darius gulped some clean water to wash down the bread. "Is that a problem?"

"The curfew. I'm not allowed."

Strange that a small, secluded town would have a curfew. He could ask the reason for it but it may rouse suspicion.

"Never mind, it can wait until tomorrow." Lyra was asleep—she'd be fine until the morning, or else he'd wake to her nibbling his arm. "The razor?"

Looking relieved, the man held out the requested implement. "If that will be all…"

"Good night," Darius said.

"Good night." The innkeeper turned to leave.

After closing the door, Darius sat down at the table and devoured the rest of the bread. Drinking part of the water, he took the razor in his hand. His mind returned to circling questions as he dampened his hair and beard and began shaving it all. With each stroke, he listed all he believed true.

One, he had the speed of an algus.

Two, Archimedes was his enemy, one that had dominated Darius in combat.

Three, Brutus said he'd been an assassin, and likely a lethal one.

Four, the soldiers in this town looked the same as those that attacked him in the forest; that meant it was safest to treat it as hostile.

Five, Margalvia was his home, according to Brutus. Maybe he and his mother had settled there.

Six, he hated blood, so much the thought of nicking his skin while shaving made him queasy. Just perfect. A warrior afraid of blood. His childhood memory welled up again, a tide of red shame. *I'm still not a real warrior.* And yet Felix had treated him as one, in spite of his revulsion.

That was all; six facts. Part of him wished Felix were still here to say more.

Once his head and chin were bald, Darius set down the razor and searched around for a bowl or container. Finding one in the corner, he poured Lyra the rest of the water, wanting to down it himself with every glug out but feeling pangs of guilt at just the thought.

Why should I care? The voice inside persisted, but he was too tired to ruminate so gave in to his instincts. Leaving the bowl of water ready for Lyra, he clambered back into bed beside her. Events replayed in his mind as he gradually drifted off to sleep.

7

Darius woke in the night to hammering on the bedroom door.

"Algus!" the old man called. "Come quickly!"

The room was dark but for a thin outline of light around the door, flickering as the innkeeper bashed it. Darius hauled himself out of bed and flung it open. His host stood with his eyebrows halfway up his forehead.

"What is this?" Darius demanded. That was the man's silver crest gone for an *undisturbed* stay.

A woman's scream echoed in the streets below.

The old man swallowed. "They need your help." He shoved an ancient, battered sword against Darius's chest. "It's all I have."

Darius took the cold metal hilt and held up the blade. Its edge showed dents and signs of heavy use. "Why do you give me this?"

"There's a rakkan in Cephos." The innkeeper pointed frantically out the window as Lyra twitched in her sleep. If only Darius were as heavy a sleeper as her.

"Fifth time this month," the man continued. "There's no other algus in town. You have to protect us."

What was a rakkan, and why should Darius care? He racked his mind but found no reason. *Illogical.*

"I'll pass."

Lantern light flickered across the old man's reddened face. His eyes bulged as if his head was about to burst. "You're an algus, it's your one duty. You're just going to stand here while people die?"

"No. I'll return to bed, but thank you for the sword." It'd save him the trouble of making someone bleed for one.

The innkeeper dared to grab his arm, wearing his patience thin. "But, the rakkan!"

Lyra started from the mattress and darted towards the door. A sudden rush of urgency set Darius's heart racing. *Lyra!* She ignored him and whisked past down the corridor. Scowling, he jerked his arm free, watching the tail of his guide to Margalvia disappear down the steep stairs. *Damn her.*

Ignoring the man's continued pleas, he dashed after his cat, muttering "useless sword" and "no armour" between his gritted teeth. Maybe he should fear this rakkan but the man seemed to suggest this was a standard duty of being an algus. Darius had likely killed hundreds. Unless they were as strong as a goman…

Relax. He'd likely killed hundreds.

Lyra finally halted in the street outside, alert and intent on action. Lamps hung from nearby buildings and trees, adding spots of light in an otherwise shadowed town. Distant clanks of armour and shouts rang throughout.

"The Guard's over there." The old man had followed him and now pointed to a group of men down the street. Darkness obscured them but the glint of armour and weapons was unmistakable. Soldiers.

"I'll do it alone," Darius said. Best to avoid soldiers even with his newly shaved head. The only algus in town was likely to draw too much attention as it was. Whatever this rakkan was, he prayed he'd make quick work of it, or wait until Lyra was satisfied enough to go back to bed.

Rakkan. He hated it just by the name. It brought images of a disgusting beast, mouth twisted and snarling at him.

"Good fortune," the innkeeper said.

The words sparked a nervous feeling as Darius turned and set off into the labyrinth of streets, Lyra quickly skipping ahead. He gripped his sword so firmly the metal chilled the bones in his palm. His escort showed no such hesitation. *Why are you making us do this?*

The muscles in his legs tingled, readying for that inhuman speed once again. He rounded another corner into a narrow street and stopped at the sight of a body, helmet caved in from a single brutal hit. The spilling brains forced his eyes skyward as he stepped over it. Soon he came across another body with a blackened slash across the man's neck, almost like the wound had been cauterised. The rakkan was tearing rampant through the town, but what did the people expect when their defences were so lax?

Another victim's agonised wail suffused in the darkness between the buildings and trees. This time it was a man's and close, echoing from the way Darius had come. It could have been the old innkeeper. Darius ran his thumb against the cross-guard of his sword, feeling every dent. "It's all I have," the man had said, gifting his last defence to a nomad. *Foolish man.* So why did Darius feel a stirring of guilt in his gut?

Darius crouched and rubbed Lyra's ear. She pressed her cheek firmly into his palm with a purr, seeming unfazed. There surely wasn't much that could take on a hulking cat like her.

If this goes badly, I'm blaming you.

Rising, he started towards the last cry he'd heard, running along the bumpy street, zig-zagging to stay shrouded by the streams of shadow between lamps. The rakkan could be anywhere, look like anything. By staying concealed, he might catch it off guard.

Sounds of bustling got closer; men shouted and weapons clashed. The noises thinned as if one by one voices were silenced. Sweat gathered on Darius's forearms and palms so he tightened his grip on the sword's hilt. A slip could mean death.

Lyra prowled slightly ahead, her tense shoulders coiling energy, ready for that first strike. She seemed to know what they were heading into. He wished he did.

They rounded the corner of a building. Two men stood grappling under a swaying street lamp. One wore the familiar armour of the town's guards. Darius saw only the back of the other, whose loose tunic and trousers bore the scraggly appearance of a slave. On the ground around them, bodies lay in the shadows—the defeated. He drew back a step, avoiding the flickering edge of light, Lyra at his heel. It was senseless to show himself before he knew what was transpiring.

The soldier swung his sword wildly, but the slave dodged every swing with empty hands raised as if toying with the man. As soon as an opening appeared, the slave slammed his palm against the soldier's chest, knocking his opponent into a wall with a crunch. Sliding forward, the slave pinned the soldier in place. The guard dropped his weapon and fought to break free, but the bony arm held as firmly as an iron bar. Was this the enemy responsible for caving in the helmet of the first body Darius had seen? He certainly seemed to possess the necessary strength, despite his frail appearance.

The soldier's scale armour shimmered orange and grew brighter. He screamed, writhing and twisting his face away from the glow. The armour bent inwards as molten orange enveloped the slave's hand, raging around it like a trapped inferno. It caused no apparent ill effect to the wielder but the victim convulsed as his armour melted. Like a sharp blade through flesh, the slave's arm sank into the soldier's chest.

The slave stepped back and let the lifeless body slump. A snicker broke the night's silence. *So, this is a rakkan.* A man so powerful the town's resistance was futile? Darius wondered how many existed. Another question to ask when he reached Margalvia.

Turning, the rakkan looked around. His eyes glowed white hot in an otherwise human face before extinguishing to a more normal set of eyes with huge black irises that sucked in the light around them. The rakkan's sunken cheeks and skinny limbs made him look like a starved corpse, but he'd betrayed his true power. The guards had no answer to the rakkan's strength, but Darius could move like an algus. If anyone stood a chance, it was him.

The rakkan's nose scrunched in a look of scorn. "I see you lurking in the dark, algus."

Crap.

The rakkan picked up the soldier's body by the leg. "Here, why don't you try and save this one." He flung the body at Darius as if it weighed nothing.

Darius dove out of the way of the hurtling corpse and skidded across the jagged cobbles. He held his sword tight as the stones grazed his knuckles, ruing his less than graceful dodge. As he clambered up to one knee, Lyra darted fearlessly towards the rakkan. *No!* He reached to stop her but the big cat pounced, baring her fangs at the rakkan's gaunt neck.

In one swift move, he side-stepped and whipped the back of his hand across her face. Her body hit the ground and tumbled like a rag doll into a wall.

Darius gritted his teeth. This fiend dared strike his escort, the one that had saved his life from the river, the only one he could trust? After witnessing the strength of this creature, self-preservation told him to run and leave the town to its fate, but he couldn't drag his eyes from Lyra's motionless body, his rebellious companion possibly lost forever. Despite urges to the contrary, he wouldn't leave her to die.

He glowered at the rakkan. *You'll pay for that.*

Drawing back his sword, Darius charged in. His first swing aimed to sever the rakkan's head but the man jumped back and watched the blade slice through air.

The rakkan flashed a wry grin. "Need to do better."

He could. Despite the dodging, the rakkan showed no match for his speed. Darius feinted then took another fast-paced swing, aiming for the rakkan's stomach.

The rakkan leapt, soared over his head and landed beyond his reach. Nice trick, but once again, Darius closed the distance between them with ease.

His opponent swung for Darius's chin but he leant to the side and easily evaded. Ducking under another swinging fist, he flashed a grin of his own. Neither of the rakkan's punches so much as grazed his cheek.

Darius chuckled at the leaden creature. He switched his sword to his off hand. When the killing blow landed, the rakkan would know just how superior Darius was.

"You're awfully slow for an algus," the rakkan said.

Darius narrowed his eyes. *Time to make this creature's smart tongue taste blood.* He lunged forward, his sword aimed between the rakkan's soulless eyes. The rakkan dodged out of the blade's path, but as he did, Darius pulled back his sword, shifted his weight, and stamped his foot onto the rakkan's knee.

Pain tore up Darius's leg as if he'd kicked an anvil. The rakkan stood unmoved.

What the…

The rakkan twisted and grabbed his outstretched arm by the wrist. Grunting, Darius tried to wrest his arm free. But his enemy's hand tightened until his grip on the sword failed. A groan of pain seeped from his lips as his weapon clattered onto the ground.

"You're no algus." The rakkan laughed.

No matter how hard Darius pulled, the rakkan stood anchored, as if ten times his size. Two specks of light glinted in the rakkan's otherwise obsidian eyes, the first hints of the power about to be unleashed.

There was no way Darius would die like a roasted hog, even if it meant chewing his own arm off. As he redoubled his efforts to break free, the light swelled in the rakkan's eyes until it consumed them in a swirling burst of fire. Why had he underestimated this monster? *Darius, you arrogant fool!* Now Lyra would pay for his mistake, too.

His arm burned under the rakkan's grip as if plunged into hot coals. He tugged so hard the limb almost tore from his shoulder. Pain seared across his flesh as he howled and collapsed to his knees.

"I knew it," the rakkan said.

Smoke fizzled from Darius's arm, the stench of burning flesh making him retch. Across the street Lyra remained motionless on the ground. Agony drowned his thoughts, spasms shook his arm.

As he succumbed, a bird swooped from the darkness. The rakkan ducked as it zipped by, sharp talons inches from his face. He grunted in annoyance as the bird darted in again with the speed of a bird of prey.

A blue-tipped arrow appeared and flashed through the air, lodged itself in the rakkan's shoulder. Releasing a yell of pain, he lost his grip and let Darius fall to the ground. Darius scooted back, his blistered mess of an arm cradled against his chest.

The rakkan spun to face the arrow's source—one of the nearby rooftops. His shoulder flared orange and the arrow ignited, turning to ash in an instant. The flames vanished as quickly as they'd appeared and blood trickled from the wound as he bent to pick up Darius's fallen sword.

"So, they sent a real algus." His voice had lost its sneer.

Another arrow darted from the roof but the rakkan twisted and dodged it. He started towards the building. With a leap, he soared upwards and grabbed hold of the second storey roof. As the rakkan pulled himself up, a shadow slid swiftly from the building and onto the street below. Darius wasn't the only one to notice. The rakkan scowled, ran across the roof then jumped down in pursuit. Sword poised over his head, he prepared to land a blow on his slippery foe.

In the street below, a blade burst into life, brilliant cobalt blue materialising out of the darkness. Its wielder thrust the weapon upwards towards the falling rakkan.

Their swords clashed in mid-air. The fluorescent blade cut through the rakkan's before it sliced through his torso with equal ease. As the rakkan's eviscerated body struck the ground, the blue light extinguished.

Darius took little comfort from the rakkan's demise. His arm still burned as if stuck in a forge. What a failure he was, defeated by a foe that another algus had slain with ease. Why had he been so overconfident?

The algus walked towards him and finally stepped into the light. Her raven hair, tied back with a strip of cloth, shone and bounced as she walked. She wore the same black leather as he and all the other algus.

Darius tried to summon the energy to fight her should she turn on him next, but the pain was too great. His eyes watered as he squeezed them closed for a second. When he opened them, she stood above him, peering down with concerned blue eyes.

"Darius."

His heart skipped at the sound of her voice, or perhaps the pain.

"Are you…crying?" Her worry twisted into contempt.

Turning his head away, Darius wiped his eyes. Tears of pain weren't weeping.

"Up! We need to leave. Now!" She bent down, grabbed his good arm and hauled him to his feet.

Bolts of pain shot through his body from the rough movement. "Get your hands off me." He pulled free and bent over, shielding his burnt flesh from the night's light breeze. Every shift of air felt like it peeled his skin off.

She spun him and inspected his injury. "How did *that* happen?"

"That fiend grabbed me and just burned me with his hand." He ground his teeth against a groan of pain.

"I guessed that." The algus touched her finger lightly across the raw flesh. "I meant how did it happen *to you*?"

All this time he'd thought himself a fierce fighter. *Fool.*

She lifted her head and looked him in the eyes, so close he felt her breath. Her look of concern had returned.

"Who are you?" he asked.

For a moment she said nothing, just stared unblinking, deep in thoughts he couldn't read.

At last an answer came. "I'm Lex. How much did he get?"

"What?"

"Archimedes. How much do you remember?"

He tried to determine whether the name "Lex" was buried somewhere in his head but all he could think of was plunging his arm into a trough of water. "I don't really remember anything."

Her eyebrows rose in shock then pressed down together. A muscle flexed on her jaw.

Without warning, she punched him in the gut. "You halfwit," she growled as he dropped to one knee. "I *told* you it was too risky to attack Archimedes. Damn you, you've put our lives in danger."

"Lex," Darius managed to croak between a fit of coughs. The pain had blunted his reactions. He needed to stand to defend himself but the blow had winded him.

Lex backed off and looked to the sky. "He had you for so little time. How could he get so much?"

Darius staggered up, finally able to fill his lungs. "Wait, you saw what happened to me?"

"Who do you think saved you? If I hadn't got Archimedes away from you, you'd be a drooling vegetable. Well, more of one. They almost saw my face too. If they'd found out who I was…"

Was she another mole like him, desperate to not reveal herself and join him among the hunted? Or was this a trick? Darius searched her face for deceit but could see no sign of it.

She paused, lost in thought, then her eyes darted up and she seized him by the shoulders. "What do you remember about your grandfather?"

Grandfather? He searched his mind but it only yielded the all too familiar emptiness.

"Nothing," he said, not sure he'd tell her if he did remember.

"Where is he? Do you remember that?"

"No."

"And what about the mine. Do you remember anything?"

How many times do I have to say it? "No."

Her jawline tensed again.

Darius braced for another assault, ready to counter this time, but her rage remained under control.

The sounds of footsteps and voices echoed around a corner on the street ahead. A group of soldiers were heading towards them.

Lex glanced in their direction. "Let me speak. Stay in the shadows so they don't see your face. And don't say a word," she turned to him, "or I'll cut your throat."

Her hard eyes said she meant it.

8

The three soldiers eyed the two halves of the dead rakkan as they approached Lex. She stepped in front of Darius, shielding him from view as much as possible.

Ducking his head, he cursed over and over in his mind, trying to block out the burning pain of his injured arm.

The leader's cloak was long and royal blue, made of finer cloth than his two compatriots—an officer, but not an algus. His belt buckle was plain metal. He crossed an arm across his chest and bowed deeply. "Algus Alexandra."

"Do you always have to be so formal, Acamas?" she replied. "How many years have we known each other?"

"'Tis reverence deserved. Is the town safe?"

"Yes. There was only one rakkan."

The soldiers' postures relaxed and Acamas removed his helmet. He was a stout man with short dark hair and a broad, stubbled jaw. "Praise Agathos. My wife and son can sleep safely again." He beamed.

"Indeed." Lex lifted a silver pendant hanging from her neck and kissed it gently like it was precious to her.

The other soldiers stared at her with mouths slightly ajar.

"It's fortunate I was passing through," she continued, as if unaware of their gaze. "I know your algus were called away recently. When will they return?"

Acamas looked around at the other soldiers and nudged them out of their reverie. They shrugged. "We couldn't say. They were expected back today but sent word of a delay to search the woods."

Darius had a guess what they were searching for.

Scratching sounded from the other side of the street. Lyra's paws twitched across the cobbles. *She's alive.* Relief temporarily overshadowed his pain.

"Is that this man's escort?" Acamas asked, looking past Lex to Darius's shaded figure.

"Never mind him," Lex said.

"Is your escort alright, algus?"

Darius drew a breath to speak but thought better of it and snapped his mouth shut.

Lex straightened her back and stood tall, drawing Acamas's gaze away. "I said leave him be." Her voice was quiet but all the more menacing for it. Despite a slender and lean frame, unthreatening at first glance, her demeanour exuded a self-assuredness only an adept fighter would have.

"The cat needs assistance," she added. "Could you take it to Ismene's? That's where we'll be lodging."

Acamas puffed out his chest. "Right away."

The soldiers shuffled over to Lyra. None dared steal a glance back at Darius. They picked up his panther and carried her limp body off down the street. As Lyra disappeared Darius felt a strange unease. Without her, there was no-one that he could trust and she had no-one to protect her in such a vulnerable state.

He stood up and groaned at the sky, spewing out the pain. Invisible fire raged along his arm. "Why did you tell them to take Lyra?"

"Because I didn't feel like carrying her, and you certainly aren't up to it. Now, sit down." Lex knelt down and started unfastening his left boot.

He didn't move. "What are you doing?"

"I said sit down." She ripped his feet from under him and his backside crashed hard onto the stone street.

"What the hell!" If he had two good arms he'd—

She pulled off his boot and touched his toe lightly with her finger. "Tell me if this hurts."

Darius jerked his foot out of her hands. "Everything hurts. What're you doing?"

She let out a long exhale. "I can ease the pain in your arm but it's dangerous. You're normally immune to algor, but I'm not sure what Archimedes did to you."

"Algor?"

"This is algor." She extended a finger and its tip glimmered with a spark of blue—the same blue that had wreathed her sword and coated the arrowheads. "It's antagonistic to ferven—what rakkans conjure. But only people with algor, like us, can touch it. To regular humans it's deadly."

Darius eyed it with trepidation. "So I may die?"

"Probably not. But it may freeze off a limb, so I figured a toe was the least objectionable. But if you have another preference…"

"I'd prefer a bucket of water." He moved to stand up, but before he could Lex grabbed his burnt arm and held him down.

Searing pain blinded him, tearing a growl from his throat. "Let go!" Darius tried to grab her arm with his free hand but she caught hold of it.

"Do you feel that burning? That will *never* cease unless I stop it. The ferven will ravage your nerves. Forever. Water does nothing."

She released his arm and he fell back, cradling it. Lex looked away like the sight of him was intolerable. So much pain. Who was this woman, and was she here to aid him or torture him? *I should burn her arm and see how she likes it.* If this was how she treated him he wouldn't stay around her for long.

"The burning will never stop?" Fear sank its claws into his chest at the thought that the only thing he had left, being a warrior, would be stripped of him as well. There was no chance he could fight bearing this pain.

"No."

"Can you help me without algor?"

"No. There's nothing we can do without it. Few humans survive encounters with rakkans and those that do are consigned to a miserable life. Or suicide." Her face remained frozen. This time, when she picked up his foot, he didn't resist. "Tell me if this hurts."

Darius braced and felt a light flick on his toe. "Was that it?"

"Yes."

"It didn't hurt." His toe looked normal.

Lex gently took his hand and held a palm over his burns. The touch made him nervous, but not for fear of further pain. He couldn't remember ever being touched by a beautiful woman. It sent a pleasant warmth through him, despite his aching arm. Her palm glowed a faint blue, then she pressed it onto the seared skin.

Cool waves rushed over his arm as if held beneath a cold waterfall. The chill spread through his veins and enveloped the arm, refreshing it more than he could have imagined. The burning sensation vanished.

Darius smiled and sighed deeply. "That feels good."

She held his arm for a few more seconds before releasing him. The limb still looked a mess—skin peeling and flesh charred—but the pain was bearable and his hand could close enough to hold a sword. That was all that mattered.

"Thanks," he said.

She stood and looked up at the roof where she'd been earlier.

"Why are you helping me?" Darius asked.

"Darius was my closest friend."

He frowned. She made it sound as if he was dead. "*I'm* Darius."

"No. I don't know you. You're not the Darius I know."

Though he appreciated her aid, he'd had enough of this woman's company and stood to go. "Then I'll leave you to—"

"No more talk."

"Don't tell m—"

"We're in danger." Turning, she reached out and touched his burn again. A cool wash of algor soothed the injury and his anger dissolved along with the pain.

"I'll get my bow then we're heading to the lodge. From now on, your name is Philippos. No one here knows who you are and they mustn't find out. Archimedes is coming for you, and he won't stop until he finishes what he started."

"You want to help me?"

Her lips pressed together in a thin line. "I'll get back the real Darius."

He grabbed her arm. "You can get my memory back?" Dare he hope?

"The journey will be dangerous and will test your limits. But I can get back Darius—the warrior who wouldn't be bested by a single rakkan, who would die for us and us for him. Is that what you want?"

Was it true the old Darius was stronger than he? Dying for her or anyone else made no sense to him, but Lex had answers to who he was before. Could he really again become a fearsome warrior?

It wasn't as if he could refuse her offer with ease—Lex's thumb rested on the hilt of her sword.

Darius avoided her question with one of his own. "Will you take me to Margalvia?" At least he could appear eager for that. It was the one place he'd most likely find allies.

She smirked. "Yes."

"Then I'll go with you." *For now.*

9

Lex wouldn't speak any further until they were indoors. She led Darius to a dwelling much more luxurious than his previous place of respite. The lodge looked deceptively ordinary outside, just another stone-walled building. However, its fine interior spoke of wealth and comfort. Fluffy white rugs ordained the floors throughout, so spotless he didn't dare step on them and leave traces of his presence.

They rounded a corner to see a well-dressed man seated at a table. His head was bent over a parchment as he scribbled on it.

"I'll take care of him," Lex whispered while Darius stepped back out of sight.

The man's creaseless clothes and well-groomed hair meant he was likely the host. Lex approached and flicked her hair. As the man looked up she leaned in close, whispering something that brought a wide grin to his clean-shaven face. She stroked his flushed cheek and laughed at his reply.

Darius had assumed "I'll take care of him" meant she'd kill the man, but watching her smile, the way she stroked a finger across the host's hand, made it obvious that wooing the man was easier for her than killing him. Was this the same woman that had just manhandled him? He wished she'd treated him with the same delicateness. She'd flipped from fearsome killer to playful beauty in an instant, a master of deception. If he wasn't careful, this woman would manipulate him like a plaything. *I'd better stay on my guard around her.*

The man grinned and stood, taking his leave down a staircase behind the table. Lex turned, the charming smile falling from her face as she beckoned for Darius to follow her.

She led him upstairs to a bedroom where he found Lyra waiting and still breathing, much to his relief. The panther lay on a four-poster bed lined with green satin drapes and silk sheets. Chairs sat plump with padding and cushions at the side of the room.

The sounds of their entrance roused Lyra. Wearily, she stepped from the bed and walked to them. Darius knelt down to greet her but she passed him and sauntered up to Lex to rub against the algus's legs.

"Hey, girl." Lex scratched Lyra behind the ear.

Charming. He gritted his teeth at the panther's snub but was grateful Lyra did seem to recognise Lex. Did that mean he should trust her, or start to doubt his panther?

"Will she recover?" he asked.

"I think so. She's been in worse states."

"Do you have one?"

"I have Tiro, my peregrine falcon."

That must have been the bird that had distracted the rakkan before Lex appeared.

"How are they so obedient?" he asked.

"They're escorts, bonded by the High Priest."

"And that means?"

Lex shook her head. "I'm not going to explain the world to you, Philippos. I've neither the time nor the patience. I'll tell you what you need to survive and get your memory back." She walked over and sat down in the largest, most padded seat.

"Sit." She pointed to a chair opposite barely large enough for an adult.

Not just aggressive, passive aggressive.

Darius pushed the chair aside and dragged a larger seat forward. Satisfied with the new arrangement, he settled on the cushions. Lex's unwavering gaze stayed locked on him making him nervous, which only worsened when she rested a hand on the hilt of a dagger at her waist.

Lyra walked over and flopped on the floor beside his chair. For a moment, he stroked her head, welcoming the comfort and distraction of her presence.

"Tell me everything that has happened—that you remember."

Darius looked up from his escort and was caught by Lex's alluring blue eyes. They beckoned for the truth, and he provided it.

As succinctly as possible, he relayed all that had occurred since he awoke, starting with meeting Brutus and Felix and their pursuit through the forest. When he told her of Felix's death, Lex stared at her lap but said nothing. He continued to his encounter with the mouthless man.

"That was Archimedes, a goman," Lex said. "He's powerful. One touch and your mind is his, to scramble and pluck out whatever he fancies. He can even embed false memories and beliefs. I can already see he's stripped you of your compassion."

Such power, not only to erase a person but to turn anyone into a slave. Darius shuddered. Thank heavens the goman needed to touch his victims and couldn't do it with a stare. Could Darius trust anything in his mind if this were true? Was that single memory about Amid real? He dared not ask her, in case it was.

"How do I know he didn't give me false memories?"

"You won't, but I'll know. Now continue."

Darius swallowed his questions and continued. Lex probed for every detail, from passing out after surviving the river to when he awoke and trudged through the forest for two days until he found the town and inn.

"The innkeeper acted strange," Darius said. "Everyone was bowing to me. Am I noble?"

Lex gestured at the panther now sleeping by his chair. "If they saw Lyra, they think you're an algus, a guardian of man. We defend the land from the rakkans to allow ordinary humans to live here." Lex continued probing further until, after what felt like hours, she was eventually satisfied. Answering her questions had worn him out, but sleep could wait. Now it was his turn.

"Why is Archimedes hunting me?" he asked.

Lex paused. "The King commissioned Archimedes to end the war, which includes stopping you. Most cities submit to Medus, King of the city of Toria and its empire; a few don't and the King wants them razed. Every algus and soldier in the Torian Empire is effectively under the goman's command."

"The algus have time to fight wars as well as defend the land from the rakkans?"

"War is the life of an algus, whether it be rakkans or humans."

"And you fight the King?"

"I take the King's coin. I'm part of the Laltos Guard, and the Regent of Laltos answers to him." She narrowed her eyes, gripped the hilt of her dagger, turning her knuckles white. "I don't trust you enough to say more."

"At least explain the interest in me," Darius grumbled.

"You must still have something important in that mind of yours."

Darius scoffed at the thought that one of the remnant pockets of information in his almost empty mind still had any value.

If he was wrapped up in a war or rebellion, he couldn't say he cared about it now, but it meant he'd have numbers behind him.

"How many algus do we have on our side?" he asked.

Lex looked him up and down. "One and a half."

He scowled at her. "Why am I half?" Was it because he'd let the rakkan best him? His mother's words rang in his ears. *You're not a real warrior.*

"You aren't ordained, which is why you still bear a slave's name."

The way she said it didn't sound like an insult, surprisingly, but the words still stung, along with frustration that they were the only ones. At least she didn't say half as a slur on his fighting ability, but perhaps she still thought lesser of him.

"Do we have any powers in addition to speed and algor?"

"No. Not enough for you?"

He held his injured arm. "Apparently not. But how is it just you and me? What about Brutus? Felix? We don't have more allies?"

Lex shook her head. "They aren't algus. There's an army, but they can't stand against Archimedes and his algus. When you ambushed him, it was as good an opportunity as you'll ever get. He'd wandered alone without the Staff of Arria, his greatest weapon. But you still couldn't overcome him."

Darius recalled the blackened staff, how all his strength had deserted him. *This is a foolish cause against insurmountable odds.*

"Why do you fight with me?" he asked.

Lex shifted uncomfortably, her stony expression telling him her lips were sealed against that answer.

He sighed, one eye still on the dagger clutched in her hand. "There's too much I don't understand. I won't last long in this state against every man and his dog." It was time to figure out how much use this woman was. "How can you get my memory back?"

"A goman must give it back to you."

"So where do we find one?" On the road to Margalvia, he hoped.

"Archimedes is the only one in the whole land."

That wasn't what he wanted to hear, yet he was a little relieved there weren't more out there given how powerful the goman was. "How can he be the only one?"

"They originate from across the Aretean Sea. Its waves are as high as the cliffs and few have ever crossed it."

How could he get Archimedes to give back his memories when he could barely stand in the goman's presence?

"There may be another that can help," Lex said.

Trying not to look too eager, he asked, "Who?"

"The Waif Magician, and you're going to help me find her."

That was certainly a grand alias. Darius was hesitant to place his life in the hands of this mysterious algus, but how much use was a man with no memories? He needed to regain them and his strength. "Who is this person?"

She tilted her head and grinned slightly. "The bald head looks good on you."

He cleared his throat, well aware she was trying to charm him to dodge the question but unable to ignore the twinge of pleasure at the compliment. "Tell me—"

Lex stood. "We've said enough for one night." The dismissal was like a parent telling a child it was time for bed. Which reminded him…

"Wait. Where are my mother and father?" He'd cared about them once and the curiosity played at the back of his mind. The absent father Brutus had said was dead, and the mother that had told him he wasn't a warrior. The rakkan had made him start to fear she was right.

"Your father's dead. Mother... Who knows? You hadn't spoken to her since you were a boy."

Darius took a deep breath, dreading the answer to the next question. "And my brother?"

She stared blankly for a few moments. "Dead. Now, that's enough."

"I disagree." He stood too but before he could catch her arm, she'd moved for the door.

The algus paused in the doorway and half turned. "I don't know if I trust you enough to say more. Get some rest and be ready for tomorrow. We're leaving Cephos at the break of dawn, before Archimedes's men arrive in full force. Don't leave this room before I return."

"Wait—"

She closed the door behind her. Darius stared at the varnished wood. Why was she helping him? She'd seemed most desperate when asking for details of his grandfather, but otherwise she hadn't seemed to care much if he lived or died. Her feelings were kept well-guarded, that much he could tell.

This woman was going to be more than a handful, with her beauty and charm that could easily captivate him if he wasn't careful. He had to be cautious, for he'd seen that beauty cloaked a violent and ruthless woman. Part of him was taken with her already. The other part wanted to wring her neck.

He looked over to Lyra. *And you snubbed me for her. I must be even more of a swine than I thought.*

10

Brutus crawled from his sleeping spot under the roots of a giant pine tree. Soggy soil slid inside his kuraminium greaves and armguards, eliciting a grunt from him. It would be a pain to clean out. The discomfort reminded him he should be grateful he'd survived and finally lost the algus that had chased him for so long. Despite that, he still fretted. Darius was missing, and Brutus had no idea where to find him.

Brutus rested his weighty hammer against a tree trunk and adjusted his helmet. Some made fun of him for often sleeping in it, but he found the cold kuraminium against his cheek oddly relaxing. It helped him forget that he was now lost and only knew the vague direction Margalvia lay in.

What a disaster the last few days had been. He had to return before Darius or it wouldn't end well for the now-mindless man. Margalvia would be a hostile place for Darius now that he'd failed to assassinate Archimedes and lost valuable information. Curse those that had accused him of being a traitor and led to him trying to prove himself.

To think that after all the years Darius had fought for the rakkans, they'd turn their backs on him. Brutus shook his head in disgust.

There was something unsettling about how the ambush had unfolded, as if Archimedes had known it was coming. Could they have a traitor leaking secrets after all? It wasn't Darius. Brutus knew that much. The man was like a son to him and would never have betrayed their cause.

He hoped Darius hadn't fallen prey to one of the roaming algus. In his current state, Darius would be easily deceived, perhaps even unknowingly led to do Archimedes's bidding. The thought brought a bad taste to Brutus's mouth. At least Darius still had his brother Felix for company. As long as they were together, they'd be fine, and Brutus could sleep a little easier.

The sky glowed orange. Sunset had arrived, the sun's rays too weak now to burn Brutus's pale rakkan skin.

A quick swipe of his hand brushed the mud from his legs and elbows. Slinging his hammer over his shoulder, Brutus set off to find Margalvia.

11

Darius awoke from a disturbed sleep in the unlit room with only Lyra beside him to calm the strain in his tense muscles. Her warm breath tickled his good arm as he rubbed his feet against the soft silken bed sheets. The comfort and safety they provided made him all the more uneasy. First he was saved by a powerful guardian, then furnished in luxury. Could it be that luck had favoured him, or was fate lulling him into a false sense of security? A faint glow came from the single window in the exterior wall. The morning sun hadn't yet risen, but soon would.

It wasn't long before a knock came at the door.

"Who—" Darius's voice cracked in his dry throat.

Lex opened the door and stepped into the room, dressed in the same clothes as before. She carried a lamp, its light touching her face just enough to reveal dark circles around her eyes. Apparently she hadn't slept any better than he.

Behind her a scruffy boy carrying a pile of clothes slinked into the room and closed the door. His beige shirt and shorts were wrinkled and smeared with grime, as if he'd been crawling around who knew where. Yet a wide grin spread across his face. Skinny and small, without a hint of facial hair—he wasn't likely over ten years old.

"Morning, Darius," Lex said.

Darius coughed and got out of bed. "You mean Philippos?"

"He knows who you are. That's why he's leaving with us."

"Leaving, mistress?" The boy placed the folded garments at the foot of the bed. "You said you needed me to help pack clothes."

He was clearly a slave; not only were his clothes shabby, but the light flickering on his arms showed criss-crossed pink scratches and scars from years of labour. Darius frowned. *Why would she tell him the truth about me?*

"I lied," Lex said. "You're coming with us and you aren't coming back."

The boy beamed. "Mistress Alexandra, that's great! Are we going on an adventure?" He waved his arm as if fighting with a sword, adding his own battle sound effects.

Darius groaned. It was too early for someone to have such energy. The boy was already getting on his nerves.

"I thought you'd need more convincing," Lex said, rifling through her bag. "And what've I told you about calling me that?"

The boy gasped, ignoring her annoyance. "I've always wanted to go hunt with an algus. Are we going to track rakkans?"

Darius shook his head at the boy's excitement. Had he never come face to face with one of those demonic men before, never looked into a rakkan's flaming eyes, so brilliantly hot it hurt to stare? If he had, he wouldn't smile. He'd cower.

"This is Omid." Lex turned the boy to face Darius. "He's one of Ismene's rat-catchers."

Darius's stomach sank at the name, too close to another for comfort. Shoving the stirred memory away, he muttered, "Pleasure to meet you."

If his sarcasm was noticed by the boy, Omid showed no sign of it. "We met a week ago."

"His memory's gone," Lex said.

Omid's eyes widened. "Oh."

"Darius, put on that fresh set of clothes." She nodded to the pile on the bed while pulling some flatbread and meat from her bag. The aroma of salted pork wafted through the room as she laid a joint on the table. A bottle soon joined it.

Lyra turned over on the bed and lifted her head. Her nostrils twitched and she eyed the exposed meat.

"Where did you get that?" Darius ignored the clothes and walked over to devour some food and water.

"Ismene's leftovers," she replied, placing some on the floor for Lyra.

Worry stole Omid's smile away. "Speaking of my mistress, won't she think I've run away if I leave?"

"Ismene owes me slaves," Lex said. "I'll get one of my men to take a few more and say you were among them." She bit into an apple and walked to the window, peering out to the streets below.

Darius swallowed a mouthful of dry pork. "The army you spoke of last night isn't all slaves is it?" It wasn't ideal if so. Unless trained to fight, a slave wouldn't be much match for any of the soldiers Darius had come across so far. They couldn't match *him* but they weren't completely without training.

"No. They're skilled warriors like Brutus," Lex replied, as if reading his mind.

"And where is this army?"

"Margalvia, one of the city states that doesn't submit to King Medus."

At last, some good news. That was his destination, the place he hoped had once been his home. Darius's connection to this rebellion made sense, but Lex's still didn't. "Why does a woman of Laltos fight for Margalvia?"

"I have my reasons."

Frowning, Darius didn't press further—for now. As he turned away from her in frustration, he caught sight of Omid. The boy's stare was fixed on the table and its small feast.

"Here." Darius ripped off some pork and handed it to the boy. "Eat something or you'll be weak travelling."

Omid snatched it and chomped it down in large, gulping bites.

"Slow down," Darius cautioned. "You're going to choke. Take whatever you want." Leaving the boy to gobble more food, Darius went to see what Lex was staring at.

Outside, the sun cast a faint red glow in the clouds to the east. Some soldiers were marching down the street. One had paused to speak with a well-dressed citizen. Further down the road, another had stopped a peasant girl and was pointing in different directions, trying to ascertain something.

Lex cursed. "They're here already." She wrenched her gaze from the street and took Darius's arm, pulling him away from the window. Algor flared on her fingertips and she caressed his burns. "How does it feel?"

"It hurts but it's not bad." He wouldn't tell her how great her touch felt.

"Can you fight?"

After the encounter with the rakkan, he was beginning to question whether he could. *Best not to let her know that.* "Yes."

The algus pulled a bandage from her bag and wrapped it around the tender wound. Looking up from her work, she caught his gaze with a sharp glare. "Can I trust you?"

Shouldn't he be asking her this? "I'm not some implanted assassin that's going to kill you if that's what you mean." *At least as far as I'm aware of.* But she would know that implication already.

82

Lex's taut lips relaxed. "You cannot die on me. Understood?" Her soft voice was devoid of the coiled rage it often restrained; instead, desperation seeped through, a glimmer of emotion escaping her otherwise steely facade.

"I won't die."

"If we get into trouble, run. Forget about me, Lyra, Omid, anyone else."

Like he needed her instruction. *Why should I care*, his mind asked. "I will."

"*Good people of Cephos*," a voice whispered in Darius's head. He knew that sinister voice, so close it was as if the goman's breath prickled his ears. His back stiffened.

"*I am Archimedes and ask your assistance with a grave matter.*"

"You hear that too?" Darius asked.

Omid winced. "Everyone can hear him."

"*A fugitive named Darius is hiding in town. If you've seen anyone foreign you must call for the Guard at once. Time is short. If anyone assists in his capture there will be a thousand crest reward.*"

Lex darted across the room and knelt down, eye to eye with Omid. "From now you do only what I tell you, without question. Understood?"

Omid paused before nodding. "Yes, mistress." He flashed a grin.

Standing, Lex drew a short sword from her waist and threw it hilt-first to Darius. He caught it and felt the comfortable weight sink into his palm. The ornamented hilt was heavy and the polished blade light, perfect balance for swift strokes in close quarters.

"Pray you don't have to use it," Lex said. "We'll move on the rooftops and through the trees out of the town."

As Cephos was littered with trees, there was no doubt some path through the branches to the forest outside. But unless they moved like ghosts there was no way they'd go unseen and unheard once the sun's rays hit in a few minutes—especially with a young boy in tow. "There must be a better way."

Lex moved towards the door, slinging her bag across her back. "There's a stairway outside that leads to a roof."

Darius grabbed the clothes laid out and began slipping the snug garments on. They weren't the attire of an algus, at least not one he'd seen, but the fine brown stitching would pass him off as a citizen rather than a slave, and they'd keep in the warmth better than the thin linen he'd been wearing since shedding his chainmail in the river.

Lyra.

She was up and ready in an instant as he fastened the buckles and slipped the sword under his belt.

"There are algus walking on the rooftops," Omid whispered, peering out of the window.

Lex cursed.

"I can make my own way out of town, mistress," Omid said. "Let you two go."

"No." Lex shook her head. "I'm not letting either of you out of my sight." She stared at the ground, lost in thought.

Banging sounded below. Some people had entered the lodge, likely beginning a search. The rhythmic stomps of boots climbing stairs didn't come yet, but they soon would. If they weren't careful they'd get pinned inside this lodging. Even the rooftops would be safer.

Darius strode to the algus's side. "Lex."

No response.

"Lex!" Darius said louder, trying to rouse her from her thoughts.

Her hand shot out and grabbed him by the cuff, tugging so hard she almost ripped it. "Shout my name again and I'll cut out your tongue."

With a scowl, Darius pushed her away and lowered his voice. "We need to go, now."

"I'm thinking. What's your idea, genius?"

His only proposal was to burst out with swords swinging, though he didn't relish the thought of fighting since being bested by the rakkan. But he had an excuse for his lack of creativity—blank memory. What was hers?

Omid fidgeted. "I know a way."

"Where?" Lex asked.

"The latrine in the cellar drops straight into the sewers. It's where I have to hunt the rats."

"Perfect." She strode to the door without any sign of hesitation.

Perfect? If crawling through faeces was her idea of perfect Darius dreaded to think what else she'd lead him through.

The algus cracked the door and glanced out while Darius and Omid held their breaths. After checking the hall, she stepped out and they followed after her into the dark corridor, single file.

As they reached the top of the staircase, Lex stopped and thrust out a palm. Light shimmered from the floor below, accompanied by banging and footsteps. Muffled voices were talking back and forth, words undiscernible.

Darius tensed. Sooner or later whoever it was would come up, then they'd have to silence them. It was hard to kill someone silently with a blade. Best to get a hand over the mouth first then stab at the neck. Repeatedly. Once wasn't enough even with the sharpest weapon. You could go for a kill in a single blow, like to the back of the head, but it was risky. A dagger would have been preferable to the sword in his belt but he'd make do.

Had his former self known anything other than killing?

Lex turned back towards them. "I'll go distract them," she whispered. "Omid, lead Darius straight down to the sewers. I won't be far behind."

Thinking back to her encounter with the inn's host yesterday, Darius wondered just how she planned on distracting them. But whatever talents she would be using, it was probably a better plan than trying to stab them discreetly with a sword.

Omid nodded as Lex stepped lightly down the stairs. The boy waited until the sound of her voice echoed up then began to creep down step by step. Darius drew his sword, not wagering on any of this going smoothly.

Once Omid had taken a few steps, Darius began his descent, grazing his hand lightly across the wooden bannister to aid his balance. *Don't make a sound, Lyra.* It wasn't as if he needed to worry about a panther though, a master of stealth. The boy was the most likely to slip and give them away.

They rounded a bend in the staircase and the backs of two soldiers came into view, both fixated on the beautiful Lex in front of them. Surprisingly, she wore a stern face, not the seductive grin he might have expected. Perhaps mere soldiers were too beneath her to charm. One was scrawny and looked like a stiff breeze would topple him, while the other could have withstood a gale judging by the size of his waist.

"I'm not impressed," Lex said. "Your algus should be here overseeing this."

Omid descended the next staircase to the cellar. Darius crept after him, toe first and thankful for the thick, cushioned rugs that softened each step. His guide was lighter and moved more quickly so was already out of sight. The soldiers were less than three yards away. Darius's hand trembled slightly. *What am I, nervous? Of soldiers?* His repeated failures in combat really had shaken his confidence, first the distant loss of Amid, then the recent humiliation by Archimedes and the rakkan.

"Archimedes ordered our algus to the eastern road," the fat soldier replied. "The fault isn't his."

Lex scoffed. "I think—"

"*Hasten the search*," Archimedes' voice hissed. "*Time is limited.*"

The scrawny soldier turned his head to move away.

Lex's eyes widened. "I'm not done—"

Too late. The man's eyes latched onto Darius's, taking a second to recognize his newly shaven face. Darius's heart thumped, thrusting his limbs into action. He flung his blade forward.

"He's—!" The soldier's cry was cut off by the sword spearing his eye.

The fat soldier turned but Lex moved faster. Her free hand plugged his mouth before he could even gasp then her blade sawed across his throat. Blood sprayed. Nauseating.

Darius fixed his eyes on a blood-free chair at the far side of the room and retrieved his sword using only peripheral vision. A thump came from Lex's direction as he pulled out the wet blade. She'd dropped the large soldier's body to the stained floor. Darius choked. The stench of blood was overpowering, as if he was drinking the filth.

"Do you think anyone heard?" he whispered, trying to think of anything else.

"Assume the worst." Lex turned and bolted down the stairs.

Omid awaited them in the cellar. Despite the room's musty smell, Darius breathed freely again.

As he took in their bloody appearance, Omid's eyes widened. "What happened?"

"Nothing," Lex said, opening the door to a bare stone room. It contained a wooden ledge at knee height with a hole in the centre—the latrine.

Lex pulled a long cloth from her bag and began wrapping it around her mouth and nose while Omid lifted the top from the wooden ledge to open the hole. The sound of trickling water echoed from below. It would have been calming at any other time. At least the smell of waste was a relief from blood. Darius grimaced as he attached his sword to his belt, not relishing the coming trek.

"In, Omid," Lex mumbled through the cloth.

The boy dropped his legs in and, bracing his feet on either side, slid down like he'd done it a hundred times before. As his head disappeared he took a deep breath.

"Lyra next," Lex said.

Darius beckoned his panther to the top of the latrine. This close to the entrance, the stench of faeces hit his nose like a stone. He twisted his head away and coughed hard to rid his lungs of the putrid air. How would he get Lyra in there? She hovered at the edge, flinching at the smelly dark hole.

Before he figured it out Lex lifted the cat's hind legs and threw her in head first. Lyra yelped as she fell and landed in the darkness with a splash.

Darius glared at Lex.

"I'll make it up to her," she said.

He kept glaring, not knowing why he cared, but aware that if she pushed his escort again she'd have more to worry about than Archimedes.

Lex returned the look with a hard one of her own. "Don't look at me like that. I'm about to go swimming in filth for you. Get in."

That was true. It was apparently his fault he was about to be knee deep in excrement. With a giant breath that stretched his lungs, he mimicked Omid and slid down into the sewer.

The stone walls soon ended and he dropped, landing with a sickening squelch in a flowing stream. Cold water—what he hoped was water—trickled around his ankles, soaking through his boots. Moving water meant it was at least fresher and less festered.

"Darius?" Omid called out from the darkness.

Darius stepped gingerly towards the boy's voice, ducking as his head grazed across the ceiling. He held his arms outstretched until he felt a bony shoulder.

Lex splashed down behind. A fluorescent blue glow flared to life. Darius winced at the sight of Lex's shining eyes, but they offered enough light to dimly illuminate the cramped stone sewer.

An ache spread through his chest as his lungs begged for air. Darius resisted a moment longer but finally heaved and took in the full force of the putrid air for the first time. He retched and cupped a hand to his mouth.

"This way leads to the river." Omid turned and started onwards.

Lyra was already ahead in the tunnel, probably eager to escape the smell. Even if the guards knew they were down here, who would want to follow?

Pinching his nose and breathing through his mouth, Darius followed after Omid at a quick pace. The boy didn't seem fazed by the atmosphere and thankfully made haste. They weaved through the passage, occasionally meeting and joining new tunnels. After what felt like hours but was more likely less than one, daylight gleamed ahead.

Darius broke into a run for the final stint and burst into the fresh air of the forest. With a deep sense of relief, he inhaled clear air and coughed up what felt like congealed grime.

The sewer poured out into the river which winded its way through the forest. Thick foliage surrounded the shore despite the discoloured waters he and his companions now stood in.

Lex scanned their surroundings but spotted no one. Not surprising; it likely still stank here, though to his dulled senses it smelt like flowers and honey. Darius washed off his boots in a cleaner part of the river and rinsed his sword. His new thick clothes kept out the worst of the morning's chilly air except below his knees where his trousers were soaked through.

"What now?" he asked, straightening as he slid his sword through his belt.

"How about we see Healer Parisa?" asked Omid. "She could help Darius with his memory. Or we can go and hunt rakkans!"

"No, we're not bothering with healer nonsense," Lex said.

Omid was so joyful and spoke to Lex like an equal, not as a slave to his mistress, yet she never reprimanded him. Their relationship puzzled Darius, as did the reasons Omid acted so content. What drove people's interactions besides serving themselves? Why did they care for one another and how could Darius know if their apparent feelings were genuine—Lex in particular?

Voices broke from the forest, followed by a man's rumbling laugh. Darius looked to Lex, expecting to see her wave an instruction or dive for cover.

She froze. "I think it's—"

Three soldiers emerged from between the low-hanging branches of a tree, Acamas from the night before at the front. His laughter faded when he spotted them, and all three halted.

"Alexandra!" Acamas smiled, as did the other two. "What an unexpected pleasure."

Damn. Darius stood like a statue in plain sight. Hiding now would only draw attention.

Lex strode up to the men and stopped a pace short. "Acamas."

"We are just returning from the southern watchtower," Acamas said. "We were given instructions to scout the forest before reporting back to Cephos. You should join us. I was just about to regale my friends here about our Denehill *adventure* when we were teens, young and precarious." The man's eyes twinkled with nostalgia.

Lex and Acamas seemed like close friends, her smile genuine. Perhaps Acamas was a soldier that could be relied on, like Brutus, to aid them in their escape, or at least keep mute about what he'd seen. If not, Darius would be forced to ensure it.

Lex stood silently. Omid was quiet too, though he scanned around the forest as if bored by whatever was happening. *Must be nice to be so carefree.* Darius's hand crept to his sword's hilt.

"I'm not going back to Cephos, Acamas," Lex said. "I must return to Laltos at once."

"But Archimedes ordered we all convene. I'll have to report I've seen you or you know what he may do to me."

She rubbed her neck and eyed the other two soldiers. "Are these your friends from last night by any chance?"

"Why yes. Percius and Diocles. And is this the man who helped you take down the rakkan?" Acamas nodded to Darius.

"I'm sorry, Acamas," Lex replied.

Then she moved—fast as a hawk. In one movement she withdrew her sword and sliced through Acamas's neck. Whirling, she brought her sword back down. It flared an icy blue as she stabbed it into the second soldier's chest, straight through his scale armour. The third man had just enough time to reach for his sword before Lex spun and drove her blade into his heart. The three bodies fell without a single cry. Three dead witnesses. One dead childhood friend. *Who is this woman?*

12

Darius looked into Acamas's dead eyes, wondering if he'd soon join him in death. Apparently, Lex didn't think twice about turning on an ally when it came to protecting herself, and Darius didn't even know if she considered him an ally. If not for Lyra's fondness of the woman he'd take his chances and run, but he trusted his panther's judge of character more than his own right now. Or did he simply *want* to trust his panther's judgement? If Archimedes could tamper with his own mind, the goman could do it to Lyra. But if he doubted Lyra, he truly would be alone.

Lex wrenched her sword from the last soldier as Omid backed away slowly, eyes wide and bottom lip quivering.

"Stop!" She pointed the bloody weapon at the boy. Red drops slithered down the steel and dripped into the soil.

Omid froze in place but turned his head away from the butchered soldiers, brown eyes filling with tears while Lex searched her pockets. She bent over a soldier's body and sprinkled a dark grey powder on the gaping hole in his chest. Then she took a flint and set the powder alight in a flash that burnt out within seconds. Her stab to the man's chest was now blackened and charred, just like a rakkan's strike. *Crafty*.

Omid looked like he was about to pass out.

"Is something wrong, boy? Don't you like the sight of blood?" Darius asked, half hoping he wasn't alone in feeling queasy.

The boy's lip still quivered. "She killed a citizen. It isn't right."

A feeling of unease stirred within Darius. Right. What did that mean? Surely it was just the blood troubling him. He sighed. "They were the only ones that saw me in Cephos with her. Seems right to protect ourselves."

"He was her friend."

Yes, but if friends outlived their usefulness... Why was this troubling the boy?

Lex straightened and approached Darius, her face wearing the same expressionless mask it so often did, but for the first time the facade cracked. Speckles of blue flickered in her eyes, eyes that pleaded with him.

"Can you finish?" She held out the pouch of powder and flint. Did it actually bother her to kill these men? Perhaps she wasn't as ruthless as he thought.

Not relishing the thought of getting close to the bloody pile of bodies, he murmured, "I'm not best placed to recreate a rakkan strike, having only seen one."

Her lips pressed together as her gaze slid away toward Omid, pointedly avoiding the slain men. "Just do it."

Darius took the flint and bag from her hand and walked to the two unburned corpses to finish the cover up. As he bent over Acamas's body, Lex knelt beside a distraught Omid and whispered in his ear.

Once again, Darius found himself wondering about their relationship. Which led his mind back to the friendship with Acamas she'd just betrayed so easily. Which led to more questions he needed answers to, questions that continued circling as he began sprinkling powder over the neck wound. Darius scratched the flint and blinked as the powdered wound flashed alight. The flames soon went out, leaving a sooty coat along with a familiar stink of seared skin. It looked a bit like his arm. He finished the grim deed on the last corpse and retreated.

"It's done." Darius tossed Lex her items.

"Go wait over there," Lex said, nudging Omid. The tiny boy's face grew paler. Could he handle the journey they were about to undertake? There would be more death.

When the boy was out of earshot, Darius whispered, "Why are we bringing him? Isn't it dangerous for him to be with us?"

"He's the only person in Cephos that can connect us besides those three. If Archimedes captured him, he'd find out I've been helping you."

"Archimedes would bother with a rat-catcher boy?"

"Yes. You don't know how easily he can do it and the lengths he'll go to. Only the algus are off limits to Archimedes. We have to bring Omid."

"Why not kill him like Acamas?"

Lex grimaced. "What the hell did Archimedes do to you? Has he stopped you caring about anyone but yourself?"

"What? You didn't think twice about killing those three."

"Three members of the town guard. I had no choice."

"Look, I don't care. If you want to bring the boy, I'll go along with what you suggest. I just want my memories and to return to Margalvia."

She stepped closer so they were nose to nose. His eyes were drawn to the tiny specks of blood on her cheeks until her sharp words yanked his gaze back to meet her own hard stare. "You follow me and do only what I say. Understood?"

"For now." He wagered she'd rather kill him than Omid, but couldn't fathom why.

"You think I won't kill you if you don't?"

Considering she'd killed a rakkan that had beaten him, she'd be a stiff challenge, but he couldn't afford to show her any sign of weakness. Instead of backing down, he scoffed as if he had all the confidence in the world.

"You think you can best me?" Lex asked.

If he didn't sound sure she'd be all the more likely to try. "Of course. On the first night I killed an algus on the riverbank."

She broke away and laughed. "I heard. She was a novice."

"Don't think because a rakkan beat me that I'm weak." His own words unsettled him, fear that it was true gnawing at his stomach. "I underestimated him, but I've seen you fight. I certainly won't underestimate you."

"Darius." Lex shook her head, scepticism dissolving into grief. "Time was when you'd best a legion of rakkans. You're a shadow of what you once were."

He gritted his teeth, not quite sure why he cared what she thought of him. "Then I must have been something remarkable."

"You were."

He must have been, to stir such reverie in her. The thought of being an even more powerful warrior stirred excitement inside him. That was what awaited him once his memories returned, a warrior that wasn't weak.

"Let's go find this Waif Magician," Darius said.

Lex nodded. "We'll head to Laltos."

"What's that?"

"The largest city in the west. Our lead to the Waif Magician is there."

"You don't know where this Magician is?" Great. A city sounded like a perfect place to get discovered. "I'll wait for you elsewhere."

Lex shook her head. "I can't trust you alone. If you go wandering off, get caught... Too much is at stake. Besides, Laltos is the capital of the West. The city is huge. The chances of Archimedes's men finding us are slim."

Her frown said she hadn't even convinced herself, but she looked away, the conversation over. With a few quick jerks, she untied an empty sword belt and handed it to him.

"This will do better than that," she said, nodding at the worn leather belt he had his sword tucked into.

The new belt was a fine piece made from glossy leather and engraved with odd patterns. It looked expensive, as did the weapon that fit it. Either she was obscenely wealthy, or she had some level of trust in him to lend it.

Darius tied it around his waist and sheathed his sword, wondering how long it would be before it was wet with blood. "Let's go then."

13

Nikolaos tried to avoid touching anything as he entered the tiny hovel. He was glad to finally be off a horse after a hard day's ride, but rest wasn't his priority. Archimedes had summoned him to this old healer's squalid abode, much to his disgust.

Shelves of dusty bottled medicines lined the stone walls. A wrinkled old woman in a blood-stained green dress sat quivering on the floor in the corner. Though she didn't appear important to Nikolaos, Archimedes had interest in her for some reason. The goman knelt beside with her palm in his hand, the Staff propped against the wall nearby. An onlooker might take him for a benevolent carer, but Nikolaos knew the mental torment being inflicted on her, stripping her mind like ripping out hair by the fistful.

Her eyes locked onto Nikolaos's, the only part of her paralysed body free to beg for deliverance. Too bad. A leader had to tolerate the necessary acts of war, and Archimedes's stomach for inflicting pain was one trait Nikolaos most admired.

A light scratching at the door to the hovel disturbed them. Nikolaos cracked it open and found a peregrine on the ground.

He'd recognise Tiro's spotted feathers anywhere. His dormouse shivered in his boot but was safe for now.

As he moved to take the message attached to the falcon's leg, Archimedes's voice boomed, "*Leave it.*"

Tiro flapped inside and Nikolaos shut the door, frustrated at missing this chance to discover what Lex was up to. He still had no idea what she and Archimedes had discussed that left her so harrowed.

Archimedes slipped a knife from his belt and pressed it flat to the woman's forearm. "*Cease resisting, Parisa.*" He dragged the knife, peeling skin as a slave would a potato. The fragile woman couldn't flinch but her eyes widened, screaming at Nikolaos to take his sword and pierce her despairing heart to end it. Resist? Like that was possible. The little resistance anyone could offer was soon quelled by pain.

A draft whipped dust along the floor as Parisa's eyes softened and faded to a vacant stare. It was finished, her mind stripped bare.

"*Nothing of use.*" Archimedes stroked his bare chin. "*I was sure she knew something.*"

"We may be ahead of Darius," Nikolaos said. "We've been riding hard and he mightn't have a horse. No one even saw him leave Cephos. He may still—"

"*He departed.*"

Nikolaos wouldn't argue. Archimedes had a habit of being right.

The goman turned to Tiro and removed the small scroll. His brow furrowed as he read the brief message before crumpling it in his hand.

"News?" Nikolaos asked.

"*Things aren't going as I anticipated. Time's being wasted and men are being sacrificed. I'm displeased.*"

"Is Alexandra well?"

Archimedes eyed him as if assessing whether he was trustworthy. "*She does what she must.*"

Nikolaos waited, but no more information was forthcoming. Apparently the goman didn't trust him enough. "Where shall we head next?"

Archimedes stood and walked towards the door. "*You will go to Laltos. Prepare the city for Darius's arrival while I see to another matter. I'll follow in a few days.*"

"Laltos? Why would he head there?" Had Lex discovered his path on her mission?

"*Don't question me.*"

Nikolaos bowed as Archimedes opened the door and stepped outside. The goman held the door open for Tiro before releasing it. It slammed shut, leaving Nikolaos alone with a hollow-faced Parisa still cowering on the floor. *I hope Archimedes is right and we trap Darius in Laltos.*

14

Darius drew heaving breaths as they jogged for the thousandth time, checking behind him for rakkans every few steps. Jog, march, jog, march was all his mind focused on now after a whole day and night travelling. The scouts' march was the fastest way to travel long distances by foot but it was a gruelling pace to keep. Omid hit his limit first during the night, and Darius had carried him until he recovered enough to continue. In contrast, Lyra didn't seem to mind at all, bounding alongside the group with ease.

At least the exhaustion took the boy's mind off the three butchered soldiers. At some point in the night Omid's tears finally dried up, though Darius still hadn't figured out why the boy was so bothered by it.

The journey also gave Darius more time to probe Lex, who continued to be cagey and short with her answers, no matter what he asked.

"If I was a soldier of Margalvia, why wasn't I ordained as an algus?" he asked.

"Your parents were exiled."

"Then why do I fight for the city?" His head ached, fatigue taking its toll, and he closed his eyes briefly as he waited for Lex's answer.

She said nothing, and he opened his eyes to find her pulling ahead again. Glaring, he lengthened his strides to catch up. What few answers she'd given him in the past day didn't fit together, which meant either she was lying or there was a connecting dot she withheld. *She still doesn't trust me.* Which was fair—he didn't trust her, either.

They slowed to a walk again and Omid groaned in relief. The sun was setting on a second day, not that it made much difference as the forest's canopy had shaded them from its heat. Darius was grateful for that; his undershirt was damp with sweat as it was.

Lyra slowed abruptly, her ears rising as she raised her nose to the air. Pangs of alarm from his escort sped up his already pounding heart. The wind carried a smoky smell, like charred flesh.

Lex drew her sword and came to a halt beside a giant fir.

Darius stopped and drew his own weapon. Though he hoped it was nothing more than smoke from a cooking fire of some hunter, he feared the worst. His gaze swept their surroundings for the source but the gusty wind was too erratic to let him pinpoint it. Omid slipped behind Darius for cover and he pushed the boy to the ground. No need to catch the boy in a swing of his sword. All Darius heard was their own panting breaths and the whir of wind through tree branches.

A soft growl came from Lyra. She stalked forward, having caught the source of the smell. Darius followed. The fading sun shed just enough light to make out a lifeless hand protruding from a ditch ahead, fingernails black and bloody like the person had clawed to stay alive. As he approached, a woman's body came into full view, steam lightly rising from a seared midriff and bronzed limbs.

It was fresh. By the ragged clothes she'd been a slave, and by the size of her stomach, she was either fat or pregnant. Chunks were missing from the arm, with clear bite marks no larger than a human jaw in size. A rakkan feast? The thought riled his stomach. He may not have cared for people, but even he felt disgust at this. What kind of creature ate a human?

One instinct told him to flee, another balked at such a cowardly suggestion.

"Darius!" Lex cried.

He turned just in time to see a bulky branch swinging for his head. Darius ducked. The rakkan holding the makeshift weapon wailed and tried to bash him again. Dodging, he readied his sword. The rakkan's loose clothes drooped from her tall frame. This one wasn't as skinny as the one in Cephos but was still slender. The long brown hair suggested it was a female and the speed she swung the hefty billet showed she easily outmatched his strength. He wouldn't underestimate her.

Hold it together, Darius. He needed a swift kill. First he'd cut the rod from her arm, then he'd sever her neck. That would prove he wasn't weak, that he was a true warrior. If only his arm would stop trembling.

The rakkan's eyes glowed as she glared at him. "Leave me be."

Her words almost sounded like a plea, but he couldn't look on that twisted face with anything but hate. He'd finally prove his worth against these creatures by killing her. Darius raised his sword.

A blue arrow speared the back of the rakkan's head and burst through her eye. Lifeless and limp, her body fell in a quiet heap, depriving him of the satisfaction of cutting it down himself. *Lex.*

"I could have taken her," he said as Lex lowered her bow.

"I'm sure, Philippos," she said.

The way she said that name gave him the impression it was meant as an insult worse than any other. He ground his teeth. She was too keen to re-emphasise that he wasn't the strong warrior he once was.

Darius looked to Lyra. *Are there any other rakkans near?* His escort briefly looked around then relaxed. He guessed that was a no.

"Why was it eating a human?" he asked.

"Starvation," Lex said. "We've been quite successful at cutting off their means of growing food. They'll eat anything they happen across on the search."

Sickening, but how many missed meals would it take to make Darius hungry enough to eat a woman?

Omid approached the dead rakkan with a look of awe on his face. "You saved us, mistress."

The boy's delight made a change from his sombre mood of late, though his chest still heaved in panted breaths. Fear? Excitement? Exhaustion? Darius guessed a mixture of the three. Weariness weighed on his own body.

"Let's find somewhere to rest for the night," Darius said. "The boy can't keep going without sleep." And neither could he. Nor did he want to run into a group of those things.

With a nod of agreement, Lex led them through the forest a little farther. She stopped at the largest tree, so broad ten men couldn't have linked arms around it. It rose high and straight into the sky, before scattering into an array of thick branches.

"Here," Lex said. "We'll spend the night up this tree."

Omid stared up and shivered as a gust whipped leaves and dust from the ground around him. Darius took off his coat and wrapped it twice around the boy, who gave him a melancholic grin of thanks. Only when the wind's chill bit his own arms did Darius question why he'd mindlessly done it.

"Why up a tree?" Darius asked. It'd be hard to sleep, balancing precariously at such a height on the swaying branches.

"It'll be safer from rakkans," Lex said.

"Isn't being sat on top of wood the worst place to be?"

"No. Trees are immune to ferven."

"Of course they are," Darius said in a mocking tone. Another gap filled, another one unearthed. "So why don't people use wooden armour and spears against them?"

"The trees are only immune while they're alive," she said, stroking the bark and peering up into the tree's reaches. It was a good place to hide, given the lowest branches obscured anything higher from view, but they started at least two storeys into the air.

"How do we get up there?" Omid asked.

Lex threw her bag onto the ground. "I'll climb up and drop a rope." She unhooked her sword belt and dropped it. Her bow and quiver followed. She dug around in her bag and pulled out a thin rope. 'String' would have been more accurate.

She caught Darius eyeing it. "It's strong." Without further ceremony, she slung the rope over a shoulder, took out two daggers and stepped up to the trunk.

Omid's eyes widened. "Mistress, are you—"

Lex leapt up and thrust a dagger into the tree's bark.

A scream burst from Omid's throat, echoing through the forest like a shrill horn calling in marauders. Darius rushed over and plugged Omid's mouth with his palm until the boy's wet cries turned to vibrations in his hand.

Releasing the dagger's handle, Lex dropped to the ground. "Don't make another sound!" She pointed her second dagger between Omid's eyes and he nodded, cringing away.

Darius slowly released the boy's mouth, ready to stifle any further cries but none came. Omid wrapped his arms around himself and shuddered. Had he finally cracked? Where was that cheerful boy that had been so keen on adventure? Even *he*'d be less annoying.

"It's just a tree," Lex said, now holding her knife against her thigh. "The myths aren't true. We'll be perfectly fine despite me stabbing it."

"Why does he care about the tree?" Darius asked.

Omid sank to the floor and buried his ruffled head in his knees.

"It's superstition," Lex said. "Some people think that the trees have some unifying connection in the forest, and damaging them turns it against us. That's why you can't walk in Cephos without tripping over a root. They won't cut the things down."

Superstition that Omid clearly took seriously. If living trees were immune to ferven, maybe there was something to it. Darius sat down next to Omid and slung an arm over his shoulder. It would be best to comfort the boy lest he cry out again.

"There, there," Darius said in as soothing a tone as he could muster. "I'm sure Mistress Alexandra just cursed herself. You and I will be fine."

Lex's eyes narrowed. "Don't call me that." With a jump, she retrieved her dagger. Her eyes flitted to the boy, then she disappeared around the trunk.

"She's gone," Darius said, scanning the surrounding trees for any hint of soldiers or rakkans drawn in by the boy's yell.

Omid lifted his head, face harrowed.

"You've looked under the weather since yesterday," Darius said, hoping to drown out the sound of Lex hammering knives into the other side of the tree. "Are you ill?"

The boy picked up a jagged stone and started scratching absentmindedly at the earth. "A slave can be crucified for witnessing a citizen's murder without reporting it. And I knew Master Acamas."

No wonder the boy was a mess. "No one's going to know you were there."

"I know that."

"Then why the gloom?"

"Like I said, I knew him."

"Why do you care? It doesn't affect you. No need to get emotional."

Omid said nothing. In the silence that followed, Lyra padded over and snuggled up to Darius. He rubbed behind her ear, now knowing just the right spot to make her purr.

"So you don't care about anyone except yourself?" Omid asked, throwing the stone into a bush.

"Why would I?"

"Would you care if I killed Lyra?"

"That's different."

"How?"

"I…" Why *was* Lyra different? "I need her to get back to Margalvia."

"What if I killed her once you got there?"

Darius grunted, imagining Lyra's silky black body cold and lifeless. He'd almost seen it that way before, with the rakkan. His jaw clenched just recalling it. Why did the mere thought make him angry? Why did the thought of not looking into those amber eyes again make him feel strange?

"I'll kill anyone that hurts her," Darius said. "Maybe I'm as irrational as all of you."

A whistle came from above, followed by the rope slithering down from the thick foliage.

Darius stood and grabbed it. "You first, tree-boy."

Omid got up and pressed his face to the tree as Darius tied the rope under his arms, knotting it tightly several times. The boy whispered something to the bark and pressed his palms in. Peculiar kid.

At the end of the rope, Darius tied Lex's bags and weapons. Reaching up, he gave the rope a few tugs. Omid slowly ascended, his hands squeezed tight around the rope and his eyes scrunched closed. The boy was thin and light but Lex was still strong to hoist him up. Unsurprising, as archers required a lot of upper body strength.

Watching the boy and bags vanish into the branches above, Darius wondered how she'd manage to pull him up. The rope was too thin to climb. After Omid disappeared, two daggers fell from the upper reaches onto the ground. That was how. He picked them up and walked up to the trunk. The daggers' hilts were curved slightly and cushioned with thick leather, ideal for the task. He'd have to dig the knives in with the flat facing the ground or they'd slip down under his weight.

Lyra eyed him as if awaiting instruction. *You can climb this, right?* She cocked her head as if to say "of course" and then leapt and sank her claws into the trunk. Paw over paw, she clambered her way toward the waiting branches.

After a final check for lurking soldiers, Darius dug in the first dagger and climbed after her.

Eventually, he caught sight of Lex resting on a thick branch high up and made his way to her. Omid lay close by, gripping the bough between his legs tightly.

When Darius reached a good spot to perch, he took a seat with a sigh of relief. His muscles ached from the strenuous climb and his head pounded. Leaning against the trunk, he waited for his swirling vision to return to focus. The ground below was shrouded but his head still spun slightly, either from fatigue or just sensing the height. He rubbed his hands together to smooth out the calluses.

Lex shuffled across the branches to sit beside him. "It's strange," she whispered. "You used to be bad with heights."

He wasn't exactly good with them now. "Scared of blood and heights. I was a *man* through and through then."

She chuckled, the first time he'd made her laugh. The sound made him smile too.

Lex rubbed her palms against her eyes. "Can you watch for a few hours? I haven't slept for days."

Neither had he, and his eyes were so heavy he'd have to physically hold them open, but she likely needed rest more than him. "Sure."

She leant her head on his shoulder and her hair brushed against his neck. That whole side of his body and face warmed as if he was sat beside a fire. Any temptation to sleep vanished, his eyes now wide open. Her hair was silky and soft, not hard like he'd imagined. Why had he expected that? Of course hair was soft. Laughing inwardly at his foolishness, he realised this was the first time he'd touched her so intimately. Darius swallowed and hoped his cheeks weren't as flushed as they felt.

"Lex, were we ever more than friends?"

She scoffed. "You mean in between all the whores you spent most nights with?"

Was that true? It didn't answer the question. Why would she bring up his promiscuity rather than give him a cold flat "no" if she felt nothing? Whatever the answer, he doubted she'd give him the full story tonight.

Choosing to change the subject rather than press the matter, he asked, "Are we really safe up here?"

"As safe as we can be. Rakkans roam at night. They see well in the dark and would easily ambush us if we slept on the ground."

"Come now, Lex." He nudged her thigh. "I'm sure you can take a rakkan in your sleep. You fight like a god." He rubbed his eyes. One touch and she already had him complimenting her? If not careful, he'd end up like Acamas, smiling as she slit his throat.

She sighed and pulled her head away. The warmth she'd been sharing lingered for a second before fading in the evening's chill.

"You remember that, do you?" she said.

"What do you mean?"

"The regular folk call us gods, saviours of man from the demonic rakkans." Lex shook her head and scrunched her nose. "They worship us. It's pathetic."

"Well, it's sort of true isn't it?"

"Would a god end up like you, Philippos?"

His fingers curled into fists, nails digging into his skin, just like that name. "Don't say *Philippos* when we're alone."

"We're not gods," she said, "and we're certainly not invincible."

He'd found that out the hard way, yet when she fought she certainly moved like an immortal. "So rakkans aren't really demons I guess."

"No. They bleed, they hurt, they feel. But don't hate them any less for it. They've taken much from me."

Much that she apparently wasn't going to divulge. "Do they have any other powers besides the strength and ferven?"

"As I said, they see well in the dark, and their skin is sensitive, enough to detect movements in the air and predict incoming blows to some extent, with training. And they live three times longer than humans."

A blinding pain seared his temples for a few seconds, before vanishing like a passing wave.

"Don't you remember?" Lex asked.

"What?" Darius rubbed his scalp. "Sorry, head keeps pounding. I don't remember anything about rakkans. I've never seen something so vile, so twisted." His arm throbbed with the scars of the rakkan's hate. "If I used to slaughter them, I'm glad."

"Mistress?" Omid finally summoned the courage to stop clinging to his perch and sat up. "May I have the rope to tie myself? I'm sleepy and worried I might fall."

"Of course." Lex stood and made her way gracefully between the branches, despite her exhaustion. As she began helping the boy bind himself to the branch, she looked up at Darius. "Wake me in a few hours. I'll sleep too."

It still puzzled Darius why she treated the boy as an equal, and why she hadn't killed him. Curious. A weakness perhaps? If only she treated Darius with such gentleness.

He leaned back against the fir's trunk and fidgeted until his back sank in comfortably. Once settled, he gripped his burnt arm, squeezing just enough to send prickles of pain to his shoulder. It was the only thing that would keep him awake for a few hours while the other two rested.

Darius watched Lex's breaths slow as she sank deeper into sleep. The sound of her exhaling was relaxing, like waves breaking on a beach. The weak moonlight didn't grant him a proper glimpse of her face, but he could picture it. Over the last few days he'd caught himself absentmindedly staring at her more and more. It had to stop. He couldn't allow himself to be seduced by a beautiful woman when he had no idea if he should trust her.

If only Felix hadn't died, or he hadn't lost Brutus. They'd had the same tattoo, which at least gave him some clue that they fought on the same side.

Lyra.

His cat didn't stir, apparently having slipped into slumber herself.

Lyra!

She jerked and turned her head towards him.

Come here, girl. I have a task for you.

Without hesitation, Lyra slinked over to him across the branches. She let out a yawn as he stroked her neck, but her amber eyes were bright and inquisitive.

I want you to search around, see if you can find Brutus's trail. It's a long shot, but if you get wind of him, go and bring him here. Otherwise, come back by sunrise.

She paused a few seconds for more petting then made her way down the tree. The quiet scratches of her claws on the tree trunk were thankfully not enough to wake Lex or Omid.

Chances were he wouldn't find Brutus again until they reached Margalvia—if he ever made it there. But he had to try. There was something off about Lex. He'd find out the truth, one way or another.

15

Brutus held the flimsy map up to the moon peeking between the clouds, as if more light would suddenly show where he was. Thank the Creator that he'd rendezvoused with Sulla in the forest. The other man at least had a map, even if it wasn't much help.

"I can't make head nor tail of this damned thing." Brutus screwed up the parchment and dropped it into the mud. At this rate he'd be an old man before they reached Margalvia. They'd left the forest hours ago, entering the southern grasslands, but every direction looked the same now.

"Don't do that, you lout," Sulla said, armour groaning as he stooped to pick up the map. "I'm surprised you can read anything through that helmet. I'll try. We don't all have brains smaller than our arms."

Brutus snorted. "Like you can use it." His brother Felix was the navigator. Without him, the pair would be marching in circles. It was a pity they'd all been separated. He counted himself fortunate that he'd met Sulla. Apart from his brothers, Brutus couldn't have chosen a better companion. The rakkan wasn't a legionnaire, only a commander in the Militia, but a loyal warrior nonetheless.

"I know where we stand." Sulla's confident grin creased the many scars on his chin and cheeks, and his eyes twinkled as moonlight caught his black irises. "I just need to find the direction to Margalvia. If we'd caught a glimpse of the sunset we'd know—"

"I've had enough of the sun. My skin can't take much more," Brutus said. The burns smarted his skin for days after. Sulla's disregard for danger too often reaped trouble, but Brutus would keep him in line for the journey ahead.

First though, they needed to choose a direction to travel. Brutus pulled off his helmet to get a better look at their surroundings.

"Come now, any rakkan can tolerate sunset." Sulla took a needle from his pocket.

"What're you doing with that needle? You can't have cut yourself again." The rakkan's body had more stitches than his undershirt, but what else did he expect when he charged fearlessly into every scrap?

"Magic," he teased.

"Don't make me punch you."

"Come to the water." Sulla walked to a nearby puddle from the day's downfall, ripping a leaf from a weed as he went. He rubbed the needle up and down the hem of the shirt poking beneath his armour, looking a bit like one of the crazed starving men that sullied Margalvia's gutters. What was he up to?

Sulla placed the needle on the leaf then carefully floated it in the puddle.

"That's a nice little boat you made for your needle, but what the hell—"

"Give it a rest. Wherever it points will be north."

Brutus scoffed. "And if I scratch your nose, will you point north too?"

"No, then my balls will swing east."

"Drivel."

Sulla ignored him, instead closing his eyes and taking a deep breath. "You smell that?"

How could Brutus not? Fresh grass and clean dry air that felt cool on his throat. Refreshing compared to the usual mists in Margalvia. "Grass?"

His companion smiled. "Smells good doesn't it?"

It reminded Brutus of only one thing. War. Grass meant human lands, and that meant algus. "Does that needle really work?"

"Yes. It's an old human trick."

Sighing, Brutus rested on one knee. "I hope Felix and Darius are finding their way easier than us."

"Maybe it's best they don't get back to Margalvia. The Warlord might have Darius's head for going after Archimedes as he did."

True, as much as Brutus didn't care to admit it. Warlord Catonius had always disliked Darius. Now the Warlord had the excuse he needed. Darius had had no orders to assassinate Archimedes and had got his mind flattened in the process. They'd take it as a ruse, proof Darius was a traitor, when Brutus knew deep down Darius would never turn on them.

He had to do something. "When I get back to Margalvia I'll have words with my brother."

"I hope we find Felix soon. This needle seems precarious." Sulla gave the leaf another nudge.

"Not Felix. Varro."

Sulla's smile vanished and his eyes darkened. "That can only mean one thing. You mean him to challenge Catonius."

Brutus chewed lightly on his tongue, unsure whether to divulge his brother's secrets, but Sulla was as close to family as one got.

114

"He's been discontented for a while. Archimedes is crushing our armies. Varro blames Catonius." If his brother could be encouraged to move against Catonius quickly, then Darius would have a chance of surviving his return to Margalvia, though it still wouldn't be assured. Varro didn't love Darius either, but at least he realised the value of someone that could walk amongst the humans.

The needle came to a rest pointing at what was hopefully north.

"Can't say my chief or any of my men would mourn Catonius," Sulla said. "And of all your commanders—hell, all of Margalvia—Varro stands shoulders above as a warrior. Even I wouldn't fight him."

"You never said that before. I thought you feared nothing?" It was Sulla's best and worst quality.

Sulla picked up the needle and stood, grin sliding back into place. "I don't fear, but I'm not a fool either. Come. South-east is this way." He strode off into the grass towards what Brutus prayed was Margalvia.

16

The sky shifted from molten red to orange. Darius had waited all through the night for his escort's return, but her search proved unsuccessful. Lyra's claws scratched against the tree's bark as she climbed onto the branch beside him, her slumped ears showing her exhaustion. He reached out and patted her head. *Maybe next time, girl. Sorry to keep you up all night.* A soft purr vibrated his hand, then she pulled away, settled on a nearby branch and shut her eyes.

Omid lay tied to another branch, shivering slightly but still slumbering. He still wore Darius's coat. The breeze was stronger this high up but at least the sun would soon soothe the chills. Darius craned his neck to find Lex's sleeping spot.

The algus sat above, staring at him with an angry expression. When had she woke and why was she looking at him like that?

"Sleep well?" Darius asked.

"You didn't wake me."

"I thought you could use a full night's rest," he lied. He could have used some rest himself but hadn't wanted her to note Lyra's absence.

"When I say wake me in a few hours, I mean it."

"Aren't people usually in a bad mood when they *don't* get a good sleep?"

"Don't get smart. Where was Lyra all night?"

How did she know? He'd checked on Lex the moment he heard Lyra's movements below, and the algus had definitely still been asleep. The panther's quiet movements must have woken her, or perhaps the growing brightness of the morning. Darius cursed his luck.

"She was out hunting," he said.

"She doesn't look full."

"No luck."

"Liar." Lex stood, fists clenched.

Darius hazarded a guess. "It was Tiro that saw her, wasn't it? I forgot about your damn bird."

Omid groaned as he roused and began sleepily disentangling himself from the rope, seemingly unaware of the argument brewing a few feet away.

"What if she was captured, or tailed? Do you know how many people want you dead?"

"I might if you told me something once in a while."

Lex dropped down the branches to Darius's perch, her face pinched. Something was amiss with her walk, like she kept her full weight from one leg. *Is she injured?*

"I can't believe you don't trust me," she snapped. "Where did you send her?"

"To find Brutus. No harm, no foul."

She moved to smack his gut but he was ready and brought up his forearm to block. His burnt forearm. Pain shot up the limb as her hand slapped against the bandage.

Pulling back, he shielded himself with his good arm. "What the... Enough with the abuse!"

Lex's jawline tensed. "Abuse?"

"Yeah, *abuse*. You touch me again and I walk."

"Odd choice of word for someone with no morals."

"It's…" It *was* a strange word for him to have used. "I don't enjoy pain."

"And why should I care what you enjoy?"

He had no answer for her smug look, only that he thought she *should* care.

"When you grabbed my arm after that rakkan burnt me. Do you have any idea how much that hurt?"

"You mean after I saved your life?"

"I'm sorry. Should I bow down and praise you, oh Goddess, for your heroic defence?" Darius bowed mockingly.

"Oh look, you remembered something for a change," Lex sneered. She turned to end the conversation, but he wasn't finished.

"Yes, I remember things if you just tell me, Alexandra."

Her head snapped back towards him, a sparkle of algor in her furious eyes. "I told you," she said quietly. "Don't. Call. Me. That."

Whatever her problem was with that name, he sensed it cut her deeply. The name formed on his lips again, but he resisted.

"Tell me, Darius, what do you want?" she asked. "Why come with me if you think you can go it alone?"

That she'd used his true name surprised him, but he didn't let that sway his mood. "Honestly? I want my memories back. You seem to be the only one that can or will help. Then I'll find Margalvia."

"Why do you want that?"

"I…" He'd not really thought about why. His desires had been lost with his memories and all that was left had no wants to speak of. "I'm a warrior. It feels like that's all I know, and Brutus said I'd be safe in Margalvia." And it was the place his mother had mentioned all those years ago; that had some sway over him. "You said I used to be an even greater warrior. I can't help but be seduced by the idea." Maybe then, tragedy wouldn't so often befall him.

Grimacing, Lex gripped her hip. "It isn't just your skill I want. It's the fire that spurred you to fight. I pray you'll get it back."

Her mood had turned sombre, which was an improvement on livid at least.

"Are you injured?" He pointed to her hip.

"It's nothing. Just stiff in the morning."

There were no signs of blood and he hadn't seen her take a blow. Perhaps an old injury she powered through by whatever spurred *her* on.

"If it's any consolation," Darius said, "when I see those rakkans, I want to hunt every last one."

She smirked. "It's a start."

They set off later that morning after foraging something to eat. Conversation was light, which was fine by Darius. His arm had returned to stabbing pains after Lex's blow. Omid seemed to find their spat entertaining, which at least took the boy's mind off Acamas's death. That boyish grin had made a reappearance too. For some reason it made the journey a little easier. Lyra also liked the boy, often trotting alongside him. His height was just right that he could pet her neck as he walked.

"Hey, tree-boy, why are you so cheery?" Darius asked. Of all the things he didn't understand, people's moods were the most confusing. Especially Omid's.

"I get to walk in the forest. Better than crawling the sewers and cellars hunting rats."

Darius slowed and put a hand to Omid's shoulder, letting Lex stride ahead out of earshot. "But you're still a slave. She owns you now. Maybe she has worse in stock."

The boy's grin faded a little. "You're a depressing git, aren't you?"

Lyra flicked her head and almost looked as if she was smiling.

Darius gave Omid a light shove. "That's how you talk to your elders?"

The boy scoffed. "I'm to be polite to citizens, but you aren't one."

"What am I then, a slave?"

"I don't think you're anything. A nomad."

That drew a chuckle from Darius. "Then I don't care how you talk, as long as you speak the truth. Was I always a git?"

Omid stopped and a wide grin spread revealing his dirty teeth. "I don't think so. I only met you once, but you promised me one day I'd be free."

His old self may have wanted something from this boy in return. "Do you know whether I trusted Lex?"

Omid frowned. "I don't know. I never saw you together. But I trust her."

Darius stopped. If Omid had never seen them together, what was Lex's reason for bringing him along? Or was there something else the boy knew? Her lies had to unravel at some point. For now, the boy proved more trustworthy than Lex, and his loyal panther more reliable than them all.

Lex had shown she was unrelenting—or so she worked hard to convey. But there were also signs underneath, the way she'd looked at him when she pleaded for him to stay safe, and how Omid spoke of her, how excited the boy had been to leave with her. A heartless woman wouldn't spare a passing comment to a slave, let alone risk themselves to bring one along. Not when killing the boy would stop him talking. There was something she wasn't telling him. There was a *lot* she wasn't telling him, and it was time to find out.

"Can you pick some of these mushrooms as we go?" Darius pointed to the littered fungi on the forest floor.

"Yes, I'm hungry too." Omid skipped off and began foraging.

Darius quickened his pace and strode alongside Lex, making sure he was out of Omid's earshot before speaking. "Why are we bringing Omid?"

"I told you, he can connect you to me, and expose me."

"I don't buy it."

"Think what you want."

"Why not kill him? You don't seem to have a problem with that."

Lex scowled. "I don't kill children."

Darius grabbed her shoulder and stopped her. "I don't believe you." He shot her a hard stare, like the ones she always gave. "Tell me the truth."

Her lips pressed into a thin line. What he wouldn't give for a glimpse of what went on in her head whenever she stared at him in silence. By doing it, she exuded dominance, usually enough to cease his objections, but this time he wouldn't surrender.

"I can't," she said at last. "If Archimedes gets you again... I can't risk giving him more."

"He already got everything."

"There are some things even Darius didn't know."

Darius relaxed his stare. Time to try a different tactic. "If Archimedes finds me then it means Omid's dead already. So tell me."

"Better dead than the alternative." Lex pushed past him with a sharp jab of her shoulder and set off at a brisk pace again.

She wasn't getting away that easily. Darius strode alongside her. "I'm not giving up. I'm tired of your secrets, and I'll hound you for however many days or weeks it takes us to get to Laltos."

Sighing, Lex shook her head. "Fine. But if anything happens, it's on you."

Finally. He gave a firm nod. "It's on me."

"Omid's like us. He has algor."

How was that possible? The boy wasn't a god that folk bowed before in the street. "Then why is he a slave?"

"Being born with algor isn't the blessing it used to be. Before Archimedes, an algus expected to be adopted by a wealthy family and would become a guardian of man. But the goman started taking the young for his army, so now they hide from him. I've helped Omid go unnoticed, but if he's discovered it's only a matter of time before he's recruited."

"You're bringing him because he can fight like us? To join our army?"

"No." Her voice sharpened. "I'm protecting the boy."

"Why?" It made no sense for her to care for him.

"Because I want to." Lex stopped abruptly. Ahead, a wide stone road cut through the forest. "We've wandered too close to the road." She turned back into the overgrowth.

Omid came running to catch them, mushrooms falling from the bulging pile in his hands. "Mistress, we're less than a league from Thrane."

"I know where we are," Lex said.

"The healer, Parisa, is just off the road outside the village," Omid continued, turning to Darius. "She has medicine. Maybe she can help you."

Lex rolled her eyes. "We haven't the time."

Omid nodded at Darius's arm. "Her remedies help with pain."

Darius touched his bandaged arm. It needed another wash of algor or something for pain. Talk about medicine stirred his mind. He strained to remember something, and all sorts of scrambled, useless information began to surface. Certain plants like Seplyga were used for wounds. Some sort of ground antler was inhaled for broken bones, elk sounded right. The faeces of one rodent or another, slathered on the face, helped skin complaints. For pain, a rare plant known as "the weeping plant" could offer relief. He'd kill for some of that. It'd help quieten his mind too.

"Does this healer have some magic that can help me?" Darius asked.

"No," Lex replied. "There's no such thing as a healer. She's nothing more than a herbalist."

One that may have access to the weeping plant then. "Good enough. Which way?"

Omid pointed, and Darius set off in that direction.

"Not you too," Lex said.

The boy followed after him and eventually Lex caught up, her scowl showing her reluctance.

"If anyone is to see her it's me," she said. "Alone."

They made their way through the undergrowth parallel to the road, Omid taking the lead with a slight spring returning to his steps.

After a couple of miles, he looked over his shoulder. "Parisa's home is just up ahead."

Soon after, they reached a small clearing. A tiny stone hovel sat under the shade of a gigantic pine tree. Darius guessed Parisa set up shop in its shadow because it lorded over all the other trees, its thick trunk bulging with age. This pine made the tree they'd slept in look like a sapling.

Lex glanced up at the setting sun. "You two wait here out of sight."

Darius and Omid sat down behind a thorny bush while Lex stalked over to the hut, eyes darting back and forth. The boy picked up clumps of hard dirt from the soil and threw them into the bush, one after another. Never still; that energy might come in useful, but right now it was a liability. Distracting him with conversation might work.

"I appreciate you suggesting coming here for me." Darius thought perhaps the boy wanted to curry favour, which would work well for his own plans.

"It's nothing. Parisa is a caring woman."

"How about we look out for one another?"

"Don't we already?"

Cute. "I'll warn you if I get wind of Lex wanting to bury you, and you do the same for me."

Omid frowned. "Would she do that?"

As far as Darius had seen, there was little she wouldn't do. "I said I wouldn't underestimate her and I meant it." It'd be the death of him. He fidgeted his legs to generate a little warmth—the evening's chill was already creeping into his limbs.

Before Omid could respond, Lex reappeared from around the shrub.

"Darius, you need to see this," she said in a low tone.

That doesn't sound good. Perhaps this herbalist wouldn't be able to help after all.

The three walked up to the hut.

"Wait outside," Lex said to Omid as she ushered Darius through the door.

He entered into a cramped room where rows of shelves lined the walls. Bottles full of red, green and black liquids covered the shelves. There were no windows and the room was lit only by two clay oil lamps at opposite ends. Their flames sputtered, sucking at the last few drops of oil. The cottage smelled rancid, like faeces and stale urine. In the corner farthest from the door, an old woman sat on the floor, shaking and huddled so tightly he'd barely noticed her.

"Hello?" he said.

The wrinkles on the woman's face multiplied as she winced and pulled her knees closer to her chest. Her wide eyes stared at him with terror, tears streaming down her cheeks.

Lex came in behind him. "This is Parisa, what's left of her."

The old woman said nothing, just shivered.

"There's no need to be afraid," he said.

"She can't understand you," Lex said. "I've tried. There's nothing inside."

"Archimedes. He did this."

"I thought you should see. This is what almost became of you. This is what may become of you if we don't succeed."

Parisa sobbed, petrified by everything around her, not understanding a word they said. Did she even have coherent thoughts? She was like a blind, lame animal left cowering in a dark and unknown world. A damp patch stained the wooden floor underneath her where she'd wet herself, lacking enough knowledge of even her body's basic functions to avoid it. Darius would rather his throat cut than end up like this.

"Why would he do this to her?" he asked.

"He must have thought we'd been to see her. I told you he'd be thorough. He's stripped everything. She's been this way since yesterday."

"But why would he leave her like this?" It was odd to leave her alive.

"I don't think he cares." Lex's voice held no trace of surprise.

Parisa wouldn't survive more than a few days. She shielded her face with an arm streaked with dried blood from where skin had been peeled off. Raw like his own. Did she even remember how to eat? Would *he* know how to eat if this was his end?

"Give me some food." He held out a hand to Lex.

She rifled through her bag, pulled out an apple and tossed it to him.

Darius moved closer to the woman, his steps light and slow so as not to startle her. He breathed shallowly to keep from retching at the stench and offered Parisa the apple.

She shrank away from him, her jaw trembling.

He took a bite out of the apple as she watched, trying to show her how to eat, that it was enjoyable, and offered it to her again. A wail scratched its way from her throat and she closed her eyes, burying her head in her hands.

"We should go," Lex said.

"What'll become of her?"

"She's forgotten how to communicate, to eat, to sleep, to survive. No one will look after her."

He turned to face Lex, unable to bear the sight of quaking Parisa any longer. "So you'll leave her like this?"

"No. I'm not going to leave her." Lex's hand rested on the hilt of her sword. "Go outside if you like."

For a moment, he hesitated while she stared unblinking at him. The thought of cutting Parisa's neck, all that vile blood gushing forth, made him want to retch more than the stink had. He stepped past Lex and grabbed hold of the door handle.

No. Something stopped him leaving. Some part of him wanted to see it, witness what may soon be his own fate. The room grew hot, beads of sweat prickling his forehead. Anger stirred inside him, wanting stoking.

"What are you waiting for?" Lex asked.

Parisa still sat in the corner cowering, too scared to even meet his eyes, cradling her arm.

"No. I'll do it," he said.

Lex frowned at him. Her mouth opened, poised to say something, but the words never came out. She turned and exited the hut without a word.

Darius pulled his cloak tight around his front, as if it would shelter him from the gore. He'd make it quick and painless. *Pointless to do otherwise.* He unsheathed his sword carefully, without as much as an audible scrape. Parisa didn't react. At least she didn't know enough to sense what was coming.

He stepped over beside her and she quivered into the corner. The angle was awkward. Dragging her into the middle of the room would give him a clean swing, but the mere thought reminded him too much of his mother being dragged outside.

Drawing back his arm, he summoned all his strength and speed to make it swift. His arm trembled and the short sword suddenly felt five times as heavy. What was happening? He'd killed before. Was it just the blood about to burst free that made him hesitate? It had to be. Why else? He pictured Archimedes, that mouthless fiend who reduced people to this.

Parisa lifted her head up and gazed at him, tears still filling her wide, innocent eyes.

Darius swung his sword so hard he barely felt it cut through her neck. The blade slammed into the wall behind with a deafening twang and sent a shudder up his arm. Silence filled the room as he walked backwards to escape the blood leaking from her lacerated neck.

His hands shook violently as he took in heavy breaths, fighting the rising urge to hurl. The stench reached an unbearable strength. He yanked the door open, unwilling to spend another moment in the presence of her butchered corpse.

Darius stepped out into the forest and slammed the door, growling under his breath. Lex stood nearby, an oil lamp in her hand to fight off dusk's shadows, with Omid waiting behind her, fidgeting. As the algus looked at Darius, he swore he saw a wistful grin flash across her mouth.

"How can you smile?" he asked.

"Because when I look at you right now, I see Darius."

Sweat trickled down his temple. "I'm angry. I don't know why." He'd killed and seen death before without a passing thought but this one felt different.

"Because it's wrong! Listen to your instincts. You have damn good reason to be angry, as do I. But this is nothing, *nothing* compared to what Archimedes has done, what he will do."

"And what has he done?"

Lex's face turned marble white with fury. "Imagine looking at your own son. Empty."

She turned and walked away like she'd said too much. Whose son? His? Hers?

He bolted after her. "What does that mean?"

"I'm not talking about it."

"You can't just say that and leave. Do you mean *I* had a son?"

She stopped and stared motionless ahead. All he could see in the lamplight was her taut black ponytail and stiff shoulders. "No. You have no children. Now drop it."

Then she'd meant her own son. What would he see if he moved in front of her? Would that steely gaze have at last softened to reveal someone full of sorrow and pain?

Omid inched up beside him and gave a sombre shake of the head.

"Fine. It's dropped," Darius said. *For the moment.*

Lex took a deep breath before she turned around to face him. There was no sadness left on her face, not even her ever-present anger. Her expression was flat and her eyes emotionless, as if all that feeling had been sucked in and buried deep inside.

"Let's go," she said, her voice faint. "We'll find somewhere close by to stay the rest of the night. Then we head for Laltos."

He still couldn't be sure what she'd meant by the "son" comment, or whether everything she was telling him was a lie. If it was, she was the best and most devious actress he'd ever seen. However, as he followed her through the night, Darius realised one thing.

He wanted to trust her.

17

Lyra led them through the forest, more at ease in the night than any of them. By the time they'd found somewhere secluded it was too dark to climb a tree so they took shelter among the large protruding roots of one.

Darius lay face to the ground, not even bothering to cover the soil with discarded leaves. The cold earth cooled his warm cheeks. The three of them lay nestled together while Lyra perched above as lookout, the only one that could see enough to watch for rakkans.

Omid shuffled backwards until pressed into Darius's arms. "Can I?" the boy whispered.

Darius wasn't in the mood to offer comfort but if it would get the boy to sleep faster... He lifted his arm and let Omid snuggle close. Thankfully the boy soon fell asleep, his breathing slipping into slow, deep hisses. Darius considered pushing Omid away but something about feeling the rhythm soothed him.

He couldn't sleep; he didn't bother to try. The image of Parisa wouldn't leave his mind but he had no idea why. Was it because soon it could be him? His hands felt dirty, covered in soil as they were. He could still feel the stickiness of blood staining them, despite having wiped them clean.

Lex's quiet, not quite rhythmic breaths told him that she wasn't sleeping either.

The night passed slowly. At the first hint of the sun peeping over the horizon he stood up and arched his back with a succession of cracks. Omid began to stir as Lex also rose and scanned the area. Her hair tie had slipped in the night and now her ponytail hung low. How long would it stay that way? She tightened that thing even when it didn't need it, like an ingrained habit. Or was it a nervous bent?

Darius ripped up some clumps of chickweed that littered the forest floor and began chewing his breakfast. Even plain bread was better than this animal feed, which tasted like a mouthful of soil and grass, but he needed fuel. Not that this was sufficient for a warrior. He needed meat and hearty meals. Without sustenance, he was less of a fighter. And if not a fighter, what else was he?

He handed some chickweed to Omid and approached Lex, holding out a handful of the meagre plant.

"I'm fine," she said.

Stuffing the rest into his mouth, Darius looked around for anything else edible.

"We should take care to sleep well the next few nights," Lex said. "We may not have the opportunity to rest once we reach the plains. It'll be difficult to hide."

Like she was one to talk, barely sleeping even when they rested. Darius watched her remove her hair band. She combed through the black waves with her fingers before tying it taut behind her head once more.

"If you're a wealthy algus why can't you get us horses?" Darius asked.

"Too rare so far west. The rakkans take them. But we'll be able to find some in Laltos."

All the more reason to hurry. A horse would give his aching feet a break. He finished foraging for snacks and they were soon underway again, passing yet more boring fir and pine trees. Their lofty branches blocked all but tiny rays of sunlight, teasing him with the warmth they deprived him of. He longed to reach the plains where he'd feel the sun on his skin again.

After a few hours, Lex's pace slowed. Her left side slumped a little as she walked like the hip had stiffened again. She wasn't out of shape; she'd proven that on their recent march. *An old injury must be acting up.*

Sounds of gushing water grew through the trees to their left and Lex stopped.

"I'm going to refill the waterskin," she said. "I'll be back soon." The algus pushed through the branches and vanished before he could enquire about her impairment.

At last he had a little time to pick Omid's brain some more.

"What do you know about her son?" Darius asked.

"He was kind."

"You knew him?"

"Yes. Before Ismene bought me I grew up in Laltos. We'd often cross paths."

"What happened to him?"

Omid looked sheepish. "Archimedes. It's not my place to say."

"What else do you know about her, and me?"

"I never knew you really, and I shouldn't speak of the mistress."

At least Darius had got something out of the boy. He was tempted to unsheathe his sword for a few swings to keep his shoulders loose, but he couldn't bear to touch the thing yet. Omid obviously had the same idea, as he picked up a branch and began to swing it lazily about.

"Hey, leaf-lover," Darius called, picking up a branch from the soil, "have at you." Time to see if the kid was what Lex said he was.

He swung the stick at Omid, who blocked his strike and gave him a wide grin before attacking with a slash of his own.

At first, Darius went easy, but soon he realised the boy was playing hard.

"Come on," Omid said. "You'll need to be faster than that to kill a rakkan."

Darius scowled. The boy was teasing, but it angered him that he had yet to prove himself against a rakkan in combat.

"You asked for it." Darius lunged forward to smack Omid's side but the boy ducked under. *Agile.* He blocked Omid's counter and brought his stick around, summoning his algus speed to dart ahead of the boy's defences. His stick rapped Omid across the backside. The boy yelped.

The sharp-pitched sound triggered the memory of Parisa's screams. Darius turned away with a grimace, scratching at his left ear as if he could claw out the echoes.

"A blow there isn't going to kill one," Omid said.

Darius glared down at him. The boy wasn't moving with the speed he was capable of, not with any algus flair. "I know you could've blocked that."

Omid frowned. "You're too fast."

To hell with subtlety. "And you're fast too. Lex told me."

The boy's gaze drifted down to the ground. His free arm hugged his stomach. That defensive posture meant Lex had told Darius the truth for once.

Darius eased over and planted a hand on Omid's bony shoulder. "Your secret's safe with me." It may end up getting them out of a scrape.

Omid looked up with pleading eyes. "Please don't tell. I don't want him to take me."

"He won't," Lex said, bursting back through the branches. She spoke with a force that reassured even Darius. "You'll be safe in Laltos with my workers until you're older."

"What happens when he's older?" Darius asked.

"Then I become an algus." Omid smiled, brandishing his stick.

"Archimedes is most interested in the young," Lex said. "When they're older some can fight back and resist his influence. Much easier to control a child with his powers. Nowadays most with algor wait until they're almost adults to reveal themselves."

"Is that what you want," Darius asked Omid, "to be an algus?"

Omid gave him a look of disbelief. "Of course. Then I'll be free."

Suddenly the boy's chirpiness made sense. Having algor meant he was destined to be free. No master could own an algus. The boy had hope, that moment of freedom to look forward to, when he'd stop chasing rats or whatever else he was ordered to do. An unfettered future lay waiting for him, a better future than Darius's in all likelihood.

"And when you're free, what will you do?" Darius asked.

"Find my mother and free her." Omid looked up at him with fiery determination in his eyes.

"Where is she?"

"In the west, Dolthea. She was sold to the city's regent."

"She was a very fair woman," Lex said with a telling look. "Lots of the algus enjoyed her company."

That likely meant she was a high-priced courtesan, a slave girl rented out to make her masters a pretty penny. Did Omid have any idea who his father was? Hell, if Lex hadn't told Darius he had no son, he might even wonder if he'd fathered the boy given his reported taste for whores.

"Nice dream," Darius said. "I'm sure you'll make a fine algus if you have her instructing you."

"I'll be the best!" Omid leapt, spinning in front of him with a burst of algus speed. The boy lifted his stick and it flared brilliant blue before he slashed it into Darius's makeshift weapon, carving it in two. Algor. The one weapon he hadn't harnessed yet.

"You *must* teach me to do that."

Lex clutched Darius's injured arm, her firm fingers sending a burst of pain to his shoulder. "He's not teaching you anything until I can trust you."

He yanked his arm away. "*You* trust *me*? Come now, if I was some spy wouldn't I have done something already? Why would Archimedes still chase me?"

She eyed him suspiciously.

"Do you want me to die the next time I happen upon those rakkans?"

She looked down at his burnt arm. "You're right. You need to know how to conjure algor to defend yourself. But we need to keep moving."

Just like that, she was going to share the secret to becoming a godlike warrior, to being like her. Then he'd be able to face the rakkans. Darius withheld a grin as they set off again.

Lex wasted little time in starting. "Give me your hand."

Darius offered his palm to Lex, bracing himself for expected pain. She took his hand and held it, light and delicate as if handling something precious. It made him nervous when she gave him such attention, when he felt her warm skin against his, but not the same nerves as fearing for his life, more like anticipation.

"Note how this feels." Lex's hand glowed and suddenly icy blood ran through the veins of his forearm. Algor spread and coated his hand and his muscles felt slow, every fibre tense like metal wire.

"It doesn't take long to learn how to conjure algor," Lex explained. "It's as natural as breathing. Eventually you can coat weapons, arrows, your enemies. Anything you touch can become an extension of your abilities." She released his arm and it returned to normal. "With practise, you could stand against a rakkan. And win."

"Cheap dig," he mumbled, catching the derogatory look she gave him. "I think you're enjoying being stronger than me, like you weren't before."

Her only answer was a wry smile.

If conjuring algor was as easy as she made out, great. He'd imagined it took months, even years of training to become proficient in it. But if a young boy like Omid could use it then surely he could learn.

Darius envisaged wielding such power, tearing apart rakkans while protected by an impenetrable shell. "Are you immune to a rakkan's attacks when you coat your body with algor?"

"It depends how powerful the rakkan is, but mostly yes. I'd never suffer a burn like you."

Another dig. He swallowed his annoyance. "Can you show me more?"

Lex took in a deep breath and let it out slowly. Her skin faded to white as if all blood drained away from it, then a blue tinge rose. It grew stronger and began enveloping her clothes and even her hair. She glowed and her irises burst in rich blue, twinkling like diamonds. The light grew stronger until her entire body radiated a brilliant cobalt blue and she left icy footprints in her wake.

Darius had never seen anything so magnificent or felt so much raw power. The cold emanating from her chilled his hands without the algor even touching him. It felt divine. She was like a goddess. He gently poked her arm out of curiosity and the algor climbed his finger as if it took on a life of its own.

He stared at her, his jaw hanging open. "Beautiful."

Her glow faded until she walked as a regular human again. She eyed him strangely, something going on behind her stare. Not for the first time, he wished he could glimpse her thoughts.

"Why don't you fight like that all the time?" Darius asked.

"While conjuring algor we are physically diminished. Coating the body completely drains speed and agility. It's as if you're a regular human."

There went his plan of fighting with algor armour.

Lex picked up his hand and held it out in front of him. "Now I want you to focus and try to put any tensions out of your mind. Repeat what you felt, when my algor touched you, only this time on your own."

"Get rid of my tension?" It'd help if she hadn't just insulted him. Twice.

"If I can do it, you can."

Darius concentrated. Shedding his mind of anger was easier than he thought; he just shoved any part of him that cared about anything out into the air. It was only a few seconds before a blue speck appeared on his index finger with a jolt like it had been pricked with a knife.

"Look at that, willow-whisperer." He grinned at Omid. "First try."

The blue swelled and spread over his entire hand, crawling up his arm and shoulder like icy tendrils. It was moving on its own. He wasn't trying anymore.

"What's happening?" he asked.

"Look at that, mindless-man." Omid laughed.

The algor didn't stop. It travelled down his chest, stomach and legs. The cold film creeped around his neck, his face, then reached down his throat into his stomach as if he swallowed gallons of freezing water. His steps slowed, each one like pushing through five feet of snow.

Darius grimaced. "How do I make it stop?"

Lex didn't look fazed. "Controlling it is the difficult part. Keep practising. It will fade soon of its own accord. Just don't touch anyone while you're like that. You'll kill them if they're not one of us. That goes for Lyra too."

This was one weapon he felt like a novice handling, but one he'd die without. Darius released a sigh of relief as the blue glow began to diminish. His training had started.

18

Another crimson sunset. Darius leaned back against the fir's rough bark and watched the sky darken through the bushy branches. After traveling for five days, they'd finally reached the edge of the forest. His gaze shifted to the scenery beyond the trees.

Miles of red-tinted plains stretched before his eyes like a sea of blood. Fields of wheat rippled in the wind. Some houses dotted the landscape with smoking chimneys, alongside bushels of harvested produce. The vast farms must have fed the region. And there, hiding in the distance, the towers of a city sprouted. Laltos. He'd have missed it if Lex hadn't pointed it out, but now it drew his attention. She said they were less than a day away.

Darius had tried to pry more details of his former self from Lex, but she was holding something back, every pause before she answered his questions an obvious filter. The mysterious raven-haired beauty offered him occasional snippets, but should he trust her?

Most of the time during their recent trek, he hadn't paid much attention to the forest around him, being either lost in his own head or trying to master the conjuring of algor. He'd managed to coat himself only up to his neck but progress was painfully slow, and every failed attempt just proved he was as inadequate as he feared.

Other memories also tugged at the edge of his mind, each bleaker than the last. Darius stared blankly at the fields, trying to unearth why Parisa's huddled form kept rising in his thoughts. She should be just another body to him.

Lex sat across from him, one hand resting on her hip, fingertips caressing her sword's hilt. Always prepared and unfaltering. When he'd pressed her about the stiffness she sometimes showed, she'd insisted she had no hip injury, and the rare times he caught a flash of the surrounding skin it looked healthy, as well as alluring.

Her face was hard, thoughts seeming to weigh heavy on her mind too. He'd gleaned some information from her along the way, though nothing more about her "son" remark, but every time she seemed to relax enough to smile at him she snapped herself out of it and returned to being cold and distant. Yet every day he could feel himself warming to her. It bothered him more than ever that his skills as a warrior were so handicapped. He hated her seeing him so weak.

Omid sat on a branch below, twiddling his thumbs.

"Hey, Omid," Darius said. "You never finished teaching me about Archimedes."

The boy glanced up at him with a pale face. "Not much more to say. I try to avoid him, hide out with the rats when he's around."

Rats certainly were more appealing. "I guess his creepy whispering gives him away before you have to meet him face to face."

Omid frowned. "Whispering? He's always loud and scary to me."

Curious.

Tiro swooped and landed beside Lex on the branch, his dotted underbelly stained red from whatever meal he'd just devoured. Darius's own escort lay on another branch, as at home in the tree as the bird. He envied their disregard for heights.

"Lex," Darius called, "tell me more of this Waif Magician."

"Her name's Shirin. She's half-goman, born decades ago to one of the first gomans to ever travel across the treacherous Aretean Sea. When the Torian king discovered the interbreeding, they hunted down and killed her family. Shirin escaped. She was only nine and has been evading humans her whole life. Such a harsh upbringing has left her hard-bitten."

"She'll be hard to find then. You're certain she can fix me?" Darius asked, wary of getting his hopes up.

"She's the only other person with goman blood in the land."

That wasn't a yes. But this Shirin was likely his only chance. He imagined what it would be like to have his memories back, to not have questions and confusion, to be a great warrior, and to not only know how to fight but why.

"Would the old Darius have gone to such lengths to get his memories back?"

"Undoubtedly. He was braver, stronger, stubborn." Lex smiled wistfully. "Rebellious yet more loyal than anyone I've met. I trusted you."

She's still using the past tense. "How was I stronger?"

"Physically, mentally."

How had losing his memories made him physically weaker? Forgetting his past shouldn't have any effect on whether he could lift a hundred pounds or five hundred.

"How—" A wave of dread washed over him, cutting off his question. Lyra had spotted danger headed their way. Darius's heart pounded. *Rakkan?*

Lex stared at him, put a finger to her lips and froze. For a while they sat in silence. Nothing on the ground stirred. Lyra's ears twitched, following sounds only she could hear.

Two scraggly figures strode from behind a tree a hundred yards away, slowly making their way through the forest. Rakkans. Darius glanced at his companions. Lex wore a grim expression. Omid's eyes were wide with interest.

The two rakkans made their way to the edge of the nearest farmland. They disappeared into the swaying crops, heading straight for a house.

Lex broke her stillness and adjusted her belt.

Darius straightened. "Are we going after them?"

"I am. I'm an algus, it's my duty."

A shadow still hung in the fields where he'd last seen the stalking forms of the rakkans. Perhaps now was the time to prove himself against these monsters. He would show all of them—Lex, Omid, his mother's memory, his own self-doubt—that he was worthy of calling himself a warrior.

"I'm coming with you," he said.

"No."

"There's smoke coming from the chimney of that house. The people inside could get hurt. You may need my help."

"No. I forbid it."

Darius glared. *Forbid?* The nerve.

He'd barely survived one rakkan, but shouldn't he stop doubting himself? There were worse things than death, like being *weak*. Weakness got those close to you killed.

Rakkans were strong but he wouldn't be so arrogant this time. He'd fight hard and show Lex and Omid he wasn't a useless has-been.

"I was in two minds about it," Darius said, "but I don't take orders. I'm not your slave."

He jumped off his branch onto one below, then to the next, and the next as if hopping down a jumbled staircase. His algus agility came naturally and he made it to the ground with a thud. Drawing his short sword, he set off marching towards the house.

A hand clutched his shoulder and jerked him to a stop.

"What do you think you're doing?" Lex said.

He grunted in annoyance and pulled away. "Doing what you forbade me—proving a point."

Lex grabbed his shirt and caught a clump of the skin on his chest too. "No. You can*not* die. Do you understand me?"

"Because my life so far has been worth living? What's the point if I can't even take two—?"

"I don't give a damn if you can take them. It's dangerous."

She said it as though nothing worse could befall her. Beneath her orders was fear, an underlying reason why she wanted Darius back more than anything, and why she was scared to relax around him. It was time to find out.

"Why don't you want me to die?"

"What?"

"You in love with me or something?"

Lex shoved him away. "You don't know anything about me."

"It explains the 'you cannot die' speech."

She shook her head. "I want to know where your grandfather is, and no one knows except you."

So they were both using each other for their own ends. "Why do you want to know?"

"I can't tell you. If Archimedes gets you again…"

Why hadn't she asked his old self about his grandfather? It didn't matter. He turned and marched once again towards the farmhouse, which was now nothing more than a dark silhouette in the fading light.

Lex followed at his shoulder. "You want to take on two rakkans? If you get injured we may not make it to Laltos, let alone to Margalvia or the Waif Magician, without getting captured."

Would he risk ever regaining his memory or reaching Margalvia for the sake of pride? What else did he have? Being a warrior was everything he knew, and until he vanquished this foe he didn't even have that. He was tired of having to be protected.

"Better dead than weak," he said.

Lex quickened her pace and strode in front of him. "You won't back down will you?"

"If I did, you'd never respect me."

She groaned. "As stubborn as ever."

19

They left Omid watching from the safety of the tree. Darius ordered Lyra to stay as well. He didn't want his escort getting hurt again. Only once he was sure the panther would stay did he turn and submerge himself in the field of crops so tall the house was barely visible through the heads of the swaying wheat.

Lex followed behind him, her footsteps a quiet echo of his. The wheeze of the wind through the crops brought a faint aroma of bread.

"They're in the yard," Lex whispered.

It was too dark to see from this distance; Tiro must have been overhead, Lex's eyes and ears. If only Lyra relayed such precise details to him. *Is that a skill I lost as well?* It was a question for another time.

They crept to the edge of the field, staying just deep enough to remain hidden but keeping within view the two rakkans now next to the farmhouse.

Lex took the bow from her shoulder and nocked an arrow, crouching lower.

The rakkans wore the now-familiar ragged clothes hanging loose from their wiry frames. Both looked male. One had a head of scraggly white hair, while the other had thick tufts, as black as Lex's. They rummaged through sacks of grain twice their size and tossed the bags around as if full of nothing but air. Just how strong were they? Could they tear down a wall with their bare hands if they wished? Yet their arms were so thin Darius winced, expecting them to snap at any moment.

The white-haired one pushed the other and uttered something, pointing to the house. The other walked over and disappeared inside for a second, before backing out again. He pulled a man by his sleeve. It must have been the farmer, ripped from his humble home. The man held his chin high in defiance, but a damp patch grew and trickled down the front of his trousers. He whimpered as the dark-haired rakkan threw him face first into the dirt.

Scratching at the dusty ground, the farmer tried to get up while the rakkan sneered down at him. The fiend muttered something and turned back to the door.

Reaching out, the farmer grasped the hem of the rakkan's leggings. "No! Please!" His cry hung in the night sky and was met with a mighty stamp of the invader's boot, crunching the farmer's face into the dirt and ending his struggles for good.

Darius grimaced. These things were as pitiless as him. Was that how Lex and Omid saw him?

Lex placed her quiver on the ground and sat, bow at the ready.

"When I go, take my bow," she whispered.

Bows were so impersonal. He wanted to feel the metal cut through these rakkans. "I should go in. I don't even recall holding a bow."

The dark-haired killer turned his back and picked up two sacks in each hand. Both rakkans now faced away and Lex seized her chance. She drew back her bowstring, and the tip of her finger glowed blue. She flicked the arrowhead, coating it in algor, and let it fly.

Lex's arrow zipped through the air leaving a faint blue streak in its wake. The dark-haired rakkan seemed to sense it coming and turned, one hand rising to block it with a sack. The arrow tore through the makeshift shield and speared his heart.

Lex dropped the bow and burst from the field before Darius moved. *Damn her.* He picked up the bow and nocked an arrow.

The other rakkan ran to his comrade's body and nudged a shoulder. No response. Looking up, he snarled as he saw Lex fast approaching.

Her bow felt as natural as a sword did in Darius's hands. Muscle memory kicking in, he drew back the bowstring until he felt the perfect tension for the distance. The light easterly breeze on his cheek told him how much to adjust his aim to hit his target.

Lex drew her blade as she darted across the hardened dirt, moving like a shadow in her black leather tunic. The rakkan backed into the wall and his eyes flared with ferven, giving Darius a bright target. He released the string with a twang. The arrow arced in the air past Lex and splintered on the wall a hair's width from the rakkan's ear. Darius cursed. Close, but it may as well have been a mile away.

Before Lex reached striking distance, the rakkan sidestepped and disappeared around the corner of the house.

Lex followed after while Darius waited, another arrow nocked. Nothing moved except the rustling wheat around him. Wait—that wasn't the wind. It rustled to his right and a tiny figure darted out of the field and towards the house. *Omid, you halfwit!*

Dropping the bow, Darius sprinted after the boy. They were both out in the open, unshielded. If the rakkan reappeared, Darius wouldn't get to Omid in time.

Dry dirt crunched under Darius's strides. He dared not shout and give them away. All he could do was draw his short sword and carry on sprinting.

Omid finally looked over his shoulder and skidded to a halt just outside the front door to the house.

"What the hell are you doing?" Darius whispered, grabbing him by the shirt and pulling him to the side of the house.

"I saw another rakkan by the house—a legionnaire! We have to warn Mistress!" The boy had a deathly fearful look and brandished a dagger, one of Lex's.

"She can look after herself—"

Darius froze as someone strolled out of the house not ten feet away. A pair of obsidian eyes stared at him. No tattered rags or loose shirts adorned this rakkan's body. He wore a tight, sleeveless leather tunic that showed off his muscular arms and the green band wrapped around his right bicep. A spatha hung from his belt, so long and thick it would cleave Darius in two in a single stroke. The sword was dark, stained by flames. This rakkan wasn't like the others; he was a trained fighter.

"Well, well," the rakkan said in a gristly tone, sauntering towards them. "Aren't I lucky to happen upon a wealthy citizen?" He looked Darius up and down and frowned. "Do I know you?"

Darius grabbed Omid and threw the boy behind him.

"It's the legionnaire..." Omid said.

"Unfortunately for you, I'm an algus." Darius's voice almost faltered as he studied this new foe.

If those bony rakkans had such strength, how strong would this one be? And how fast? That spatha had no sheath. It'd be quick to release. But no cross-guard either, leaving the wrists vulnerable.

Scars from many a battle adorned the rakkan's arms and legs, most concentrated on the left arm. That must be his weakest point, and Darius would capitalise on it.

He lunged and thrust his blade forward, willing his supernatural speed to end the fight before it began. The rakkan dodged to the side and batted the jab away with a metal armguard.

Taking the spatha in his hand, he swung at Darius's legs. Darius jumped back, almost crashing into Omid. The rakkan's blow struck the wall and smashed through a foot of stone as if it weren't there.

Pushing the boy back farther, Darius kept his gaze fixed on his foe. The rakkan was fast, but not algus fast. *I can win this fight.*

The rakkan growled and his hand ignited sending tongues of ferven whirling down his blade, as if the weapon weren't dangerous enough. A single hit with that rakkan strength would cut Darius's bones like thread. Conjuring algor would counter the ferven, but it'd slow him too much without control.

Darius feinted to the left. Then the right. The rakkan didn't flinch, just stared with soulless eyes, reading his every move.

When Darius burst forward in a true attack, the rakkan parried his stroke in a haze of sparks. His next swing glanced across the rakkan's thinly covered chest causing the warrior to grunt in pain. Darius followed through and swung down from high, aiming to rend the rakkan's neck. His blade met only an unyielding spatha.

He pushed on the steel, only a few inches from rupturing the bulging vein on his foe's neck. It didn't budge, and the rakkan growled. Darius was sure his opponent had the strength to push him away, but instead the rakkan frowned and searched his eyes as if seeking something.

Trickles of blood seeped from the warrior's chest wound. A few inches deeper and it would've been over.

Darius's arms were high, midriff exposed. He stood so close he almost tasted ash from the flaming blade. One wrong move and he was dead.

"I thought you were an algus." Scowling, the rakkan thrust Darius's sword away. Taking a step back, the warrior spun his blade around, fire still licking the razor edge now headed straight for Darius's belly.

There wasn't time to dodge. Darius brought his sword flat to his stomach and flared algor, the icy coat engulfing his body and blade.

The spatha slammed into his sword with the force of a bucking horse, sending Darius flying through the air.

He barely felt himself hit the ground as every rib shot pain through his chest. The world spun as he looked back, the flaming spatha dancing in his swirling vision but getting ever larger as it approached. *Get up.*

A blue spark erupted and darted towards the flames. The two lights clashed.

Darius dug his knuckles into his eyes and rubbed. He opened them and a tiny boy came into focus, seized in the death grip of the warrior. *Omid.* The boy should have let them be.

"Let him…go," Darius coughed out, struggling to stand under what felt like a boulder crushing his chest. He forced a deep breath and picked up his sword.

"You've got baby algus fighting for you now?" the rakkan spat.

Omid tugged at his wrist caught in the rakkan's clutches, but the warrior paid no heed.

"Let the boy go," Darius repeated.

The rakkan's eyes narrowed. "Toss the weapon."

This situation was eerily familiar. Darius's hand trembled, squeezing the hilt of his short sword. Without a weapon, he stood no chance against this monster. A warrior's weapon was his life. He should have laughed at the demand yet found himself caught by Omid's pleading eyes as his heart raced.

"Drop it." The rakkan's impatience intensified in his voice and his grip on the boy's arm.

Omid grimaced and fell to his knees.

"He won't surrender for a slave," Lex shouted, walking from behind the house like a gladiator entering the arena. Her sword pulsed blue with algor, raised and ready to clash.

A deep snarl came from the rakkan, like a fire pit crackling in his throat.

Lex stopped a few feet short. "I'll end this one quick, Darius."

The warrior glared at Darius, trying to pierce his resolve. He raised his sword and pointed it between the rakkan's eyes. No. This was his battle.

"Have it your way." The rakkan flung Omid towards Darius then lunged at Lex.

Omid screamed as he crashed into Darius and the pair rolled on the ground.

Blades clashed together. Lex hammered her sword onto the rakkan's fiery spatha and drove it into the dry ground. Then she slid her blade up towards the warrior's unguarded wrists. He released the spatha and kicked her in the hip, but only landed a glancing blow. It was enough to send Lex skidding across the ground.

Darius rolled Omid off him, blocking out the screams. The boy's forearm had snapped from the force of the throw, and now bone protruded from the skin. *Oh, hell.* Darius clambered to his feet and stood between Omid and the rakkan. He needed to put this monster down before he could help the boy.

Lex glared at the rakkan with a ferocity Darius had never seen in her before. He'd thought she looked at him with contempt, but this was pure hatred, glints of the rakkan's flaming weapon flickering in her eyes. For the first time, Darius was seeing her true feelings. No mask, no concealment. Just pure, utter loathing. She wanted this rakkan dead and every one that followed.

Darius took heed. He wouldn't rush in and underestimate this warrior again. Keeping his distance, he circled around them. The rakkan picked up his spatha and stepped back to keep them both in sight, waiting for them to make a move. Rakkans couldn't match their speed, but this one had the reflexes of a predator, and every attack left them vulnerable to a thunderous counter blow. Darius had endured one hit, somehow, but probably wouldn't survive a second.

The balance of his sword felt off. Darius glanced down. Dozens of notches now spoiled the edge, scars of fiery blows it was too weak to withstand. One had sunk deep and threatened to split the blade clean in two. It'd have to hold a little longer.

Darius surged forwards with a flurry of swipes. Each stretch pained his aching ribs and slowed him a fraction, a fraction that allowed the rakkan to manoeuvre the hulking blade to block every one.

Lex pounced with an arcing blue swing for the rakkan's legs—no, she'd feinted. Her sword reversed and slashed at his neck. The rakkan dropped to a knee, letting the swing sail overhead. His flaming spatha rose to block any follow-up blow.

Darius leapt, sword overhead, poised to unleash every last drop of strength he had onto his foe's weapon. He smashed down with full force at his blade's weakest spot. It snapped in two and followed through to bury its jagged remnant in the rakkan's shoulder.

The warrior roared, his eyes ablaze, but that light was extinguished by Lex's icy blade through his mouth. Darius clutched the stub of his sword embedded in the lifeless body as it slumped, still growling even in death. No, the growls were his own.

"A legionnaire." Lex's nostrils flared as she gazed down at the corpse. "You picked a tough one to prove yourself against." She sheathed her sword and sprinted over to where Omid lay sobbing.

Darius tugged out his blade, now half its length and more of a blunt dagger. Three dead rakkans, one a more than worthy foe. Somehow, it didn't feel like enough, and Omid had paid a heavy price for this victory.

20

"Calm him down," Lex ordered as Darius approached the boy.

Like that was possible. Darius knelt and buried Omid's head in his chest to muffle the screams.

"Hush. We'll fix you," he said, unconvinced himself. Blood trickled from the protruding bone in Omid's arm, primed for infection and bad enough to bleed out if they weren't fast.

"Do you know anyone that can fix this? A healer?" Darius asked.

"No. He needs a surgeon," Lex replied.

"I don't suppose surgeons have powers like us, but for healing?"

"No. Such powers don't exist."

Great. "Then you need to straighten his arm manually." The boy needed knocking out. Would the farmhouse have any firewater in it? They didn't have time to check. Darius found a clean patch of his cloak and pushed it into Omid's mouth while Lex inspected the arm. "Bite down. It'll help."

Lex took hold and pulled, and the fractured bone snapped back inside with a crack. Omid howled, sending shudders through Darius's still painful chest. He squeezed the boy closer, so tightly he worried about breaking another bone in Omid's fragile little body. Those cries, they reminded him of Amid. Could this have been avoided if he'd laid down his weapon as the rakkan asked?

Omid's wails barely eased. Frowning, Lex drew a vial out of her pocket. She held the tube of tar-like liquid up to the moonlight. He recognised it immediately. A vial of blackened tears. The weeping plant's gift for pain.

"Have you had that all along?" Darius asked through gritted teeth. Why hadn't she offered him some when his arm was on fire?

"Never without it." She brushed the boy's hair from his face. "Silly boy. You should have stayed out of it." Lex opened the vial and tipped a drop of black liquid into Omid's mouth.

"If we hadn't gone after those rakkans…" Darius said.

"It's always worth it to kill a Viridian Legionnaire." She spat the last words.

"A legionnaire? I didn't know they could look so human. Never mind so brawny. He spoke like one of us."

"He was nothing like us."

But if not for the eyes and strength, that warrior would've passed for human.

Lex leaned forward and whispered in Darius's ear, "I've only enough tears to numb this kind of injury for a few hours."

Laltos was at least twelve hours away. Her cheek brushed his skin, sending gooseflesh down his neck. Now wasn't the time. "Got anything else? Firewater?"

"A little, but I should use it to burn the wound clean."

"Do you have bandages?"

"In my pack back at the tree."

"I'll get Lyra to bring it." He retreated into his mind and gave his escort the instructions.

"I'll save the weeping plant's tears for when we reach Laltos," Lex whispered. "I want Omid asleep. We can't risk him drawing attention to us with Archimedes's eyes and ears all over the city."

Sitting back, she pulled Omid away from Darius and into her arms. The boy's sobbing slowly quieted as the medicine soothed his troubles. Or perhaps it was Lex's touch. She gazed down and wiped sweat from the boy's brow, looking almost maternal.

Darius moved to stand when pain stabbed at his ribs. That rakkan blow had taken its toll. If only she had enough tears for him. Glancing at Omid's shuddering body, he shook that thought away. *He needs it more.*

"Look in the house," Lex said, her tone soft now, the anger chilled again.

Mustering his strength, Darius hauled his aching body up and walked towards the door. It still swung gently on its hinges from when the rakkan had emerged. The farmer's body lay sprawled in the earth not far from the dead rakkans. What carnage had they left inside? A butchered family, limbs askew and walls sprayed crimson? The mental image conjured by his imagination turned his stomach, and Darius hesitated before pushing open the door.

Hinges whined and floorboards moaned as he eased into the house. A glimmer of embers in the central fireplace cast little light on the simple wooden furniture, unvarnished and sparse. The farmers weren't well off, which suggested the chances of finding firewater were slim. The place looked eerily familiar, like the house of his parents all those years ago.

Dodging the splintered pieces of chairs on the floor, Darius crept farther into the house. As he rounded the overturned table, a girl's body came into view, stained red and still, not a day over five years old.

He turned, marched out of the house and slammed the door closed behind him. The image wouldn't leave his mind as he walked over to Lex's hunched figure. She sat attending a bloody Omid, whose eyes looked half taken by slumber. Or was that death creeping in, just like with the girl? Just like with Amid. He'd failed again.

Acid rose to the back of his throat and this time he couldn't swallow it down. Darius lurched to the side and hurled into the dirt.

As he straightened, wiping his mouth with the back of his hand, he caught sight of Lyra slipping out of the field. She carried Lex's pack over to the algus and sat beside her.

"Anything?" Lex opened the pack and pulled out bandages.

Darius spat out the last of the bile. "A body."

"The rakkan's doing?" She narrowed her eyes at him as if expecting that he'd slit the girl's throat.

"Yes."

A hint of relief on her face, Lex focused on bandaging Omid's arm.

"Maybe we should have let those rakkans be," Darius said. At least then Omid wouldn't be writhing in pain.

All traces of warmth fled Lex's face and she glared at him. "They need slaying, lest more end up like this farmer and his family."

"Even if it means the boy almost gets his arm snapped off?"

She didn't blink, her eyes seething. "Even if. And if what he did to Omid bothers you, take it out on the next to cross your path."

The way she spoke of rage was like a fuel, a companion she'd kept close for so long she didn't know life without it. Did he dare ask what had ignited it within her?

Beads of sweat crept across Omid's forehead despite the cool night air.

"The boy needs medicine," Darius said, "but it'll mean travelling through the night." His voice held steady, despite the fear coiling in his aching chest. Travelling in the dark also meant giving any other rakkans in their path the advantage.

"Then that's what we do." Lex finished bandaging Omid's arm and stood. "There's an old tunnel system into the city. I'll take us there. Carry him."

Darius scooped the boy into his arms, the copper smell of blood and sweat hitting his nose immediately. He swallowed. Another injured boy in his arms. This one would *not* die. They'd best make haste.

Lyra ran ahead, the best scout of a path in the dark. They sped after her. It was a good thing Omid was light, or Darius couldn't have run. They'd knock hours off the journey at this rate.

Progress was swift and no rakkans disturbed them. After a few hours the black tears began to wear off and Lex had no more for the boy until Laltos. Omid began whimpering and sweat dripped from his brow. The sound was almost as intolerable as the blood. Not for the volume, which was at times no more than a quiet moan, but for the dark feeling it triggered that was impossible to shake off. Darius would have preferred a harpy's shriek to the tiny boy's sobs of agony.

"Hold on. Just a little further," he said.

21

Sunlight bounced off the gleaming white towers that reached to the skies. Darius winced at the glare. Nearby, Lex surveyed the rubble plugging what was once a tunnel entrance shrouded in bushes and dug into the side of a small hill.

"Archimedes must have sent word ahead," Lex said. "The tunnels are blocked."

Hundreds of soldiers patrolled along the towers and crenelated walls, and those were just the visible men. This city was a fortress.

"He knows I'm coming here? It's risky my being so close." Darius glanced up at the wall again, squinting. "We can't linger here." The leafy shrubs around them were the only thing preventing them being spotted.

Omid lay on the ground whimpering. He had been without any relief from the pain for hours, and the strain showed in his pale, sweaty face. Darius tried his best to block out the noise so he could think straight.

"We'll have to go in the main gate." Lex grabbed at her hip with a grimace. Strange the injury hadn't slowed her through the night, or perhaps his mind had been elsewhere and he hadn't noticed.

The main gate was definitely too close to danger for comfort. "If it's all the same to you, I'll pass," Darius said. "Get the boy a surgeon and find the location of this Waif Magician. I'll meet you back here in two days."

"I can't let you out of my sight. If anything happened to you... You're coming in."

"Oh, well if you put it like that," Darius said sarcastically, waving Lyra over to him so they could head to safety and catch a much needed bite to eat.

His cat didn't budge.

"I'll aid you no further if you walk away now." Lex glared at him, her eyes shadowed with fatigue.

"It's too risky." Darius shot an angry look at his disobedient panther. Lyra was his guide to Margalvia, and at this point he was considering heading directly there. Lex had saved his life but yielded precious little about his former self. "Tell me a better way in and I'll reconsider."

"There are sewers or the river, but if Archimedes knows of the tunnels he will have thought of all other routes. They'll be expecting it. They won't expect you to go through the gates."

Because it's suicide. "No."

"I'd rather you dead than roaming free." Lex's hand moved to her sword as she took up a fighting stance.

The odds of her trying to kill him were even—he still had information she wanted, after all. How much would that hip hinder her if she did make the attempt? Was it worth the risk?

Lyra sauntered over to Lex and gave him a pleading look with her big amber eyes.

You too? You'd desert me?

His escort wavered for a second then trotted back over to him, unwilling to take it that far. Somehow he knew he could always rely on her, trust her with his life, but why was she so trusting of this reticent woman? He supposed trusting his escort's instincts hadn't failed him so far.

Darius hesitated. Walking away now would mean he'd likely never get his memories back and would be cursed to spend the rest of his days wandering in ignorance. "You truly want me to walk through the gate?"

"Not walk. Tiro has seen something from the sky. A prison wagon you can join."

He scoffed. "Even better. I'll put the chains on for them!"

"It's the best way. No one will suspect. I'll collect you once in Laltos."

"Too risky."

"Did Archimedes take your gonads as well as your memory?"

He growled under his breath, all too aware she used his manly pride against him but unable to shake off the insult regardless. Lyra thought he should stick with Lex. Perhaps he should trust his escort's judgement. "If I get caught, I'll name you, Alexandra."

The colour drained from her face, but she didn't even blink. "You won't be caught."

She sounded confident. Either that or she was a gambling woman. To hell with it. "Then let's go before the boy succumbs to fever."

22

Omid's blood filled Darius's nostrils again as he carried the boy towards the prison wagon. How was it possible that a warrior had never got used to the smell?

The stone road was wide and its cobbles hurt his bare feet. It had been a shame to toss his nice clothes away and make himself look like a ragged vagabond, but Lex had promised him better garments once they were in Laltos. Lyra had left, too much a risk to be seen with them in the city, and he felt all the more naked without her. Lex's presence, stalking along at his side, was no comfort at all.

Two large oxen tugged the wagon at barely a walking pace which made it easy to catch, not that he was in any rush to join its festering inhabitants behind those iron bars.

Omid's scraggly-haired head drooped, out cold from the last of Lex's tears. Ironic that "cold" was an appropriate word for someone drenched in sweat and as hot as fire.

"You there!" Lex called to the wagon.

A gruff-looking soldier walking alongside turned towards them. When he caught sight of Lex, he stopped and bowed. "May we be of service, algus?"

"Take my slaves to the prison. I caught them trying to escape." She gave Darius an unexpected shove in the back and he shot her a displeased glance over his shoulder.

A whip lashed his side and he dropped Omid to the ground with a groan.

"You dare look at your mistress that way?" the soldier barked.

The side of Darius's ribcage stung as if cut by a sword. Blood dribbled from a shallow scratch. He turned, ready to snap that whip-wielding arm in two, but caught himself in time. Eyes to the ground, he feigned a sheepish look lest he invite another flog.

"Apologies, mistress," he said.

He hadn't even spotted the whip in the man's grasp when they'd approached. What happened to the ever-prepared warrior? Being so lost in his own thoughts would get him killed.

The soldier whistled, and the wagon ground to a halt with the clank of iron chains. Darius recovered Omid from the road, taking a chance while the soldier looked away to get a good look at the man's dirty red hair and over-bitten jaw. Darius would remember that face and pay the oaf back in kind later.

Lex stood close by while the soldier and another fixed shackles to his ankles and arms. Could this be how it ended, voluntarily locked in irons? He could kill them with his algor if necessary, but it would give his ability away. Hopefully he wouldn't be forced to do so.

"The boy's been beaten. He doesn't need chains," Lex said.

Over-bite looked dubious but dared not question. His companion opened the wagon door while he waved Darius in, looking eager to dispense another lash. Thankfully Lex stood close enough to put him off. Couldn't catch a god by mistake.

Darius clambered in, the warm, moist wood slippery under his shackled feet. Urine. *Nice.* He slumped beside an elderly man on a free stretch of bench and planted Omid on his knee. There were at least ten other men in the wagon crammed together like animals. As the soldier locked the door, a fair-haired man opposite knocked knees against Darius's and eyed him and the boy like a hungry vulture. The prisoner had thick sideburns stretching down to a grimace half made of blackened teeth.

A jerk shook the carriage as it got underway, the rattle of wood on the uneven road almost deafening inside. Darius closed his eyes, breathing as deep as he could without retching. It wouldn't be long until Laltos.

23

The gateway came ever closer, its white stone towers and archway like the upper jaw of a gaping mouth ready to swallow the carriage whole. Darius fought to keep his expression impassive and cradled Omid close.

The man opposite still stared with the glint of madness in his eyes. Better to watch the approaching gate. The worst thing Darius could do was attract attention while passing the lines of soldiers on the border of the city. One glance from someone who recognised his face despite the shaved hair and beard, and that would be it. This was possibly the most dangerous thing he had done to date, entering a walled city with the full knowledge that his enemy knew he was coming.

Now that he thought on it, this was his way in, but how was he to get out? He'd been so concerned with their entry it hadn't occurred to him how they'd leave the city. He cursed under his breath. *Too late now.*

The stones forming the thick city walls bore the dents and scars of wars long passed. Lex had mentioned a little of the last war to topple Laltos, not with rakkans but amongst humans. King Medus's father had besieged the city three decades ago. Without a seaport to replenish supplies, the city was quickly forced to surrender but not before heavy losses. The Queen of Laltos was executed and replaced by a regent to oversee the rebuilding of the city, subservient to the new King of the Empire of course.

Lex didn't seem to harbour much bitterness over the defeat, which was unusual for her. If anything, she talked of the Regent fondly. The rakkans had attacked not long after, and Laltos had had to stand united with the King. Lex's grievance was with Archimedes's methods and with King Medus for sending him.

The wagon jerked to a stop in the gateway, jolting Darius out of his thoughts. Rows of soldiers stood on stone balconies flanking the entrance, glimmers flashing from their iron scale armour and the razor-tipped spears in their hands. Omid remained unconscious. Lex was ahead in the street but was still watching. Darius glanced away, not wanting to draw attention to her.

"They trying you as a runaway slave?" the black-toothed man opposite asked in a hoarse voice.

Why choose now to speak? Darius gave a quick nod.

"You don't look a slave to me. Too well-fed."

One of the Laltos guards walked past and peered inside at the sound of voices, too long for comfort. Darius needed to shut this man up. He waited for the soldier to pass on then muttered, "I was a gladiator," hoping it would end the conversation.

The man chuckled to himself so long he coughed up phlegm, spitting onto the floor and Darius's feet. At least it was a change from urine.

"Strange," the man said. "Laltos' arena has been closed for some time."

Curse his blank memory. "I'm from Marg—"

Something rapped on the iron bars of the door. The guard pressed his helmet to the gap. "Quiet. Save your voices for your trial," he stared intently at Darius, "and perhaps you'll have a chance to avoid hard labour." His gaze didn't waver but Darius averted his.

Bending over, Darius mimicked kissing Omid on the cheek to bury his face behind the boy's tousled hair.

A shout came and the wagon jerked ahead again, the head at the door slowly disappearing as they entered the streets of the city. Darius sighed in relief.

It was less than half an hour before the wagon halted on a busy street. Lex was nowhere to be seen as Over-bite yanked them from the wagon one by one. Passers-by peered at the prisoners with curiosity and gave them a wide berth as if fearful of catching something. Judging by the look of some of his companions, Darius had the same worry. His chains scratched across the flat stone underfoot as they were marched toward a tall building. An axe-wielding man was carved into the stone above the entrance. An executioner? Something he'd ask Lex about later, if she showed up.

They were quickly ushered downstairs into the underground jail. Two guards removed their shackles as they all filed into a large cell. A hole in the corner, ringed by brown stains, served as a latrine. Bar that, the cell was bare dirt surrounded by stone walls with iron bars on one side. The two guards stood outside muttering to one another while watching over the prisoners.

Darius found a spot to put Omid to rest and sat cushioning the boy's head. Already Omid had begun to fidget. The tears were wearing off. How much attention would Omid's cries draw? Darius caught sight of the man with blackened teeth crouched nearby, staring at them.

If his unwanted attention drew that of the guards, Darius feared they might not make it out alive.

Hurry, Lex.

24

Nikolaos strode quickly down the street. If he'd heard right, Archimedes would arrive imminently, and though Nikolaos had been in Laltos for days, he hadn't managed to secure an audience with the Regent yet. His next best route to power was capturing Darius. That would surely impress Archimedes enough to earn the promotion he desired.

A raven-haired woman heading swiftly towards the courthouse caught Nikolaos's eye. "Lex!"

She turned as if aggrieved at the interruption but grinned when she saw it was him. Nikolaos had that effect on women. She walked over, her fatigue obvious as she neared. Whatever mission she was on for Archimedes hadn't granted much time for rest.

"Niko, a pleasure."

"So glad to happen upon you. I need to speak with your father urgently."

"Why?"

"Given the Laltos Guard needs a new leader, I—"

Lex laughed. "Let me guess, you want my father to name *you?* He hates you."

Nikolaos clenched his fists. He'd known Regent Theodoros disliked him but *hate*? "If you put in a good word, perhaps I can do you a favour in return." Nikolaos took Lex's hand in his and gazed into her arresting eyes.

A smirk played about her lips as she pulled her hand away. "What favour?"

"I'm sure I can think of something. But later. Archimedes arrives in the city at this very moment."

Lex's grin vanished.

"He commanded all algus to report," Nikolaos continued.

"I can't right now. I'll speak with him later."

Archimedes wouldn't be pleased about her absence but Nikolaos could make it go unnoticed. "Very well. I won't mention you've arrived."

"I'm sure he'll do some recruiting in the meantime." She scowled.

Probably true. No one dared question Archimedes taking children for his Numbered army, though many murmured in resentment. Just because the goman limited his kidnapping to the slaves and lesser citizens didn't mean the algus didn't curse him. It gave powerful families fewer to adopt as their own to strengthen their ranks.

"I still think you should come," Nikolaos said. "Whatever Archimedes has you doing, you can—"

"I'll see him when I'm ready to." With a flick of her cloak she turned and strode off into the courthouse.

What had gotten into Lex? She was always reticent but this was another level. Something must have been deeply troubling her, and he hoped he didn't have to prevent her stepping off a balcony again.

Lex wasn't usually so unwise as to snub Archimedes, even with the protection of her father. The Regent valued her above all else since she wasn't merely an adopted daughter, but one by blood. To be born with algor was rare, so an algus fathering another algus was almost unheard of. Not that she needed her father's backing, given her fighting prowess.

The wind brought a chill to Nikolaos's neck as the sound of marching boots grew nearer. People in the street began to shuffle away with cautious looks over their shoulder.

"*Nikolaos*," Archimedes's voice boomed in his head.

He turned to see the goman almost upon him with ten of the Numbered to his right, including the seductive Thirty-seven. Nikolaos bowed.

"*Is the city readied as instructed?*"

"Yes. When Darius arrives, this city shall be his tomb." Now all they needed to do was wait.

25

Darius's head slumped, fatigue weighing down his shoulders. Omid's whimpers had returned, but the boy was still half unconscious. The sounds grated as if the pain were his own but why did it bother him so? Cradling the boy, he squeezed his eyes shut as if it would make his thoughts clearer. Was it his fault? No, Omid had chosen to fight to save him. Why should Darius mind? He'd felt nothing when cutting down other men, but now... First Parisa, now Omid. Their suffering haunted his mind for no fathomable reason. Had Archimedes done something to him?

"You, with the child," a guard called, opening the cell.

Frowning, Darius looked over. The guard was staring at him.

"Move it!" The guard waved him to the door.

Darius staggered up, legs weak from a day and night with no rest. It took all his strength to lift Omid off the dirt. If the boy had been more than skin and bone he wouldn't have managed it.

One slow step at a time, he trudged out of the cell, stepping over the unconscious black-toothed loudmouth on his way. The guard led him to a staircase where Lex waited.

"I'll take them from here," she said. The algus grabbed Darius's elbow and ushered him up the stairs.

He struggled to keep up, vision wobbling the higher they climbed. They made it outside to the street which looked more deserted than when he'd arrived. Lex pushed him on until they were deep in a maze of narrow streets. She picked her way through carefully but with haste, clearly having planned the route ahead of time. The fresh air brought a little energy back to Darius's arms and legs, and the journey became easier.

They finally arrived at a large square with an enormous fountain of a winged woman at its centre. Before Darius could study the statue, Lex pushed him through the narrow doorway of a nearby building.

Inside it was dark and quiet, with soft wooden flooring and an unpleasant floral scent masking something in the air. The ceiling was low and brushed against his head. Ducking, he hunched his shoulders. There'd been more space in the prison.

A woman appeared from a doorway to the right. Her light brown hair curled across her shoulders and her warm eyes looked soft enough to soothe a rabid animal. Her cream apron bore many reddish brown stains, old and new. This was a home of the sick and the woman was a carer. The scented air was meant to mask the death and decay but failed.

"Through here," she beckoned, as if expecting them.

Darius followed her into a room with four beds, one at each side. A table stood in the middle of the room, rows of instruments laid across its centre, almost like a carpenter's workshop but clearly for surgery. The wooden slab was stained dark but that didn't mask the blotches of gore.

At the woman's direction, he placed Omid gently on one of the beds and felt a weight lift from him. The boy was safe for now. Only one other bed was taken, but its occupant had a sheet covering them from head to toe.

"I'm Nasrin," the woman said.

Lex strode into the room, eyes fixated on the other occupied bed.

"I said we were to be alone," she said, tense as ever.

"You needn't worry about her. She has no family to come for her."

Darius sauntered over and lifted the cover to reveal a chubby woman's head staring dead into the ceiling. The skin still had some colour and traces of sweat. She'd died recently. "Another rakkan victim?"

"No," Nasrin replied. "She died in childbirth. It was her sixth."

"I thought you said there was no family."

"There isn't. Their fathers are unknown, and the child didn't make it either. She wanted to rear an algus so badly. Many do, but for her it wasn't to be."

"As long as you're sure her other children won't pay us a visit."

Nasrin took the sheet from his hands and covered the woman's head again. "Not unless they traverse the grave. She had no use for them and no way to provide. They were left to succumb like many are."

How morbid. Darius looked around for something to drink, unsure how to respond and in the mood for firewater. He was far from being the only one in this world without a care for others, but it surprised him that a mother could be so pitiless towards her children. Not even Lex treated a child so poorly, and she was doubtlessly one of the most callous women around.

"Forgive the questions," he said, "but my memory—"

"Mistress told me," Nasrin said with a hollow smile. "I will see to the boy until the surgeon arrives. You should eat and rest upstairs."

173

Darius gave Nasrin a nod and followed Lex upstairs into another room with beds and chairs, this one vacant of dead bodies. The fatigue had eased and, now that Omid was safe, his mind was free to absorb all he'd seen and heard in the last day. He didn't know where to begin processing.

Lex let out a sigh and sat on a bed, running a hand through her hair.

"Your plan worked," he said.

She didn't seem to take any pleasure in the fact, not giving him as much as a smug grin. "I'm glad Omid's safe. Few survive a Viridian Legionnaire."

"Why do you call the rakkan that? Their skin is white as chalk."

"Their legion's battle standard is viridian."

A standard meant organisation, tactical minds, and not just a band of roaming barbarians. It meant armies. A legion of rakkans was surely almost impossible to stop unless they had adequate numbers of algus, but so far he'd only seen a handful of the guardians. How had the rakkans not wiped the humans out?

"I share your disdain for them." Darius could think of no greater cause than slaughtering them one by one. A deep part of him burned with hatred towards the rakkan. "But I can't say why. Why do you hate them?"

"They killed my husband," she said, so slow, almost whispering, like every word was forced out. "Imagine. A widow at eighteen."

Her bitterness suddenly made sense. What could he say? He sat in silence and watched her.

Lex stared at the floor, unable to contain the sorrow welling in her eyes. "You remind me of him."

"He was a mindless warrior too? Lucky you."

A weak grin formed on her lips but her eyes didn't lose a drop of sadness. "Sometimes he was fierce, sometimes he was kind. He calmed me with the mere utterance of my name. Alexandra."

The name she hated him speaking. Because it reminded her of her husband, or because she didn't want to be calmed?

Grief darkened her expression. He'd best change the subject and spare them the insufferable dwelling on painful memories.

"Why haven't the rakkans wiped us all out yet?" he asked. "I don't understand how we humans can have time to war amongst ourselves when such strong enemies exist."

"The algus are strong. We can take them even when outnumbered, but that's not the main reason we're winning the war. Archimedes is."

"He's at war with us and the rakkans too?"

She sighed. "Yes."

"And he's powerful enough to stop a legion of rakkans?"

"Yes. With the Staff of Arria."

The goman was stronger than he'd imagined, fighting wars against multiple enemies. Felix's collapsed figure flashed across his mind, a mighty warrior reduced to nothing in the goman's path in their first encounter. Poor man. How many more had to die for Darius's sake?

Archimedes wouldn't stop until Darius was his, yet if Darius killed him would it be like handing the Torian Empire to the rakkan invaders? Would Margalvia fall and leave Darius nowhere to call home?

"So what does it mean if we kill Archimedes? That's what you want, isn't it?"

Lex lay down and closed her eyes. "The King will find someone else to lead the war against the rakkans."

Did she not care? Was revenge worth more than the lives of all those around her, including her own? "Why is he not king, if he's so powerful?"

"I don't know. He's loyal to King Medus. Some men don't want the throne."

Darius related to that desire. He had little ambition himself. He would be satisfied being a feared warrior, one who fought for a glorious endeavour, not for recognition.

Lex turned her head towards him. She looked peaceful when resting, beautiful even, without the angry stare. How did the pair of them fit into all this?

"Why don't you care if we kill the one man holding the rakkans at bay? I feel there's something you aren't telling me."

Her breathing paused.

Pain lanced through his head like a nail driven into the back of his skull. His vision lost focus and a hissing noise drowned everything out around him. He grabbed his head and massaged it roughly. The attack eased as quickly as it had come and Lex's figure came back into focus. She'd opened her eyes and was looking at him cautiously.

"Did you hear what I just said?" she asked.

He rubbed his forehead, slick with sweat. "No."

Lex cursed. "Get some rest. We'll talk more later."

There was something she wasn't telling him but what could he do, beat it out of her? That wouldn't endear her to help him reach Margalvia and get his memories back. No, he had to win her trust, make her believe his old self was in there somewhere, the fierce warrior that she'd said fought for what he believed in. But how? Fighting he could do, but trust was something bewildering.

Darius lied down and rested his head, a faint headache still plaguing him. He understood the concept of trust, but eliciting it in someone was nothing short of magic in his mind. The only one he had faith in was Lyra because she obeyed his commands, and mostly because she wasn't human.

There was Omid, too, and he'd almost grown fond of the boy. *I hope the surgeon can save his arm.* While wondering why he dwelled on the boy so much, he drifted off to sleep.

26

Darius sat by Omid's bedside, coughing up a lungful of the smoky air that filled the cramped room. Heavy scents lingered on his tongue and nettled his throat. Lex had left them so she could chase down her lead on the Waif Magician's whereabouts. Now that he was alone, he could mine Nasrin for whatever information Lex was withholding. But he'd have to be careful. He didn't know how much the carer knew, or was allowed to know, about him.

"Is this smoke really helping?" he asked, holding Omid's sweaty little hand at Nasrin's instruction. *She may as well stuff dandelions up his nose; he'd breathe easier.*

"The incense purifies the air." Nasrin rested a palm on the boy's forehead. She had gentle hands, even for a carer, and Omid couldn't have asked for better treatment, but she believed some nonsense. It was a wonder the boy didn't choke.

She walked over to the table and prodded the smoking herbs. They had spoken a little since Lex's departure, but Darius wasn't sure how to gather more sensitive details from her. He had to find a way, something she wanted that he could trade for information.

"Have you known Lex long?" he asked.

"All my life."

"Has she always been so withdrawn?"

Nasrin sighed. "Yes, and she gets worse with every tragedy."

It was a relief to know it wasn't just Darius she was reserved around. Lex had mentioned her son and her husband. Were there others she had lost? Had the loss of Darius made her worse?

"Omid's sweating," Nasrin said.

Darius dipped a rag in some water and wiped Omid's brow. The boy looked peaceful in his sleep, despite the sweats. If only they could keep him under like this until his arm mended, but the risk of giving him more numbing black tears was high. Tears were lethal in sufficient quantities. More than a couple of drops and the patient may simply stop breathing. Even if that didn't occur, people could sleep for days and die of thirst.

It'd be a few more hours until Omid's sobbing and gnashing of teeth returned. The surgeon would arrive soon and Darius would have to make himself scarce. The fewer people that saw him, the better. Before then, he wanted answers.

Maybe the boy's pain was a way to connect with Nasrin. She seemed to care, and he couldn't stop thinking about Omid anyway.

"What do you make of his arm?" Darius asked.

Nasrin sighed and adjusted her scarf. "It's a bad break. Omid may lose it."

If Darius had been faster, stronger, that rakkan would never have got his hands on the boy.

"It's my fault." Would Omid still become an algus with one arm? Possibly. The boy's mother still had a chance her son would come rescue her.

"It's the rakkan's fault," Nasrin said.

She didn't know; she wasn't there. "Is that what Lex said?"

"In effect."

"That's a no then. What *did* she say?"

"As much as usual."

"A real warrior wouldn't have let it happen, wouldn't let a child die."

Nasrin's face showed a mix of confusion and pity. "Omid isn't dead."

No, *Omid* wasn't, but his baby brother... "Thanks to Lex." He coughed up another cloud of scented mist. Why had he begun speaking about this? Dwelling on it made him feel uneasy. "Got any firewater?"

"No." She sat next to him and straightened Omid's covers.

Too bad. He could use something to numb these feelings. *Numb.* An idea struck him.

"Do you have tears of the weeping plant?" Lex was bound to need some more later on their journey, and he'd use them to barter for information.

"I do." Nasrin reached into her apron and withdrew a tube of tarry gel.

"May I take it?" Darius gripped the tube but she didn't let go.

"Not for free." Nasrin gave him a whimsical look, cheeks round and plump with youth.

"Sorry." He reached into his trouser pocket for one of the crest coins buried there.

She grasped his arm. "I don't want money." Her eyes weren't threatening, more puckish.

"Then, what do you want?"

"You're not like the other men my mistress associates with."

He frowned. *What other men?* Whoever they were, he didn't like them already.

"She doesn't treat you the same either," Nasrin continued, "doesn't toy with you like the others."

What? She never did anything but toy with him, orchestrate her words and beatings to elicit her preferred response, and the worst thing was half the time he was likely oblivious.

"I've only seen her like this with one other man," Nasrin said.

"Who?"

She didn't reply. If she meant who he thought she did—Lex's dead husband—she was barking up the wrong tree.

"You haven't answered my original question," he said. "What do you want for the tears?"

Nasrin smiled. "You can't flee your troubles."

"Hey, I'm not trying to flee anything. I'm no coward!" Darius ripped back his sleeve and bandage, brandishing his scarred, raw skin. "My arm hurts. I just want some pain relief."

Her hand flew to her mouth. "I'm sorry, I didn't mean to offend. I don't judge. I know you're like her."

He was standing. When had he stood up? He sank back down onto the stool and straightened his sleeve. "Forget it. I overreacted." Darius paused. He'd missed something. "What do you mean, 'you're like her?'"

"She has constant pain." Nasrin circled her hip with her hand.

Lex's mysterious ailment that plagued her travels and seemed to flare up from time to time. Such a curse for a warrior like her, to have her fighting ability hindered.

"That's grim," he said. "What happened to her?"

"She has no injury." Nasrin leaned in, lowering her voice. "The pain started after her son was taken. It's come and gone ever since, particularly when something troubles her."

What was it like to lose a son, to care for someone enough to be affected when they were gone? Worse than losing a companion, or a brother. He couldn't imagine.

"Would she mind you telling me all this?"

"I tell you so you'll help her." Nasrin placed the vial of tears in Darius's hand and stood. "That's my price. Her ailment had improved a lot, but it seems to have grown worse again. At times she can barely walk without medicine."

181

If Lex would let him in on her thoughts once in a while perhaps he could help, but as it stood all he could do was soldier on to reclaim his memory. "What can I do to get her to talk to me?"

"You can start by learning about that statue in the square outside. And care about others. Show her Archimedes hasn't completely corrupted you."

"I don't think caring is something I can learn. Why do *you* care for people here?"

"I'm moved by their suffering."

"Why?"

"It's a feeling, from the heart. Don't you care whether Omid is well?"

Darius felt *something*, but didn't know if it was caring, or why he should take notice of the feelings that threatened to overwhelm him if he let them free. "I don't understand how I feel. I cannot think of a reason why I should care about anyone else."

"Sometimes the answer isn't in the mind." Nasrin gave him a sombre look and left the room, a cloud of mist swirling after her.

He'd got what he wanted, a little more insight into Lex. Hopefully it would give him some way to break through to her. First, he'd make sure to find out about the fountain Nasrin mentioned.

27

Brutus chewed tobacco leaves, savouring the picante taste. The dark halls of the Margalvian garrison gave one the illusion of secrecy but that was all it was, illusion. You never knew who was listening, as even whispers carried far down the stone passages. Still, it was as secluded as one got in Margalvia, and thus the best place for a covert meeting. He pressed against the cold wall to cool his sweaty back.

A figure rounded the corner. *Sulla.* Brutus recognised the swagger a mile away.

He didn't dare utter a word until his mouth was to the rakkan's scarred ear. "Where is he?"

"Coming." Sulla grunted. "What's the word from the Warlord?"

"Sour." Brutus scowled. "Catonius has had enough, thinks Darius is a traitor. When Darius gets back to the city, he's a dead man."

Sulla cursed and began pacing. "He's no traitor. Why can't Catonius see how useful he is? None except him can get close to the humans without them seeing what we are."

It was the same conversation he'd had with the Warlord ad nauseam. "That's just it. Catonius hates Darius because he isn't one of us, always has. He was just looking for an excuse to end him, and he's not alone."

"The commanders?"

Brutus nodded. "Most want to see Darius at the end of a rope and not just because Catonius wants it."

"Then our only option is challenging Catonius." Sulla's eyes stared wide and black. It was as they'd feared but not so simple. There was only one strong enough to challenge Catonius.

"Why don't you speak louder," a voice echoed behind them. "I don't think everyone in Margalvia heard you."

The pair started and turned to see a rakkan standing behind them. Half a foot taller than Brutus and Sulla, the newcomer was clad in a kuraminium cuirass and two swords rested at his waist. His blond hair was slicked back and his face scowled.

"Varro," Brutus whispered. He hadn't even felt his brother approaching in the air.

"No need to scare the crap out of us like that, blondie," Sulla whispered with a grin of relief.

Varro gave him a hard stare that wiped the smile off Sulla's face. "This is serious. If the Warlord gets wind of this, he'll end it before you can open your mouths to challenge."

"Let's speak plainly." Brutus folded his arms. "Even if we had many allies outside us three, you're the only one that can stand against him, Varro."

Tall and lean, his brother wasn't the biggest rakkan, and lacked the raw punch of Brutus. As a fighter however, Varro was unrivalled. Over a century of training, discipline, blood and sweat had made the name "Varro" feared far outside Margalvia.

"I don't know why you hesitate," Sulla whispered into Varro's ear. "Issue the challenge, fight him one on one, and he'll be the one bleeding out into the dirt. Catonius is against us but he's honourable. He'll meet an official challenge."

Varro stared blankly at the floor. "And then what? If I kill him?"

Wasn't it obvious? "You're warlord. You control the Legion," Brutus said. "You pardon Darius."

"It's not so simple."

How could Varro even consider otherwise? "You have to. You know he's like a son to me. Even you treated him like family."

"He's a danger to us all. And Archimedes seems to know too much. What if it's true and Darius is a trait—"

Brutus grabbed Varro by the neck and pushed him into the wall. "Don't you dare speak like that."

Varro looked into his eyes, veins bulging at the neck but otherwise unfazed. They both knew Varro would win in a fair fight, but Brutus also knew that a big brother's threats didn't lose all their fright in adulthood. And he didn't fight fair.

"I'd have to lead the commanders to lead the Legion," Varro said as Brutus slowly released him. "I can't do that by fear alone. I need their support and I don't know if I have it. What's to stop each of them challenging me too?"

"You can take any that challenge."

"And after I kill them all, what is left of the Legion?"

Brutus stepped away, knowing there was little more to be said now. He'd hoped Varro would be on board; his brother hated Catonius after all. If he wasn't, then he wouldn't be convinced. Stubborn little brother.

"I need to think on this," Varro murmured, then he turned and walked away.

Shaking his head, Brutus muttered curses under his breath. If only every problem could be solved by the blunt force of his hammer. Too bad they seldom could.

28

What's taking so long? For almost an hour, Darius had sat still on the hard wooden stool. His backside ached, but the surgeon was checking Omid below and any movements might draw unwanted attention.

Grumbling under his breath, Darius peered through the narrow gaps in the shutters to the square outside. He'd studied the fountain in detail, as Nasrin had suggested. A statue of a woman stood at the centre, reaching up to the sky with a look of agony upon her face. Two wings of water sprayed from her back and splashed into a pool below. Some sort of god they worshipped, perhaps?

He twiddled Nasrin's vial of black tears in his hand, unopened. Just a tiny bit would help him relax but what if Lex wanted it later? Better to save it. Maybe he'd score some points with her if he offered it in a few days. Maybe he'd see whether Nasrin was right about Lex seeing him differently. Already he'd made the mistake of thinking that he'd been anything other than a means to an end for Lex, that she'd cared for him. She never smiled at him like the men she charmed, but she had other

186

conniving techniques. Did that mean he should trust her more or less?

What was Nasrin seeing that he wasn't? Had his old self seen it? If only he could have five minutes with the old Darius.

Needing a distraction, he focused on his finger and summoned the cold touch of algor. A blue spark lit and crawled up his hand. Darius pushed back, willing the icy film to stop but still it crept up his arm and onto his neck. Jaw clenched, he pushed harder with a force that pained his temples. The spread halted halfway across his chest.

I've done it.

No. The spread continued, exploiting his break in concentration, and coated his legs in seconds. *Stop!*

It slowly faded until the only cold touching him was the draft from the window. Failure. He could banish the algor now but still had no control. *I'm still useless.*

Enough with practise. The surgeon shouldn't be taking so long. Something was wrong with Omid; he'd lost the arm, or—

A light tapping sounded on the door.

"Master Philippos?" Nasrin called.

"Come."

She entered and offered him a gentle smile. "The surgeon's gone. Omid is fine and my mistress is waiting for you downstairs."

That was a relief. Darius stood and pointed out of the window. "What is the fountain you mentioned? I've seen people kneeling before it."

"It is Dianoia, Goddess of Mind. Her thoughts brought the world into being."

These gods confused him. First the sacred trees of Cephos, now this. What was real?

"In the fountain," Nasrin continued, "she reaches out to her husband, Agathos, the arbiter of good and evil. She asks for justice in a world teeming with cruelty."

There was definitely an abundance of cruelty. "I take it he ignores her then. So Lex cares about these things?"

"Yes." Nasrin gave him an uncomfortable look. "You may have seen Agathos's image at the courthouse, wielding the executioner's axe."

That was the carving he had planned to ask Lex about. Now he had his answer. "Has anyone ever seen these gods? Where are they?"

"I haven't, but some claim to have. They are everywhere and nowhere."

Did that even make sense? "How many other gods does she believe in?"

"No others. Some say the algus are gods, but not her or me. Come, let's return."

She led him back downstairs to Omid's bed. Lex sat on the edge, fiddling with the boy's clothes. She'd changed from her black tunic to a grey cloak.

Omid looked up with a beaming grin. *Euphoria. Lucky sod.* It'd last maybe an hour until the tears wore off completely.

"How's he doing?" Darius asked.

"He'll live," Lex said, as if that was all that mattered.

"Will his arm?"

"Time will tell," Nasrin said. "But it looks good."

The little man wasn't out of the woods yet—not that you'd know looking at him as he gaped in awe at a floating bit of fluff. Darius smiled, a little envious of the boy's happy mood.

"Nasrin." Lex took the carer's hands in hers and pulled her aside. "I need you to tell me something."

"Of course, mistress. Anything."

"I wouldn't answer so fast, dear."

The pair sat down, arms still linked, an odd sight for a slave and her mistress. Lex looked poised to work her charms on the girl.

"Do you remember when we were young?" Lex said. "You would go off on Sundays for hours, sending your mother hysterical?"

Nasrin giggled. "Yes. She always was a worrier."

"I know where you went."

The carer's face dropped and she fidgeted, as if pulling to break away from Lex's clutches but unable to.

"Don't worry," Lex said, "I haven't told a soul. But now I need to know how you found her."

Darius moved closer to the pair, finally alert to what Lex was after—the Waif Magician. This girl was the source they'd been after, the one they'd risked life and limb for, literally. But if the source had been here all along, what had Lex been doing out in the city besides changing clothes? She'd brought food and supplies, but had that been all? Why lie to him?

Nasrin frowned. "Why do you seek her?"

"I just need to talk to her," Lex said. "I don't want to hurt her. I'm not interested in the reward for her head."

Darius cursed under his breath. She'd neglected to mention the woman they sought was a fugitive as well. That'd make finding her all the more difficult, and possibly dangerous.

Eyes full of conflict, Nasrin gave a slow shake of her head. "I can't."

"Please." Lex brought a palm to the girl's cheek, and Nasrin melted at her touch like a bewitched plaything.

"I didn't find her. No one can. That's why they're still searching after decades and haven't so much as seen the tail of her cloak."

"But you did meet her?" Lex's face was a fine-tuned balance of compassionate smile and unyielding, piercing eyes.

"Yes. I'd wait and she'd come to me."

"Where?"

Nasrin took a breath. "South of Denehill, in the shade of a leaning willow."

"The start of the Uxon Trail?"

Darius frowned. *Why does that sound familiar?*

"Yes. Hang a dead mouse from one of the branches and wait."

"Why a dead mouse?" Darius asked.

"Thank you." Lex kissed the carer's cheek and stood. "Did you ready my supplies like I asked?"

"Yes, mistress, and I have your—"

"Thanks. Give it to me."

Nasrin palmed something to Lex who slipped it into her pocket. Darius had a good idea what it was but no idea why she hid her pain from him.

"Philippos, we're leaving at once." The algus grabbed a pack of supplies from the floor.

Nasrin left the room while Darius pulled on a new woollen cloak Lex had brought for him. First they needed a plan for getting out of the city.

"The Uxon Trail is the path to Margalvia," Lex said.

That's why it sounded familiar. "Good. So the Waif Magician is on our way to meet Brutus?" Finally some fortune.

"Yes. I'll send Tiro to...tell Brutus where to meet us."

"What's your plan for getting out of Laltos?"

"It'll be dark soon. We'll find a quiet part of the wall, shielded from view, and make our way down the outside."

"Those walls are as high as ancient trees with barely a foothold from what I saw."

She cocked an eyebrow. "You afraid?"

Swallowing his annoyance, Darius fastened the new sword belt she'd given him around his waist. That was her answer to every fault he found in her plans, to emasculate him into submission. One of these days it wouldn't work, but right now it wasn't like he had a better idea for escaping the city.

Outside, the streets grew busier, the hustle and bustle disturbing the once tranquil room. This was it. They'd leave Omid here to live out the rest of his youth as one of Lex's workers in Laltos. Lex had said the boy would do better than chasing after rats but Darius wasn't sure whether to believe her. One day he may be curious enough to come back and see for himself. And see if the boy still had two arms.

"I'm glad we're leaving." Omid bounced off the bed and almost fell head-first into the table. "This place smells."

Darius pulled him upright and ruffled the boy's hair. "Sorry, no tree-nuts allowed on this part of the journey."

Omid sniggered as Lex shook her head. The boy was out of it, high as a cloud.

The racket outside continued to grow. *What the hell is going on?* At least thick masses of people would be easier to dissolve into.

Lex frowned. "Let's go. I don't like the sound of those crowds. Nasrin, we're leaving!"

Without waiting for the carer, Lex took off and was outside in a blink. Darius squeezed through the door as Nasrin came past. With a quick wave of farewell, he plunged into the crowds in the square.

Even in the commotion, Lex's figure cut a wedge through the people. She turned onto a narrow street leading back towards the courthouse. The silver caps of soldiers' helmets mixed in with bobbing heads and Darius pulled up his collar to his cheeks.

As he kept his eyes peeled for any soldiers drifting too close, Lex stopped and turned so fast he walked straight into her.

"He's here," she whispered. "Get back."

Darius caught sight of swaying dreadlocks behind a slave. Heaviness washed over him as if he'd been coated in iron. *Archimedes.*

29

Darius tried to turn but his legs barely obeyed. Lex planted a palm on the small of his back and pushed him around. His slowly beating heart would have raced if it had the energy. Other people shoved past him and skipped out of the way, unencumbered. Why was it only him? Did Archimedes know he was here and target him with whatever magic it was that had reduced Felix to a crawling insect?

Lex threw an arm around his waist. "I've got you."

She had. If not for her, his legs wouldn't bear him.

"*Search there. I saw one.*" Archimedes's whisper sent a jolt through Darius's legs and he quickened his pace. Every step still felt like wading through sludge.

Wrapping both arms around Darius, Lex pressed her strides into him, her thighs moving his. This wasn't how he'd imagined her holding him like this for the first time. He couldn't be any more pathetic if he tried. *So much for the mighty warrior.*

"Down here," she said, dragging him off the street through a narrow gap between buildings.

A staircase loomed ahead, leading up to a rooftop, and he collapsed onto it like a ragdoll. Lex bent down and checked his breathing, her own breaths short and sharp. If she was afraid, he should be terrified.

"I can't," he croaked.

"I know." Standing, she faced the street. The gap was so narrow her cloak shielded him almost entirely from view.

Darius's head slipped from the step and clapped the cobbles. Feet flickered past his vision as he gazed beneath Lex's cloak. No one stopped.

His heart bashed his ribcage with a single explosive beat. A pause. Another bash. Each time it felt like a pocket of air caught in his chest. His heart's strength was struggling to return. After a few seconds, his heart pounded freely and Darius breathed deep. His forearms and calves twitched as bursts of energy returned.

He scraped his hand across the stone to a spot underneath his chest and tried to push himself upright. Too frail. After another couple of breaths, he tried again. This time he shifted, his chest parting from the cold ground.

Lex came and knelt beside him. "He's moving away."

As she moved to help him up, he batted away her hand. "No. If I'm going to survive, I've got to be able to fight this weakness." *And salvage a shred of dignity.*

"You can't." She grabbed his arm and pulled him up to his knees.

Darius jerked away and steadied himself against the wall. More strength returned every second, his muscles hardening one fibre at a time. He planted a foot and threw his body upwards, bracing against the wall to stay upright.

As he moved to the next step, her words sank in. Darius's brow furrowed. "Why? Don't *you* resist the weakness?"

She frowned. "No. It doesn't affect me. Come." She helped him up the stairs like a frail old man, onto the roof of whoever's abode this was.

"Why just me?"

"You're special," she said with a wry grin.

Darius gave a sarcastic grunt to her evasive reply. No one else had seemed to be suffering with weakness. Why him? Archimedes couldn't have been targeting only him, otherwise the goman would have known he was here and not moved on. Lex was hiding something from him, as always.

The roof gave them a crows-nest view of the square below, where hundreds of people shuffled about unhindered in the fading sunlight. He ducked behind the low wall encircling the roof. Decorative crevices offered good cover and a view below to see anyone coming. Perfect. He just needed a few minutes to regather his strength. Now if only Archime—

There he was, dark dreadlocks hanging still as he surveyed his surroundings from beside the fountain, one hand gripping his staff. Some of the townsfolk held lanterns high to light their way in the dim streets while the rest gave the goman a wide berth, creating a crater of gloom around him.

A group of soldiers burst from a nearby house and began barging their way through the crowds.

"We found one!" a soldier cried, waving a flaming torch above his head.

Another soldier emerged from the building, dragging a little girl, and passed her on. The torch-wielder took her by the scruff of the neck and threw her at Archimedes's feet.

Lex grabbed Darius's wrist and pinned it to the ground. "Stay low," she whispered, a tone higher than usual. Her eyes didn't leave the square.

The girl must have been a potential algus ripe for recruiting. She sat up on the ground and held what looked like a stuffed animal tight to her chest, biting down nervously on its ear. Every clank of metal or shout from the crowd made her flinch.

Archimedes stepped forward and pushed the soldier's torch-bearing hand away with his staff. *"That's how you treat a goddess?"*

Jumping to her feet, the little girl darted like a startled mouse with algus speed. But Archimedes shifted and blocked her path, scooping her into his arms. She wriggled but couldn't break free of the death lock. The goman held her out, inspecting her like a lamb for sacrifice.

"Forget the nasty soldier, my dear."

Her struggles stopped, as if all her upset were wiped away in an instant.

Somewhere in the crowd a woman cried out. Onlookers jostled aside as she barged her way through to the front in such a frenzy her ragged headscarf was torn from her head. She shook off the cloth and stopped a step short of Archimedes.

Arms outstretched, eyes red and swollen, she pleaded, "Please, don't take my Anousheh."

Lex's grip tightened on Darius's arm so hard he winced. As much as he wanted to pull away, he could tell this was more than keeping him put. She wanted someone to hold, so he remained still and bore the pain.

Archimedes placed the little girl down with all the gentleness one would use for a delicate flower and took her hand in his.

"Your daughter is needed for the war. I'll allow you to say your goodbyes in a moment."

The woman collapsed to the ground and wailed, the only sound that filled the crowd's silence. Even in her most desperate moments, she apparently feared the goman too much to touch him or her child.

Lex put her lips to Darius's ear. "Every minute he touches the girl, more of her mind is replaced with lies."

The girl's life was being sucked away without harming a hair on her head. Anousheh stood so innocently, holding the goman's hand, her other arm still clutching the stuffed bear. A few weeks ago that was him, and Parisa too. Darius clenched his fists, wishing they were around Archimedes's neck.

"Shouldn't we get out of here while he's distracted?" Darius's strength had returned enough, and there was nothing to gain by watching this. Yet he couldn't pry away his gaze. Lex didn't answer, didn't even look at him.

After a silent period holding the goman's hand, the little girl released the bear and let it drop to the ground.

"*Say goodbye quickly*," Archimedes told the woman. "*Try anything and you die*." The goman released his victim and her mother leaped up and embraced her.

"Anousheh," the woman sobbed, "Anousheh. Anousheh."

The girl patted her mother on the back with the stiff face of a puppet.

"You won't take her!" The woman jumped up and ran, child cradled in her arms. She dove into the crowd and pushed through horrified onlookers, no one moving to stop her.

Archimedes didn't stir, not even his eyes shifted in a look of surprise. How many other mothers had Darius's enemy watched try to spare their children from his clutches?

The woman still pushed through the swarms, but ahead of her amongst the bobbing heads lurked soldiers. There was no chance she'd make it, not with at least ten, no, twenty enemies in her path. Unless there was a distraction. And what better distraction than the man they hunted? Darius could do something to assist, but it'd surely be a death sentence. *Why am I even considering it?*

Archimedes shifted the Staff to his other arm and paced slowly after the fleeing woman, the crowd parting before him. No one down there would cross the goman to help a desperate mother.

The anger burning in Lex's eyes showed her desire to do so.

"Are you going to do something?" Darius asked her.

Again his words hit a wall of silence, but something flickered in her gaze. She was considering it. All it would take was one arrow.

Someone in the crowd tripped the woman as she ran past, and she collapsed to the ground with a squeal. Soldiers dove in and pinned her down as Archimedes approached. She sobbed into her child's curly brown hair, all resistance smothered.

Archimedes held out a hand. Anousheh unravelled herself from her mother's arms and grasped his fingers.

"*When will you people learn that it's pointless to resist?*"

The girl stood at his side, gazing impassively at her mother, all emotion sucked from her tiny young mind.

"No. There are too many," Lex said, finally answering Darius's question. Had she spent all this time contemplating it?

"The child's lost forever," she added.

"Couldn't the woman take her to the Waif Magician?" Darius asked.

"No. When they're so young, you can't get them back. Even older, it's a long shot."

Good to know. She'd neglected to mention how stacked the odds were against him ever getting his memories back.

An elderly man stepped gingerly forward, earning looks of terror from those close by. "Please, Master Archimedes. She's hysterical. She doesn't know what she does." He stopped several paces away and looked ready to flee if Archimedes so much as blinked.

"*Give me a dagger.*" Archimedes held out a hand.

The soldier with the torch hopped forward and held out the hilt of a knife.

Wind whistled through the street as Archimedes took the dagger. He knelt down and passed it to the little girl.

"*Your daughter is an algus now and bids you farewell.*"

Whimpers were all the woman mustered now, tear wells run dry. Why did all the city-folk stand by and watch, but do nothing?

"Mercy, Master Archimedes," the elderly man begged, his arms shaking as he bowed, not from age but fear.

"Didn't I say if she ran she would die?"

The old man's mouth moved but no more words spilled from his lips. His stricken expression showed he knew there would be no mercy from Archimedes.

"Gomans can't lie. Kill her."

Anousheh rushed forward and thrust the knife into her mother's neck. The woman's arms fell lifeless to her sides as blood gushed down the girl's front and showered her snarling face.

Lex turned, still gripping Darius, and jerked him away in tow. Her gaze fixated on some distant point, her hand shaking but squeezed so tight his arm flushed purple.

What had he just seen? A child turned into a ruthless killer in moments by a simple touch. And a puppet master, with no pity, no mercy, no qualms. Why did it make Darius feel…angry?

"This goman's too powerful." He seized Lex's arm and stilled her shudders. "I've seen enough."

At last she met his eyes, with a look that lay her pain bare before him. Darius doubted he'd ever seen so much sorrow battling so much hate, her mind torn in two over whether to grieve or avenge. Did it stir memories of her son? Her husband?

Red motes speckled her forehead and Darius wiped them away, smearing his palm.

"What the hell, Lex. You're sweating blood."

If only he could wipe away her agony so easily.

"To the wall," she whispered.

Lex released Darius's arm and walked low towards the stairs. He wiped his hand on his sleeve and followed.

They made it down the steps into the quiet back street and were about to disappear into the city when Archimedes's voice sounded again. *"Search that house too! There's another one there."*

More shouts rang out from the crowd, soon followed by the crash of doors being burst from their hinges.

Darius and Lex ground to a halt as roars swelled again behind them. The sounds of splintering wood were too close for comfort, like they were from the square next to where Omid was recovering.

They looked at one another and hesitated for far longer than they should have. Surely Archimedes couldn't know who or where the boy was…

Then the crowd suddenly quieted.

"We found another!" a man yelled.

"Bring him here."

Lex balled up a fist, knuckles white, abating tremors by force of will. They turned and sprinted back up the stairs, but Darius's weakened run felt as if it took longer than when they'd crept.

As he approached the wall of the roof again, he tensed and stayed low. The goman, then the crowd, came into view.

Lex gasped.

"Let me go!" Omid cried as two guards manhandled him into the empty space around Archimedes. The boy's face flushed as a man's hand took hold of his throat, and Darius felt as if his own skull was fit to burst. *How?*

Archimedes reached out in the same way he had with the little girl.

Darius's heart stopped.

But a bright flash erupted from Omid as he flared algor across his body. The guards hadn't even time to cry out before their bodies froze and fell, giving Omid the second he needed to dart away from the goman's reach.

Darius had to do something. "Give me the bow."

"He can't be hit by an arrow." Lex ducked down and planted her body between him and the bow on her shoulder. Her hand still trembled as she pulled a linen mask out of her bag.

Below, as Omid fled, he ran past the little girl. She pounced suddenly and locked arms with him.

"Let go!" Omid shouted. He tugged but to no avail.

Then she snarled and grabbed him with both hands.

Darius withdrew his sword, as if it would help. Should he jump down? He barely had the strength to leap, let alone fight. He gaped at Lex, who was now masked with only her eyes visible.

Again, Omid writhed with an ever-increasing panic in his eyes, but the girl held him in place as Archimedes walked towards him.

"Let me go! Please!" Omid cried.

Darius reached for Lex's bow, but she flinched away and readied it herself.

As she hurried, Archimedes lunged forward, and his hand grabbed Omid's bare wrist.

"Do something!" Darius shoved Lex so hard she almost toppled. Her bloodshot eyes seethed, but he didn't care.

She ripped an arrow from her quiver and nocked it.

"*Northeast roof!*" Archimedes's voice hissed, and all heads turned towards the rooftop where Darius and Lex were.

Darius crouched lower. *Impossible.* The goman couldn't have seen them behind the wall.

Lex jumped to her feet and drew back her bowstring. The trim of Archimedes's cloak disappeared into a nearby building, leaving a wooden-faced Omid standing in the square. His arm remained outstretched, but the girl had long since let go of him. Now he just stood, as if he were a statue holding hands with an invisible friend.

Darius stood with his sword ready. "Archimedes is gone. I'll take the soldiers. You grab Omid."

Lex let the arrow fly. It tore down into the square below, straight towards Omid, and ripped clean through his tiny head in a burst of blood and bone and hair.

His life, that childish grin, those playful jabs, his cries of pain, his dreams of freeing his mother, all bled out before his body hit the ground.

"He won't take another of mine," Lex whispered, her voice threatening to falter. The bow quivered in her hands.

Darius's chest seized up. Fighting for breath, he gazed down at the limp, prone form sprawled on the cobbles. *What has she done?*

30

Unable to look away, Darius stared at Omid's body, still clothed in the rags of a slave. The boy would never wear the algus's fine attire he'd so craved. It didn't feel real. How could he be dead, when he'd been so full of life just minutes ago? And Lex, why had she...?

Darius couldn't think. These foreign feelings made no sense but overwhelmed him nonetheless.

What if Omid had still been in there, a small part lingering? That would mean—

The thunder of boots rose from the stairs and dragged Darius back to reality. Glints of metal helmets came into view, along with sharp blades swaying, ready to slash them like that little girl's mother. These soldiers had done nothing to stop Archimedes, some had even brought the lambs to the slaughter. *To hell with them all.*

Darius turned and charged before even considering how he'd take out the dozens approaching. He slammed shoulder first into the lead soldier's thighs before the man could swing his sword and toppled the men into one another.

They tumbled down the stairs with a deafening rattle of metal and stone. The crashing bodies hit the ground and Darius lay buried in a pile of kicking feet, barging elbows and flailing swords, all looking to score a piece of him.

They wouldn't get as much as a hair. He summoned algor and his body radiated its icy tendrils. A man pressing into his stomach screamed and was quickly silenced as if his throat had frozen shut. More shouts erupted and soldiers scrambled to get away, cowards without their cruel master nearby. They'd find no mercy from Darius. Men that aided Archimedes deserved only death.

Darius clambered to his feet atop the frozen corpses while survivors hobbled away clutching frozen limbs. His sword lay on the ground by the stairs and Darius snatched it up. Though his cobalt blue body felt as if battling a gale, he still had the speed to outrun any of the men around.

A masked Lex landed a few feet away, her sword drawn, like an executioner thirsting for blood. All he saw when he looked at her was Omid's head speared by her arrow, but he couldn't look away. Her eyes were glazed over as if her mind were elsewhere. Regardless, anyone close enough would recognise their allure.

"Tiro sees algus coming through the streets from all directions," she said. "It's a trap. We need to find a way out of the city."

His throat wouldn't summon a word to her, but she was his only ally. Now wasn't the time to argue. Darius shoved away whatever it was he felt and gave her a nod. Closing his eyes, he focused his mind on the algor and banished it from his body. His muscles still felt sluggish, tingling as their energy fled like vapour in the air, growing heavier by the second. Wait. That wasn't the algor. Archimedes was coming for him.

Whirling, Darius started up the stairs before all his strength was lost. Lex zipped up past him to the top and leaped to an adjacent roof, away from the square. Every step gained him a little more energy, a step farther away from his pursuer.

He jumped to follow Lex. The gap was only a couple of yards but he barely landed a foot on the edge and tripped. His sword screeched as it scratched across the cold slates. Without pausing to breathe, he scrambled back up and leaped to another roof, finally with enough strength to land without stumbling.

A figure darted across the rooftops to the right, at most a hundred yards away and closing fast. Another two to the left skipped across the city's heights with the distinct adeptness of algus. The light grey slate used to line the rooftops made it easier to spot his pursuers as he ran but would make him stand out like a blot on a page too.

If the other algus were as fast as Lex, they'd catch him. The weapons they clutched were stubby and dark, not the glinting iron of swords. *Clubs.* To pacify, not kill. Archimedes still wanted him alive.

The roofs grew sparser. Darius leapt with all the strength left in his legs and soared over a wide gap, landing so hard his foot almost speared through the slate roof. The two algus following ate away at the distance between them with ease. They were short and slender, looked like teens. Lex was pulling ahead, her strides long and swift. At this rate, she'd make it, but he wouldn't.

Even worse, they were running out of buildings. Only a few roofs still lay before them. Darius began to doubt they'd make it to the wall at all. He tightened his grip on his sword, ready to fight to the last breath if need be.

An arrow screeched past Darius's thigh and he side-stepped as he watched it whip past. He wouldn't be taken alive to serve as another puppet after Archimedes pillaged his mind. A glance back told him there was an algus wielding a short bow to his left, already aiming another arrow. They'd be lucky to hit within ten feet of him running at this speed, but he didn't dare avert his eyes, ready to dodge the incoming projectile. He couldn't afford to falter. The closer they came, the greater the risk of Lex being recognised, despite her mask.

He heard a scurry of steps too late. An algus rammed Darius from the right and sent him tumbling across the roof. His shoulder slammed into a stone chimney and a snap of pain shot through it like a bolt. He spun and skidded, shredding his knees on the sharp tiles as he came to a halt. His attacker loomed over him, ready to beat him to a pulp.

A few paces behind the algus, Lex raised her bow.

"Nikolaos, duck!" a girl algus screamed from across the rooftops as Lex unleashed an arrow.

Nikolaos dove to the side as it darted past. In the blink of an eye, he regained his footing and charged at Darius. The algus swung a club for his head but he ducked and rolled away. He got to one knee but Nikolaos was there again. The club hammered into his injured shoulder. A shout of pain broke from Darius's throat and he ducked to shield his head as Nikolaos drew back for another attack. Agony shot through the shoulder. It was dislocated for sure, barely moveable.

Darius dug his knee into the rooftop, fighting to stay upright. If he went down, it'd be over. Nikolaos pummelled his shoulder again and again. The algus's face twisted in a grimace, eyes burning bright with hatred.

An arrow slammed into Darius's thigh but it barely registered over the jolts of pain from his shoulder. The two teens knelt on a nearby roof, firing off more low shots towards his legs. He twisted to dodge.

Nikolaos swung the club but this time Darius caught it with a slap to his palm that almost snapped his wrist. Growling, he tightened his grip on the weapon. The algus grunted and tried to rip it free.

Lex tore in from behind the teens and cleaved both their heads in a single stroke. Nikolaos's eyes widened with fear as she turned towards him. Had he recognised her? Darius yanked the club and slammed his forehead into Nikolaos's nose as the algus stumbled forward.

Tremors echoed through Darius's head and his eyes refused to focus as Nikolaos's fuzzy form dropped. Darius smashed his fist into his opponent's chin for good measure. He owed the algus a dozen more but his vision darkened. Shaking his head, he tried to brush the shadows from his eyes.

Another figure landed in front of him. "Don't you pass out on me." Lex grabbed his shoulders and shook him.

Bolts of pain dragged him from the enveloping darkness and his eyes eased back into focus. "My shoulder," he groaned, clutching it.

Lex took his hand and held out his injured arm to the side. With a sharp yank, she cracked it back in, sending another jolt through his arm. After a few seconds, the pain in his shoulder eased, but that only made the ache in his punctured thigh more prominent. An arrow still sat buried in his flesh. Yet another wound to add to the list; another he was lucky hadn't killed him. Teeth gritted, he ripped the arrow out and snapped the damned thing in his hand.

Blood trickled out of the puncture and down his thigh. *Not gushing at least. It's a non-lethal wound.* Darius held his breath to choke the sickness rising in his throat as he ripped a thick strip of cloth from Nikolaos's undershirt. He tied it over the wound as best he could with only one good arm.

Lex looked hesitant to come close again to help, as if he were a wild animal. The rage building inside certainly felt feral but he couldn't lash out at her while he still needed her to get out of the city. After that, all bets were off.

"More will be coming," Lex said.

Like he didn't know. Darius struggled to his feet and tested how much weight his thigh could bear. Enough to get away from Nikolaos's unconscious body. Odd that Lex hadn't slit the algus's throat yet given how quick she was to snuff out people's lives. Darius should count himself lucky she hadn't finished him off already. To think the only thing keeping him alive was some information on his grandfather...

His eyes took a second to bring the edge of the roof into focus, where the lines of buildings halted. A river swerved through the city. At the perimeter, it traced underneath a stone bridge where lanterns flickered, extended over the water. Darius picked up his sword as Lex eyed him. If he wanted to try and gut her for killing Omid, she was ready.

"We go out on the river?" he asked. It must have been where she was headed, but the guards would surely see a boat, even a small rower.

"Not on it. In it."

Just what he needed, another midnight swim escaping Archimedes. His beaten body ached at the thought but it didn't have a choice. He wasn't dying here.

Darius hobbled to the roof's edge and peered down the two-storey drop to the hard cobbles below. "I can't jump with this leg."

Tiny shadows darted on rooftops towards them, like insects flitting from point to point. More algus. They'd be swarming all around him in minutes.

Lex pulled out her rope and tossed him an end. He held it and watched her wrap the rope around the chimney few times. After giving it a few sharp tugs, she returned to his side with the second end. Not even a wisp of smoke rose from the chimney on this chilly evening. Odds were good there was no one home to notice them clambering down the side of the house.

"You're leaving him?" Darius nodded to Nikolaos.

"Yes."

"That mask doesn't hide those blue eyes you know. Better finish him like you do the rest."

Lex looked over the edge as she wrapped her end of the rope around one hand. "I know Nikolaos. I can't take his life after he saved mine."

So there was a shred of humanity inside her after all, something that felt loyalty or debt to other people. Too bad Omid hadn't been one of them.

Darius sheathed his sword, then wrapped the rope three times around the hand of his good arm. At least the same arm kept getting injured, leaving the other usable, even if it was his weakest. He backed up to the roof's edge, Lex echoing his movements.

Their newest pursuers were only a few rooftops away. *Time to go.* Darius leaned back and the rope groaned as it took their weight. He stepped down onto his strong leg, trying to steady the wobbles in the rope. Lex was already level with his ankles, her climbing swift and efficient. He loosened his grip and slid down in bursts to catch up, wincing as the rope bit at his palm and trying to avoid putting a foot through a window.

Shouts echoed through the streets from soldiers not yet within sight but not far away. Darius dropped the last six feet with a thud, the impact jarring his injured leg. Lex tugged the rope down from the roof while he listened for approaching footsteps and looked for those flitting insects upon the rooftops. There was definitely movement nearby, but it was hard to pinpoint from the darkened streets. If only Lyra were here, she'd spot them with ease. What he wouldn't give to feel her warm fur in his hands now.

The evening air was eerily still save for the river lapping at the banks ahead. Moonlight flickered over the waters, showing the river's quiet but rapid movement. For a split second he worried that Omid wasn't there, and then he remembered what had happened in the square.

They stalked along the paved banks. Lex's gaze was fixed ahead, like she had an escape route planned. After a couple of minutes, she stopped at a tiny building at the end of a tall block of houses. It wasn't a home, more of a stone shed without even a single window. She pulled out a key, unlocked the door and slipped inside.

Darius moved to follow, expecting it to lead to some underground tunnel or hole to hide, but Lex came out holding what looked like two canes. She closed the door and handed them to him. They were wooden and light, thin enough to wrap his hand around, and about as long as his forearm. They were hollow through both ends. *Pipes for breathing underwater.*

Lex began tightening the straps of her bag and armour. "You haven't forgotten how to swim, have you?" she whispered.

Another time, the concern in her voice might have been flattering, but he still could hardly bear to look at her.

"I can swim," he said, though there was no Lyra to save him from drowning this time.

"Tie that bandage as tight as you can."

He pulled it taut. "Why?"

"Wolf-fish in the river."

Darius's stomach sank. "Wolf-fish" brought to mind flesh-eating fish.

"The river's shallow at the edges and the current will carry us." Lex snatched one of the hollow sticks from him. "Stay underwater and use the rod to breathe. Don't use algor underwater."

And don't get eaten alive. At least that'd be a better way to go than to the dreadlocked devil.

Lex stepped to the edge of the riverbank, taking out a hoop of rope, and slung it over her wrist. "So we don't lose one another." She held out a hand, the same one that'd loosed the arrow that shattered Omid's head. It may as well have been coated in blood.

An arrow clattered against the cobbles beside them. Shadows whipped across the nearby rooftops. Time had run out.

Darius ran to the river and leapt in. He hit the water and dropped straight to the riverbed. The water wasn't as cold as he'd feared but the current was stronger. It towed him along before he could raise the end of the pipe above water.

He opened his eyes to try and gain his bearings but all he saw was the murky surface and endless black in all other directions. As he struggled to get the pipe clear, his foot hit a rock and the current rolled him over. Who knew where Lex was. Who cared?

Pain constricted his chest. Another few seconds and it would cave in as he sucked every last drop of air from his lungs. If he didn't get back to the surface he'd drown.

Kicking against the riverbed, he thrust his body upwards and broke free of the water. Darius sucked in a huge breath. His panic eased, only to be replaced with dread as he realised his head was now a floating target. Luckily he couldn't see farther than a few feet which meant no one would spot *him*.

He took one last deep breath, jammed the pipe into his mouth and dropped back under, his wet clothes helping pull him down. The thick cloak hindered him but he was loath to shed it. He'd need it for the journey to the Waif Magician and Margalvia.

Thanks to the strong current, he barely needed to swim. The pipe let him breathe though it was a struggle to pull the air into his lungs. Something brushed against his hand and he froze. It wasn't

Lex, too small. A plant? A fish? A wolf-fish? It didn't return and he drew another breath through the pipe.

Darius made his way along the river, keeping to the shallower parts where he could easily poke the pipe out into the air. Now and then the pipe bucked against the current. Its light weight made it more difficult to control.

The pipe dipped under briefly and a gush of water made its way to his mouth. Spluttering, he pushed to the surface and stole a breath as quietly as he could. Lanterns flickered only a few yards away in the hands of soldiers and fishermen forming a search party. They'd be on the lookout for boats but hopefully not swimmers. How soon would word make it around that they'd dived into the river?

A large stone bridge arched over the river ahead, its far side joined to the outer walls of the city. All he had to do was cross under it and he was free, but lines of torches showed men marching up and down that area like ants.

Darius sank back below when something tugged at his leggings. He looked down, half expecting to see Lex. Nothing but darkness. Another tug, this time near his thigh, like being pinched by an angry…wolf-fish.

He punched at the water but hit only his own thigh. The current dragged him on as something nipped his bad arm. Another snap on his leg, this time most definitely a bite. Teeth clamped around the pipe, Darius waved his arm to try and shake them off. Only a little longer until he was outside the city, then it would be safe to get out.

More hungry mouths snapped at his leggings, tearing the bandage and inviting bites to his exposed skin.

Lights flickered overheard, the lanterns sketching out the arched bridge. Darius's body tensed, bracing for an arrow or spear from one of the watchers. He wouldn't be able to do anything if one came, even his algus speed wouldn't save him underwater.

His foot sought the riverbed and he pushed off, trying to speed up and get through the gauntlet faster but the pipe threatened to go under again. He was too close to the bridge to risk rushing to the surface now even if he took in water.

More nibbles at his leg, drawn in by the blood now seeping out. Flaring algor might kill them all, but Lex had warned him against using it in the river. He had to endure.

Dribbles of water ran into his mouth as the top of the pipe flirted with the surface. Too high and it'd be spotted, too low and he couldn't breathe. Just a few more strokes and he was through.

A fish bit his throat and he spluttered in a flurry of bubbles. Dropping the pipe, Darius batted the fish away. At least he'd finally managed to hit one. It didn't feel any bigger than his palm but by the sting of their bites they were half jaw muscle. His own mouth clamped shut and yearned for air. He couldn't be sure how many seconds he had left but he'd stretch them out as long as possible. The lanterns were too close, casting their searching lights onto the surface above.

Darius tried to relax and let the current take him to conserve his air and energy. More fish nipped his thigh but he blocked out the pain. His chest began to cave and his ribs stabbed into his lungs, urging him to rise for a lungful of fresh, life-giving air. Each extra second he endured got him closer to safety.

When the pain reached unbearable heights, Darius pushed for the surface. His head broke out of the water and he gulped down breath after breath. The lantern lights swayed behind him, some held high above soldiers' heads as they walked across the bridge and wall, but they hadn't spotted him. He'd made it, but alone with only the wolf-fish for company.

31

Darius let the current wash him farther downstream, its waves rocking him like a worn, twisted piece of driftwood. Soon only the moonlight was left to trace the banks as the city's lights receded.

There was still no sight of Lex, though he wasn't sure whether he wanted to see her or not. If she'd made it, surely she'd have lingered near the river when beyond the soldiers' sights. Or perhaps she was dead. Which would he prefer?

He'd prefer if she was alive. She was his guide to Denehill, to the Waif Magician and his memories. Why did he have to pause to answer? So she'd killed Omid. He had no reason to care.

Yet he did. Why?

Another wolf-fish nipped his thigh. *Little git. Time to get out of the water.* Darius woke his tired muscles and stroked for the bank. As his feet found the riverbed, a wolf-fish sank its teeth deep into his thigh and he clamped his jaw against a yell. Arm finally out of the water, he snatched the thing and held it up as it squirmed and tried to wriggle free. Despite its oily skin, his grip didn't relent.

Darius tossed the fish onto the shore and limped out after it with a sigh, letting the water drain from his heavy clothes. Finally, he was free of the gnawing wet. He strode through the mud lining the river with slow, heavy steps, past the flapping fish trying desperately to fling itself back into the water. Maybe its chest was caving in just like his had underwater. That'd teach it to bite him.

Bushes littered the riverbank, and he found a somewhat dry spot near one. Settling on the ground, Darius cradled his arm to give his shoulder some much-needed relief.

A foreign sense of concern drifted through his mind, and he smiled. *Come to me, Lyra.* She was close. Somehow, his escort had known he was in danger and set off at once to meet him by the shore. How lucky he was to have her. Being alone right now was the last thing he wanted.

The bush's leaves would give him some cover, but not so much Lex wouldn't spot him if she'd made it. Stars speckled the cloudless sky and he watched for any shadows passing overhead that might reveal Tiro searching.

Slapping sounds came from the muddy bank where the wolf-fish still struggled. The wretch deserved it. But still, it was pitiful. Darius got up and kicked the fish back into the river, having seen enough death for one day.

The light splash soon faded to leave a desolate silence without hint of the enemy or of Lex. She was lost. Omid was dead. The thought kept striking him like a blow to the chest. He wanted to yell at Lex until her eardrums hurt, and then some.

A few minutes passed before Lyra emerged from a bush, her pace slow and sombre as if she shared his mood. Grateful for her presence, he wrapped his good arm around her and pulled her in tight. If only everyone were as loyal and obedient as her.

Lex. His mind couldn't string together the words he wanted to say to her. Lyra could try to find her, or his escort could guide him straight to Margalvia. Choices, choices.

The panther snuggled her nose into his neck. She'd stay with him no matter what, and *she* wouldn't kill a child.

215

He clenched his jaw. Things couldn't be left like this. There was too much he wanted to say to Lex, and at the least he wanted to know why she'd done it. Then he'd choose whether to turn his back on her.

Lyra. Find Lex.

His escort's wide eyes sought his as if to check he was sure, then she set off along the muddy riverbank.

More questions circled in Darius's mind as he followed her. How much of the boy had been left when the goman fled? Who had really killed him, Lex or Archimedes? Regardless, that mouthless fiend would get what was coming to him.

It wasn't long before Lyra slowed and he sensed they'd found Lex. *She's alive, then.* Darius eased his steps to dampen the squelch of mud and stuck to the bushes which were becoming thicker along the river. Another forest loomed in the distance among the hills, and on its edge he noticed a dark figure standing below a medium-sized conifer, still as a lurking crocodile. If not for the bright moon, he'd have missed them and wandered too close.

Their face was shrouded in the night, but he made out long hair pulled back behind the head. *Lex.*

Darius paused, unsure whether to be relieved or nervous. Walking away was still an option. He could let Lyra lead him back to Margalvia and forget the Waif Magician. Trusting Lex seemed impossible now. But somehow, part of him still did. No one else had risked so much for him or possessed the answers he wanted.

He stepped out from the cover of the bushes, brushing them aside with a rustle to draw her attention. Her head turned towards him then held still. His boots squelched as he hobbled towards her, the filth seeping in. He didn't stop until she placed a palm on his chest and lowered her head, not meeting his eyes.

"You…killed him." His voice was quieter than he'd imagined it would be.

The hand pressing against his chest curled into a fist. His own fist was clenched so tightly he felt the bones in his palm.

"Well?" He grabbed a thick branch on the tree to have something to squeeze. "You're not going to say anything?"

"It had to be done," she said, her back pressing into the tree trunk.

Did she not care? Was she so cold that she couldn't give him a single reason?

"I knew you were heartless but—"

"You're one to talk."

Darius snapped the branch off with a roar and slammed it into the trunk, sending a shower of splinters over her.

Though Lex flinched, she didn't move to stop him. Perhaps she wanted him to smash it into her head, to make it bleed like Omid's had.

Scowling, Darius pressed the split end under her chin. "I should ram this through your neck."

"As if you care for anyone but yourself anymore."

"Then we're just two peas in a pod," he sneered. "At least I have an excuse. You say Archimedes took my empathy; well, who took yours? You act like you're some righteous fighter for justice, for your god, Agathos, or whatever his name is, but you're no better than that damned goman. You're lucky I need you to get my memories back. Maybe after I'm whole and done feeding Archimedes's guts to the worms I should slay *you* so I don't need to worry about a dagger in my back. I'd die a happier man never hearing the name *Alexandra* again."

Lex's face was still shrouded in shadow, her chest rising and falling with heavy breaths. He lifted her chin with the branch, wanting to stare down those steely eyes and show her how furious he was.

His scowl softened as she met his hard gaze with none of her usual barriers. Her eyes welled with sorrow and her hand fell from his chest to grab her hip.

He took a step back.

"Go to hell," she whispered.

It was as if her fight was spent, and it made him feel hollow. He never thought he'd yearn for her cold parries but seeing her surrender, seeing her sweat blood in Laltos, was like watching someone waste away to a cursed illness.

Did he really want to see her dead? If she fell, he might feel that same anger he felt over Omid's death.

"Just tell me, why did you do it?" He had to know the reason, and it had better be good.

"Omid was as good as dead."

Darius had hoped for more. "How can you know?"

"You saw him standing there like a statue. He was already gone."

"What if he was in there, even just a remnant like me? You don't know—"

"I know! I've seen it so many times it's burnt into my mind." Lex groaned and clutched her hip with a grimace.

"You can't know!" He flared algor across the branch in his hand and smashed it into the tree trunk again. The wood shattered into pieces. Even the small part left in his hand crumbled under his fierce grip.

"I know." She choked out the words, still watching him with that sorrowful look.

Darius bowed his head and stared at Lyra, hoping her loyal eyes would calm him enough to think straight. Why did he want to throttle Lex and comfort her at the same time?

She began searching through her pockets, patting herself all over as concern began to knit her eyebrows together.

"What's wrong?" he asked.

She scowled at him and kept searching. As each pocket turned out empty, she sighed, whether from pain or frustration he couldn't say, but he knew what she was looking for.

Darius slipped a hand into his pocket and grasped the vial of tears Nasrin had given him. Should he give it to Lex? Part of him wanted to watch her squirm, feel pain like she deserved to.

A curse escaped Lex as she gave up searching. She clutched her forehead and squeezed her eyes shut. Usually she never made much of the pain.

Must be in agony. He watched her, listening to her heavy, pain-laden breaths. Each one made his own chest tighten in sympathy, despite everything. Perhaps they both deserved the punishment, but after a while he'd had enough.

He pulled out the vial. "Here."

She looked up, eyes widening as she caught sight of the black nectar. "Where did you get that?"

"You have your secrets, I have mine."

Lex eyed him as if suspicious he was trying to poison her. To prove her wrong, he pulled off the cap and placed a drop on his tongue. It'd ease his shoulder and thigh for a good few hours.

The bitterness made his mouth twist in disgust. He sucked and swallowed hard repeatedly to rid his tongue of every trace, then took her hand and placed the vial in it.

She wasted no time, carefully measuring two drops on the back of her hand before licking them up. Two drops. Darius frowned. She'd better be careful. One had been enough to make Omid groggy. Two had flattened the boy for eight hours.

Lex dabbed another two drops on her hand.

Darius started. "Hey, wait—"

Before he could snatch the vial back, she licked the spots off.

219

"Four?" Darius hissed. "That's enough to fell a horse. What're you thinking?"

She scoffed. "Don't be so dramatic."

If only he was being dramatic. She tried to turn away, but he grabbed her shoulders and spun her back around.

"So much could kill you." A cloud had drifted over the moon, rendering its light too dim to see her eyes clearly. He couldn't tell if she was already slipping under.

Lex placed her palm on his chest. "Don't worry. I have a high tolerance. I need a lot for it to work."

What could he do? Sticking his fingers down her throat wouldn't help. Some herbs might, if they were even around, and if he could see far enough to spot them. Even then, she'd have to eat pounds for it to work fast enough to counteract the tears. Damn her, but what was done was done.

Lex sighed and leant her head against his chest. It had been a few minutes and the tears were kicking in. First fatigue, then dizziness, then spiralling nothingness. He knew a lot about this, somehow.

Darius took her hand and squeezed it, wondering whether she still had enough feeling to notice. "Tell me, which direction do I go if you fall under? I can carry you to Denehill." They couldn't linger here for long. Archimedes would widen the search and they weren't far outside the city.

Lex scoffed. "Aren't you going to feed my guts to the…worms, was it?"

Half of him still felt like it. "I'll see how I feel after a night with you on my shoulder."

"We aren't here by accident. There's a cave ahead. The plan was to wait there until dusk tomorrow then head for Denehill on horseback when Nasrin…"

"When she what?" Darius didn't know the first thing about horses and sure didn't know how to ride one.

Lex leaned into him and almost knocked him over. He steadied himself and pushed her upright.

"Lex, have you ever taken this much before? Will you be fine?"

She closed her eyes and frowned. "Yes."

Damn her. She acted invincible but these tears were lethal. Darius slung an arm around her waist to steady her. "Show me the cave."

Pointing through a tangle of leaves, she stepped forward and pushed away his arm. "I can...walk." She took a wobbly step and winced, her hand clutching her hip again.

Stubborn as a panther.

They set off through the mess of branches with Lyra quietly following. Darius watched the algus closely for any sign she might be about to collapse. What if Lex fell asleep and didn't wake up? She was the only one that could help get his memories back.

A rocky outface with vines creeping down it loomed out of the dark ahead, no opening obvious. He broke into a limping jog along the face, looking high and low at every patch of shadow. This damned cave was hard to find.

"Lex, where is it?"

"Heere." The word slurred from her mouth. She kicked at a stone face, causing it to ripple, then beckoned him over.

Odd. Darius reached out an arm, expecting cold stone, but instead touched a coarse fabric. The façade was barely a foot across and half concealed by a mess of ivy. It would hide them, but for how long? Lex had mentioned Nasrin. He needed to get word to her somehow, explain the algus's condition. Perhaps Lex's falcon could help.

"Where's Tiro?" he asked.

Lex leaned against the rocky surface and shut her eyes. "Close."

Darius turned to his amber-eyed panther. *Lyra, find Tiro and get him back here.*

His escort set off into the thin trees. He wasn't sure whether a panther and peregrine could communicate, but surely Lyra could handle a bird.

Lex slipped through the fabric into the passage and he followed. The narrow way opened into a larger space, so dark his hand wasn't visible in front of his face. Focusing on his fingertips, he willed the icy touch of algor and it sparked on his hand. Stone walls glimmered around him, reflecting the algor's subtle shine. The hole was barely six feet by six. It wasn't a natural cave; the chunks in the wall looked carved by pickaxe—a hideout.

The algor began its familiar uncontrollable spread up his arm to his neck. It crossed his back to his injured shoulder. Recalling the branch he had coated during his confrontation with Lex, he wondered if he'd ever have that kind of control deliberately.

Lex dropped to one knee with a thud and leant back against the rocks. Not long until she fell under. Darius knelt and began stripping off her weapons, putting her bow, quiver and sword at the back of the cave. She sat down and loosened the belt around her leather tunic, head hanging back. Darius settled next to her, slung his good arm around her shoulders and pulled her close in case she fell.

Safe at last, from soldiers and algus at least. Lex still battled her own internal torment. Her mind was a mess, perhaps scrambled enough by tears and grief to answer some of his questions.

"You never told me why you chose to fight with Margalvia instead of your city," he said, "or about our army."

"I told you enough," she said without opening her eyes.

Damn. Even moments from unconsciousness her barriers were up.

"You'd better not die," he said through gritted teeth.

No response, and she'd stopped moving. He'd never seen her relinquish control like this, leave herself so vulnerable. She was hurting more than he knew.

Darius took her hand and pressed his fingers to her wrist. Her gentle rhythmic pulse drew a sigh from him and he fidgeted to get comfortable. Sleep would elude him tonight; his back was wound tight and his nerves were on edge. The one downside of catching up on all that sleep in Laltos was he was no longer exhausted enough to sleep on cold, hard stone despite fretting that tomorrow would be his last day.

Lex's pulse slowed and he kept his fingers firmly in place. If it slowed further or stopped he'd have to do something. What 'something' was, he had no clue. Shake her, scream at her, punch her chest and hope her heart sprang back to life? He wasn't letting her slip away. Maybe it was best not to let her sleep at all.

"Lex?" Darius shook her gently.

Nothing.

"Lex." He nudged her again.

Still nothing.

He took her face in his hand, and when she still didn't stir, he pulled open an eyelid. Her eye looked responsive; she was still in there. Checking her gag reflex would help see how far under she was but she wouldn't like it. And for some reason that stopped him from doing it. Did that mean he cared about her? Did the fact he hoped she didn't die despite the anger still clenching his jaw mean he cared?

Perhaps they deserved each other; both were responsible for the death of a young boy now. The memory of Amid was so distant, yet that baby's blood still felt wet on his hands. The feelings of guilt and despair had been unrelenting at the time and lingered even now, though he questioned their rationality.

But they didn't wane. It was as if the feelings needed no discernible reason to exist. Was that the point he was missing? Perhaps it was time to ask Lex about the conflict within him. He'd assumed her hip pain had driven her to take so many of the tears, but could it be the guilt over killing Omid had made her long for sleep? Maybe she knew of guilt too.

Lyra pushed through the hideout's covering with Tiro skipping underneath her. The falcon looked at his mistress and then turned to Darius as if to ask, "What did you do?"

"She took tears." Darius mimicked licking the back of his hand the way Lex had taken them.

Tiro skipped forward and pecked at her boot like he was checking if she slept.

Darius waved to get the bird's attention. "I need you to find Nasrin. Nasrin. Do you understand?"

The peregrine's gaze shifted to Darius and he cocked his head.

What am I even asking? Darius had no idea what Nasrin was supposed to do for them, but he didn't know anyone else that could help.

"Nasrin. Bring Nasrin to us." Darius motioned with his hands. "Make sure you aren't followed back here."

Tiro turned and headed for the exit. Darius could only hope that meant the bird had understood his instructions. *Damn you, Lex.* She could have made arrangements before knocking herself out. Or had this been her plan all along? The algus had said they would lie low until Nasrin…did what?

He nodded to Lyra. *Good work, girl. Keep watch outside and warn me if someone comes.*

As she left he looked back at Lex. This was the first time he'd stared at her for so long. Usually she caught his glances and chased them away with a stiff look. A woman as beautiful as Lex made him realise he had no memory of being with one. Lex's cheeks glowed blue in his algor's light, soft and unblemished, tempting him to run a finger across her skin. He pulled his hand away and banished the algor, plunging them into pitch blackness. There was clearly some part of him that felt something for her. Maybe showing her that was how he'd win her trust and get some answers.

32

Surrounded by his protectors, Archimedes led Nikolaos through the courthouse to one of the grand state rooms adorned with fine varnished furniture and enviable royal blue seating. It was unoccupied, but even had a magister sat there Nikolaos had no doubt they would have vacated for the dreadlocked servant of the King. Nikolaos dreamed of having such influence.

Archimedes indicated for the others to wait outside and placed the Staff of Arria down carefully on a table as the door shut behind them. "*Snuff out the candles.*"

Frowning, Nikolaos looked around. On some of the tables, candles were still alight from the night before. He walked around and snuffed them out as Archimedes watched. Was it Nikolaos's imagination, or was there a trace of nervousness in the goman's stare and slightly more sweat than usual visible on his forehead? Nikolaos had heard whispers that Archimedes hated fire, or feared it, but though everyone muttered about it, no one dared make fun of the goman.

When the task was complete, Archimedes motioned for Nikolaos to sit on one of the padded chairs. As he sat, Nikolaos gently touched his tender nose. Hopefully the paste he'd applied hid the bruising from Darius's head-butt.

"*Report.*"

"The guard has been tripled at the gates and over the river. Patrols along the walls are doubled and our reserve forces walk the streets in plain clothes."

"*You've lost him. And one of the algus is aiding him.*"

Nikolaos swallowed. "No one saw their face. We have no idea who the algus is, but Darius won't escape. I had all escape tunnels blocked days ago, even the Regent's own." They'd catch Darius and that traitor algus, whoever they were.

"*I fear Darius has already left. The city's defences were inadequate. Perhaps I have stretched myself too thin heading the Laltos Guard.*"

Nikolaos didn't respond. He'd assumed Archimedes would be livid, but it sounded like the goman placed the blame for failing to capture Darius at his own feet. Nikolaos certainly wouldn't object to that. Especially if—

"*I may consider appointing you to lead the Guard after all.*"

Nikolaos had to suppress a grin. "You can entrust me to follow your commands, Archimedes."

"*You weren't my first choice. I can't help but mourn the fact Alexandra turned down the role.*"

His eyes narrowed. "What do you mean?"

"*I asked her before I hung your uncle, but she sent word not long after declining due to ongoing duties. I feel she'd be more effective.*"

That was the message Tiro had brought? That was why Lex was so harrowed? He'd assumed she'd been given some unofficial duty, but all she'd been ruminating on was leading the Laltos Guard? It was a huge responsibility but still. No, something more was amiss and he'd discover what. Thank Dianoia she'd turned down the position though. He wouldn't relish killing her too.

"*You will do. I need someone the Guard will trust and that can deal with the politics of a large city.*" Archimedes rested his eyes on Nikolaos and they misted over. "*I see disaster in the future. Cities burning with ferven. Humanity needs unity.*"

Their worst fear was the rakkan invaders taking the city. Against ferven that melted rock, how could they defend themselves without Archimedes? Nikolaos knew that, but he also knew that if the goman wasn't careful he'd be viewed as a conqueror, not a saviour. Yet despite his power, Archimedes never seemed to hunger for it. Oddly.

"I have always wondered…" Nikolaos paused, choosing words carefully for fear he was prying too much. "You speak often of seeing things. I wonder if you mean it literally."

Archimedes's expression softened for the first time Nikolaos could recall. "*My cogi powers do more than give me control of the mind. I see the future as clear as I see you now.*"

Nikolaos gasped. Was that how he always seemed to know where Darius was heading, such as when he insisted that the fugitive would end up in Laltos? Nikolaos had always assumed Archimedes somehow had rakkan informants that kept him updated, but with a power like cogi, who needed spies?

"*I don't always see what will come to pass, but what may, sometimes different outcomes of the actions I or others could possibly take so I can act wisely and influence the result. There is no certainty, but it's how I knew what to do to stand the best chance of luring Darius out. I tell you this so you understand why you must follow my commands without question. Knowledge of my abilities is not to be passed any further.*"

That was the least of Nikolaos's concerns. "Do you see who the traitor is?"

"*No. I only see them masked. They're careful, but they need only make one mistake. Neither do I know where exactly Darius is. Yet. But I soon may. My cogi has its limitations.*"

"What limitations?"

"*That's not your concern.*"

Nikolaos couldn't blame the goman for keeping his weaknesses a secret. "Do you see our city razed?" Hatred burned in his stomach at the thought.

"*In the past I've seen most of the Empire burning. It is why I have fought with everything I have for so many years, raised an algus army greater and more focused than any other. That reason and…*"

The goman stood and removed his leather tunic slowly, wearing only a humble grey vest underneath. Nikolaos winced as the goman uncovered his left arm, the dark skin so scarred with burns that no patch of untainted skin remained. The whole arm and shoulder were a wrinkled mess, as if they had been drenched in scorching oil.

"*I had been in this land not three days when a rakkan descended on me.*"

That explained the fear of a naked flame. Archimedes had never allowed his scars to be seen by anyone that Nikolaos knew, always instead exuding the air of an invincible colossus, untouchable. But when he'd first arrived, he hadn't had the Staff of Arria, the weapon that had finally thwarted the rakkans. Should Nikolaos be honoured to share this knowledge, or concerned? He settled for the former, for now.

"How did you survive?" Ferven never ceased burning and the goman couldn't touch algor without more serious injury. Was he in constant agony? It explained the continual sweating and the goman's unending hatred of the rakkans.

"*I am perhaps fortunate that some of the burns are due to my clothing catching alight. I fought off my attacker with only steel. It was then I confirmed they were immune to all my cogi powers.*"

"And now you fight so that no other has to suffer as you have. You're noble, Archimedes, to carry such a heavy burden."

The goman slipped his tunic back on as his eyebrows forked in irritation. "*I don't show you this for your pity or honours. Whilst it's true I aim to save humans from suffering the same fate as me, I do confess my motives are also vengeful. I see no other resolution than for every last rakkan to be wiped out; each is as barbaric as the last. And with Darius, that end is in sight. Once I retrieve the location of the mine from his head, their only kuraminium supply will be ours. We'll win the war and I can finally be at peace.*"

Nikolaos's heart quickened. A world without rakkans in sight. "What do you see of Darius?"

"*We'll see him again somewhere south.*"

Unable to contain himself, Nikolaos jumped to his feet. They would head south at once.

33

Darius sat in the dark cave with Lex still one step from death whilst lying against his lap. He focused on the icy film crawling up his arm. *Stop.*

It didn't obey, but he wouldn't let it beat him this time.

Stop, damn it.

Still paying no heed, the algor crawled to his neck. He growled under his breath and clenched his fist. The spread faltered, as if wary of approaching his snarling mouth. Darius growled all the more. It retreated a fraction and he stretched out his arm, willing the algor back. Familiar warmth prickled his skin as the algor receded, first past the shoulder, then the elbow, until only his hand flared blue in a fist of triumph.

He'd done it; after so long trying, it was responding to him. *Control.* Just like balancing a ball on the back of his hand.

Darius sighed, watching the whisker of light that flickered through the thin gap in the cave's covering. Over the course of the day, a thin ray of sunlight had traced its way across the floor. Soon the sun would be setting again. *Thank the heavens.* The light made it that much easier for Archimedes's men to find their hiding hole.

He took Lex's wrist again and felt her pulse, still slow but strong. Another shake didn't rouse her and butterflies continued to flutter in his stomach as they had all night and morning. What if she never woke? What if her heart rate halved again like it had in the night, giving him cold sweats? And why was he having such a reaction to people dying?

Closing his eyes, Darius resolved to get some rest, if not sleep. Deep breaths. She'd wake.

As if answering his prayers, Lex twitched. Her fingers moved, gently touching his arm as he held her wrist.

"Are you awake?" he asked.

She sighed and snuggled a little closer. "No."

Darius grinned, too relieved for the moment that she wasn't dead to reprimand her for being so reckless. They sat in silence for a while, and he tried to string together the words he needed to ask her about what had been circling his mind all night.

"I worried over you." He tensed as he spoke, like he was lowering a shield and exposing himself.

Lex flared algor in her eyes, lighting up their immediate surroundings. A smirk played about her lips. "You think some drops can kill me?"

Was she joking or did she really believe that? She'd risked her life, and his own, for what? So he could spend a night desperately clinging to her hand for signs of life, clinging to the hand that had killed Omid?

"I'm so angry I could wring your neck," he said. "Yet I know it would hurt me all the more if I did. I don't understand these feelings."

"You're angry that Omid's dead?" Lex squeezed his arm a little tighter, to comfort him or to prevent him striking her?

"Yes. Why am I? The boy should mean nothing to me."

"Because you cared. You know what Archimedes did to him wasn't right."

She'd conveniently left out her part in that tragedy. "What does that even mean?"

"You know in your heart what it means. No goman can take that from you, they can only make you disconnect from it, which you seem fairly adept at doing." Her voice had become taut but she still sat in his embrace.

"I wish I understood. Omid reminds me of…" He hesitated, letting his voice trail off. Should he tell her about that single memory still lurking inside?

"Of what?"

"Of my brother. I think it's the name."

Lex's breathing paused. "You remember something?"

"It's the only thing I recall. I guess Archimedes left it there to haunt me, if it's true."

"You never told me exactly what happened, but I know the gist. I can try to verify."

The more his mind veered towards the memory of Amid's body, the more it revolted at further ruminating. "My brother got killed. It was messy."

"That's it?"

"That's all you're getting."

"Tell me." She squeezed his arm again.

"No!" His forehead was burning up. Why did she have to make him think of the past?

"Well, I know that did happen. And your reluctance to talk about it is very *Darius*."

He breathed deep again, trying to figure out why he'd even begun talking about this. It only stirred useless emotion. Maybe he'd gained some favour by being open with her. Perhaps she'd return the favour. It was time to root out the reason she'd plunged herself into oblivion last night.

"It was reckless of you to take so many tears. Your heart barely beat at one point."

Lex frowned. "I'm surprised it still has the will to beat." She slipped his arm off her shoulder and stood.

It hadn't taken him long to strike a nerve.

"I'm being serious," Darius said, remaining hunched against the wall.

"So am I." Weariness etched shadows across her face. She looked almost ready to crawl into her own grave. "I was in a lot of pain, after everything that happened in the square. I just wanted peace for a few hours."

"Do you have a death wish?"

Lex picked up her sword and squeezed the hilt as if embracing a long-lost friend. "I'm not ready to die yet."

Was she so sorry to be alive she had to block out the pain? Was the fear of getting hurt why she treated everyone either like a tool to be exploited or as a means to an end? Except Omid. Darius had never seen her treat Omid like that, despite the boy being her slave. And then she'd killed him. Darius couldn't connect the two.

He shook his head. "Say we somehow manage to take down Archimedes. Get my memory back and kill him. What will you do then? Take a whole vial of those tears and end it all?"

Lex's eyes narrowed. "It's not just Archimedes I need to punish."

"Who else? The Viridian Legion?" Darius recalled how she'd looked at the legionnaire at the farm, how much hate she'd bore. He knew how she felt; he felt it too. Just imagining those vacuous eyes brought a sickness to his stomach.

"I swore to my husband's grave I wouldn't stop until I'd wiped that filth out."

"And I was helping you?" Maybe she was still groggy enough to give him more crumbs of information.

"Yes, you were most useful."

That was probably the nicest thing she'd ever said about him, even if it was about his former self.

Darius stood and grunted as his thigh reminded him it had an arrow-shaped hole in it. He'd bandaged it during the night and the bleeding had stopped, but it still ached as much as his shoulder.

"It doesn't make sense," he said. "Archimedes fights the Viridian Legion, and so do you—we. Why fight him? Why not wait until he wipes them out or dies trying?"

"You gave me another way to take out the legion." For some reason, she looked ashamed. She turned and slithered through the cave's narrow entrance.

Darius followed her into the bushes outside. "I did?" He was flattered to have earned the loyalty of such a fearsome woman.

"*You* convinced me to join you to fight Archimedes. But don't forget that goman took my son. The sooner he doesn't breathe, the better." Lex sat and pulled some flatbread Nasrin had given them from her bag. "Do you remember the square we saw Archimedes in yesterday?"

"With the fountain of the winged woman?"

"Yes. Do you know who that woman is?"

Darius thought back to his conversation with Nasrin, remembering that she'd said it was important to Lex. "Dianoia, the mind that created the world."

Lex's eyes widened with surprise. "Yes."

For a moment she studied him as if his eyes would tell her how he knew it. Her expression finally softened. He hoped that meant he'd won some favour with Nasrin's titbit of knowledge.

"In the fountain," Lex continued, "Dianoia reaches out to her husband, Agathos, for justice in a world of cruelty. For years I searched for my boy, until so much time had passed I wouldn't have recognised him even if I did find him."

"What happened?" Darius sat on the grass in front of her.

"We were in the square." Lex turned her head and stared at a pair of fallen leaves wrestling in the wind.

No wonder Lex had been so distressed. Watching Omid in Archimedes's clutches must have brought it all flooding back for her. Darius stared in silence at her beautiful but solemn face, still avoiding his gaze. He could think of nothing appropriate to say.

"Archimedes took him," Lex said, "as punishment for my father's hesitation in supplying men for his cause." She took a bite from the bread that she'd all but squeezed into a ball in her hand.

Darius wanted to say something, do something to comfort her, but was afraid she'd bite off his head.

"I tore the city apart for three days and nights," Lex said, still chewing the lump of bread. "But that monster is artful at making his recruits disappear." She spat out the bread and threw the rest into dirt.

"If you'd had a shot at your son, like Omid, would you have taken it?"

"Yes."

The swift reply surprised him. She'd obviously thought about it before, perhaps before even meeting Omid.

"I wasn't searching to bring my son back. I was searching to end his misery. I've seen how Archimedes's Numbered are, stripped of their humanity. At the first sign of regaining it, they're stripped again. When they're so young even a goman can't bring them back."

Was it really an act of kindness then, what she had done to Omid? Darius wanted to believe it, and part of him already did. What Archimedes had done made his blood boil. That goman stole everything Darius was, everything he would have been, then sucked out Omid's mind and stole away the only remaining person Darius cared for. Lex may have been lying and spinning a web he was all too eager to leap into, but surely no one could mimic sweating blood or the deep sorrow that had filled her eyes the night before. He had to believe her.

Lex stood and sighed, looking keen to get away and end the conversation. But he couldn't leave it on such a defeated note.

"Lex." Darius rose to his feet and she met his gaze, as if wary of what his next words would be. And what words could he choose?

"I don't care what it takes," he said, "or what it costs. We're going to find Archimedes, and he's going to pay for what he's done to us. You'll have your justice, god or no god. I'm going to run a sword through his gut and rip a hole in that face of his so I can hear him scream when I twist the blade."

Lex closed her eyes and pressed her forehead to his chin. "Darius."

34

Darius leaned back against a tree and closed his eyes as the cool night's wind washed over his face. It was pitch black and time to leave. Lex had planned all along for Nasrin to meet them with horses, and hopefully Tiro would guide her to them safely.

They'd ride south to Denehill and reclaim his memories with the help of the Waif Magician. He couldn't imagine how it would feel to suddenly become a different person, but anything had to be better than being on the run and having his allies picked off one by one.

"As soon as we get to the next town we'll join the Royal Roads," Lex said. "We'll be in Denehill before sundown tomorrow."

Darius sighed and stroked Lyra lying beside him. One of the few things still floating around in his mind, the Roads were the official courier and messenger routes between the cities. Relays of horses on flat stone and mortar roads meant swift travel. He guessed Lex's algus status granted her access to it, though to use it so close to Laltos was risky. If Archimedes found him, he'd end up like Omid, or worse.

"Can I ask you a favour?" he said, barely able to make out her silhouetted head in the darkness.

"I'm listening."

"Don't hesitate if he gets me. I don't want to end up like Parisa or Omid. If my mind is too far gone, can you…" *Why is it so difficult to say?* He swallowed and tried again. "I don't want to see it coming. Make it quick."

Lex stood so still he had to squint to be sure she hadn't vanished into the shadows.

"Only if there's no hope," she said.

"What do you mean 'no hope'? You just split Omid's head…" He couldn't even finish the sentence. Did she refuse because Darius was actually asking for it?

"Omid was a child. He was gone, and I can't let you die, not as long as there's even the smallest hope."

"You really want whatever was in my head. My grandfather?"

"More than anything."

"Why?"

He waited for an answer, but none came. The silence made it easy to hear a horse neigh in the distance. Not daring to assume it was Nasrin, Darius rose and drew his sword, straining his eyes to make out any movement.

Lex released a weak flash of algor that soon faded while Darius hobbled away, putting enough distance between them that they'd stand a chance if the horse's owner wasn't friendly and sent a barrage of arrows.

Steps clapped through the mud. The four rhythmic hooves of a horse and another pair of light footsteps. Just the one pair. He risked a little hope. Soon a light flickered between the leaves of the trees, a clay lamp held just over head height.

Once free of the foliage, the lamp cast light onto the patchy white and brown coat of a horse and Nasrin's unmistakable dark bushy hair.

Darius started towards her. By the scared look on her face, his sudden movement had given her a fright so he slowed his approach.

"Hello?" she called.

"It's us, Nasrin," Darius said.

If anything, she looked more afraid at the sound of his voice, but she lowered the lamp a little.

Lex emerged from the darkness to Nasrin's left and grabbed the girl by the neck with the speed of a pouncing cat. Darius rushed over, fearing the algus would tear Nasrin's throat out.

"How did Archimedes know about Omid, Nasrin?" Lex hissed. "Did you let him be seen through the window?"

The girl dropped the lamp, spilling oil over the ground. Her eyes welled with tears, but she didn't resist. It was as if she'd come knowing this would happen.

"Stop it, Lex," Darius said, trying to wedge an arm between them. "This won't bring Omid back."

The veins on Nasrin's forehead and neck bulged as Lex squeezed tighter. Still, the girl didn't raise a hand to try and loosen the chokehold.

"Enough!" Darius grabbed Lex's hands and prised them from the girl's neck. For all that spiel about right and justice, he couldn't let Lex give in to her anger and take it out on Nasrin. Lex wasn't innocent in this either. But Archimedes was to blame, and he'd pay.

Nasrin coughed and choked on her tears, her voice hoarse as she whispered an explanation. "I don't know how they found Omid. The shutters were closed, yet they just forced their way inside before I could react. I'm sorry!"

"Are we safe to travel the roads?" Darius moved to stand between the pair. "How many men does Archimedes have searching for us? And where?"

"...I'm sorry."

"Nasrin, focus!"

She bent and picked up the lamp, blinking a few times to clear the tears. "I heard Archimedes is to leave at dawn and take the Royal Roads. Scouts are already searching outside the city. I was lucky to make it out without being seen."

Lex began stripping her weapons and attaching them to the horse's saddle. "He could be headed anywhere, but I'll wager he knows where we're going."

"You only brought one horse?" Darius tugged at his hair, welcoming the pain in his scalp as it distracted him from the ever-tightening web they were caught in.

"I couldn't take more," Nasrin said. "And that's no mere horse. It's a swift."

It sure looked like a horse. Whatever it was, it'd have to do.

"We'll have a few hours' lead on Archimedes. That'll be enough," he said hopefully. He wasn't as concerned over scouts. Those he stood a chance fighting against.

Lex grabbed the saddle and leapt on the swift's back.

"Will you be safe heading back alone in the dark?" Darius asked Nasrin.

"I'll be fine," she said with a forced smile. "The rakkans will know Archimedes is in Laltos. They won't dare come this close."

"I hope you're right. It was brave of you to come meet us." And not just due to the threat of rakkans.

Nasrin turned without waiting for a farewell from Lex and vanished into the trees.

"Get on," Lex called, sliding forward on the saddle.

"I don't know horses, but that doesn't look built for two."

She shrugged. "We'll fit. I have a small posterior."

"I hadn't noticed," he lied.

Darius grabbed the saddle with his good arm and hauled himself up. It was a tight fit. Lex's backside pressed into his groin, sending a nervous flutter through his stomach.

"This won't be comfortable," she said. "We'll have to ride hard."

"My thigh will be thankful for any rest it gets." He wrapped an arm around her waist. Their bodies squashed together as he pulled himself close. The horse stamped a hoof and Darius gulped. "Can this thing ride when it's so dark?"

"He'll be fine once we get on the road. And don't hold me with that arm."

Darius quickly retracted it to his side. "I just didn't want to fall off."

"No," she turned a cheek towards him, "I meant use the other arm."

Darius lifted his other elbow slightly and winced. "But that shoulder still hurts."

"Then take a drop of tears. I want your strong arm free for your sword." She held up a hand with the vial.

"Thanks." Darius snatched the tube and uncorked it. He'd been wary about taking too many but the thought of hours on horseback holding on with a recently dislocated shoulder was enough to sway him.

"One drop," Lex said, like he needed advice on dosage from *her*.

Darius carefully measured a drop onto the back of his hand then sucked the bitter liquid off.

"Do you ever grow used to that foul taste?" he asked.

"Not really."

After tucking the vial away, Darius adjusted his sword belt, ensuring the hilt was within easy reach of his strong arm. He wrapped his other arm around Lex's waist, feeling her stomach rise and fall as she breathed. Being so close to her, he didn't know whether to be relaxed or nervous.

"Will Lyra be able to keep up?"

"No. She'll have to follow as best she can and meet us near Denehill."

You heard her. Stay safe, girl. Pace yourself.

"Let's ride," he said.

They set off and raced through the darkness atop the mighty beast. Now he saw why it wasn't a mere horse. At first Darius held his breath at the sensation of so much raw muscle thundering beneath him, but awe soon faded to weariness of the endless dark and the rocking gait. A low-hanging branch would take off his head at this pace. He prayed the horse saw better than him.

It didn't take them long to join the road. Once upon the hard surface, Lex unleashed the full power of her steed. He'd thought algus ran fast, but this was something else, as if the creature possessed the same powers they did.

Lamps suspended beside tiny outposts flew past like fireflies as Darius clung to Lex, trying to keep a vague sense of the minutes and hours passing. It wasn't long before the dotted lights of a town appeared ahead.

"We change steed here, at Patros," Lex shouted above the drumming hooves. "It's tiring."

Not for the first time, the back of his thigh seized with a cramp. Wincing, Darius jerked it straight and prayed Archimedes's men weren't awaiting them at the town.

35

Brutus stepped across the bare room in the bowels of the Margalvia arena. He handed Varro a twin set of blades with a grunt of encouragement. The warrior took the hilts of the fine kuraminium swords, every muscle on his bare forearms bulging as he clutched them. Varro wore only trousers and boots. No armour or shields were allowed in a challenge for either party.

Now that he'd talked his younger brother into it, Brutus was beginning to have second thoughts. Varro was the most skilled fighter Brutus had seen in over a hundred years, one of the few rakkans that rivalled an algus singlehanded. But this was Catonius he was facing, warlord for twenty years, an honour defended against a dozen challenges. Now Varro was to fight him one on one to the death. So many things could go awry.

However, this fight was a necessary one. Catonius was a poor leader and had ordered Darius dead—they already called him a traitor in the streets, which pained Brutus as he'd watched the boy grow up loving Margalvia.

"You can do this, brother," Brutus said.

"Can I?"

The thundering of feet echoed from above as the crowd stamped in anticipation of the coming fight. Sweat dripped down Varro's bare chest. Even his blond hair looked damp.

"I believe in you," Brutus said. "But if not, I'll see you in the afterlife."

36

Wafts of manure attacked Darius's nostrils and he coughed as they rode up to the stable. The place looked as if it hadn't been mucked out for at least a day.

"You there," Lex called to a lanky man sitting against a wall with a flat cap tilted across his eyes. "Are you the stable-hand?"

"That I am," said the man, lazily rising from his wooden stool. "And who might you be?"

Lex leapt from the swift and landed with a flick of algor from her hair.

The man removed his cap and bowed. "Apologies, algus. I thought—"

"I have urgent business," Lex said, already unfastening her belongings. "Bring me two fresh swifts."

Darius scanned for signs of anyone else. The stable and nearby town appeared quiet, not surprising considering the time of night. He dismounted and grunted as his weight collapsed onto his injured leg.

"Algus, we have no swifts, only shire horses." The man shuffled towards the stable. "Two algus have already been here yesterday."

Archimedes's men on the hunt, with more likely following. Darius needed to be ready to fight. He flexed his stiff muscles as he waited for their new mounts.

"Then I'll take the reserve." Lex's voice dropped to a forceful tone.

"Reserve? No, only on the King's orders."

"I have the orders."

Somehow, Darius doubted she did.

The man's face grew concerned. "I'll have to wake the master."

"Hurry."

He scurried off towards the house to the side while Lex wandered into the stable.

Anticipating a wait, Darius grabbed bread from their supplies and stuffed his face. He washed the quick meal down with a few gulps from his waterskin.

Lex emerged with a new horse, this time white, and jogged towards him, already hooking her weapons to its saddle.

"Get on," she said with one foot in a stirrup.

Darius loaded their bags and jumped on. His backside barely touched the leather before Lex whipped the reins and sent the swift forward.

He grabbed her collar just in time to stop himself tumbling backwards. "Lex! Give me a second."

The swift picked up speed and Darius wrapped his bad arm around her waist.

"I take it you stole this?" he yelled above the rushing wind.

"No choice."

He glanced back but the stable was long gone. That stable-hand had seen her face despite the night.

"Will they give chase?" Darius asked in Lex's ear.

"Soon enough."

With Lex now in more danger than ever, Darius found himself becoming increasingly worried for her, as well as for his escort. He hoped Lyra wasn't far behind, and didn't get caught by those that would soon ride in pursuit.

37

Nikolaos stood in the grimy dungeon, trying his best to ignore the other two sweaty bodies at the far side, prisoner and torturer. He brushed a finger down his cheek and smeared more pale gum to cover the hideous purple and green bruising. A few more dabs and only subtle hints remained on that dashing face in the cracked mirror, though it was hard to tell by the dim candlelight. Still, he wanted to look his best. No need to display the fact he'd been beaten in Laltos.

A rakkan's cry of agony echoed from the walls as he struggled against the chains. The heavy-handed torturer, Thirty-seven, cracked the beast in the jaw with an iron post.

"Quiet, please," Nikolaos said. He needed time to think and this suffocating room made it difficult. One never got used to the smell of sweat and blood.

Thirty-seven huffed and kicked at the naked rakkan.

Archimedes would arrive at the outpost any minute and Nikolaos needed to show results. They'd captured this rakkan less than a league from Denehill whilst hot on Darius's trail. If Nikolaos extracted valuable information from the prisoner it would secure his position as leader of the Laltos Guard.

Unfortunately, pain never seemed to work in breaking a rakkan, at least not one that had any useful information. He had to be smarter.

Nikolaos turned and looked the rakkan in the eyes, his huge black irises still defiant. Such strength was admirable given the hours of torture. Thick kuraminium shackles cut rings of blood around the wrists and ankles, the only metal strong enough to withstand a rakkan's monstrous strength.

"Perhaps we should try another nail through his last remaining fingertip," Thirty-seven said.

Nikolaos looked over the bloodied stumps on the rakkan's hands and shook his head. "He won't talk."

"I already told you, I don't know anything," the rakkan said weakly to his beautiful torturer.

Thirty-seven knelt and poked an algor-tipped dagger into the rakkan's groin. "Then I'll enjoy being left alone with you, without expectant onlookers." She twisted the blade in and the rakkan howled as blood trickled down his thighs.

Nikolaos winced at the gleeful look in his fellow algus's eyes. It was curious how the Numbered sometimes came to enjoy inflicting harm. Perhaps Archimedes made them savour it to make them more eager. To put it mildly, it wasn't Thirty-seven's personality that attracted Nikolaos. His interests were purely venereal.

As for more important matters, he needed to open this rakkan another way. Time to play the benevolent partner to the sadist.

"Didn't you hear me say enough?" He walked over and slapped Thirty-seven across the cheek.

She scowled but backed off, unable to respond to an outranking algus.

Nikolaos knelt down to speak with the rakkan at eye level. "She won't hurt you any further."

The rakkan eyed him nervously, but look relieved his torturer had been rebuked.

"Here, have some water." Nikolaos took a cup and held it to the prisoner's mouth. The rakkan guzzled it down, probably hoping it was poison to end his suffering.

"What's your name?" Nikolaos asked.

"Ennius."

"Well, Ennius, I take it you don't know anything of where Darius is heading, or where the kuraminium mine is?"

Ennius shook his head. "No idea."

"What city are you from?"

The rakkan narrowed his eyes with suspicion.

"This isn't a trick. Surely it's no secret where you're from?" Nikolaos kept his tone friendly, hoping this attempt to build a rapport through simple questions would work.

"Margalvia."

Nikolaos had guessed as much. It was the nearest city to Denehill, though still some ways away. "You're a long way from home."

"Looking for food."

Odd. Reports said a large supply convoy was hijacked only days ago. It would feed the city for a while, unless they were stockpiling for something.

"You don't look so starved," Nikolaos said.

"I do as I'm ordered." Ennius gave a slight shake of the head, a subliminal clue that made Nikolaos smile. Discontentment with leadership perhaps? He could work with that.

"Don't we all," Nikolaos said with a sigh, then he leaned in and lowered his voice. "Sometimes those in command become too distracted."

Ennius scoffed. "That's one way of putting it."

"And how would you put it?"

"Doesn't matter. Soon, our warlord may be de—" Ennius's eyes widened then he snapped his mouth shut.

Nikolaos puzzled over that small clue. Had Ennius been about to say "dead?" Sounded like their leader was in mortal danger. The algus were nowhere close so it must have been from illness or mutiny, but which? Ennius wasn't certain, which suggested a power struggle. That would mean the leadership of Margalvia was temporarily weak, which made it ripe for an attack.

It wasn't a lead on Darius or the mine, but it was something he could take to Archimedes. Intelligence that led to the fall of a city was sure to secure Nikolaos's position as head of the Laltos Guard.

"This is what you summoned me for?" Archimedes's voice boomed.

Nikolaos jumped. The dreadlocked figure emerged from the narrow spiral stairway, unusually bereft of his Numbered guards.

"With every passing minute, Darius could be fleeing farther from our grasp."

"He has valuable information." Nikolaos straightened from his crouch. "The Margalvians are fighting over the leadership."

Ennius's horrified face told him he'd guessed right.

"That's what he said? Surely any fool knows that torture only elicits lies at best."

"It wasn't torture that drew it out of him." It was frustrating that rakkans were immune to Archimedes's powers over the mind. His abilities would make life easier.

"Then how?"

"I was gentle, lured him into a slip of the tongue."

Archimedes raised an eyebrow. *"Impressive, but it doesn't help us find Darius."*

"We should head to Denehill. We heard a swift was stolen by a female algus on the Royal Roads so we've tracked them. It must be the traitor. We'll have them soon, and, once we do, there are enough algus stationed in Denehill to raise an army quickly and attack Margalvia. We can besiege the city in only a few days' time."

"*You think the leadership contest will sufficiently distract them?*"

"It did when we razed Gerunda," Thirty-seven said.

Archimedes seemed to weigh the idea. "*I'll consider our options once we reach Denehill.*"

"You can leave this rakkan to me and we'll have some fun." Thirty-seven smirked at Ennius, her fingers playing with the dagger she held. Its blade still dripped blood.

Archimedes motioned to her. "*No. Leave us at once and head for Denehill.*"

The algus frowned at the goman's dismissal but left as ordered.

"*I don't like it when they become so sadistic. They remind me too much of the rakkans we fight.*"

"You don't make them like that?"

"*No. I need obedience, not monsters.*"

For all Archimedes's pitiless actions, Nikolaos had never seen him enjoy causing pain like Thirty-seven. The goman was driven by the end goal, defeat of the rakkans, and would stop at nothing to achieve it. His cruelty always seemed to come from indifference. Those that enjoyed the suffering of others had their uses, but a good leader knew the time and place.

"Should I begin rallying troops?"

"*Yes. Gather as many of the algus as you can and head south of Denehill. There's a chance we'll meet Darius on the Uxon Trail.*"

"You've seen it?"

The goman raised his eyebrows. "*I have, though it isn't clear. In a gorge adorned with crystals.*"

Nikolaos didn't recognize the description, but few algus were familiar enough with the trail to the rakkan lands to know where that place may lie. Not that it mattered. They'd search until they found it.

"Any insights on the algus assisting Darius?" It was almost painful to think one of their own was aiding the man.

"*I've now seen who it is.*"

Nikolaos started. "Who?" It was probably one of the southerners. Surely it couldn't be one of Laltos's own algus. "We'll hunt the traitor down. I can spare twenty algus from the Laltos Guard. We can take their family, lure them out that way."

"*No. I want all algus pursuing Darius.*"

"But we need to make an example of them. The algus will want immediate action, all of the traitor's friends and family rounded up in case the betrayal runs deeper."

"*No. I'd rather keep the algus focused on preparing to face Darius. You'll see who the traitor is for yourself soon enough.*"

He could understand keeping the others focused on Darius, but surely Archimedes had to tell someone. If Nikolaos crossed paths with the traitor he wouldn't hesitate to gut them.

"Can you at least tell me——?"

"*No. The consequences will be far-reaching and distracting. Our window to catch Darius is slim. For now, it stays with me.*"

It must have been someone important. The rest of the algus would be in uproar. Hopefully it wasn't one of Nikolaos's own family.

He pushed away that thought, unwilling to contemplate such a betrayal.

"I'll finish off this rakkan and head out."

Archimedes eyed Ennius with an unusual look of sadness. "*Pitiful rakkan. I look forward to the end of this war when I can join him in a serene exit from this painful world. We're close to winning this.*"

Nikolaos didn't say a word, didn't even look at the goman. He needed to retrain his focus onto Darius. His men couldn't be more than a day behind the fugitive.

38

Darius hobbled along a small patch of grass. His knees struggled to bend with each step, stiff from so many days atop horse after horse. *How far away is Archimedes?* It couldn't be far.

Behind him, the sun peeked over the towering snow-capped mountains whose high peaks guarded the valley they waited in.

Darius studied the outer walls of Denehill as the morning light brushed over them. They stood high and thick, with scars and blackened chunks cleft from the stone. Denehill had seen its fair share of battle. He'd thought Laltos was forbidding, but Denehill's walls made Lex's home city look like a wooden fort. This was a fortress, and with good reason. The city stood as the gatekeeper to the plains they'd just travelled across. Anything moving from the south had to come through this valley, and therefore through Denehill.

A soft breeze swept through the reeds in the bow lake next to him. They'd stopped amidst a scattering of trees with a willow standing at the centre. Its slender branches dipped into the water, forming tiny ripples as the wind stirred them.

Here was where Nasrin had said she'd met the Waif Magician. They'd already hung a dead mouse they'd caught from a branch, for whatever bizarre reason. It hopefully wouldn't be long now until he was whole again, his full fighting ability restored. Then he'd hunt down the mouthless fiend.

The lush green foliage hugging the lake stood in stark contrast against the bare hills beyond. Now that they'd stopped, Lyra could finally catch up. Darius kept scanning their surroundings for a sign of the panther. He longed to stroke her soft fur again. His own clothes were hard with congealed dirt and sweat. The soft lap of water on the lake's shore beckoned. His skin would enjoy the cool touch of cleansing water and the thigh wound needed cleaning too; it was starting to smell.

"Any wolf-fish in that lake?" Darius asked Lex, who sat near the shore.

She glanced away from the water and shook her head. "No, but I wouldn't be so eager for a swim. That water is not long from the mountains; it's cold as ice in the morning."

The cold would wake him up, and one of them needed to keep watch while the other got some much needed rest, but his already seizing muscles couldn't take more stiffness. Darius cast the water one last glance before turning away. He'd have to stay dirty.

"You can rest. I'll keep an eye out," he said, sitting down next to Lex. "It's day, so no rakkans at least. Your hip looked like it needs a respite."

Lex's gaze dropped to her lap and Darius realised his hand was grasping her thigh. She looked back up at him and stared, clearly unsettled.

With a nervous cough, Darius gave her thigh a friendly squeeze then pulled his hand away. His heart-rate picked up. Why had he done that? He didn't even remember being with a woman, how to act, what it was like to touch, to kiss.

Lex still stared. "Fine. I'll rest." The algus shuffled down until she lay almost flat, her head leaning on a tree root. "You're wrong about rakkans though. They can come in the day, they just prefer the night."

That didn't help calm his heart. "Good to know. Sweet dreams." Darius sat forward to make sure he didn't doze off and took in their surroundings more carefully, noting every bush capable of obscuring an assassin and every visible route towards them. As Lex slept, he wouldn't be caught unawares, and he wouldn't be caught staring at her thigh, either. Forcing his eyes away from her leg, he gave his own a sharp pinch of warning. Enemies weren't the only thing he needed to remain alert for. His own heart seemed determined to betray him as well.

***

Darius's sword screeched as it clashed with Lex's, sparks of algor flying. He pushed her away and re-adjusted his stance. Having one bad leg made practising all the harder.

"Don't lose focus. Keep your arms strong," Lex said.

He could coat his sword in algor now but it still required a lot of concentration. That wasn't good enough; it needed to be second nature.

"Again," he said.

Lex lowered her sword. "Let's take a break."

Darius sighed. They'd been at it a while but the skill wasn't ingrained yet. At least it offered a distraction from the unending wait. Who knew when, or if, the Waif Magician would surface? Lex had said the woman was a ghost, on the run from the algus her entire life. With enemies on their tail, it reduced the likelihood they'd ever find her.

Lyra had re-joined them and lay sleeping under the tree. He'd wait a few days at most, then head to Margalvia if there was still no sight of the Magician.

He sat on a patch of grass with Lex sat opposite, staring into nothingness while clutching the pendant around her neck. Darius caught her gaze a few times and she eventually stopped avoiding his. She seemed somewhat comforted by his watchful eyes since he'd sworn to cut a hole in Archimedes's chest.

Darius leaned in to get a closer look at the pendant cupped in her hand. "You touch that a lot."

She frowned and looked down at it. "Do I?"

"What is it?"

Lex plucked the chain from around her neck and tossed it to him. "See for yourself."

He held the light metal up. It was a silver figure of a man, no larger than a coin but so detailed Darius could barely discern all the intricate carving. It looked like it was worth more than everything on his person. The man held an axe in one hand and a set of balancing scales in the other, a vaguely familiar symbol.

"Justice," he said. "Agathos?"

"He judges with balance and punishes the guilty."

"You've seen him?"

"No."

Then why believe he existed? Where was he to punish Archimedes? To punish Lex?

Darius tossed back the pendant. "You really believe those stories?"

"I do," she said, looping the necklace around her slender neck.

"And the trees being sacred? The curses of the forest?"

"No. They're just superstitions."

He smirked. "But yours aren't?"

Lex's eyes narrowed. "Careful, Darius. I never tolerated your mockery before and I still won't."

He used to mock her? Old Darius really was brave.

"I'm not mocking, I just don't understand. Why one and not the others? Why are yours true but not Omid's"—it still felt numbing to say the name—"Omid's gods."

She shrugged. "Mine are plausible."

"More so? If your Agathos, God of Justice, exists, why do *we* suffer such injustice? Why does an innocent child like Omid get caught by that goman? Seems Agathos either doesn't care or isn't so powerful."

Lex stood slowly. "Or the judgment hasn't begun. We're given free will to do both good and evil."

"He could stop the injustice, stop a young boy getting killed."

"And make us what? Puppets like Archimedes's minions? Wouldn't you rather be free, capable of choice, of love?"

He supposed that was true, but he wasn't really thinking of himself as the target of judgement. Maybe she had a point. It was what he'd been fighting for all this time, his freedom to choose who he was and not be a mere vessel of Archimedes's will.

A bird soared towards them from the east and soon Darius made out Tiro's arched wings and spotted breast. The peregrine swooped down beside Lex, a folded scrap of parchment tied to his leg. Darius hadn't seen him since they'd hit the Royal Roads.

"You sent word to someone?" It couldn't be the Waif Magician.

Nodding, Lex bent and retrieved the message.

"Why didn't you say? Who?"

"Our allies in Margalvia. I didn't think it worth mentioning." The algus unrolled the parchment.

Darius scowled. What would it take for her to trust him enough to share the small things? "Brutus?"

She scanned the note. "Yes. He'll meet us on the Uxon Trail when we're done."

The road to Margalvia, just as he'd hoped. He caught a glimpse of the parchment's corner. The note was written in unfamiliar characters. Brutus hadn't spoken another language and he hadn't heard one spoken anywhere. Was the message encoded, then?

"Can I see it?"

Lex raised an eyebrow. "You don't believe me?"

She was annoyingly seductive when she looked at him like that. He wanted to believe her, but a little evidence wouldn't hurt considering she had barely mentioned Brutus until now and he was beginning to doubt she really knew the burly warrior. However, if the note was written in code, he wouldn't understand it and she likely wouldn't explain it. Better to feign trust.

"No, of course I trust you." It took effort not to lapse into sarcasm. "I'm still here after you killed Omid, aren't I?"

"I'm not..." Her sigh sounded more frustrated than anything else. "I want to tell you more, but when I try, you don't take it in."

"What do you mean? When have you tried?" As far as he'd seen, she was always cagey.

"I tried in Cephos, then on the road, in Laltos. I've tried saying it, writing it. You wince, grasp your head then don't seem to recall anything I've been saying." She stepped closer and took his hand in hers.

Darius did recall occasional headaches throughout the journey. He couldn't remember any skipping of time, but if she spoke the truth he'd be none the wiser.

"So you're saying I'm incapable of hearing something? That you're lying to me?"

"No." She squeezed his hand gently, as though trying to comfort him. "I just can't seem to tell you the real reason why we're fighting, who you are."

"I thought we were rebels, fighting against Archimedes kidnapping children and turning them into his personal army."

"We are, but that's not the whole story."

Darius pulled away and turned towards the lake, once so tranquil and open but now rippling under the force of an icy wind. The cold crept into his chest. "This is just *great*."

"You're—"

Pain shot through his temple and he grasped his forehead. By the time it had dissipated and the ringing in his ears ceased, Lex was standing in front of him, one eyebrow raised as she studied his face.

"You see?" she said.

He couldn't recall her moving, and the wind had died down a bit. Something *was* blocking his mind. What was she trying to tell him?

"I've tried writing, hinting. Nothing works, but the Waif Magician will be able to help."

"I hope—"

A tawny owl caught his eye. It sat on a branch of the willow, picking at the dead mouse. *How long has it been there?* He hadn't seen it before or heard it, though that wasn't surprising for an owl.

Lex frowned and turned in the direction he stared.

"That's hers," she said.

"The Waif Magician's?" An owl escort would certainly suit a reclusive figure. Silent in flight and hearing second to none.

"It must be. We'll follow it," Lex's voice dropped to a murmur, so quiet he didn't think she wanted him to hear, "and hope we don't run into Brutus."

"Why are you worried about Brutus?"

"Let's just say he won't be best pleased about us going to see her. I'd rather he didn't know."

It wasn't just him she kept secrets from then. "We'll take care." *Lyra, let's go.*

They hurriedly gathered their few possessions before the owl finished its meal and took off. It flew away from the lake, leading the way up a dirt trail that ran through the large stony valley. Darius had expected to play catch up with the bird, but it maintained a slow glide overhead as if purposely guiding them. He didn't know whether to be relieved or concerned.

"We're not taking the horse?" Darius asked, glancing back at the beast grazing by the lake.

"The terrain gets too rocky. It's faster on foot."

"That's if you've got two good legs." His injured one still caused him to limp, but he kept pace with her as they walked along.

The hardened dirt trail soon became littered with loose rocks. As it started to slope upwards, Darius could feel his wounded thigh begin to burn from the exertion.

Most of the trail ahead was hidden behind a ridge but he had no doubt it would be steep. The valley ran deep, with sheer cliffs flanking it in the distance. At the top of the ridge stood a mound and wooden post. A banner hung from the pole, probably marking the start of the lands of Denehill. He knew the Uxon Trail led to Margalvia, but who knew how far away the city was. How long would it take them to get there after they met with the Magician?

More importantly, would she be able to help him as he hoped?

"What's this Magician like?" Darius asked. He'd like some idea of what they were walking into. "She has some special power?"

"Hardly. Her name comes from exaggerated stories." Lex took a sip from her waterskin. "Half-goman, half-human. That's why her parents were hunted down and killed. She and her brothers escaped but only she remains."

Which meant gomans *could* be killed. "If she's only half-goman, is she less powerful than Archimedes?"

"I don't know. Her goman powers don't sound diminished and she's one of the lucky few born with algor as well."

Goman powers with the speed of an algus? This Magician sounded even more threatening than Archimedes. Darius's lost memories and abilities better be worth the risk.

The trail passed through a steep, rocky gorge. Darius clambered over yet another boulder blocking the road, a difficult feat with only one good arm and leg. Lex perched on the rock and grabbed his belt to drag him up.

"Thanks," he said, rolling over the top. "I get the feeling this woman is worse than what we're running from." And if Brutus hated her, he wasn't holding out much hope of her helping him willingly.

"She's our only hope."

"Well, at least she doesn't want to kill me," Darius said with a laugh.

Lex threw him an unamused look. "You really mustn't tell her who you are."

He stopped. "Please don't tell me she wants to kill me."

Lex leaned in and put her mouth to his ear. "She knows the name Darius but she doesn't know what you look like, and she'll have no reason to suspect."

Darius scowled. "Are you the only one in this land that doesn't want me dead?"

"Choose your words carefully or they'll be your last," a woman's voice croaked from a dark crevice to their right.

Darius and Lex both turned, their hands rising to sword hilts in unison. *The Magician. How much did she overhear?*

"Show yourself," Lex called.

"Why are you here?" The woman's voice was high and shrill but had the hack of age, not of a waif.

"I'm Alexandra, daughter of—"

"I know who you are, otherwise I wouldn't have met with you. I asked why, and who is this man you've brought?" She either hadn't heard their conversation or was feigning ignorance.

"We've come to speak with Shirin. We're in need of her assistance."

A silence followed, disturbed only by the gentle wheeze of dust stirred by the wind. The fissure where the speaker lurked was only a couple of feet across. An arrow into the dark had a good chance of hitting the hidden woman if things turned bad.

"Am I right to assume that's who I'm speaking with?" Lex asked.

The soft pats of footsteps came from the crevice and Darius tightened his grip on his sword. A tiny figure eased out into the light, cloaked in shabby charcoal robes. She had no visible weapon. Across her head fell a black veil that failed to contain long locks of deep red hair. The colour was fake, so stark it had to be dye. She stood not much over five feet and was as scrawny as Omid had been. The lines across her brow and crow's feet around her eyes betrayed her old age.

Lyra hissed and bared her teeth.

"I am she," the woman said.

We found her. Hope stirred in Darius's chest, brighter than it had been since he first became aware in that bloody battlefield. All he had to do was not reveal who he was. He flexed his fingers and arms, checking for any signs of weakness. None were present. Perhaps the weakness wasn't a goman thing, but he'd be careful nonetheless not to let her anywhere near him, fearing the touch of those wrinkled hands that could suck out the remnants of his mind.

"My friend Nasrin asked me to find you," Lex said. "She needs—"

The Magician held up a palm. "Hush. We'll talk further from the trail. Follow me." She turned and walked back into the crevice.

Darius and Lex exchanged a glance. She gave a nod and followed the Magician into the darkness. Before he went after them, he looked up at the sunlit sky. *This could be the last time I see the light of day.* He soaked in a little warmth then stepped through the opening, Lyra close behind.

39

The Magician led the way through the dark with a faint tint of algor glowing from her head. The blue light turned her hair a curious shade of purple. This was it; Darius could be only a few steps away from having his memories restored. What would it feel like to suddenly remember?

A razor-sharp rock scraped his elbow and he conjured algor in his palm to shed more light. The crevice was narrow, forking every few steps, and odd glittering crystals lay embedded in the stone. Darius brushed his hand against one of the crystals and it crumbled a little. He licked some of the dust from his finger. *Salt.*

A couple of rats scurried out of their path as they walked. He gave the creatures a wide berth and continued on. Not even Lyra spared the rodents a second glance, though a growl still rumbled in his escort's throat. For some reason, she didn't like this woman.

At last the Magician brought them to an open cavern, walled on one side by a towering face of fractured rock. Cracks spread across it like a spider's web, threatening a collapse. Hunks of rock were scattered around the edge of the cave, along with a few candles. She'd been expecting them, but this wasn't where she lived—too bare.

The taste of salt in the air settled on the tip of his tongue, as if they stood next to an ocean. But unlike the sea, there was no stirring of air here. It weighed heavy, stagnant in his lungs.

The Magician motioned for them to sit on two flat rocks and stood in front of them. In silence she scanned them up and down with hungry eyes, as if wondering how many days their bodies would feed her.

"Thank you for speaking with us," Lex said with a nod.

Lyra paced slowly along the perimeter of the room, amber gaze never leaving the half-goman. The Magician eyed her for a moment then returned to staring at Darius. She'd dismissed the algor and the flickering candlelight made her red hair look ablaze.

"I know that my people have sought you for a long time," Lex said.

"Yes. To kill me." The woman's lips were thin. When pressed together, they seemed to vanish, as though she had no mouth at all.

"I can assure you that had nothing to do with me."

"If it did, you'd already be dead." The Magician crossed her arms, exuding confidence.

She must have been assured in her skills to best both of them should it come to a clash of swords. *How unnerving.*

"So." The Magician narrowed her wise eyes on Darius. "You want me to help this one."

Perceptive. Even more unnerving.

"A goman took my memories," he said, "and I want them back."

"You bear the scars, the half-vacant eyes. Obvious to a goman." She shook her head. "There's nothing I can do; only the one that severed your memories can repair them."

The air drained from Darius's lungs along with his hope. Gomans couldn't lie, which meant she spoke the truth. He'd travelled so far, foolishly let Lex encourage his hope that this Waif Magician could help him, but she couldn't.

"There's nothing you can do?" Lex asked. "Not even undo what the goman did to him, the callousness, the mental blocks?"

"I'm afraid not. He will never be himself unless the goman who did this restores him."

"What about—"

"Never."

What could he do now? Archimedes wouldn't give him his memories back.

Sensing his inner turmoil, Lyra came and rubbed her cheek against his leg. He looked to Lex, expecting to see the same defeat in her expression that he felt inside, but instead she gave him a resolute look that told him she'd go to any length to get his memories back. The fire inside her belly seemed limitless and made him all the more determined himself. He wanted his memories, his ability back. He wanted to be a fierce warrior. He wanted to get revenge on Archimedes the best way he knew. If that meant facing the goman as a weakened Darius, then so be it.

"The goman that took his memories is named Archimedes," Lex began, "and—"

The Magician nodded. "I've heard of him. Where did you last see him?"

"Laltos," Darius replied.

"How many others are there?"

"None that we know of," Lex said. "Apart from Archimedes, there hasn't been a goman in the land for half a century. Not since your family."

A grimace twisted the Magician's thin mouth. "One is one too many. I'd like to see what you've seen for myself." She stepped towards Darius and reached out a hand.

He leapt backwards over the rock and whipped his sword from its sheath.

Lex thrust herself in front of him with a palm outstretched as a snarl rumbled from Lyra's throat.

The old woman paused and retracted her hand. "My, my. Aren't we guarded? Too many secrets left swimming around in there?"

"No offense, but I don't trust the touch of even a half-goman," Darius said, lowering his blade an inch. Not to mention she'd discover who he was, and he didn't want to find out what would happen if she did.

"I just wanted to look, to see what you have seen."

Lex frowned. "Tell us about what you see with your goman powers."

The Magician's wrinkles deepened as she frowned. "Why should I?"

Darius wasn't surprised she didn't want to divulge her abilities. It was surprising how forthcoming she'd been up to now. Something wasn't right; this was all too easy compared to the slog it had been so far. He didn't trust the Magician enough to even blink lest he miss a sudden lunge.

"What do you want? Money? Safety?" Lex paced between them, kicking some loose stones on the ground. "Tell us how to reverse what Archimedes has done and I'll give you anything."

The Magician scowled. "Money can't buy what I want."

"And what's that?" Darius asked.

She turned to him with the vicious eyes of a coiled snake. "The algus, dead. Every last one of the swine. I want humanity to fester without its guardians, torn apart bite by bite by the rakkan hounds at their gates. I want payback for a lifetime running, and this." She ripped back her sleeve to show a semi-circular scar on her forearm, white twisted skin forming half a skull. "The humans branded me for death. Do you know what it's like to spend your life on the run since you were a little girl? To never have a home, never time to mourn your parents, never a moment's rest without wondering when the next bounty hunter will find you?"

Darius looked down at his own arm, still pink from the rakkan's ferven, and imagined the same searing pain he'd felt, only from a branding iron. Half a skull because she was only half worthy of death? He'd been on the run for only a few weeks. Decades of it would be too much to bear.

"I pray every day that it will be another the algus don't find me," the Magician said.

Darius glanced at Lex, who stood still now, her face an unreadable mask. The Magician must have thought from the moment she saw them that they were algus, yet she met them anyway. Was she toying with them?

"You know we're algus," he said. "Are you going to try to kill us?"

The Magician traced a tongue across her thin lips as Lex's hand inched closer to the hilt of her sword.

"If I wanted to kill you, I wouldn't wait."

Darius believed her, but that still left the mystery of why she was answering their questions.

"You should help us," Lex said, her voice a tone louder than before. "We need to stop Archimedes or soon he'll wipe out the rakkans and the algus will win the rakkan war. Now that he has the Staff they can't stand against him. Only we can."

The Magician shifted her stare to Lex and her grin vanished. "What staff?"

"Archimedes found the Staff of Arria."

The woman's eyes widened. For a moment she stood in silence, ruminating. When she spoke again, her voice was calm and controlled. "Fine. I'll answer some of your questions."

"And what do you want in return?" Darius asked.

She sauntered over to a rock between them and sat down with a sigh. "If you succeed, I want the Staff."

Lex turned away, seeming to consider the request. Darius waited with bated breath for her response. The weapon sounded powerful, the source of Archimedes's domination and surely best kept out of foreign hands. Whatever Lex's concerns, it'd be best to lie to the Magician and deal with the consequences if they ever got their hands on the Staff. Perhaps she would pose no threat if they had it.

Lex faced the Magician, fingers still brushing the hilt of her sword. "You think your information worth that?"

The woman sat still, like a spider on her web. "It could make the difference between life and death. I'll tell you about Archimedes's powers and his blind spots."

Darius strolled up to Lex and put his mouth to her ear. "Say you agree. We don't have to give her the Staff."

Lex looked at him with concern, like she'd rather do anything than make an enemy of this woman.

"Deal," Lex said quietly.

Darius had a feeling she was being sincere, though he couldn't ascertain why. The Magician had already stated her intent to wipe out the algus, which included himself and Lex. Why give her a powerful weapon?

"Splendid," the Magician said. "The first thing you should know about the goman art of cogi is that it allows one access to future memories. With it, you can effectively see the future."

Darius and Lex gasped.

"Many possible futures in fact. If you want to defeat Archimedes, understand your task is akin to outmanoeuvring someone that can see five moves ahead. Or a hundred. Depends if he's a long or short cogi."

"And that means?" Lex asked, moving to stand at Darius's side. Her fingers grasped the hilt of her sword firmly now.

"A long cogi can see memories far into the future whereas a short cogi can see only the imminent. We only see at a certain distance, and it is always a range of possible futures. I saw this conversation, though it was a while ago and my memory isn't what it once was. I also saw myself severing both your heads at the willow as you sparred, but like I said, possibilities. Only one becomes actual."

Their situation was more dire than Darius had realised. He should have just asked Lex to bury him there and then by the willow—better than having his hope crushed so thoroughly.

"If you want the Staff, you'd best tell us how to defeat him," Darius said.

The Magician's eyes narrowed. "We see the memories as visions. No sound or feeling or taste. That is the weakness."

"How's it a weakness to see the future?"

"They're *memories*. We see them through our own eyes as we will see things to come. We can't see something from the future if we won't see it *in* the future, like if we're dead or—"

"Blind," Darius said. *A literal blind spot.*

"Yes. Simple in theory."

He leaned forwards, eager to scavenge more details. "Tell us more about this cogi. When you touch someone, how does it work?"

The Magician carefully slid her tattered sleeves up from her wrists. "I'll show you."

A rat scurried across the ground towards the Magician's foot. She snatched it up, swift as any algus he'd seen despite her frail appearance. With her gaze locked onto Darius, she held out the motionless rat in the palm of her hand while the creature remained still as if dead.

"It's alive," she whispered. "I just have complete control of it."

The rat nodded its head, an eerie movement that reminded Darius too much of the puppet motions of the girl in Laltos. He shuddered, his own hand moving to his sword hilt now, for comfort more than anything. Lyra pressed close to his legs, her eyes fixed on the rodent.

"I'm rifling through its memories," the Magician said. "It takes time and it's chaotic—there's no order. I can steal from its tiny mind for myself, but first I must sever memories so it has no knowledge of them."

The rat still stared with vacant black eyes at Darius. *Haunting.*

The Magician chuckled. "If I want it to obey me afterwards, I simply give it false memories, false beliefs. Rats are easy, but humans are much more difficult, beyond my power. And worst of all—"

"There's worse?" Darius growled.

"Oh yes."

A hissing exploded in the room, screeching high as if a hurricane passed through the eye of a needle and straight into his ear. A second later it was gone, leaving only a monotonous ringing.

Darius jabbed a finger in his ear and rubbed. "What the hell was that?"

The Magician dropped the lifeless rat onto the ground with a light thump. "That's worse. When the mind is ripped completely from the body. Ironically, it's the easiest skill to master."

He stared at the dead rat, its feet askew in the air. That could soon be him if Archimedes got his hands on him, or Lyra, or Lex. He had to become stronger. "How do you fight it? How can you block it?"

"There is no way to fight, or block. Not unless you're a rakkan."

"Rakkans are immune to goman powers," Lex said.

"Yes, a curious thing," the Magician said. "Makes them hard to control or kill."

Lex stepped over to Darius and gave him a nudge. "I think it's time we went to meet our friend. Night's falling."

He gave a short nod. "Well—"

"I don't need to warn you what I'll do if you don't deliver the Staff should you succeed, Alexandra." The Magician's voice was sharp with warning.

Darius could imagine what she'd do, but he had no intention of honouring Lex's deal himself. She could do as she wished once he was restored in full.

"I know," Lex said.

"And young man," the Magician said, tilting her head slightly at Darius as one would a child. "When you have to choose between yourself and her, for all our sakes, choose her."

There was no grin on her face now, only a wrinkled frown and piercing eyes.

Choose between myself and her? "What—"

"You'll know what I mean, when the time comes. Now I really must leave you, and I think this is the most opportune time to warn you that Archimedes will be here shortly."

Darius took a moment to process what she'd said. Lex reacted faster, whipping out her sword, but the old woman moved like someone a quarter of her age. She darted to the other end of the cave, well out of reach of the blade.

"Is this a trap?" Lex said.

The Magician scoffed. "I play no games. He tracked you here, and you're lucky I didn't kill you for it. But don't worry, I'll get away fine." With that, she zipped out of the cavern and into the narrow maze of pathways.

40

With a roar of frustration, Lex wreathed her sword in algor. She hammered it through a rock, sending a cloud of dust into Darius's face.

He coughed and wafted away the salty grit, rubbing his stinging eyes free of debris. His vision went blurry. Archimedes was coming and Darius's first instinct was to run after having done it for so long, but the goman was his only chance now at his memories. He'd have to face him sooner or later, so why not now?

"I've got an idea." He crushed one of the crystals in the walls with the hilt of his sword and collected the falling dust. "We can use this salt and throw it in Archimedes's eyes."

Lex took a breath, exhaling slowly until her snarl faded. Her eyes shifted to the grey powder in his hand.

"Not bad, Darius, but not good enough. He'll see you throw it." She ripped her mask out of her pack and threw it over her head. "We have to get out of here."

Where was left to run to—Margalvia? They'd find allies there, which might improve their odds of success. But Archimedes had lost the advantage of surprise this time, thanks to the Magician's warning.

"We're in the middle of a dark maze, Lex. Isn't this our best chance for taking Archimedes?"

"*Our*?" Lex held out her glinting blade before his face. "Unless you've stopped collapsing when he's around, I'm the one that has to do it."

True, but once Darius had his memories back, he'd be the warrior he wanted to be again. He'd finally be able to protect himself.

A faint clatter echoed through one of the openings in the rock to their left. They both froze, standing so still Darius could hear the wind whisper as it wound its way through the fissures. It carried the faint but distinct patter of footsteps. Many footsteps.

"They're coming this way," he said, "and I'm tired of running."

Lex took a step as if to bolt but instead stopped and blew out several deep breaths. She stared upwards, lost in thought, then lowered her chin and met his gaze firmly. "You're right," she whispered and walked to the fractured wall. "If I climb high and wait, I can shoot from directly overhead. He won't see it coming."

Now that she was willing to go along with his plan, Darius began to doubt it was a good one. "He'll see it if you don't kill or blind him, and I want my memories back."

"I can hit his spine, paralyse him. We don't have time to plan anything better."

Darius grunted. "Fine."

"We need to get up this wall." Lex waved him over with an impatient glare.

He knelt next to Lyra and took her head in his hands. "Get out of here however you can."

She'd have an easier time escaping than him. His escort looked at him and lifted her nose in a defiant "no."

"You can't help us. Go. That's an order." He gave her one last pat before shoving her towards a narrow gap on the right side of the cavern, away from the oncoming enemy.

Lex leapt up and began climbing the huge wall. Knowing he would need relief from the pain in his shoulder to follow her, Darius pulled the vial of tears from his pocket and took a drop of the bitter liquid. The footsteps were getting louder. He didn't dare wait for the pain relief to kick in. Gritting his teeth, he grabbed hold of a crack and hauled himself up.

It wasn't hard to find anchors for his feet and hands in the badly fragmented rock, but it was difficult to find ones that didn't threaten to bring the whole wall crumbling down. One handhold at a time, Darius found a way, testing each stone and ignoring the pain still biting his shoulder. Soon the tears numbed it and he pushed on with more ease.

Lex had disappeared above and he kept climbing in hope that she'd found a perch. The higher he went, the thicker the shadow around him grew. When he could no longer see his way in the dimness, Darius conjured just a speck of algor on his fingers to find the cracks.

At last he reached the ledge Lex waited on and she helped him up.

The cave down below still flickered in the candlelight. Even the slowest of soldiers would know they'd been there, but there hadn't been time to snuff the lights. Darius's vision lost focus for a second and he blinked. The tears were kicking in and his heart slowed to a steady pace.

Lex slid over a fraction and freed her bow and quiver. Her eyes glowed slightly through the mask as she looked down and nocked an arrow. There was barely enough room for them on the ledge and the only way out was the way they'd come.

If they were forced to fight their way out of here, Lex may have to split Archimedes's skull with an arrow. If by some miracle she managed it, Darius's memories would die with the goman. If that happened, he might never regain his strength, never be a true warrior. *If, if, if.* Things weren't looking good, but he felt oddly calm about it all, watching Lex's glowing eyes. The tears were working their magic.

"What?" she whispered.

He realised he'd been staring at her. "Sorry."

With a blink, she snuffed out the algor.

"Will you take a shot to kill Archimedes if you need to?" Darius whispered.

Lex sat still, her figure now bathed in shadow. "I don't know."

That makes two of us. These could be his last moments but death didn't scare him. Of all the things to run through his mind right now, he wondered if he would die without any memory of what it was like to kiss a woman. *Why am I thinking of that now?*

A dark-haired algus ran into the space below. The man gave the empty area a quick scan and ran out the way he came, probably for backup. At least Lyra was on her way to safety.

They sat in silence as Darius waited to feel the weakness in his knees that would announce the goman's arrival. He took out a dagger and drove it through the armpit of his cloak into a gap in the stone behind. With a shove, he forced it deep so that it pinned him to the wall. Now he wouldn't fall even if all his strength deserted him.

The dark-haired man returned, followed by three—no five algus. They wore the same outfits as Lex with swords at their waists. It seemed they'd given up on clubs. Now they were fighting to maim him. *No bows. Yet.* Lex could pick them off from the ledge if she was fast enough, but not without alerting Archimedes to their presence. Where was the goman?

An algus pointed at the candles and they whispered amongst themselves. One looked up but it was too dark for the man to spot them. Darius held his breath and froze. The tiniest of movements may send a loose pebble down and alert the men.

Archimedes entered the cavern, black dreadlocks swaying and the Staff strapped to his back. Darius felt Lex tense and he strained to tighten his grip on the ledge as his arms and legs weakened. Her elbow brushed his; she was drawing her bowstring. Below them, Archimedes paced, his dreadlocks swaying back and forth. All the algus were silent. Archimedes wasn't talking either, or Darius would hear him. *What are they waiting for?*

Lex aimed her arrow down. Would she try? What if she missed? Archimedes wouldn't see anything if she hit him; he'd be dead or paralysed. But if she might miss, Archimedes would see that. He'd seen in Laltos. Perhaps they should hide and wait until everyone left, but it was too late to tell Lex.

Darius didn't blink despite the salt in the air prickling his eyes. *What will she do?*

Lex loosed her arrow as Archimedes darted to the side. The projectile clattered into the ground and all the algus jumped back and looked upwards.

"*You'll need aim truer than that,*" Archimedes' voice whispered in his ears as the goman pulled the Staff from his back and pointed it toward them.

All strength poured from Darius's muscles and he slumped, his cloak tugging against the dagger. Lex shot another arrow but Archimedes dodged again. Darius groaned as his weight crept forwards, giving him an ever clearer view of the hard stone ground below that his skull would soon be splattered against. He couldn't fight it. No strength was there to summon.

Again it only affected him and not Lex. Why wouldn't Archimedes target her as well?

With a screech, the dagger's hold failed. Lex dropped her bow and grabbed his shoulder. Her arms shook from the strain. Groaning, she struggled to pull him back against the wall. Somewhere below her bow clattered on the ground, their only defence lost.

"Surrender yourselves and I'll let you live."

Live, but as what? Empty shells? Puppets? Darius grunted a "no" to Lex.

"Never!" she cried out in a voice much shriller than her own. Even so close to discovery she shielded her identity. She still had hope and fight left in her. Her fire kept his own burning despite the weakness that gripped him.

"*Why die for them*?"

"We fight for—"

Darius's head split with pain and hissing drowned out the shouts from the room. The next thing he knew, Lex was standing on the ledge and a new knife pinned his cloak to the wall. *What the...* His mind was blocking something, skipping like a story missing a few pages. Just as she had described before. He drew in a sharp breath, having just enough strength now to lift his head.

"We'd rather die." Lex held out her sword, radiating algor.

Archimedes had moved to the far side of the cavern, a step from the crack he'd entered through. Was he about to run? The goman's eyes bulged with rage.

Lex raised her sword above her head, the tip pointed at her feet, ready to splinter the rock they sat on and bring the whole wall crumbling down. So this was how it ended. *Not the worst way to go.*

Darius conjured algor on his face and glared at Archimedes. The goman's eyes shifted to the new light source and Darius bared his teeth, emanating all the hatred and disgust he felt. He spat at the fiend as Lex brought down her sword with a cry and smashed it into the rock beneath them.

The fragmented rock yielded with a crack of thunder. Archimedes dashed through the gap as man-sized boulders rained down. Darius's weight ripped his cloak free from the dagger and he plummeted. Strength returning, he twisted and clawed at what remained of the wall as he fell, trying to slow his fall. Pain seared his fingertips as nails ripped off against the rough stone. His attempts did nothing and he slammed into the ground with a force that felt like it flattened every bone in his body.

Darius's vision blacked out as cries echoed around him. Deep breaths brought dust and salt into his lungs and he spluttered. His muscles twitched as he lay, only some obeying his will to move. He lifted an arm and rubbed his eyes weakly to try and get back his sight. Any second a sword could slice him in two. How was he still alive?

A blue light burst to his left. Of course, he wasn't blind. It was dark. He flared a little algor and looked down his torso, vision blurry from the salt stinging his eyes. His foot was swelling and he couldn't move it. It didn't hurt thanks to the tears still in his system. More fuzzy blue lights sprang up, accompanied by the rattle of stones as men rose from the debris.

To his right lay a masked head, half buried in rubble, wet with blood and motionless. Darius tried to call out "Lex" but only managed a desperate moan. He dragged himself towards her, stroke by stroke, still numb and barely feeling the rocks digging into his forearms. Reaching out, he touched her head. The warm blood was slick against his fingers. Lex flinched. She was alive, thank Agathos, or Dianoia, or whoever it was she bent her knee to.

Darius struggled upright and looked around for the sword no longer at his waist. It could have lain buried anywhere under the hunks of rock and dust.

A boulder now covered the crack Archimedes had fled through. The goman was kept out for now, but it wouldn't be long before he found another route in. Or would he risk it while the salt blurred all sight in the room?

Three men now stood in the cavern with algor-coated swords in hand. Another four were still scrambling to their feet. One began walking towards Darius as he clambered up to one knee. A flicker of metal caught his eye, and he saw his sword buried a few yards away. *Too far.* He picked up a rock and lobbed it at the advancing algus.

The man dodged it with ease and kept coming. Two others joined him in stalking forwards. Even with a sword, in this state he couldn't take three algus. Lex lay groaning, unfit to fight.

Darius balled his fists, ready to punch, kick, bite, whatever it took to survive. The three algus paused while their four companions brushed themselves off and scrambled over the loose rocks to join them. Seven versus one. If he survived this, he really could call himself a warrior.

The algus fanned out in a semicircle only a few paces away. Maybe they'd try and take him alive, in which case he'd rather die.

A crunch of metal came from the far side of the cave. The algus all stopped and looked back. A thud echoed in the dark, followed by another—heavy footsteps.

"It's a good job you made a racket," a deep gristly voice said, "or we may never have found you."

"Who's that?" one algus said to another.

The second man picked up a rock, coated it with algor and threw it to the voice in the dark. It hit a burly figure's metal cuirass with a clank and bounced onto the floor, illuminating the dark man and his black helmet. He wore similarly dark armguards and thick greaves over his shins. A familiar hammer was slung over his shoulder.

"Ouch," the man said sarcastically.

Now Darius remembered that voice—Brutus. But so what? One warrior was no use against so many algus.

Another figure climbed through a narrow gap in the rock behind Brutus, similarly clad in armour. He had a dark sword at his waist and two red bands across his bicep rather than a single black band like Brutus. The algus all shifted toward these two newcomers, seeming to have forgotten all about Darius. Why? There was something he wasn't seeing.

"What're you waiting for, old man?" said the new figure. This one was tall next to Brutus and looked wiry but strong. A monstrous scar cut across his upper arm, visible even in the faint light.

"There's seven of them, Sulla," Brutus said. "We need to wait for the others."

Sulla chuckled. "Where's the fun in that?" He bent a knee and sprung high into the air at the waiting algus.

Pain seared through Darius's head again and he was suddenly on the ground face down with someone as heavy as a bull standing on his back. His damned mind was blocking out huge chunks of what was happening. Groaning, he pushed at the foot on his back but couldn't budge it. Had the algus got him?

A cry from Brutus echoed, followed by a thunderous crash. Blood splattered across the stones around Darius. His head ached, vision going dark as a buzzing sound filled his ears.

Now he was standing, hands pinned behind his back by someone and the sharp pain in his head now constant. The bloody corpses of men and seven algus lay on the ground, some with split skulls, others in foetal positions with blood seeping from their bellies. The algus had been overcome but not before cutting down many men. At least twenty warriors still stood around the cave.

Several carried flaming torches. All of them wore the same armour as Brutus, the same helmets, the same weapons. Darius's allies.

Lex stood leaning on the shoulder of one for support, her face unmasked and dripping blood. "Darius's mind won't accept it. I've tried. It's why he goes insane and then blacks out. Archimedes did something to him."

Darius tried to wriggle free of his captor's hold on him but the iron grip didn't relent. "What's going on?" What was his mind avoiding?

Brutus growled. "Damn him. It's happened again. We need to make it so he can't avoid it."

"Talking won't do it." Lex remained slumped against the warrior as if she was about to faint. She couldn't have been the one to kill the algus.

"Lex, are you alright?" Darius said.

"Then he'll have to see it." Brutus stormed over, craned his neck until Darius's nose felt the cold metal of the warrior's helmet. In the weak light, all he saw through the grating was darkness.

"Hold his head," Brutus said, "and hold his eyes open!"

Strong hands caught Darius's head from behind. Fingers prised open his eyelids. The salt in the air made his eyes ache and yearn to blink.

Darius grunted, unable to wriggle an inch now. His heart beat on his ribcage. This had better be for his own good.

Brutus took a step back and slowly pulled off his helmet, first revealing a stubbled chin lined with dribbles of grimy sweat, then a pale, crooked nose broken one too many times, then eyes, black as coal.

A spear of pain slammed through Darius's head. He writhed against his captors as his stomach twisted so much that bile rose in his throat. Brutus was a—his vision flickered.

Brutus's face was suddenly so close Darius inhaled the man's hot breath and coughed. Still those obsidian eyes stared and his own eyelids were held open.

"Two minutes, Brutus," Sulla called from behind the warrior. "If Archimedes finds his way in here, we're all dead."

Brutus couldn't be… If he was, it meant Lex and Darius were fighting for the *rakkans*. The headache ceased and he groaned in relief. It felt like a tense cord in his mind had snapped. He was loose, free.

But he preferred oblivion.

"Brutus," he said.

"Yes?"

"You're a rakkan."

Brutus flashed a grin dotted with metal teeth. "We got him, boys."

The hands unlocked from Darius's head and eyelids. Blinking in relief, he scowled. "This doesn't make sense." He jerked again, trying to rip free of the man still gripping his arms but unable to slip an inch. A rakkan's hold, far stronger than him.

"Why would I help you? I *hate* rakkans. You attack us, kill people." Darius looked over to Lex and she stared back, holding a clump of rags to her head. "Lex?" Why would she help them, of all people?

"Tell him, Brutus," she said.

The other men—rakkans—began regrouping into a formation and headed out.

"There's more to us than you've seen." Brutus pulled his helmet back on. "How many of us have you come across: one, two, a dozen?"

Darius didn't want to accept this truth; it went against everything his gut told him. "Why would I fight for you?"

Brutus pressed a metal fist into Darius's chest. "Because you're one of us. Your father was a rakkan."

Bile burned Darius's throat again, and he swallowed it back down. It couldn't be true. He didn't have the eyes, the strength or the power. His arm had been scarred by ferven in his first encounter with a rakkan. He felt betrayed.

"It's a lie," he said.

"Ever wonder why only you are weakened by the Staff?" Brutus said.

The weakness had crossed Darius's mind a few times but Lex wouldn't tell him why it affected only him. No, not just him. Felix had been weakened on the riverbank when they first met. The Staff was responsible, not the goman's powers?

"The Staff only affects rakkans," Brutus said.

Sulla hurried over. "Brutus, we must move. Let's get back to Margalvia."

"With Archimedes on our tail? That'd be inviting him to attack the city."

"Not much choice with the state of these two. We've been preparing for months. We'll survive."

Brutus shook his head. "Your lack of fear has a habit of getting us into trouble. The Warlord is angry enough at Darius as it is."

"He's angry anyway after the challenge. What a fight though. Your brother—"

"We've got more important things to discuss."

Darius was only half following their conversation. Margalvia was a rakkan city? All his friends, all rakkans? He'd been a fool not to see it. But then Archimedes had made it so he could never think it, so he wouldn't fight for them again. Had Darius really been such a threat?

"I can't be a rakkan," he said. "I'm not strong like you."

"Oh, but you were," Sulla said, pushing his way between Brutus and Darius. The rakkan pulled off his helmet and the flickering torchlight fell on his scarred face. His right eyebrow was cleft in two by a thick scar and his breath smelled of ash, same as Brutus's. Despite the scar, his cocky grin made him look somewhat striking.

"You had the strength of ten humans," Sulla continued, "fire in your eyes and in your belly. Speed of an algus with the strength of a rakkan. What a warrior. Only thing you were missing, apparently, was our immunity to that mouthless freak." He patted Darius's cheek.

"My headache's gone, and I'm talking to you without losing my memory."

Sulla threw his helmet back over his head. "I guess you've broken whatever mental block was in there. Time's up, Dar. You coming willingly, or will one of these grunts have to manhandle you all the way?"

For all this time Margalvia had been his goal, the one place he'd be safe, and now it beckoned. But he couldn't accept the rakkans. "No. I'm not one of you."

Sulla didn't appear to hear his refusal. "You're coming." The rakkan held out one of the algus's swords to him hilt first. "Take it. A warrior's weapon is his life."

Darius started. "Where did you hear that?"

Sulla shrugged. "It's an old rakkan proverb."

The only link Darius had to his father had turned out to be a maxim of the enemy. What little he thought he knew was worthless. Could it be true? The more he thought on it, the more it made sense. Archimedes was after him because he was half rakkan, the only one not immune to cogi, whose mind could be tapped for secrets. How had he not seen it before? The fact he heard Archimedes as a whisper, when Omid and Lex said his voice was loud, the fact he was weakened by the Staff when everyone else was unaffected. How had he been such a fool?

What other options did he have but to accept his past?

"Fine. I'll come with you." *Finally, I'll learn the truth.*

41

Darius breathed a lungful of wet air. The mists at this end of the Uxon Trail continually settled in his throat, causing him to cough up the moisture while trying to remain quiet lest anyone be tailing them. His stomach ached for food but the rakkans had none. They'd said Margalvia was close—over an hour ago.

No stars lit the sky and all he had to see by was the torchlight of their band. Only rocks and stone cliffs were visible, the barren lands devoid of any life besides the rakkans. *This is the refuge I've been seeking all along?*

Darius winced as he put weight on his injured foot and leant more into the rakkan helping him walk. It still felt odd to touch them as allies. His instinct was to slay them all, an impulse he had difficulty shaking off.

Beside him walked Lex, her legs wobbling with each step. She had refused to let anyone carry her, instead struggling on with an arm around one of the rakkan warriors. *Same old stubborn Lex.* Much longer and she'd *have* to be carried, but Darius prayed it didn't come to that. With her head almost split open, if she went under there was a good chance she wouldn't wake and he'd lose one of the only constants in his life as he remembered it. He was trying to listen to these unfamiliar feelings he had towards other people, just like she'd told him, but he was still unable to explain them.

Thankfully, he at least knew Lyra was still alive and well. Their connection was as strong as ever. He'd called for her countless times, but she had yet to appear.

Sulla dropped back and paced alongside them. "There's an algus tailing us atop the right-hand cliff," he said in a low voice.

Darius scanned the top of the deep gorge they trudged through and caught sight of a ghost-like shadow. "Will he catch us?"

"If he wanted to, he would have already. If you haven't noticed, we aren't blessed with algus speed."

"So he's seeing where I head."

"Likely. He won't dare come far into the legion's reach alone. But more will follow."

Legion… The word brought back Lex's tales of war and her hatred of the rakkans. Something still didn't make sense.

"You speak of the Viridian Legion?" Darius kept his voice quiet and steady to hide the contempt wanting to spill out.

"Viridian?" Sulla slapped Darius's chest with the back of his hand. It would have knocked him over had another rakkan not been holding him upright. "We're no green-flags. Margalvia's standards are of the Black Legion."

Maybe Brutus was right about Darius judging all rakkans by the few he'd seen. Perhaps Sulla and the others weren't like the Viridian Legion. But still, it all felt surreal.

"Any of those green-flags come around here," Sulla continued, "and they get their heads cut off. One day we'll end their vile legion."

Suddenly his and Lex's alliance made sense.

"I didn't come to chit-chat," Sulla added. "Just keep your eyes peeled and if you feel an arrow heading for your nut, get out of the way."

The warrior upped his pace and left before Darius could ask how to *feel* an arrow coming. The rakkan helping him walk had yet to utter a single word. Perhaps he was mute, or just surly. Either way, hopefully *he* could 'feel' any incoming arrows.

Brutus held up a fist ahead and the group halted. One by one, the rakkans turned back towards Darius with disturbed looks, as if sensing incoming danger.

A feeling washed over him, familiar intense relief—his escort. "It's Lyra. Don't harm her."

Sure enough, his panther sped up the trail towards them, bringing a smile to Darius's face. She bounded to his side without a moment's pause at the rakkans surrounding him. Rearing back, she pounded her paws into his chest and almost knocked him over. Apparently, she didn't share his discomfort amongst these warriors.

"Hey, Dar," Sulla said from ahead. "Save the lovers' reunion for when we're safe and sound."

"Keep moving," Darius growled.

Sulla gave a mock salute. "Aye, Commander."

The group set off again. Dark blocky outlines soon took form in front of them, too straight and orderly to be natural rocks. They had to be buildings. Darius took a deep breath, readying himself to dive into the city he'd longed for, one he had hoped would welcome him with open arms. A city of rakkans, as it transpired.

They passed through a narrow fissure in the rock ahead, a natural bottleneck into the city. Sheer rock cliffs surrounded it on all sides, a city built in a crater. It wasn't the ideal position for one, with the possibility of being surrounded from high ground, vulnerable to siege and bombardment. *Just perfect.*

A couple of thick-muscled guards grunted at Brutus as he walked by. The soldiers waved Darius's group on, though not without curious glances at him and Lex. They stepped into streets paved with badly cut stones arranged in random patterns, nothing like the neat roads in Laltos. The ground was damp and slippery, as though covered in mildew, and Darius took careful steps. All this time, he'd been longing for *this*? Hell would have been more appealing.

Most of the buildings were no more than two storeys high and made of loose, blackened stones fused together with something that looked like hardened lava. Apparently ferven could melt not only flesh and bone but also solid rock.

Three skinny rakkans walked towards them from an adjacent street and were the first to meet Darius's gaze. Their clothes hung loose, much like those on the other rakkans he'd seen. They were thin, though not skeletal, and when they saw him their noses scrunched in disgust. Muttering to one another, they turned away from the group of warriors.

Another man drew closer. Brutus stamped his foot and growled, but the man's gaze was fixed on Darius.

"Traitor," he hissed through haphazard teeth.

Charming.

A woman stepped to the man's side and pulled him back. "Leave him be. The Warlord will take care of *him* soon enough." She shot Darius an angry glare before leading the man away.

Darius did his best not to flinch, not to let his inner turmoil show. This wasn't right. They should be welcoming him, not hurling insults. Was there anyone that didn't think of him a traitor, anywhere that would have him without spitting at him? If even hell rejected him, where else was left? *Darius, what did you do to turn everyone against you?*

Brutus led them on through the city. More jeers rose at every turn from young and old alike. Darius stared down a few until they looked away. It was getting harder not to listen to those killing instincts.

"He's doomed us all!" someone shouted.

"Hang him!"

Brutus didn't stop to argue, just kept marching along. Darius glanced at Lex. The algus had her head down and seemed to have gone unnoticed so far. *Probably for the best.*

They arrived at what looked like a garrison with black banners hanging on all fronts. The walls of the entrance stood tall and sank into the ground like a bunker. Perhaps most of the city was underground. That would explain why they didn't mind settling in a crater. The garrison doors were plated with the same dark metal the rakkan soldiers wore, covering wood four feet thick.

"Get them inside," Brutus said. "They need rest. Watch who goes in or out. I'll find the Warlord."

"I'm off to report to the Militia chief." Sulla strutted away without a backward glance.

Rest. Nothing sounded better. Darius needed to regain his strength and start getting answers. Brutus slapped a hand on Darius's chest as he headed for the entrance. "Before you go inside, you're going to tell me exactly how my brother died."

Oh damn.

42

Darius sat on his bed, mopping up the last few drops of stew with a piece of stale bread so hard it could knock someone unconscious if wielded as a weapon. *Might come in useful if they try to hang me.*

As it happened, rakkans ate similar food to humans, and he did too, now that he was apparently one of them. His father had been... Darius shook his head. He had no memories of the man—the rakkan. How could it be true? They had much more strength and power than he did. The question had paced endless circles in his mind for days.

They hadn't let many people in to speak with him over the last few days. He was a prisoner confined to one room with only a bed, table and a single chair. He'd heard whisperings of Archimedes amassing an army to assault the city. No one would tell him why everyone thought he was a traitor, or how long it would be before Archimedes attacked. They'd said Lex was alive and resting, but he hadn't been allowed to see her.

Brutus had shown little reaction to the story of his brother's death, simply ordered Darius taken here. Perhaps it was punishment, or perhaps for his own protection.

The confinement didn't bother him too much. Darius needed the time to regain some strength and hadn't felt much like getting out of bed, out of reach of Lyra's warm, furry body, when she was around. *She* was allowed out, and good thing because he had her scavenge extra food for him. The allotted meals were never enough to fill his aching stomach for long.

What was he supposed to do now that Margalvia had forsaken him? All he had left driving him on was revenge against Archimedes for Omid and himself. The only thing left to do was get his memories back, or die trying. Maybe Lex would come with him. *Maybe.*

A knock at the door announced Sulla's arrival, the warrior strutting in without waiting for a response. He looked slimmer without armour but his body was nothing but muscle, lean and strong.

"Thought I'd visit the prisoner," he said, nudging the door closed. "Hope I'm not interrupting."

Finally some company and a familiar face after a week of nothing.

Darius set his empty bowl on the bedside table. "I get the impression you'd love nothing more than to catch me doing something untoward."

Sulla grinned. "I do need more anecdotes."

"Sorry to disappoint. Maybe if you brought me some ale or firewater you'd have more luck." Darius raised an eyebrow.

"Ha! Keep dreaming, Dar. You aren't in some cushy human town now. We're on rations here. Food and drink are scarce. But I do have one treat I've called in for you. It should be here any minute."

That sounded like a much needed distraction from his current situation.

"Something's been bothering me." Darius swung his legs over the side of the bed. "If I'm truly half-rakkan, why does everyone spit in my face?"

"Word's spread over your failed attempt on Archimedes, losing your mind along with our secrets. Some suspect you meant to betray us all along. Archimedes always seems one step ahead of us."

Great. He should be grateful for the support of those few that protected him at least.

"For all I know, I was a traitor."

"Take it from me, you were loyal. I counted you as a friend."

They always spoke in the past tense. "And now?"

Sulla's grin widened. "Still a friend. I knew you'd lost your mind before I leapt into a fight with seven algus to save you, despite the fact they would have cut me to pieces had help not arrived soon after."

Darius couldn't argue with that. "I guess I owe you my life. Wish everyone else was so welcoming."

"Don't take it to heart." Sulla placed a hand on his shoulder. "People are hungry, looking for someone to blame. The war's not gone well."

"Why are the people on rations?"

The rakkan's face sank. "We're starving, my friend. Farming isn't easy in the mountains. We eat whatever we can get from the humans while trying not to get killed by Archimedes's men."

"You raid human towns?" They sounded no better than the Viridian Legion. "Eat people?"

Sulla scowled. "No. But the humans are the ones starving us out. They burn our crops, watch on with smiles as our people wither away to skin and bone. Faced with that, I'd consider our actions tame. *Raid* isn't the word. We mostly take from military supply routes. Good way to get food in bulk, and it deprives our enemies' soldiers."

Darius was lucky to get crusty bread in such lean times. All this time he'd seen the rakkans' thinness and frailty as part of their defiled wickedness when they really deserved pity? These emotions were confusing. Whatever the treat Sulla had said was coming was, it couldn't arrive soon enough.

"Brutus doesn't look so starved," Darius said. That rakkan's thighs were like tree trunks.

"Aye, well, legionnaires get full rations, as do warriors in the Red Militia like me."

"What's that?"

Sulla brandished the red bands around his bicep. "We get a white band when we sign up to the Militia. Once we're experienced, and it's stained with blood, you're classed as Red Militia."

"And let me guess. When it's so stained it's black, you can join the Black Legion?"

"Right. Only for the most battle-hardened. Strongest legion there is, for all it matters now with Dreads and his staff." Sulla screwed up his face and shook his head. "Evil weapon, created for one reason. To kill us. It saps a rakkan's strength making him weak, and Archimedes can somehow bolster its power until we haven't even got the strength to stand. You must've noticed."

Darius remembered all too well. So did it prove he truly was half rakkan? But then why...

"I felt it. And I also felt this." Darius ripped back his sleeve to show his burns. "A rakkan did that."

Sulla's brow furrowed and he held up his hand. With a flick of his fingers, his hand was coated in a molten film. "With this?"

Darius nervously drew his arm back and pulled his sleeve down. "Yes."

Sulla's hand extinguished as quickly as it had flared. "Impossible. You're a rakkan. You're immune."

"Could *I* do that before?"

"Of course. Most rakkans can. Isn't rare like those pompous algus, acting like they fell down from the heavens." Sulla drew his sword and held out the hilt to Darius. "Take this."

The blade was the same dark metal Darius had seen the other rakkans use in weapons and armour. He took the hilt and Sulla released the blade. His arm gave under what felt like a ton of metal and the sword fell to the floor with crash.

"Damn," Sulla muttered. "You've lost your strength too. It's like you're not even a rakkan."

Darius rubbed his aching muscles. "That weighs more than an anvil. What's it made of?"

Sulla snatched his sword from the ground. "Kuraminium. Strongest, hardest substance ever found, and the only thing that can withstand ferven and not melt. It's too heavy for humans. Gives us an edge. Takes the power of at least ten rakkans in unison to smelt it for casting, down in the Urukan Mine."

That name sounded familiar but Darius couldn't quite place the name. "Where's that?"

"Don't know. Its location is secret."

Darius pushed himself up from the bed and relaxed his weight onto his bad leg. The movement stung his thigh a little but it would loosen up as he walked around.

"Try conjuring ferven." Sulla grabbed Darius's hand and held it out so tightly Darius wondered whether he intended to break it. "Start with your fingertip and imagine a tiny inferno raging on it. It helps if you're angry."

Not more practising with new conjuring. Holding back a groan of frustration, Darius closed his eyes and concentrated. It was probably similar to conjuring algor, only willing heat instead of cold. He strained, throwing all his focus into creating flame.

"Come on," Sulla said impatiently.

Darius pushed harder. Opening his eyes, he was unsurprised to see nothing but dirt on his finger.

"You can't. If you could it wouldn't be difficult." Sulla turned away with a deep frown.

Great. Only rakkan thing I retained was vulnerability to the Staff. Archimedes had sucked out all the benefits. That or his mind had just forgotten how to tap into the ferven. Could he even be called half-rakkan anymore?

"So when will I know if I'll hang? Can I leave here and see Lex?" Darius began pacing around the room. If he had to wait much longer, he'd be tempted to fight his way out.

Sulla raised his scarred eyebrow. "Missing her? What went on between you two out there?"

Darius sighed. "Battling. Arguing. She seems to hate me." *No need to mention her incident with the tears, or Omid.*

"Ha! Sounds like before. She doesn't hate you. You two need your heads bashing together, or something else bashing together if you know what I mean." Sulla chuckled. "Tell me you haven't thought about it. She's a fine specimen."

Darius shrugged. "Yes, she's gorgeous. And fierce."

"Fierce! Dar, you spend a night with her and I'll bet you'll be recovering for a week." Sulla howled and patted Darius's shoulder, his eyes twinkling with mischief like a young boy. Despite him being a rakkan, Darius felt oddly at ease around him.

Their chatter was interrupted by a light knock at the door.

"Enter!" Sulla bellowed before Darius opened his mouth.

"You realise it's my room?" *Even if it is virtually a cell.*

The door opened and in strode Lex, walking freely as if she hadn't been flattened by a ton of rocks a few days before. For once she wore no armour, only a tight-fitting shirt and trousers. A sword still rested at her waist though. Her hair was tied back except for a strand hanging across her face and the shirt was unbuttoned just enough to suck in a man's stare. Darius had to force his gaze up.

"Speak of the…" Sulla sniggered. "You're looking as ravishing as ever."

"Been talking about me, handsome?" Lex sauntered over to Sulla and ran a thumb across a scar on his chin. Her teasing wasn't confined to the humans then.

The rakkan scoffed and shook his head, though his smile widened. "You know that isn't the scar I got saving you that time, Lex."

"I know, but I'm not touching *that* scar."

Lex kept walking until she stood by the bed. She placed a hand on Darius's injured shoulder, giving him a faint smile. Maybe she'd missed him this last week. She squeezed his shoulder and moved it around, watching his reaction. He didn't flinch. Why didn't she ask how he was if she wanted to know?

A trail of hardened sap sealed shut the gash on her forehead. It had been a nasty wound, but it was all fixed up and seemed to be healing well.

"Darius was just saying how gorgeous you are," Sulla said.

Lex's hand stopped squeezing.

"Uh…" Darius's mind was even more blank than usual. *What should I say?* He shot Sulla a glare but the rakkan just grinned.

Lex smiled as she lifted his arm. "Did he now?" The algus drew back his sleeve and inspected the burns.

"I think my exact words were…" Darius hesitated, "gorgeous and fierce."

Her eyes stayed fixated on his arm but a little colour surfaced in her cheeks.

"You're blushing." he said, surprised by the reaction.

She dropped his arm and looked at him with those sparkling blue eyes. Did she purposely conjure a little algor in there to make them twinkle or was it an unconscious thing?

"You think you can make me blush?" Lex raised an eyebrow in challenge.

If he leant in and kissed her, that would make her blush. Or smack him. Sulla folded his arms and made himself comfortable against the wall as if watching a private play.

Another knock came at the door.

"Get lost," Sulla called. "It's just getting good in here."

The door opened and Brutus strode in, as surly as ever.

"No one visits for days and suddenly I'm popular," Darius said.

The warrior stared at him, chewing something that tasted of rotten egg if his expression was anything to go by.

"I take it you met with the Warlord," Sulla said.

"No." Brutus frowned at the three of them. "I see word spread fast that these two are to meet with the commanders."

Sulla shrugged. "I may have mentioned it to Lex."

Shaking his head at the incorrigible rakkan, Brutus turned to Darius. "The commanders are the highest ranking warriors below the Warlord."

His tone was grim, but that seemed to be the warrior's default. *Should I be worried?*

"When am I to meet them?" Darius asked.

"In an hour."

As Brutus spoke, a tall, blonde woman came to the doorway and waited patiently behind him.

Sulla coughed. "That's your treat, Darius."

"I'll be back in an hour." Brutus turned and stepped past her as Darius's startled eyes traced the skimpy strips of leather across her torso, waist and hips. Her skin was rakkan pale with a slight sheen, like it had been oiled to highlight the curves and aid hands sliding across it. The leather barely contained her chest and her eyes stared, black and piercing, straight at him. The mischievous grin playing about her lips set his nerves on edge. She was stunning, for a rakkan. He'd never thought those perilous eyes could be alluring, until now.

"Darius," she purred. "How great it is to see you again, sweetheart." The rakkan stepped farther into the room and paused when she caught sight of Lex, who was glaring at her as if weighing whether to rip out the woman's throat. "Sulla, you didn't say we'd have company."

"This is Flora," Sulla said, his grin as toothy as ever.

"She's a whore," Lex added in a sneering tone, not taking her eyes off the woman.

Flora flicked her blonde hair and pricked her nose into the air. "Not always for my dear Darius. He didn't always have to pay." She grinned at Lex.

Why had Sulla hired a whore for him? Lex wouldn't like it, and Darius would much rather go to bed with her, but that didn't seem likely. Darius looked between the women, torn. In an hour he may be sentenced to hang, like everyone in this forsaken city wanted.

"Are you alright, my dear?" Flora drew him over to the bed and sat him down. Her warm hands cupped his cheeks then the woman brought her mouth to his and kissed him before he could answer. She smelled sweet like she'd soaked in honey.

Darius glanced at Lex, who was now glaring at Sulla with eyes that could kill.

"I'll leave you to it," the algus said then marched out of the room.

Sulla smiled and winked at Darius. "I'd love to watch but I've got business to see to. Don't forget, commanders meet in an hour." With that he left and closed the door behind him, leaving Darius alone with Flora.

Darius swallowed.

"I've not seen her around for a while," Flora said, pulling off Darius's tunic. She wasn't wasting time. This was more nerve-wracking than facing a rakkan wanting to kill him. At least then he knew how to react.

Despite his reservations, Darius couldn't help but admire Flora's flat, bare stomach. She was slim but athletic. "You're not starved like the rest. Do whores get full rations too?"

Flora looked taken aback and pulled her hand away.

Damn it. Perhaps he shouldn't have called her a whore. "Apologies. I didn't mean to offend."

Smiling, she shuffled herself closer to him. "I think that's the first time I've ever got an apology from the mighty Darius."

The mention of 'mighty' Darius made him sit up straighter, though he didn't relish filling the legend's boots right now.

Flora slipped a hand onto his chest and kissed him again. As her lips caressed his, warmth tingled through his whole body, nervous excitement. It was like when he'd first slid onto the horse behind Lex, only this woman wanted him. Or perhaps she just wanted the money.

Drawing back, Flora gave his eyes a few seconds to study her smooth body in all its magnificence. She ran two hands through her hair and gave him a sultry look that suggested she wanted to rip the rest of his clothes off and sink her nails into his back.

"I went back to blonde."

He hadn't been too focused on her hair. "Looks fine, like rays of sunshine."

She winced, a flicker of displeasure soon replaced with that warm, beckoning smile. "We're not big fans of the sun, but I'm

glad you like it now. Before, you always asked me to dye my hair black."

Black? He could guess why. How he wished it were black right now.

"How many times have we done this?"

"I didn't keep count, honey."

That meant more than a handful. Lex had once said Darius had a liking for whores but he'd wondered if it was true. Women hadn't seemed a priority for the last few weeks.

"Did I see a lot of other women, too?"

Flora gave him a disapproving look. "You'd lay anything that moved. And some things that didn't too."

Darius scratched his head. It hadn't been *him* exactly that had been some sort of whore addict, but he couldn't help but feel awkward. This was the Darius he was fighting so hard to get back.

She traced his jaw with a finger. "I think I was your favourite though."

"Is it true you didn't always charge me?" He was a little flattered, though who wouldn't want to curry favour with a 'mighty' warrior?

"Sure. I think that's why I was your favourite." Flora ran her hands down his stomach, breathing deep as she got lower.

"I guess I was tight-fisted."

"No, it was because I actually wanted you." She shoved him back and pinned his shoulders to the bed. Bending over, she touched her nose to his with a teasing smile. He was totally at her mercy; he couldn't fight her off. To think that she could melt his arms with ferven. Darius's logical side insisted he should be in a fighting mind-set, devising ways to escape her. But instead her strength made his heart palpitate. Her black eyes weren't fearsome, they were wide and inviting. He just wished they contained a blue tint of algor.

Again and again, thoughts of Lex wouldn't leave him be.

The Waif Magician's last words to him rang in his head, 'when the time comes, choose her.' He doubted this was what she had been talking about, but it felt oddly relevant.

"Is something wrong?" Flora tilted her head. "You look confused."

Darius paused. What did he really want? All he kept thinking about was Lex. Part of him despaired that he was here with Flora instead of her. It made no sense but she'd told him to listen to his instincts, and right now they were telling him this felt wrong.

"I'll take that as a yes." Flora released his shoulders and sat back on the bed.

"I'm just concerned. Most people, humans and rakkans, want me dead."

The woman stood, giving him a good look at her strong thighs. He knew they would have felt good wrapped around his hips. He also knew that wasn't what he wanted right now.

"If you're not in the mood," Flora said, "then I'll leave."

"No." Darius grabbed her hand. "Stay, just to talk. I need someone to ask about what's going on here."

She nodded and sat down again. "Sure. I'm paid up for the hour."

Sulla had already said as much, but it still stung to hear that the only reason she was near him was because she'd been paid. He drew away and folded his hands in his lap. "Tell me about Sulla, Brutus and the others."

"Alright. Sulla likes to talk and has cared for me over the years better than my own brother. He cares about you too, despite the bravado, and I think if anything happened to you he'd be distraught. But be careful. He's dangerous. There's no fear holding him back and while it makes him a demon in a fight, it gets him into trouble."

From the little Darius knew of Sulla, *trouble* rang true. "And Brutus?"

A warm smile spread across her face. "You seemed like a son to him. Stay close to him and you'll be fine. You can trust them both. You were all thick as thieves the past few years."

That put his mind at ease a little, to hear it from someone that didn't seem to have skin in the game.

He smiled back. "Now tell me everything else you know about this city and the old Darius."

43

Darius followed Brutus into a smoke-filled room, dimly lit by lamps on the walls. Pipes glowed in the mouths of six rakkans sat around a large circular table that could have seated at least twenty. The commanders' ranks must have been thinning but that only made each one more powerful in Darius's opinion.

There was a murmur of conversation as he entered but it soon faded to silence. The thick air made him sweat and carried the scent of aged wood. He missed the sweet smell of Flora's skin.

An hour had gone by quickly and all Darius had gleaned about his past self could be summed up as overindulgence in drink, women and fighting. By the sounds of it, old Darius hadn't been a happy man, but he had been a ferocious warrior. Darius was itching with anticipation at the thought of becoming that warrior again.

As he approached the table, he noted etched patterns on its surface. None of the six rakkans rose or gestured to greet him. All had thick eyebrows scrunched over deep frowns. A muscular man to the right blew a smoke ring while the others let their pipes kindle. Those with bare arms all wore two black bands around the bicep, similar to the red bands Sulla wore—a symbol of rank, Darius guessed.

A large cushioned chair at the farthest side of the table was vacant, probably meant for the Warlord.

The rakkans' chalk-white skin made them glimmer in the weak light. Each had a sword leant against the table by their side. The big rakkan had two and a dagger in front of him that was small enough to throw. Darius would keep an eye on that one.

Squinting in the dimness, he tried to make out the patterns on the table. Lex had said rakkans saw better in the dark and Darius guessed that was one more ability stolen from him.

The algus walked up and stopped to his right, facing the panel alongside him. Her presence made him feel slightly better. He would have preferred Lyra too but she had to stay behind. The plan was to stay polite and quiet, let Brutus do the talking and avoid death. Their ultimate goal was to convince the commanders to help him take down Archimedes and his algus. *No big ask then.*

"Here he is, commanders," Brutus said.

The group shifted slightly and a rakkan to the far left pulled the pipe from his mouth. He had a bald head and a thick grey beard that resembled a bird's nest.

"Good to see you again, Darius," he said. "I'm Gaius, and these are Faustus, Habitus, Iuba, Lunaris and Julius."

The big rakkan gave a nod at the last name.

They didn't expect Darius to remember all their names, did they?

"I was your commander," Gaius added. "I sent you on missions."

Darius placed his hands on the back of the empty chair in front of him for support. His aching leg made him eager to sit, but it would be best to follow Brutus's lead and stay standing.

Despite his intention to remain silent, he couldn't help but ask, "Missions, Commander? You mean assassinations?"

"Aye. You and Lex were the only ones able to mix with the humans." Gaius's tone was relaxed, not hard as Darius would expect for a traitor's interrogation. Perhaps his former commander had his back.

Try not to ruffle his beard, Darius.

"I guess I should apologise for having tried to assassinate Archimedes."

Gaius grimaced. "You went rogue and you've landed us in a mess."

"Mess?" Julius pressed his pipe into the table. "That's an understatement. This traitor gave us up to Archimedes."

Damn. Hadn't taken long for someone to fling accusations. As he considered how best to respond, Darius kept his eyes sharp in case someone went for their sword. Persuasion most certainly didn't come to him as naturally as fighting. *Best leave the talking to Brutus and Lex for now.*

"Traitor?" Lex said. "It isn't like he gave Archimedes anything voluntarily, Julius. Is it you that's been spreading that lie?"

"That's what he says," Julius said, his voice rising and hand still pressing into the table.

"You can trust Darius. I didn't at first but I've been with him for a while. I'd know if he meant to betray us."

Darius was moved to hear her voice confidence in him for once.

"The fact is Archimedes got our secrets," Julius said, "our strategies, our defensive positions, our escape routes."

Brutus grunted. "We don't know what he got. He can't have got everything or he wouldn't still be after Darius, would he?"

"Maybe he's after the mine." Julius scrunched his nose in disgust. "I knew we shouldn't have trusted him with the location."

310

The commanders sat in silence.

"If Archimedes wants the mine, we need to warn all the cities and legions," Gaius said. "Even the Viridians."

"That's the Warlord's decision," Brutus said.

"The mine's treaty demands it. The mine is greater than any one legion."

"Let's not get distracted." Julius narrowed his eyes on Darius. "We need to deal with this traitor."

Every time the rakkan used the word, Darius felt the urge to cut out Julius's tongue. He squeezed the back of the chair, wishing for a sword hilt instead.

Gaius hammered his fist on the table. "Enough, Julius. We knew the risks letting these humans in but the benefits outweighed them. Don't forget, without them Margalvia would already be in ruins."

The commander's voice echoed from the walls and rang in Darius's ears. Lex leaned in close and nudged him. A signal? He looked to his left and saw a dark stone wall with a black banner hanging across two spears. *Weapons.* Sulla was leant against the wall under the glow of a lamp. When had he slinked in?

"If Archimedes is still after Darius then we can just ensure the goman gets nothing else." Julius placed a hand on the blade in front of him.

Darius braced himself, ready to dart for the spears should Julius's hand so much as flinch in his direction.

"Is that why you summoned us here?" Brutus growled, eyeing Gaius who avoided his gaze.

No one spoke.

Darius was ready for a fight, but he had nowhere left to run, and by now, he'd had it with people trying to kill him. "You want me gone, then kill me. But just remember she's the only one here that stands a chance against Archimedes." He pointed to Lex who was giving Julius one of her icy glares. "And she won't help you if I'm dead." *I hope.* All she seemed to want was his grandfather. Even if that wasn't true, she'd at least play along with the bluff.

Julius stared hard for a second then shook his head. "Kill Archimedes? Boy, we gave up on that long ago. All we're trying to do now is survive extinction."

Darius was just trying to survive too. "I'm not a 'boy.'" He dug his nails into the chair.

The big rakkan grinned. "We've got almost a millennium between us around this table, *boy*. You're not even half a century. We'll decide if you make it further."

A millennium—a hundred and sixty years per man? That was a long time to train how to fight. The rakkans must have been fierce, experienced warriors. By the look of their bulging arms, they had the strength of young men to boot.

"If you want to kill Darius then you'll have to go through me." Algor flared in Lex's eyes.

"And me," Sulla said, still leant against the wall.

Some of the commanders chuckled.

"You may be a Red Commander, Sulla," Julius said, "but you know the law. Black Legion is higher up the food chain than the Militia. Even you wouldn't be foolish enough to challenge us."

Sulla shrugged. "Maybe we'll see."

"Enough of this bickering." Gaius waved a hand at Sulla dismissively. "I think we should give Darius a chance, but he should at least pay for his insolence."

"I say hang him," Julius said, slamming a fist on the table like a hammer of judgement.

"That's not what I had in mind."

"I second it," one of the other rakkans said with a huff of smoke.

"Aye," another two grunted in unison.

Darius's life was going to come down to a vote? So much for Margalvia saving him.

"Nay," the last one said, like it mattered.

"Four against two, Gaius," Julius said as Brutus grabbed Darius by the arm and pulled him back.

Darius instinctively grabbed for his sword but only clutched air, having forgotten he was weaponless. Sulla moved forwards, a spear in hand. Another spear stood on the wall behind him, ready for Darius to snatch.

"This isn't a democracy," Brutus said with a clenched fist.

Julius smiled. "No? So how do we operate?"

"Might is right," a voice spoke calmly from the door behind them.

Darius turned to see a tall blond rakkan striding into the room. He wore a vest made of brown leather with three black straps across his right, muscular arm. His skin bore none of the scars and scratches that Sulla and the other rakkans had.

A hush fell over the room as the rakkan walked forwards. Even the hovering smoke seemed to part for him, pushed back by a cool, fresh breeze from the corridor. His blond hair was slicked back with oil, tidy like a Laltos nobleman.

He walked up to Darius and gave him a hard look. "And I'm the might."

"Varro," Brutus rumbled over Darius's shoulder.

"I hear you don't know who I am anymore," Varro said, his stare not softening a fraction. "So let me introduce myself. I'm Varro, Warlord of the Black Legion, and brother of Felix, who's dead. Because of you."

Darius's stomach sank as he braced for a punch to the gut or a fist to the chin, but the Warlord just stared. *Stay quiet or speak?* Varro's face showed no trace of sadness or even anger. Whatever

313

he felt was masked, and that worried Darius more than a snarl or spit.

A warlord without a visible scar on his body? Only a battle-hardened warrior would rise to warlord, so a lack of scars could only mean foes had rarely landed a blow on the man. This rakkan scared him.

Darius stood tall and tried to keep his voice calm. "Both your brothers fought hard to save me that day. Let me assure you I want nothing more than to avenge Felix's death."

Without a flicker of reaction, Varro turned to his right. "Alexandra."

She looked away, jaw clenched.

"Good to see you, too," Varro said, moving past them. "Brother."

Brutus bowed his head. "Varro, you've recovered from the contest quickly. I'm sor—"

"Weren't my orders to ensure you brought Darius back to the city without Archimedes's knowledge?"

Brutus stammered, "I, er, it wasn't possible. They were both too injured."

"You've led the dogs right to our door. We might have had weeks—months—to vacate the city. Now we have days."

"It wouldn't have mattered," Darius said. All eyes turned on him like he'd spoken out of turn. Perhaps he had, but it was his life they were deliberating over like it was nothing. "Archimedes's cogi powers show him his future. If I was here, he'd probably know it even if we weren't tailed."

Varro walked over to the large chair and sat, planting his elbows on the thick armrests and steepling his hands. Rings of all shades—silver, black, grey—adorned his fingers like brass knuckles.

"How do you know this?" Julius said, relighting his pipe with a fingertip.

Darius looked to Lex who gave the slightest shake of her head. She'd warned him not to mention the Waif Magician to Brutus and the others because of whatever feud raged between them.

"We figured it out on the run," Darius said.

The commanders groaned and Gaius waved his hand. "That means nothing."

"The algus confirmed it to Lex." Darius held a hand out to her and she nodded, still avoiding Varro's gaze.

"Strange that none of the algus we've captured mentioned it." Julius released a cloud of thick smoke. "And we're very good at making them talk."

The fact they'd actually captured an algus made Darius all the more wary of these warriors.

"It would explain how Archimedes is always one step ahead," Brutus said. "Maybe there is no traitor, no one leaking our plans, it's all this cogi."

Varro's eyes narrowed. "You're lying, Darius."

Everyone sat so still Darius could hear the light crackle of burning tobacco.

"Tell us," Brutus said in a harsh tone.

"Fine." Darius glanced at Lex. "I was told by the Waif Magician."

The commanders gasped and Brutus growled. "That witch?"

Sulla cursed while Lex backed away a fraction. This was her bed yet she looked ready to leave Darius to lie in it.

"Yes. So?" he asked.

"Ah, so you didn't tell him?" Brutus said, rounding on Lex. She squared her shoulders but the rakkan held himself back, though his glare was dark and ominous. "That witch has been

315

kidnapping our kind—your friends, Darius—for decades, for her depraved sorcery, experimenting on us. We've tried to find her for years. If you saw her you should've strung her up with her own bowels."

The commanders all murmured in agreement except for Varro who stayed mute. Darius decided not to mention he and Lex had promised to give the Magician the Staff of Arria if they defeated Archimedes.

"What experiments?" Darius asked.

Lex wouldn't meet his eye.

"We think she's trying to create a mirror of the Staff of Arria," Gaius said. "Only instead of weakening rakkans, she wants to weaken algus. Our ferven opposes their algor and she wants to harness it, in the same way legend says the Staff was created..." His voice trailed off like the tale was too ghastly to utter.

Yet another detail Lex had declined to divulge. Should he feel bad for all those tortured rakkans, or would she be happy for him to listen to the voice that told him he shouldn't care?

"I didn't know," Darius said. "But we needed to find a way to undo what Archimedes did." He kept his voice quiet, pleading. A few more minutes and maybe they'd expect him to get down on his knees. "It was the only way. But she told us how to kill him and that's what I'm going to do."

Silence hung heavy in the dreary room. Lex still gazed at the floor like she'd rather be anywhere else. This wasn't just about the Waif Magician; she hadn't said a word or lifted her eyes since Varro had entered the room.

"I'm afraid that's not going to happen," Varro said. "We can't risk Archimedes getting anything more from your mind. We're immune to his powers. You're not. You're a weak link."

The Warlord's words rang in Darius's ears like a curse. Without their support, he'd never get his memories back. He'd never be Darius again. Instead, he'd be left an oblivious fool until someone put him out of his misery. *To hell with that.*

"We just have to neutralise Archimedes first," Sulla said, coming forwards to join them properly. The spear leaned against his shoulder. "Then we bring in Darius when it's safe. We can get the old Darius back."

Julius laughed. "Like it's that simple."

"Sure it is." Sulla grinned. "All we need to do is get him away from the Staff. Without that, we can stand and fight. We outnumber the algus at least ten to one. It's enough."

"Doesn't mean we can take Archimedes though," Gaius said, running a hand across his bald scalp. "If Darius is right and he sees his future memories, it explains how he's such a formidable fighter. Even without the Staff, Darius couldn't take him."

Darius hung his head as the commanders murmured again. What a colossal failure he'd made as a warrior all those weeks ago.

"I'd wager Varro could take Archimedes," Julius said. "He made short work of Warlord Catonius."

Everyone looked to Varro but the Warlord continued staring down Darius.

"His weakness is that the future memories are only based on sight," Darius said. "If he doesn't see something, like if we blind him or take a shot out of his line of vision, then he won't foresee it coming. Except that it has to be perfect with no chance of failure. If there's a chance we miss, he'll foresee it and be prepared."

Sulla pulled out a chair and sat down. "Blind you say. It's a good thing we can see in the dark then."

Darius hadn't thought of that, but it made perfect sense. If they could get Archimedes in the dark against the rakkans they'd have the upper hand. Except that it was futile so long as Archimedes had the Staff.

"You're forgetting the Staff," Varro said, echoing Darius's thoughts. The Warlord stood and withdrew a cane from under the table like a father about to straighten out his children.

"Has he ever let the Staff leave his possession that you know?" Brutus asked Lex.

"Once," she muttered. "When we ambushed him and Darius lost his memories."

"Enough fantasising." Varro pointed the cane at one of the etchings on the table.

The lines formed rows of squares and circles, with thicker lines around a mass in the centre. All at once, it made sense to Darius. It was a map of the city and the surrounding mountains and trails.

"I want to know the latest reports on Archimedes's forces," Varro said. "I came back to the city via the Markan Gate here. There were five algus already there watching, with a battalion of soldiers just over the crest of the hill."

"What about Darius?" Julius snarled.

"I'm sorry," Varro said, turning to the beefy rakkan, "is there something more important to discuss than the defence of Margalvia?"

Julius wilted under the weight of Varro's eyes and the Warlord turned back to the table. At least someone had their priorities right. Did this mean Darius wasn't to be hanged? Dare he feel relief? *Best not to ask.*

"Our scouts report dozens of algus setting up camp only a couple of hours from the main gate." Gaius pointed to a narrow groove that looked like where Darius had entered Margalvia. "They're heading a growing army already five hundred strong."

"More like a thousand," Lex said, finally breaking her silence. "I have eyes in the sky."

Julius scowled. "We should attack while we can, before they're at full strength."

"Where's Archimedes?" Varro frowned as he scoured the map.

The commanders looked to each other and shrugged.

"Another few thousand soldiers and algus are a few hours behind," Lex said. "Archimedes is with them."

"It's tight, but possible," Julius said.

"Blah." Brutus shook his head. "If we attack, there wouldn't be time to kill a thousand men, plus algus, and get back before Archimedes arrived."

Sulla lifted his feet onto the table and leaned back in his chair. "There'd be time to kill the algus."

"We'd outnumber the algus," Gaius said, "just enough to overcome them."

Varro set aside the cane and sat back down. Fingers steepled again, he stared at the map in concentration. Was he concocting a strategic defence of the city, distributing his army in his mind, or was he just wondering what the hell to do? They couldn't wait and defend the city against a full army; Archimedes was too powerful.

"I've got it." Julius thumped his fist on the table. "We send Lex to assassinate Archimedes while a team attacks the main forces."

"How's that a solution?" Darius said. "She can't kill him alone and your men can't help."

Julius shrugged. "It would delay him and give our men enough time to wreak havoc and get back. We can dispatch some men to bombard Archimedes from a distance."

Darius shook his head. Did Julius not understand or did he just not care? "Archimedes will already know about your bombardment. He'll have algus ready and waiting. You won't get close."

"Alexandra's not going anywhere near Archimedes," Varro said, throwing Julius a hard stare.

Lex crossed her arms and let out a heavy breath towards the ground.

"She can't help," the Warlord continued, dark eyes now fixated on her though she still avoided his gaze. "She should leave us and go back to her human friends."

Lex finally looked up. "I'll take any excuse to avoid another moment with *you*." Her voice was quiet and cold. She turned and walked out while the rakkans—Sulla and Brutus included—looked blankly at the table, as if Lex's sudden dismissal was nothing out of the ordinary. There was something else going on that Darius wasn't privy to.

The handle clanged against the wall as she threw the door open and left.

Varro fixed his gaze on Darius. "And you. Stay in Margalvia. No one's leaving to face Archimedes."

Darius guessed it meant he'd escaped the noose, but they were never going to help him capture Archimedes and get back his memories. Arguing further would be fruitless.

"Then there's nothing left to say." He turned and followed Lex out of the room. *Looks like we might have to do this ourselves.*

44

A horde of rakkan soldiers stood in line at the blacksmith to ready their weapons and armour for the battle ahead. Despite the tension in the air, their voices never rose above a murmur, so low Darius heard every cough and every bash of the blacksmith's hammer. *Men wondering how soon death will come for them, because of me.*

The smell of fear and sweat hung heavy on the wind. Some passers-by still gave him dirty looks. It made him uncomfortable, even the eyes that weren't on him. Guilt—things had been easier when he'd discarded these feelings.

He hadn't seen Lex since she stormed out of the meeting, and he kept checking around, hoping to see her saunter up. It'd kill him if she'd left the city as Varro had suggested, but part of him would be glad she was safe. He guessed that meant he cared about her now.

To distract himself, Darius sucked another mouthful of smoke from a pipe Sulla had given him and let the warm, ashy taste sit on his tongue.

"So the long and short of it is Varro believed you, that Archimedes sees the future, so we're agreed you aren't a traitor," Brutus said, finishing his summary of the meeting after Darius had left. "You're pardoned. But we aren't attacking Archimedes's forces."

Pardoned. He should be happy, but it only prolonged his life until Archimedes assaulted the city. They had to take the fight to the goman.

"We have about six hours until the sun rises," Brutus added. "They won't attack at night when we can see better than them, staff or no staff; its influence only extends so far. But Archimedes won't wait long after dawn to attack now that he has enough algus. Evacuation's already started."

"What happened to your brother's balls?" Sulla said, heating his sword between his palms so it would be ready for sharpening.

"I hope you're not criticising my pardon," Darius said.

Brutus grinned. "No balls? Say that to his face."

Sulla shrugged and looked away. "I would." His glum mug said otherwise, though.

"Ha! I remember what you said all those weeks ago. Varro's twice the fighter you are. You don't fight your way to warlord without being the best."

"So we just wait here to die?" Sulla shook his head. "We should draw Archimedes away from Margalvia, sneak out a group and attack Denehill."

"No. Archimedes would never allow Denehill to be taken and there's no way we can hold it. Varro's orders are to hold them up in the city for as long as we can while the women and civilians escape south."

This whole city was in danger because of Darius—thousands of people. And what hope was there? Maybe if he gave himself up it'd buy them more time to flee.

That's odd. Now he gave a passing concern for strangers, and rakkans no less.

Knowing how to defeat the goman was useless if he didn't face Archimedes. The city was already lost so what more would the goman get from him? The risk was his, and he wanted the old Darius back.

"If it's me Archimedes wants," Darius said, "I'll go out and face him. Get my memories back or die trying. I presume Archimedes sleeps sometime, and I'm not above cutting his throat in bed."

Sulla grinned, deepening the scars in his cheeks. Even a suicidal suggestion seemed no more odd to the rakkan than proposing a day out hunting. Darius liked this man.

Brutus scoffed. "You'll be out of here in a couple of hours, as soon as it's clear."

Darius leaned in close. "I'm serious. I want my memories back."

"My man," Sulla growled.

Brutus shook his head. "We have our orders. You're still a Black Legionnaire and you obey your warlord."

"I'm sorry, Brutus, but I can't," Darius said quietly. "I'll go it alone if I have to."

The warrior eyed him. It was often hard to tell exactly where the rakkan stared with his obsidian eyes, but this time Darius knew they lanced his own. Brutus's iron-dotted teeth ground tobacco as he mulled.

"*My* chief hasn't given me orders yet," Sulla said. "The Militia are weighing their options."

"Militia falls under Varro's command," Brutus said.

"Our chief does, but he is still to issue the command to us. I've made other plans."

Brutus's eyes narrowed as his chewing ceased. Darius didn't like the thought of mutiny, but he was out of options. If Sulla was leaving, he was going with him.

Sulla leant in and lowered his voice even more. "My men'll be less than half an hour from Denehill now. Two hundred strong."

Brutus's pipe snapped between his fingers. "You've sent them on a suicide mission." He cursed and wiped the ash from his chest. It pattered on the ground around the stool he sat on.

"Only if the Staff is there. He's taken all the algus away for this army. Word will get to Archimedes quickly. He'll send the Staff to defend the city."

"Maybe he won't. At best he'll leave with it and you'll buy us a day or two, at the cost of two hundred of your own men."

"Archimedes won't leave if he's got Darius sitting on a platter somewhere else. My men were ready to risk their lives for the chance to kill Archimedes. And kill him we will. Once the Staff leaves to defend Denehill, we'll stage an attack on the camp and make sure Archimedes knows Darius is there. Then we'll withdraw into the old tunnels to the north. We'll take the goman and algus in the dark."

Darius would be as powerless as a worm on a hook if Sulla's plan went to pot and the Staff stayed in Archimedes's hands. But the chance of running the goman through and getting back his memories was too enticing.

"You're treading on thin ice, Sulla," Brutus muttered. "You think you'll get away with treachery against Varro on a technicality?"

"I'm in," Darius whispered. "As long as we confirm the Staff leaves for Denehill."

Brutus raised his eyebrows and stared at Darius for a second, but it didn't take long for the rakkan's face to twist into a surly expression again. "I shouldn't be listening to this."

Sulla's eyes turned serious as he shed his permanent grin. "You know what the Magician told Darius. Archimedes is the only one that can bring him back."

Brutus twisted his neck, as if trying to wrestle off an invisible arm strangling him.

"What more can Archimedes get from me that would change things?" Darius asked. "The city's about to be razed. The worst has happened. Our only way out is to kill him. At least don't tell anyone we're leaving."

Muttering under his breath, Brutus rose to his feet. Darius gave him space to think while Sulla held his blade to a grinder, sending sparks flying. The smell of iron—or was it kuraminium—was oddly pleasant.

Brutus's snarl smoothed into a frown. Darius tried to read those black eyes but it was so much harder than a human's gaze. Before he could speak, the rakkan grabbed Darius by the neck and pulled his ear close.

"I'm not leaving you in this madman's hands. There's a reason he got all those scars. He doesn't know when to turn from a fight and he's lousy when he gets into them. You need me. Now, let's find Lex." Brutus dragged Darius into a one-armed bear hug. "I've got your back, son. Let's go kill that fiend."

45

Sulla knocked on Lex's door as the three of them and Lyra waited in the hall. Brutus and Sulla took twice the space now that they'd clad their chests and limbs with dark plates of kuraminium. The cuirass they'd given Darius was smaller and lighter. It would protect him better than an algus's mail but it made movement a little less free. It did make his chest look fuller though. He still felt small next to the rakkans and was almost loathe to stand next to them, especially meeting Lex. *At least I'm taller.*

Lyra nudged his hand with her head, seeking pets. It was good to have his escort back at his heel. She never showed a trace of fear and almost deluded him into thinking this foolhardy plan had a chance of coming off. *It must be nice not to know what's coming.* Or perhaps she did and had bigger balls than them all.

Sulla's knock received no answer. He cranked the handle. "I'm coming in. I don't care if you're nude." Despite his brave words, the rakkan eased the door open slowly to reveal a small bedroom, the same as Darius's except for the female garments piled on the bed and table. Lex wasn't there but it didn't look like she'd run out on him. The room was bright with lamps, hurting his eyes that had grown used to the dim Margalvian streets.

Sulla chuckled. "You look disappointed, Dar. Hoping for bit of skin?"

"I'll wager you were," Darius said, brushing past him and taking a closer look around the room. A half-eaten bread roll sat on the desk next to rolls of parchment, some with notes scrawled across. A ten-inch blade lay sheathed on the bed and her bow stood balanced at the foot. She'd be back but where had she disappeared to? Had it anything to do with Varro?

Lyra jumped on the bed and made herself comfortable while Sulla snatched up a parchment from the table.

"What have we here? 'Dear Darius, I want to write this to you before it's too late'"

Darius and Brutus both stepped forwards to get a glance but Sulla backed away, shielding the parchment.

"'I want you to know that I'll always love you, even though you aren't half as good looking as that sex-god Sulla and—'"

Lunging forward, Darius snatched the parchment from Sulla. He turned it over and found only a single line, *Weakness is sight.*

"Very funny," he said, scrunching it up while Sulla and Brutus chuckled.

Darius threw the parchment at Sulla's head. The rakkan ducked and caught it, laughing all the louder. Flora had told Darius about the apparently swift rakkan reflexes. *Apparent* because they weren't fast at all; rakkans felt subtle movements in the air, like when things flew towards them. That explained why they left their arms exposed bar the armguards, to feel incoming attacks.

Perception wasn't without its price though. Flora had explained their skin's sensitivity left them vulnerable to the sun. Darius wondered whether they were more sensitive to a sharp blade too. He hadn't thought to ask her.

"Those scars on your face," he said to Sulla. "Did they hurt more because you're a rakkan?"

Sulla's eyes widened. "Like hell."

"Ferven protects us somewhat," Brutus said, "from hot and cold especially if we need it. Varro walked for half a day in the blazing sun once by conjuring it over his body."

"Show off," Sulla muttered.

If conjuring ferven was anything like algor, keeping it up for half a day was an impressive feat. It was tiring in long stints, just like running or lifting.

"Speaking of Varro," Darius said, keeping his tone casual, "what's the situation between him and Lex?"

Brutus took a deep breath. "I wouldn't bring it up with either of them if I were you."

"Noted. But I'm bringing it up with you."

"They had a thing."

Darius had guessed as much. The venom she spat at Varro, she'd only been like that with him. *Does that mean we...?* "How did she end up with a rakkan?"

"We came across her a few years ago: me, you and Varro. He almost killed her but you stopped him. You always had a weakness for pretty girls. She was most curious about you, being half human. You two had some sort of thing brewing but you went off for a long time and they sort of happened."

So, old Darius had let her go. What a fool. "And now?"

"Let's just say he broke her heart. She doesn't talk of it, and she's been even more closed off since." Brutus gave him a look of warning.

Would he be a fool to try anything with her?

The door swung open and Lex strode in, her hair loose and falling down over her shoulders. She showed a distinct lack of surprise at seeing them in her room.

"Hey, blue-eyes," Sulla said.

"I thought I heard voices. I guessed only you three would be stupid enough to set foot in my space."

Darius craned his head towards the bed. *Lyra. Off!* She didn't move, apparently quite at home in Lex's bed.

"You all look ready to go somewhere," Lex said, heading straight for the dagger lying next to Lyra. She scratched the panther's ear before snatching up the blade.

"We've lost all sense and are going after Archimedes." Brutus paced around the room.

Lex began putting on her armour. "I thought I'd have to convince you."

Lucky for her and Darius, Sulla had done the convincing.

"Where did you disappear to?" Darius asked. An algus wandering a rakkan town was surely abnormal.

"Picking up these." Lex tossed him four small pouches, altogether no bigger than the palm of his hand.

Sulla took one and sniffed it while Darius loosened the string of another and sprinkled some of the dark powdered contents into his hand. It was so fine his breath swept away a small wisp of particles. It rose like steam, dissipating in the lamplight.

"Ground sprugenroot," Sulla muttered.

The powder began tickling Darius's palm and he shifted it to reveal a slightly red patch on his skin.

"A dash in stew gives it a kick," Sulla said, "but I don't see what use it is. And all this must have cost you a small fortune."

Darius doubted the rakkans took crests. Most likely she'd stolen it but he wasn't going to ask in front of the others. *Is this for fighting Archimedes?* He poked at the dust more, wondering how difficult it would be to use. As he considered testing it out, pain seared his eyes and he snapped them shut with a loud curse.

"Irritating, isn't it?" Lex said. "Better than salt, especially in the eyes. We get this in the air in front of Archimedes and it'll be barely visible but will burn his eyes in an instant. He won't be able to open them."

Darius tried to open his eyes but they seared all the more with every tiny movement. "And how do we stop it blinding *us*?"

"Conjure algor in your eyes."

Focusing, Darius coated his eyes and breathed as the pain vanished. At least he knew the powder worked well. They finally had a plan for taking down Archimedes. Darius's memories were no longer a dream, they were within grasp. He'd remember so much more of how to fight, why he was fighting…and all his old self had known about Lex.

The algus swung her bow over her shoulder and stood ready. "Where are we going? What's the plan?"

Sulla stepped forward while Brutus planted his backside on a chair with a clunk.

"There's a peak just to the north," Sulla began, "a stone's throw from a tunnel we dug through the mountain last winter. Archimedes's forces are in the valley below, in full view of the hilltop, and you or Darius should have no trouble making your presence known."

"Draw Archimedes and his army to us?" Lex looked sceptical.

"We draw him into the tunnels. They're narrow, with only a few wider caves where the shafts hit natural pockets and pits. He can't send much of an army in so his numbers will be constrained. We know the passages well. We can tear his algus apart in the dark."

Lex remained unconvinced. "Aren't you forgetting the Staff?"

"My men are attacking Denehill as we speak. The town will fall unless Archimedes sends someone with the Staff and it'd be too big a strategic blow for him to allow that."

Lex's brow furrowed, but she didn't voice any immediate objection. That could mean the plan had half a chance of working.

He might actually become old Darius again, that great warrior everyone spoke of. *How thrilling.*

"It won't take long for word to reach Archimedes about Denehill," Brutus said, rising from his chair. "We dangle the bait, reel him in, Sulla and I will pump him with a face-full of sprugenroot in the dark. If it's destined to work, he'll have no memories to foresee after that point. Then we fry him bit by bit until he gives Darius his memories back."

"It won't be just us facing him," Sulla said. "I have another group of men coming with us."

Lex looked Darius in the eye, as if assessing whether he was still worth risking her life for. After all this time, he was beginning to wonder if his life was worth more or less than hers too.

"Lex, you don't have to come if you don't want to." He was loathe to say it but he hated to drag her into this fight as well. "I have these guys now. They'll need to keep the tunnels dark so we won't even be able to help much."

"You need me," Lex said, taking a step towards him. "If Sulla's wrong and Archimedes comes with the Staff, I'm the only one that can stand and fight."

"We'll make sure it leaves. But if Archimedes somehow tricks us and brings the Staff we're all dead anyway."

"You need me."

"I don't..." Truth be told, he did need her, and for more than just her skills as a fighter, but part of him wanted at least one of them to survive. Everyone close to him had died so far. First Amid, then Felix, then Omid. The thought of adding another name to the list unsettled him. Soon there'd be no one left.

"We'll wait for you outside. One minute." Brutus turned and shoved a reluctant Sulla out of the room, the door slamming shut behind them.

Lex sighed, her expression solemn as she gazed at Darius. "I can't wait here. I have to make sure I get Darius back."

"Because you want to know where my grandfather is. That's all you want?"

"And no one knows except you. I want a lot, but this is more important than anything." Her eyes widened, a hint of desperation leaking out.

"Is this all about information to you? Do you actually care if I die, if old Darius is gone forever?" He took a step closer until their bodies touched, his cuirass pressing against her armour.

Her eyes shifted, conflict clear in their wary blue depths as she ruminated on thoughts he doubted she'd ever share.

"I care," she whispered, her gaze flicking down to his lips for a second.

"Nothing happened with Flora," Darius said, hoping it would weaken those shields she always kept so high. Maybe that encounter played on her mind. It'd certainly be on his if Lex had a half-naked man alone with her.

She scoffed. "You expect me to believe that? I know you, Darius."

"Well, as you've made perfectly clear, I'm not the Darius you knew. I didn't feel like being with a whore." There was more he wanted to say, but the thought of laying out his feelings towards her only to have her stomp all over them sent beads of sweat running down his temple. *Should I?*

"Darius, I—"

"Not just that." To hell with it. Fear was for the weak. "I couldn't stop thinking of you. Even though you've treated me like dirt, even though you're reticent to the extreme, I can't get you out of my head. That's why I didn't do it."

Her frown vanished and her lips parted a fraction, breath held. The longer she remained silent, the more he wanted to look away and brace for a blow that would hurt more than any he'd taken so far.

Lex reached up, but instead of striking him, she stroked the back of his head. "I'm coming with you, and that's that. But don't hold out for me, Darius. I'm done with men. They only bring me pain."

Had she really given up on men or was she letting him down gently? "What if I'm willing to hold out for the few hours left of my life?"

She squeezed her eyes shut. "If I was certain… I want to… I hope—"

Taking her by the waist, Darius pressed his lips to hers. Her eyes still shut, she closed her mouth around his and lightly sucked his top lip. He ran his hand through her soft raven hair, brushing his fingertips across the back of her head as their kiss deepened. It was everything he'd imagined, and more.

Lex's eyes opened, sparkling with blue algor as she gazed at him in a way she never had before, in a way that said she cared.

She pulled her head back and drew a breath, mouth slightly parted in shock.

"I thought a dead man deserved a last kiss," he said, letting his hands fall through her silky hair.

A bang resonated on the door. Brutus was getting impatient.

Lex stared silently at him, her expression suggesting that she was contemplating kissing him again.

"We should go," she finally said, blinking away the algor and brushing past him.

If only he'd kissed her before now, they'd have had time to talk or take it further. It still felt like so much needed to be said but time was something they didn't have. Darius straightened his back. If all went well, they'd have all the time in the world. And if it didn't… The memory of her lips against his lingered, warm and thrilling. *At least I'll have that to accompany me into death.*

"Lyra, come." He beckoned his escort, smiling as the panther leapt off the bed and padded towards the door. "Let's go finish this."

46

Nikolaos leapt over another fallen rock as he raced up the treacherous Uxon Trail. Thirty-seven sprinted two steps ahead, her black hair waving wildly in the wind as she set a pace he barely matched. There wasn't a second to waste. From peace to chaos within minutes, Denehill was under attack and falling fast. Walls melted into lava. Buildings pelted with boulders. Men screamed as they were torn apart by the attackers, too many to fend off for the few algus left there. They had to reach Archimedes or the fortress would fall.

Thirty-seven had gone first and it didn't take two to raise the alarm, but Nikolaos wasn't staying in that town to die. The southerners could fight their own battles, just as they always let the westerners. Besides, it was only right that he be the one to break the news, given he'd convinced Archimedes to weaken the town's defences for the attack on Margalvia. *Curses, what a poor turn of events.*

A flaming torch rose into view. A tent lay just beyond it. Nikolaos groaned in relief. They'd finally made it to the camp; now to find the goman. Thirty-seven at his side, he raced through the tents, dodging soldiers as they searched for the largest where

Archimedes resided. Two guards at the entrance stepped aside as they burst in.

"Master!" Thirty-seven yelled as they shoved past the thick tent flaps.

Archimedes sat at a long table with algus crammed around it. The goman rose to his feet, eyes narrowed at the intrusion. "*What's wrong?*"

"Dene—"

"Denehill is under attack," Nikolaos interjected. "An army of rakkans attacked less than half an hour ago. Without reinforcements, the fort will be destroyed."

Archimedes sat back down as half the algus around the table murmured to one another. The tent was grand, made of fine royal blue cloth. It must have belonged to a wealthy southern family; Archimedes rarely travelled with such extravagance.

Half the algus watched the goman, awaiting instructions. Some couldn't have been older than fifteen but all wore the stares of hardened warriors. *The Numbered.* They'd only respond to orders when their master was around.

"*I can spare ten algus.*"

"But there are at least a couple of hundred rakkans," Nikolaos said, still panting from the strenuous run.

Archimedes glanced around the table. All of the algus now sat silent. Despite the large number there, none seemed eager to volunteer to fight a rakkan army without *him*. Now that Nikolaos thought of it, it was odd the goman had convened so many algus. Normally he simply sent orders.

"*Fifteen then,*" Archimedes conceded.

It was risky to send so few. Nikolaos was loath to argue but Denehill was too strategically important, the floodgate to the southern rakkans. "Why don't you go, Archimedes? Margalvia can surely wait a day."

Some of the algus raised their eyebrows at him. Wind slipped through the tent flaps that hung askew from Nikolaos and Thirty-seven's hasty entrance. The chilled air raised the hair on the back of his neck.

"*I can't leave. Soon Darius will leave himself vulnerable and I need to seize my opportunity to strike. My only lead on the Urukan Mine is tantalisingly close.*"

So it was Denehill in exchange for the Urukan Mine. Nikolaos couldn't argue it wasn't worth it. Without the mine, all the major rakkan cities would struggle to arm and defend themselves.

"Why not send the fifteen with the Staff?" an elderly algus said.

The room held its breath while the goman didn't answer, just sat with a furrowed brow.

"Master Archimedes," a soldier called as he walked into the tent. "She's arrived and is asking to speak with you."

"*Show her in. I'll deal with Denehill in a moment.*"

All the algus stood and turned towards the entrance. Those not among the Numbered looked nervous, some even clutched the hilts of their swords. The chilly air howled through the tent flaps and sent shivers across Nikolaos's sweaty body as the heat from the run faded. He stepped away from the entrance, wondering who it was that would rouse such anxiety when Archimedes was here. Was this woman the reason all the algus were congregated?

A frail woman wearing the ragged robes of a beggar hobbled into the tent. Locks of fiery red hair fell over her shoulders. It couldn't be… As far as Nikolaos knew, no one had laid eyes on her for years. She was thought to be dead.

"*Forgive my men, but I don't trust easily.*" Archimedes stayed seated at the opposite end of the tent.

337

"Then let me set your mind at ease," she said. "I won't harm you or your men unless they move against me." Her wrinkled face was slightly veiled by hair but Nikolaos could see her thin lips. Pressed together as they were, they almost made her look like a goman.

"*Am I supposed to trust your word?*" Archimedes cocked his dreadlocked head.

"Of course. I am half goman, I cannot lie. I am Shirin, known to your knuckle-draggers as the Waif Magician." Shirin hobbled a step closer. She looked like an old woman, hardly a threat. But Nikolaos knew an act when he saw it. This woman could move like the wind wafting her cloak.

"*I confess, I'm a little confused. I knew you would come, but I don't know why.*"

The Magician frowned. "I'm here to help you catch Darius. I can tell you where he is, where he'll be and how he plans to take you down."

"*And why would you help me?*"

"Because in return the King will pardon me. I want to live out my old age in peace."

Archimedes's eyes brightened. "*Done.*"

"And I want fifty thousand crests in bullion under my name at the Laltos Bank."

The goman stared motionless. Nikolaos clenched his jaw to stop it from falling open at her audacity. So much wealth would buy a quarter of Laltos itself. The King would need to impose heavy taxes to pay for it.

Taking a deep breath, Archimedes stood. "*Agreed.*"

47

Darius held the flaming torch up to the ceiling of the cavern. Finger marks in the rough stone showed where rakkans had chipped away the rock with ferven-coated hands. It looked as if a hundred people had been trapped in a mass grave and tried to scratch their way out. *Hopefully it won't become our tomb.*

"This place is perfect," Sulla said. "I'll have my men flush Archimedes's algus into here."

Darius stepped to the edge of one of the gaping chasms in the ground. The floor looked like a honeycomb, thin strips of walkway between sheer drops so black not even torchlight could reach their depths. The darkness threatened to suck him in.

"Can you see the bottom of that?" he asked Brutus.

"No."

Maybe if he fell in, he'd never stop falling, or he'd land in hell. Darius stepped away and pressed his back to the wall, comforted by its dry, safe touch. Lyra walked past, brushing against the sides too. *Smart girl.*

Sulla grinned. "We'll barely have to fight them. Half will race in here and see the drops too late. The other half we can give a nudging hand."

Lex crouched with one of Sulla's men in an alcove they'd specially carved out. Both had bows with an arrow already nocked, the tips carrying light cotton-wrapped balls filled with powdered sprugenroot. The pair chatted quietly. Darius couldn't see Lex's expression through her mask, but the rakkan was grinning at her over some inside joke. Was she flirting, like she always did? His blood heated at the thought. At least Nasrin had said she never flirted with the ones she cared about.

The other bags of sprugenroot were with Brutus, Sulla and Darius. His pouch was burning a hole in his pocket. If Archimedes wanted him, the goman would have to come within arm's reach, and when he did, Darius would conjure every ounce of strength in him to blind the fiend as a last-ditch effort, however short his odds. He'd stick it in his mouth and spit it at the goman if he had to.

Brutus sauntered over, helmet now firmly in place. "You and Lex will need to speak with Archimedes when we have him. We're immune to cogi so we can't hear him."

"Don't get ahead of yourself." They had to catch the goman first.

The thought of Archimedes's cogi voice burrowing into his ear again sent shivers down Darius's spine. Lex had told him Archimedes sounded normal to her, not the whisper Darius heard. Perhaps that had something to do with his rakkan half. Perhaps some immunity still burned in his veins. Not that it had made a difference so far.

Brutus slapped a beefy hand on his shoulder. "The scouts have confirmed the Staff has left for Denehill. Archimedes stayed behind. It's time."

Darius and Brutus made their way out of the tunnel and crept a couple of hundred yards to the peak of a hill. The night cloaked them but they still crawled the last few feet. Darius raised his head just enough to see the hundreds of torches illuminating tents stretching across the valley. Half of Sulla's men were already positioned around the encampment, ready to begin raining fiery rocks from all sides. With their rakkan strength, they were as good as ballistae.

Mist hung in the air, tickling Darius's throat. He quietly nudged aside the loose jagged stones digging into his elbows.

"See that big tent with the four braziers outside?" Brutus whispered.

"I see the braziers," Darius said, wishing he had the rakkan's vision.

"That'll be where Archimedes is. You and I will fight on this slope to make sure he gets a good view of the bait."

"You mean me."

"Exactly. We only turn back to the tunnels when we know we'll draw in Archimedes. This has to look like another ambush gone awry if he's to give chase without suspecting a trap."

Once all the focus was on Darius, the other rakkans would try to slip away. Any number of things could go wrong but Darius was done running away like a coward. It was time for either him or the goman to die, and if it was going to be Darius he'd go out like he came into this world, screaming and kicking.

He ran over the plan again in his mind, wishing all the while that Lyra was by his side. The panther sat waiting in the cavern with the others. Everyone was in position, the snares laid.

"You ready?" Darius whispered, grabbing the cold hilt of his sword for comfort.

If Archimedes saw his future, he'd already know they were on this hilltop. His men may be somewhere close, waiting to strike as soon as Darius and Brutus revealed themselves. Brutus better move fast to the tunnels because Darius didn't have the rakkan strength to drag the warrior's hefty backside along.

"Let's start the fun." Brutus's eyes glowed orange through the slits in his helmet and he chuckled.

The laugh brought Darius a fleeting moment of calm before the conflict. This plan might work and he'd soon be the one smiling with blazing eyes, old Darius back in full force. What would it feel like? Like a blind man suddenly seeing? Would his new self vanish into the void?

Who cared?

Brutus picked up a rock and it erupted in a blaze of ferven. The rakkan stood and loosed the stone along with a stomach-trembling roar. It echoed through the valley and hung in the air long after Brutus fell silent.

The molten projectile crashed through one of the smaller tents and bounced into another. Shouts echoed from the camp, smoke and flames rising from the fabrics.

More fiery rocks flew in from all sides as the other rakkans joined in. Brutus held a second flaming stone in his hand, letting it sit a moment to give the algus more of a chance to spot him.

Figures began bursting from tents and were soon heading up the slope towards them. Only a handful for now, but more would follow.

Now it was Darius's turn. He crawled in front of Brutus, getting into position to launch a surprise first strike at the incomers. The rakkan tossed a handful of molten pebbles down the hill that shed enough light for Darius to track the defenders.

A long-haired algus was fastest and already almost upon them.

Darius lunged at her and flared algor across his sword. She saw him too late as he cut through her waist, both chainmail and flesh as if it weren't there.

Averting his eyes from the spilling blood, he darted towards the next algus. This one was more prepared and their blue swords clashed. *Perfect.* All Archimedes needed to see was algor battling algor and he'd know Darius was here.

The pair traded blows as Brutus's shadowy figure leapt overhead. The rakkan brought his hammer down on another approaching algus with a crunch of bone.

More tents were catching fire and smoke began filling the sky. *Damn.* Too much and Archimedes wouldn't be able to see them fighting on the hill. Plenty of other algus had spotted them though and were heading their way. Much longer and they'd be overrun.

"I see Archimedes," Brutus called. "He's looking over here."

About time. Darius swung his glimmering sword in a few huge swings. His foe easily blocked the blows but they were meant to alert the goman to his presence, not kill. Satisfied he'd done enough, Darius extinguished his blade and bolted for the tunnel.

Air blasted his face as he sprinted. The ground shook as Brutus landed just behind with a thunderous crash, having leaped after him.

A blue-tipped arrow darted from the darkness and Darius ducked before it skewered his shoulder. He was running virtually blind, following the path from memory. Though it would give his position away, he conjured a trace of algor below his feet. Better to dodge arrows than twist an ankle on the uneven stony ground. The clanking of armour fell back and he tempered his pace to keep Brutus close.

The whip of arrows sounded all around. Brutus's muscular arm shoved him to the left, guiding him to the tunnel entrance. After every step he half expected to slam into stone but trusted Brutus's eyes to guide him true.

"There!" Brutus kicked a hunk of stone, ferven bursting over its surface. It flew straight into the narrow mouth of the tunnel.

Streaks of blue flew by from all angles. One grazed Darius's neck, an inch shy of ending him.

The pair dove to the ground and rolled into the tunnel in a cloud of shingles and dust. *Graceful.*

Darius regained his feet quickly. They'd made it back and no trace of weakness had seeped in his body. His muscles pulsed with energy and his hand still clutched his sword with an iron grip.

Brutus rose and they ran on. Darius flared algor across his sword, holding it out to light the way through the meandering passages. He didn't dare wrench his eyes from the ground lest a pit swallow him whole. The dark tunnel walls closed in at the edges of his vision, suffocating, raising the fear this would be his grave. He pushed those thoughts away.

A clash of metal rang from behind and Darius skidded to a halt. Brutus roared and smashed his fist into an algus's stomach as a blue-edged sword lacerated the rakkan's arm.

Darius lunged at the staggering man and drove his sword clean through the algus's throat. Blood gushed down his blade. His mind flashed back to the little girl in Laltos, dagger in her mother's neck, showered in blood. Algus like this were helping that monster Archimedes. He twisted the blade and ripped it free, choking down his sickness and light-headedness.

"Go ahead," Brutus growled. "I'll be better off in the dark."

Blood dripped from the rakkan's arm but it wasn't gushing. He'd live, and there wasn't time to argue. Darius sprinted off deeper into the tunnels.

The passage broadened, giving him extra breathing space. This deep, the air was dry and stagnant, like it came from the depths of the earth rather than the mists outside.

Sulla's warriors would be waiting in the dark nooks hidden at the edges of the tunnel. Darius prayed they'd know him from Archimedes's men. As he navigated the twisting, forking passages, sharp pains stung his injured thigh. The muscles were tiring already, still not recovered from the arrow wound. He gritted his teeth. They'd have to damn well power through until he found Lex and the others.

The sounds of footsteps grew behind him, along with a dancing blue light. Darius rounded a bend and stopped, back pressed to the wall. He extinguished his sword and lifted it high, poised to skewer the next shape that came around the corner.

An algor-coated hand was the first thing he saw before thrusting forward. The algus twisted instinctively as she caught sight of him, her raven hair swinging behind her head. Darius averted his thrust and sliced across her stomach, narrowly avoiding disembowelling her. *Lex?*

Taking advantage of his hesitation, the algus swung at him with her cobalt blue sword. Darius blocked with his armguard, flaring algor to stop it slicing clean through. The light flashed across her face. She scowled and bared her teeth in a snarl of rage. *Fetching, but not Lex.*

Darius kicked at her front leg but she blocked with a heel to his knee. He lunged, grabbing for her sword-bearing hand. The algus spun away, too fast to catch. Her fist smacked into the back of his head and he fell forwards with a groan onto the ground, metal digging into his forearms as they hit solid stone. Damn, she was quick. He needed to utilise some of those warrior smarts.

Her sword swung down at his neck. Rolling away, he regained his footing. They faced each other with algor-coated swords raised, tips touching. Every muscle in his body tensed, ready to act, as his heart pounded energy through his veins. The rush of the fight. But she was too fast.

Brute force would have to do. He slapped her sword aside with his own and charged forward, head dropped and aimed at her chest like a charging bull. The algus tried to dodge but he caught her in his arms and slammed his shoulder into her stomach, crunching her into the wall behind. A cry of pain was followed by the clatter of her sword on the ground.

Sharp, desperate pants shook her frame. *Winded. Now end it.* Darius pulled away and drew back his weapon, ready to drive it through her heart.

Raven hair fell across her face. She eyed him, breathless, her stare blank. No fear, no emotion.

His sword's glow flickered in her eyes as he paused. This woman looked so much like Lex. The thought of spilling her blood made him nauseated. But she was the enemy. Why did he hesitate?

Darius withdrew his blade and punched her across her jaw. Her head swivelled and she collapsed out cold, face first on the stone floor.

Picking up her sword lest she use it against him later, he set off into the passages. Just a few more turns and he'd be in the cavern with the others. A speck of algor on each foot helped guide him but he didn't dare conjure more. Just a few more turns and he'd see a flicker of ferven, or smell the ash of rakkan breath.

The turns came and went and his heartrate picked up. Surely he couldn't be lost, all alone in the black passages just waiting for another algus—or worse, Archimedes—to find him. Where were Sulla's men?

Darius came to an abrupt stop as the ground dropped into an abyss ahead. Holding out his sword, he sent algor trickling down its length until the blue glow illuminated a chasm two steps in front.

"It's Darius," whispered a voice, one of Sulla's men.

Lyra stalked over to greet him with a rub against his leg. He breathed a heavy sigh and nudged her away. *Go back to your position.* She didn't budge. Something was amiss.

"Movement behind!" the same rakkan called.

His escort turned and darted into the tunnel as Darius whirled around. His sword illuminated the straining face of an algus whose own raised blade was already slicing forwards to carve him in two. Their swords clashed and the algus jumped to avoid Lyra's jaws. The cat slid across the ground, biting nothing but dirt.

Darius kicked the algus in mid-air, smashing the full force of his heel into the man's thighbone. The algus landed and his damaged leg buckled, bringing him to one knee. Darius brought down a hammer blow that the man blocked just in time to stop it cleaving a shoulder. Metal squealed as Darius pressed down until his arms shook from strain and the blades touched the algus's mail, pinning his enemy in place.

Lyra roared and sank her jaws into the man's arm. He screamed as his bones crunched and blood spurted out, the attack weakening his resistance enough for Darius to slice the man's throat.

Darius hadn't the time to retch before two more algus, a man and a woman, burst from the shadows of the passage behind Lyra. The panther didn't have time to react; their lofted swords were only a second from cleaving her.

No one was going to lay their damned hands on his Lyra. He dove on top of her and banished the algor coating his weapon, plunging them all into darkness.

Two strikes lashed his back. He clenched his teeth, waiting for the cold sharpness of steel but only sensing dull pain. His cuirass had held. Lyra wriggled from under him and darted into the shadows, hopefully somewhere safe.

He kicked at the algus' legs, hoping to knock them off balance and somehow regain his feet. His foot connected with nothing but air. Sharp pain lanced through his left forearm as a blade pierced it. Darius cried out. Algor flared to life, revealing his opponents.

347

As the male algus pinned him to the ground, the woman's glowing blade aimed to spear his eye.

A molten fist flared from behind them and smashed into the woman's skull with a hiss of searing flesh. Her eyes went blank from the thunderous blow and her body flew back into the tunnel wall. The other algus ripped his blade from Darius's arm and ducked under a fiery sword's swing, dodging the blow by a few hairs.

Darius grunted and grabbed his punctured arm to stem the leaking blood. The wound was bad. How much blood could he lose before passing out? He already felt faint.

Pull yourself together, you wuss. Darius grabbed his sword but his hand wouldn't close enough to touch his fingers to his palm. He shifted and snatched the hilt with his other hand.

A clash of icy algor and flaming kuraminium sent sparks across his head. Sulla stood in front of him, scowling at the algus. The rakkan took a swing that the algus sidestepped with ease. The enemy's blade sliced across Sulla's face, drawing a sharp hiss and a thin flow of blood.

Darius pushed himself to one knee. Behind the two fighters, Lyra crept along the tunnel wall. Body low, she watched unblinking as the algus's gaze flitted back and forth between Darius and Sulla. *Wait for it, girl.*

As he rose to his feet, Darius slashed at the algus's ankle. The man flicked his leg away and backed up a step, straight into Lyra's jaws. She sank her teeth and claws into the man's calf. Screaming, he whipped his head around at the sudden attack and raised his sword. Darius dropped his weapon and grabbed the man's wrist with his one good arm just in time to stop the blow.

Sulla seized his chance and raced forward. He grabbed the algus by the neck and squeezed until his knuckles grew even whiter, muting the man's cries. The algus's arm went limp just before a crunch of vertebrae. Sulla dropped his arm to his side with the algus still dangling from his hand, the dead man's tongue hanging loose from a gaping mouth.

The rakkan narrowed glowing eyes at Darius, blood trickling down the latest addition to his scarred face. "I had him."

Like hell he did.

Sulla bent and grabbed the female algus's body by the hair then walked down the passage. Darius followed just behind Lyra, clutching his arm again. He'd risked his life to save her, taken two swords to his back without knowing if his cuirass would hold. It was the first selfless act he recalled doing. And he didn't regret it, even with his arm bleeding out. *Perhaps I'm capable of compassion after all.*

Sulla tossed the bodies down a pit. "Don't want to put the rest off coming in."

They'd made it back to the cavern. Sulla extinguished his ferven and walked away, leaving nothing but silence.

Darius conjured algor across his feet, making sure to tread carefully. He reached a narrow strip of ground between two pits and made his way across the quasi-bridge to the far side, the position Brutus had assigned him in the master plan. Touching the wall, he made sure Lyra was on safe footing then banished all algor, plunging the cavern into pitch black.

Things could have gone better but also a lot worse, so Darius had hope. Now it was up to the rakkans. One breathed heavily to his right. *Nerves.* These rakkans were here facing death for Darius. They were Militia, not legionnaires. The thought of the Staff still lingered in his mind, a weapon against which they faced certain death. It set his heart racing, and it must have been the same for them.

It was an odd feeling, that so many risked so much for him.

"Don't fret," Darius whispered.

The rakkan's breathing quieted a little.

Scuttling footsteps sounded from one of the passages leading into the cavern, accompanied by a faint light. Hushed whispers reached Darius's ears, announcing the first humans to the trap. But where was Brutus?

48

Three algus walked into view, the one in front holding a flaming torch overhead. All three held their swords ready and their heads flicked in all directions for any sight of a foe. The torch gave them light, but not enough to see every nook of the cavern; they had no chance of surviving the rakkans who lurked in wait.

Still no sign of dreadlocks, but hopefully Archimedes would not be far behind. He'd never missed a chance to find Darius in person yet.

The frontmost algus caught himself before stepping into a chasm. Algor flared in his widened eyes. His allies stopped and peered for a second into the abyss.

Brutus's hulking figure emerged from the shadows behind them. Darius had never been so happy to see a rakkan. The warrior leapt forwards and smashed his fists into the two closest skulls. The third algus side-stepped and swung his sword. Brutus's armguard flared with ferven and he blocked the blow inches from his helmet.

Darius couldn't help but admire the rakkan's fighting ability. Hand to hand combat and anticipation of moves like he'd never seen. He itched to have such power again himself.

Another two rakkans emerged from the dark. They caught the last algus by the hair and arm from behind. Before the man could flail, his neck snapped back and his arms drooped. The cavern flickered in the light of the torch now lying on the ground as the other rakkans returned to their hiding spots. Brutus tossed the bodies into another chasm so deep no impact sounded. Anything living down there was going to have a feast for sure.

As he turned from the abyss, Brutus grunted and froze. His left leg gave out and he dropped to one knee. Weakness seeped into Darius's own thighs and his heart skipped a beat, knowing the feeling all too well. *No.* He shoved his good hand into his pocket and grabbed the pouch of sprugenroot while he still had strength to clutch it. The powder might be his only hope, and what a longshot it was if his fears were true.

Clanks and thuds sounded around the cavern along with curses and growls, more rakkans falling under the weight of their heavy armour. *It's the Staff.* Darius crouched before he lost all strength and stumbled into one of the chasms on either side of him. One long, narrow strip of ground was all that separated him from Brutus but he couldn't reach the rakkan.

They'd failed. The scouts had been tricked or wrong about the Staff. It had always been risky but that didn't make his impending death any easier to swallow. There'd probably be a dozen more algus following. He'd foolishly let himself believe this plan would work.

Brutus dropped to all fours just as his brother Felix had, only an inch from the gaping pit. His arms trembled as he fought to stay up, while a blue glow grew in the tunnel behind him. Darius felt his shoulders sink. He leaned forwards and fell onto his hands, one step shy of the abyss himself. *I can't let Archimedes reach me.* Perhaps he should jump to his death now.

Each inch was a struggle, but he crawled forwards with his pouch still clutched tightly. The rock grated his knuckles as he slid them across the ground. His arm ached from the stab wound. Growling deep in his throat, Darius pushed on despite the pain. Eventually his hands met the jagged edge of the pit.

An outstretched staff slid into the cave from the tunnel, followed by Archimedes's mouthless face. The goman's eyes speared Brutus. Darius's arms drained of strength and he dropped to his elbows, right hand slipping perilously over the chasm, still squeezing the pouch.

Archimedes was flanked by algus. To his right walked Nikolaos from Laltos, still sporting a bruise beneath his glowing eyes. Maybe Darius should have finished the noble off when he'd had the chance.

"*This is the best they can do?*" Archimedes's voice hissed in his ears but the goman hadn't spotted Darius in the dark yet.

Stopping a few steps short of Brutus, Archimedes waved Nikolaos forward. The algus approached Brutus with a look of disgust and stooped to pick up the flaming torch.

He placed a leather boot on Brutus's trembling shoulders. "Not so tough, are you?"

Darius had to do something or Brutus was dead. If he drew their attention, maybe they'd forget about his rakkan friend long enough for Lex to get a shot off at Archimedes. He strained to conjure algor in his eyes but barely felt a flicker. Air slipped from his lungs weakly as he tried to cry out. The Staff's power pressed down on him, stripping any chance of aiding his ally.

Nikolaos shoved Brutus towards the pit. The rakkan barely wobbled and instead Nikolaos lurched off balance with a huff. He couldn't shove the warrior under the weight of all that armour. With a growl of anger, Nikolaos kicked Brutus's arm. The rakkan buckled, his chest slamming against the ground.

A smug grin spread across the algus's face as more men and women filed into the room. At the rear hobbled a small woman with a tattered cloak and fiery hair. The Waif Magician.

Darius clenched his jaw, curses screaming in his mind. Why was that witch helping Archimedes? He focused on his right hand. Stopping the sprugenroot falling into the pit was taking all his will and any waver would be the end of them. He needed to pull his hand back. There would be no giving up, not until every hope of revenge was lost.

"*Search the cavern. He's in here.*" Archimedes retracted the Staff to his chest.

A little strength returned to Darius and he tugged his right arm away from the chasm, grateful for the cold touch of stone on the back of his hand.

A rakkan cried out at the other side of the cavern as an algus's cobalt sword speared his gut.

"*Leave some alive. I want to question them.*" Archimedes glared at the algus, who bowed her auburn head and moved on.

Nikolaos still hovered over Brutus, torch aloft in one hand, sword lazily hanging down in the other. The blade scratched across the warrior's back with a thin screech.

Darius pushed with his legs and eased forwards. He had to get farther onto the thin strip of rock between the chasms. The depths were the only out he had should it come to that, and if he was perilously close to falling, Archimedes would back off with the Staff. Beyond that, he had no plan.

Lyra. His faithful friend brushed against his feet. *Push me.* Lyra's head pressed into the back of his thighs and shoved him on. Inch by inch, he crawled along as another rakkan was uncovered by an algus and shoved to the ground.

Darius struggled back onto his elbows, each hand flirting with the chasms' edges. His breaths grew sharper, heart slow but pounding. Warm blood pooled at his elbow from the stinging puncture in his arm. That was far enough. *Back up and hide, Lyra, until I need you.*

Even more algus and soldiers filed into the squat cave and began probing its dark corners. He counted at least thirty. Archimedes stood and watched it unfold, like a lion waiting for the pride to bring back the kill.

The Waif Magician shuffled away from the centre, stepping carefully to avoid the chasms. Another ten rakkans had been uncovered and lay helpless at the feet of sneering men and women. Shirin knelt by one and squeezed his dirt-smeared chin.

Lex still hadn't been found, thank goodness. Neither had she loosed an arrow at the goman. Perhaps she needed a better shot, a distraction. The rakkans needed one for sure. Darius had no new ideas, but it was time to quit hiding like a coward, time to live and die like a warrior. After all, that was what he wanted.

Flaring algor in his eyes, Darius lurched up on his knees with a shout. His seething gaze locked with Archimedes's and he let algor seep from his legs, highlighting the inches that separated him from death on each side.

The room fell silent. All of the algus turned to watch him kneeling like a beggar before their master. Archimedes pulled the Staff behind him and pointed it away. As if a belt loosened from Darius's chest, he finally breathed deep and tightened his grip on the sprugenroot.

"*Darius,*" Archimedes's voice whispered. His flat tone never carried any emotion to Darius's ears, but if it did, he imagined it would be one of triumph.

"Anyone moves…" Darius called out. He paused to catch a breath. "I fall into one of these pits." The idea was strangely inviting compared to this hell.

Archimedes's eyes narrowed and the algus exchanged sceptical glances. "*I don't think you will.*"

Wrong. He'd rather split his skull on the bottom of a gulf than end up an empty shell like Parisa.

The Waif Magician stood less than ten paces from Lex's alcove, so close it made Darius sweat. Luckily Shirin's eyes were on him now. He had to keep them there.

"Tell your algus to back off," Darius said, in as deep and threatening a tone he could muster.

"*Or what?*" Archimedes took a half step towards him, daring him.

Darius strained, pushing off the ground, and stood shakily. He swayed, balanced on rock not a couple of feet wide, wishing he dared wipe the sweat dripping down his forehead. Sway too far, and he was gone. If only he were close enough to Archimedes to toss the sprugenroot. *Lex better hurry and shoot.*

Archimedes shook his head. "*Don't be so foolish.*"

"Come any closer and I'll fall." Darius's shaking legs would barely take his weight any closer to the Staff. His gaze dropped to the black chasm again and he beat down the fear that threatened to overwhelm him. Turned out death wasn't so inviting when it was staring you in the face.

"*Enough. We both know you're afraid to jump.*" The goman's dreadlocks swayed gently despite the still air.

Darius chuckled. "If I was too afraid, your algus would already have me in irons." The only reason the goman hadn't given the order was because there was a chance he would jump.

"*You either leave with me, or down there,*" Archimedes whispered. "*You're outnumbered.*" The goman turned and gestured to the algus and soldiers lining the cavern, their weapons ready to gut his allies.

An arrow darted from the shadows near the Magician and smashed into the cavern roof just above Archimedes's head.

Ducking, the goman flung his cloak up over his head as fine sprugenroot dissolved into the air.

Finally, Lex had struck but Darius only had the energy to watch on as their plan failed to hit its target, now safely cocooned beneath a cloak.

The Magician flared algor across her hands and dashed to the arrow's source. Her flickering blue light revealed Lex's masked face pressed against another nocked arrow. This one wasn't tipped with sprugenroot but steel. Lex eyed the Magician surging towards her and shifted her aim until the arrowhead pointed at Darius.

"Any closer and Darius dies." Her voice was high, breathing sharp. Was she serious or buying time? But time for what? She was so close to the algus discovering who she was.

The Magician halted a few yards away. Some of the algus closest to Archimedes flared algor in their eyes to protect them from the sprugenroot.

The goman whipped the cloak from his head and stood tall again, eyes red and bulging, whether from rage or any lingering sprugenroot, Darius couldn't be sure. All that mattered was they were open. He wracked his brain for ways out of this mess but knew when it came to ingenuity he was out of his depth.

"*You cretins still think you can surprise me?*" Archimedes took a step forward and Darius's knees shook.

Clenching his teeth, he fought to stay upright, not taking his eyes off Lex, off the metal tip about to meet his forehead. Her arms were firm without a hint of trembling. She was serious. He braced his neck and prayed he wouldn't feel it. But still she didn't shoot.

"*Enough of the charade. You won't do it.*"

Lex pulled back the bowstring another inch. She'd done it for Omid, now it was Darius's turn.

He waited.

Lex swung to the right and loosed the arrow at Archimedes but he dodged. The Magician lunged as Lex dropped the bow and reached for her sword waiting by her knee. Shirin's foot pinned the blade with a clank.

Darius gasped for breath. Why hadn't she done it? Archimedes's unblinking gaze didn't waver from him. He had only the strength to stare back with as much hate as he could.

The algus flew back into action, uncovering more subdued rakkans in the shadows on their way to Lex.

"Thirty-seven, seize her!" Nikolaos shouted.

Lex's doppelganger sprang forwards and batted her across the back of the head. She fell face first to the hard stone. The algus's boot pressed into the back of Lex's neck as she ripped off the mask. Lex glared up, her cheeks flushed, struggling to breathe.

Nikolaos's face drained of colour.

She'd been discovered by the woman Darius had spared no less.

It was over. Darius couldn't even imagine what would happen to Lex now, because of him. He eyed the chasm while Archimedes continued to watch. The goman surely knew about the pouch in his hand. There wasn't any use resisting. The abyss beckoned, not a true warrior's death but it'd have to do.

Pain suddenly shot through Darius's right arm and his grip failed. Lyra screeched behind him as the pouch fell from his fingers and was swallowed into the black chasm.

He looked down but his hand showed no trace of blood or injury. Lyra squirmed in the corner of his eye. Her right paw was speared with a sword and pinned to the bloody ground. *No!* Anger squeezed his temples. He wished he could hack and slash at the red-haired algus standing over his panther. The man smirked down at the writhing cat, contemplating whether to finish her off. Darius couldn't watch anymore.

"You want me to jump? So be it," he yelled, raising a foot over the edge of the chasm.

"*Wait!*" Archimedes held out his palm. Genuine fear showed in his eyes for the first time.

Darius paused. Everyone in the cavern fell mute, the only sound Lyra's whimpers echoing around the claw marks in the ceiling.

The Waif Magician had left Lex pinned by Thirty-seven. Now she stalked towards Sulla with Lex's bow in her hand. The rakkan was on one knee, fighting for breath and yet another cut dripping blood down his chin. Darius hoped it was just the Staff weakening him and not a mortal wound, but what did it matter now? They were all dead.

Darius dreaded to think what Archimedes had promised the Waif Magician for her aid. He scanned the room, rakkan to rakkan, counting. All of his allies were caught. His eyes fell on Brutus last, the once mighty warrior still pinned under the weight of his own armour.

There was no way out. The chasm beckoned, black and inviting. If he could have dragged any of his friends in with him, out of Archimedes's clutches, he would have, but all he could do now was fall.

Lex's blue eyes glowed, wide and pleading, begging him to…what? Jump, or stand his ground? Why hadn't she killed him when she had the chance? Nikolaos looked at her, algor-coated eyes shimmering with unshed tears, his mouth hanging open in disbelief.

"*If you jump,*" Archimedes's voice hissed, "*I'll take your friends, your precious cat and this traitorous woman and make them suffer more than you can imagine.*"

Darius met the goman's fiendish red gaze.

"*Do you know how long an animal can survive when skinned alive?*" Archimedes's eyes ceased bulging and narrowed on Lyra. "*I confess I don't, but I know how long a human can, on average.*"

Lex's lip quivered slightly. She looked to Nikolaos, pleading silently, but the other algus turned away. Darius tasted bile. He'd seldom seen that look in Lex's eyes. Fear. Nikolaos couldn't save her. Neither could Darius.

Some of the rakkans growled in defiance and Sulla gave Darius a weak forced grin. At least one of them was prepared to meet their fate, but how could he doom Lex to that? And his poor innocent Lyra, who now had a sword pressed to her abdomen. Why did this keep happening to him, to the ones he cared for? Lex had told him to trust his instincts, to care about what happened to people, but it only brought him pain. Not feeling was easier.

"How do I know you won't do it anyway?" Darius spat, looking around as if there were a way out.

Archimedes brushed back his dreads. "*Because, if you give yourself to me, I promise they won't suffer. I cannot lie.*"

Darius gritted his teeth. "Not good enough." His knees shook, threatening to relent to the Staff's power.

"*Join me and I'll make you the most powerful warrior Toria has ever seen.*" Archimedes turned his hand as if inviting him like a friend.

A warrior? It was what he'd wanted all this time, to be powerful, feared, unrivalled. The goman had taken it and could give it back. He'd be a dog on a leash, a puppet on strings, but what a puppet. If the goman poisoned Darius's mind, unlocked his rakkan powers along with his algus ones, no one could stand against him. In spite of everything, the offer tempted him. *I would be a true warrior.*

He met Lex's gaze again. Her eyes pleaded with him and now he knew what she was trying to say. She didn't want Darius to be under the thumb of another, and deep down, neither did he. He longed to be a warrior, but why? So that he could protect Amid, protect Felix, protect Omid, and now, protect Lyra and Lex. Being a warrior wasn't worth the cost if he wasn't himself, if he couldn't fight for his own allies.

But neither did he want Lex and Lyra tortured to death. How he wished he was strong enough as he was, with the strength to fight fate.

Darius straightened his back and faced the goman head on, showing a little strength while he could. At shoulder width, his feet touched the chasms at each side. "I'll give myself over if you let the rest of them go."

"*No. You're in no position to negotiate. I've offered them a painless death out of kindness.*"

Kindness? Archimedes? "Then once you have my mind, kill me with them."

Archimedes looked at the ground, eyes almost glazed over as if lost in another world. "*I don't think so. You're too valuable.*"

No. I can't let this happen. He couldn't bear the thought of Lex killed, never mind that beautiful face skinned. The frustration heated his blood until his forehead burned. No one could stop this monster from his depraved crusade, and it twisted Darius's insides into knots of cramping muscles. How he wished Lex's God would appear and execute justice.

"*I'll be generous,*" Archimedes whispered. "*Come to me and I'll let one of them go.*"

Darius grimaced. "I think you just want the pleasure of seeing me choose which one lives and which die."

"*Then I'll choose. Alexandra, but if she's ever seen in the Empire again she'll be shown no mercy.*"

Nikolaos gasped. The other algus shot disgruntled looks to one another. Darius could guess their thoughts. Archimedes must want him very badly to let a traitor go free.

The Magician stared at him, now standing at the far side of the cavern. Crow's feet wrinkled the corners of her eyes as she squinted. Her words came back to him, 'when you have to choose between yourself and her, choose her.'

Damn the Magician to hell. He should have known she'd be here watching this unfold. How else would she have known? Why should he listen to anything that witch said? He dug his nails into his palm, fighting the urge to jump into the chasm just to spite her. The blackness beckoned, offering to carry him away.

But if Lex had a way out, he owed it to her. They were all dead anyway, all the rakkans and Margalvia. Only she had an out.

Darius sighed. "Fine. You can have me."

Sulla growled, arms shaking, and Brutus's armour scraped the ground as he twitched. They wanted him to jump. Lex stared blankly, as though she couldn't believe he'd chosen to give himself up for her.

"Just tell me one thing," Darius said, still watching Lex. "Where's my grandfather?"

She blinked and her face hardened. It was all she'd wanted to know and the least he could do was try to find out before his free will was gone forever.

Archimedes's eyebrows drew together, as close to a frown as his mouthless face allowed. "*Why do you ask this?*"

It sounded random but Darius had nothing to hide, not when the goman would soon be digging through his memories. "I tried to find him but couldn't. I'm just curious if you sucked that knowledge from my head."

Archimedes's suspicious eyes searched his own but found nothing untoward. "*It's of no consequence. You didn't know his whereabouts. You rendezvoused on the first of each month, at an abandoned whaling station ten miles south of Margalvia.*"

Lex closed her eyes and looked as if a ton had been lifted from her shoulders. Hopefully she was satisfied to get what she'd fought so hard for. Her last secret, one more he'd never understand, and how he wished he knew more about her, about them, about the future they might have had if it hadn't all gone to hell here.

Archimedes waved over one of the algus and held out the Staff as everyone in the cavern watched. The woman grasped it, Archimedes still clutching the shaft as if hesitant to let it go. The goman released it and pointed to a spot behind them, clear of the other algus but close enough that the rakkans still wouldn't have the strength to fight. With each step she took away, Darius felt his muscle fibres twitch, eager to move once again as energy flowed through them.

Archimedes turned to him and held out a hand. *"Come."*

Darius took a step forward, still wobbly at the knees. The Magician smirked from behind the goman. *Witch.* He took another step, then a third, each one carrying him deeper into the cloud of weakness surrounding the Staff. He'd fought so hard, they all had, and the strain finally weighed heavy. All the bodies crammed in the cavern had raised the temperature and sweat dripped from his brow. The only gentle air movement seemed to wash up from the chasms. He could still change his mind.

A few steps closer to oblivion and he stopped, wondering whether it was safer to crawl the rest of the way lest he fall, but there was no way he'd go to Archimedes on his knees.

Darius looked over to Lex while he still could. "I hope you got what you wanted." It was sincere, no sarcasm this time. At least one person he cared for would survive.

She just stared. No 'thank you,' no 'I'm sorry,' no 'Darius, I love you.' Her face was flushed, either from stress or from Thirty-seven's boot still pressing into the back of her neck. Perhaps she wanted to speak but couldn't.

The chasms ended at either side. Only a few feet separated him from Archimedes, whose hand was still outstretched, as unmoving as an iron post. What would it feel like, to have everything else sucked away? Painful? Elating? Maybe Archimedes's Darius would think he was happy.

"To the rest of you," Darius said to all the brave rakkans that had risked their lives for him. "I'm sorry."

As he took another step, he allowed the pity to well inside him, not ignoring it or holding it back anymore. Darius felt especially guilty for Brutus and Sulla, who he guessed were among his closest allies at this point—friends even. He seethed at the thought of soon being poisoned against them. Emotions were so foreign and difficult to control, but he wanted to die caring, to die as Lex told him he was before.

Some of the algus were shifting their feet, stepping to and fro in agitation. The Waif Magician had backed into the shadows behind Archimedes, sparing Darius her sneers as the end approached.

He put another foot forward, and tussling sounded behind him.

"Darius, no!" Lex cried, having managed to shake free of the algus.

Within a second, her throat was clamped by a filthy boot again. Darius paused as her face turned purple, veins bulging on her forehead. His gaze shifted to the goman. *At this rate, she'll be dead before he releases her.*

Archimedes's eyes narrowed. "*Better hurry.*"

If she wanted Darius to stop, it was too late now. He walked on, his last few steps of his own free will, and paused within arm's reach, lifting a hand that Archimedes eyed greedily.

Before the goman could touch him, an arrow darted into the stone over Archimedes's head from behind. A cloud of fine powder burst and melded into the air. The goman screamed and his eyes snapped shut as the Magician burst from the shadows, throwing Lex's bow to the ground.

Darius felt the powder bite his eyes and flared algor to save them. Shouts echoed around the cavern and algus moved towards their leader, leaving the rakkan prisoners to writhe on the ground.

Darius's arms still drooped from the Staff's power but this was his only chance. Who knew how long that powder would last? He lunged forward and plunged his thumbs into Archimedes's closed eyes. The goman's screams rang as monotone whispers in his ear, hands waving wildly in an attempt to latch onto his skin. They found nothing but his armour. With a sharp push, Darius gouged out the slimy balls and kicked the goman in the groin, hoping it hurt as much as it would any other man.

Energy spent, Darius collapsed to his knees, out of reach of Archimedes for now.

Blood sprayed as the Magician sliced a sword through two algus necks with a single stroke. She moved like a whirlwind, not needing to parry a single incoming blade, instead ducking and weaving as if performing a rehearsed dance. Using her cogi gift of foresight, Darius guessed.

The Magician rounded on the algus with the Staff, eyeing the woman with an intensity she'd never shown before. In one lightning move, Shirin carved off the woman's arm and snatched the Staff.

Screaming, the algus dropped to the ground. She desperately tried to stem the torrent of blood gushing from her stump while the Magician pulled the Staff to her cheek and sighed. A wide grin of utter joy spread across the half-goman's treacherous face.

"*Don't let them escape,*" Archimedes hissed.

The two algus restraining Lyra and Lex still held their captives, but the rest circled nervously around Shirin, each unwilling to be her next victim.

Her eyes latched onto Darius and she started towards him.

The Staff's power felt like vines gripping his ribcage. He struggled to stay upright. An algus jumped in and took a swipe at the Magician's face, but she ducked and plunged her sword deep into the man's chest. He spluttered and fell, the impact ramming the embedded blade deep into his torso.

No other algus dared intervene as the Magician came up to Darius. She was so short that even on his knees they were almost nose to nose.

"And now you die, Darius," she said with mocking sympathy.

He knew by the look in her eyes it was all over. At least he'd had his revenge on Archimedes.

Shirin grabbed his sweaty forehead. Noise blasted his ears and threatened to burst the eardrums, sharp like a hurricane passing through the eye of a needle. Just like that rat, only now it lanced his mind.

One last thought hovered as the pain grew overwhelming. *Please let Lex and Lyra live.* He could do nothing more for them.

Darkness swallowed Darius as his mind and heart gave up.

49

Lex stole a gasp as the foot on the back of her neck shifted a few inches. Hard rock pressed against her throat again and hair fell in her eyes, blocking her view of Darius and Shirin. Her chest strained like it was gripped by crushing hands. Another minute starved of air and the pain would overwhelm her. But she'd fight every damn second of it.

Hissing air pierced her ears like needles, a sound she'd seldom heard yet was burnt into her memory. A mind being ripped from its body. All too soon, it silenced. *No.*

Scurrying footsteps sounded, then came a thump and the pressure on her neck ceased. She heaved in air like her lungs were bottomless, spots circling her vision.

"You're going to kill her!" Nikolaos's voice cried above.

Thirty-seven replied but Lex didn't hear. She ripped the hair from her eyes and stared at Darius, his head gripped in Shirin's claw-like hands, arms limp at his sides. The Magician sneered at him as she let go. His legs folded, no life within, and his body hit the floor with a thud. Lex's newfound breath froze in her lungs. *No.* Darius's head lolled to the side, vacant eyes rolled back until only the whites showed.

Loss strangled her chest, squeezing her heart until it ached. She looked to the ground, her nose grazing against the stone and tears swelling in her vision. He couldn't be…she'd fought so hard to get him back.

She tried to stand but pain speared her hip. Why was she never strong enough? *Dianoia, why?* Lex squeezed her eyes shut. This was no time for sorrow. Her daughter was all that mattered. She could meet Darius's grandfather ten miles south of Margalvia at a whaling station. At last she'd find the rakkan she entrusted her daughter's life to, whose location she hadn't even trusted her own mind to hold. It had seemed the only safe place for her daughter, deep in rakkan lands, safe in the wilderness with a guardian to whom Darius was the only link. If only she'd known Darius's mind wasn't safe.

She forced down the tears like hammering nails.

A cackle dragged her back to the cavern. The Magician had Archimedes's face in one hand; her other smashed an algus across the jaw with the Staff. Shirin dropped the goman's head, still laughing, and darted for the exit, prize in hand and greedy eyes wide.

Lex's face burned. Anger clenched her jaw so hard her teeth threatened to crack. That hag wouldn't get away with this. Lex would hunt her to the ends of the world, search every tree, every cave herself if she had to. Another name on the list scorched in her mind for retribution.

The tail of Shirin's cloak disappeared into the tunnel as Lex clambered to one knee, blocking out the pain.

"What do we do?" Nikolaos sounded panicked, not at all like the brave leader he always presented himself as, the coward.

Go to hell. Lex reached to her breast pocket for a vial, for relief from the pain to fight. A few of the algus had gathered around

Archimedes, helping the blind goman to his feet as he patted their arms like a helpless invalid.

"*Get me out of here,*" the goman said.

So, that twisted mind was still in there. It didn't surprise Lex that a goman couldn't destroy another goman's mind, but what then had the Magician been doing to Archimedes?

As Lex dabbed a drop of black tears on her tongue, a hand grabbed her shoulder and threw her back onto the ground. Thirty-seven's eyes narrowed as she loomed over Lex. She raised her sword, ready to jab through Lex's neck. *Try it, scum.*

A deep roar echoed through the cavern like a lion rousing. Brutus slammed a fist into the ground and pushed his chest free. Ferven dripped from the grating over his mouth and he thundered a battle cry. More groans and clunks sounded as metal sprang into motion. The rakkans rose, free of the Staff's grip.

The algus regrouped and began escorting their now feeble leader out of the cave. Thirty-seven stared at Lex, her tiny mind probably unsure whether it was worth risking getting caught alone in a rakkan frenzy just to run the traitor through.

The algus thought better of it and rushed back to the group, Nikolaos at her cloak's hem. At least fifteen algus still stood, too many for the rakkans to take. That damned goman would escape. Pain lanced Lex's hip all the harder as if someone twisted a blade buried in it. Her vial was gone, flung off somewhere. That drop needed to kick in fast. She had to fight. She had to survive.

Brutus stood, eyes blazing and fury howling from his mouth. He lifted his fiery hammer. He'd fight to the last man, just how she liked it. Lex struggled to her feet, almost blinded by the pain. *You won't restrain me.* She grabbed a sword waiting nearby, as if laid out by Agathos for her to execute his justice.

Light danced around the cavern, ferven igniting everywhere as the rakkans vented their rage. The red-orange glow flickered in

Darius's once striking eyes as he lay motionless on the ground. *Safe journey, my dear Darius.*

The flickering in his eyes brightened. Twinkling flame turned to swirling clouds until it engulfed his eyes. *Odd.* What was happening? It almost looked like that hint of fire when he used to see her. It couldn't be...Darius?